The Empire of Kalman the Cripple

The Empire of Kalman the Cripple

· · · · ·

Yehuda Elberg

Translated from the Yiddish

Syracuse University Press

First Edition 1997
97 98 99 00 01 02   6 5 4 3 2 1

The paper used in this publication meets the minimum requirements of
American National Standard for Information Sciences—Permanence of Paper
for Printed Library Materials, ANSI Z39.48-1984. ⊗

Library of Congress Cataloging-in-Publication Data

Elberg, Yehudah.
[Ḳalman ḳaliḳes imperye. English]
The empire of Kalman the cripple / Yehuda Elberg ; translated from
the Yiddish by the author. — 1st ed.
p.   cm. — (Library of modern Jewish literature)
ISBN 0-8156-0448-3 (cloth : alk. paper)
I. Title.   II. Series.
PJ5129.E534K313   1997
839'.134—dc21   96-37265

Manufactured in the United States of America

To Renia

The author expresses his sincere thanks to Barbara E. Galli
for her editorial assistance on this volume.
The contributions of Max Rosenfeld, Nathan Elberg, Shaindle Elberg, Eve
Elberg, Kathy Roth, and Gilah Langner are also gratefully acknowledged.

Yehuda Elberg was born in Zgierz, Poland, in 1912 to a rabbinical family and is himself an ordained rabbi. He was active in the Jewish Underground throughout World War II. He established the Writers' Union and *Dos Naye Lebn,* the first Jewish newspaper in his homeland, and is the author of numerous novels, short stories, Hasidic stories, and dramas in Yiddish and Hebrew, including *Ship of the Hunted, Under Copper Skies,* and *Jeftah and His Daughter.* Elberg now resides in Montreal.

Barbara Ellen Galli is assistant professor in the Department of Religion at Concordia University and associate faculty of Religious Studies at McGill University. She is author of *Franz Rosenzweig and Jehuda Halevi: Translating, Translations, and Translators,* as well as numerous articles on Rosenzweig's thought.

The Empire of Kalman the Cripple

Book One

1

When the community elder Reb Jonah Swerdl passed away, he left only one heir, his young grandson, Kalman, who dutifully recited the Kaddish at the open grave. But when the townspeople came to the deceased's house to conduct evening services, as is the custom, they found the doors locked. Kalman did not show up at the synagogue to say the mourner's prayer. An outrageous thing like this had never once happened since Jonah had built the prayer house, making Dombrovka a respected Jewish community. But who can argue with Kalman the Cripple?

Only recently was Lowicz Road, the main thoroughfare of Dombrovka, renamed Lowicz Street in recognition of its role as the commercial center of the town. Here a professionally constructed building could be found alongside an old wooden structure a peasant had built for himself, with the helping hands of neighbors. No one knew whether the little wood house, smack in the center of the street, was the oldest, but it certainly looked ancient. Stooped and sunken into the ground, it would have toppled long ago if not for the wooden posts, and the supporting beams holding up the ceiling. Rarely did a sunbeam reach so low that it crawled through the tiny windows. Several crooked steps led from the street down to a little store; from the store, a door opened onto a series of dark rooms. Jonah had purchased this old house when he was still poor, and now his heir, Kalman, considered it the choice business location of Dombrovka.

People did not recall ever having heard sounds of merriment coming from this gloomy old house, but now suddenly, in this period of mourning, strains of music burst through the open window— music was being played on the first gramophone in town. Kalman the Cripple had assembled it from parts of broken-down machines he had acquired from God knows where. When asked about it, Kalman

1

would laugh and say that his grandfather had a part in the music, for after all it was the spring from Jonah's timepiece that made the gramophone work.

"You didn't take apart your grandfather's cherished clock?!" they asked him in disbelief.

"I resurrected it in something that gives much nicer melodies than the chimes of that old clock."

Childhood diseases had cut down old Jonah's entire household. His son, Boruch, had attended six funerals before he turned thirteen: five for his younger brothers and sisters, and the sixth for his mother, who followed these five children of hers into the next world.

Boruch left home very young, and settled in another town, where he married and had a son, Kalman. After a childhood disease crippled the boy, Boruch vanished without a trace. Some years later, Jonah rode off to the funeral of his daughter-in-law and returned with his orphaned grandson.

When Jonah died it was rumored that he had left a lot of money, but that he had hidden it away so well that Kalman would probably never find it. It seemed, however, that Kalman did find something after all. New shelves appeared in the store, filled with new kinds of merchandise. In Dombrovka, people were accustomed to buying food in a grocery store, linens and materials for making clothing in a dry goods store, and leather and shoe fittings in a leather shop. But Kalman was offering so many new things that old Jonah's grocery was transformed into a sort of general store. One could still buy a kilo of flour, a few chunks of yeast, a liter of oil. But one could also find a pot or a baking pan, or dish towels with a red stripe for meat and a blue stripe for dairy dishes. One could order a whole trousseau from Kalman, even a wig for the bride and a *shtrayml* for the groom, a fancy fur hat for the Sabbath. One could certainly order a gold wedding band, for there was no goldsmith in Dombrovka. When a peasant needed a new scythe, plough, pitchfork, or thresher, he could buy these from Kalman on credit and not pay until after the harvest. Kalman sold tools for every trade and, if necessary, he could even repair them.

• • • • •

The custom of crowning people with nicknames had its rhyme and reason: Moyshe Longlegs was tall and skinny; Matus Pulpit always wanted to lead the services from the pulpit in the synagogue; Sarah Stargazer was constantly murmuring some prayer, her eyes raised piously toward heaven. Generally, a cripple would not be humiliated this way, but they dubbed Kalman "the Cripple" only because he himself invited it. "Ask Kalman the Cripple," he would say, or "You can depend on Kalman the Cripple!"

Kalman expanded his shop into the long room behind the store. Soon a barn was erected in the courtyard behind the house, full of shelves with even more merchandise. Although the old, sunken house could not be lifted out of the ground, it no longer looked so drab. The tiny windows near the ground could not be made into showcases, but a big sign across the front proclaimed: BUY EVERYTHING YOU NEED FROM THE CRIPPLE.

One day Kalman gave some candy to a group of schoolboys, in exchange for which they walked the streets of the town shouting, "Buy from Kalman the Cripple!" "Kalman sells cheaper!" The people of Dombrovka weren't used to such wild innovations, but Kalman enjoyed making people open their eyes and turn their heads.

2

Kalman seemed to remember an illness in his childhood but wasn't sure whether it was then that he had become paralyzed. The good years, when he was like other children, had completely flown out of his head. He only remembered himself as a cripple.

Did he love his parents? He had no recollection of when his father disappeared or when his mother died. Maybe that was why he vented all his bitterness on his grandfather. He remembered the trip to Dombrovka with Old Jonah very clearly. He had resisted his grandfather's efforts to remove him from his house. They had promised him many wonderful things, but he struggled with his grandfather and clung to the doorknob. When Jonah pulled at his hand, he had sunk his teeth into the old man's fingers. That was the beginning of the feud between them. During the trip he had fought incessantly with his grandfather, and he tried to jump out the train window. He couldn't run anywhere, of course. At that time he couldn't even move around very well on his behind. All he knew was that he had been happy "there" and "back then." Here, in Dombrovka, in his grandfather's house, he always felt miserable. To annoy Jonah, he would yell, "Pissin' shittin'—bah!" and stick out his tongue like a goat. He learned his spitefulness early.

Kalman's years in *heder* were filled with dreaded days for him. The other kids played terrible pranks on him. At night he would stuff his pillow into his mouth so Jonah wouldn't hear him crying. He kept biting holes in his pillowcase until he discovered he could use his head to get even. At first he only avenged himself on those who had wronged him, but he soon decided that if others could play dirty tricks on him for no reason at all, he could do the same. And when Kalman the Cripple did a thing, he tried, successfully, to do it better than anyone else. Up to that time Kalman had only pretended to laugh, but after each of his successful pranks he laughed freely, genuinely, and with all his heart. After all, he had a right to laugh too . . .

In *heder* the teacher would go over the same portion of the Bible from Sunday to Friday, and on Saturday the children would be examined by one of the town's learned people. One day—it must have been a Monday, because they were going over the section for the second time—the teacher noticed that Kalman wasn't looking at the book. The teacher motioned to the class to stay quiet, and told Kalman to read the next part. Kalman had no idea which sentence they were at. All the boys burst out laughing.

The teacher twisted Kalman's ear. "A boy must always follow the reading in the Bible; a boy must study even if he is not going to be examined by anyone at all!"

Kalman's ear turned red and his face grew white from anger. "If the rebbe wants to examine me," he challenged, "let him examine me right now!" Without waiting for the teacher's response, he turned back to the beginning of the chapter, read the Hebrew words flawlessly, and translated them into Yiddish.

The teacher couldn't believe his ears. "Is your grandfather tutoring you? We only started this section yesterday."

"Once is enough for me," Kalman replied brazenly.

The children roared with laughter, certain that this was impossible.

"If I want to," Kalman continued, "I can learn the section all by myself. It's all in the Yiddish translation, printed right here."

This infuriated the teacher. Usually the children understood the Bible text only when it contained a story, such as Joseph and his brothers. The rest they learned by rote, word for word. When they grew older they would understand the meaning.

"Really?" said the teacher mockingly. "Maybe you also know the portion for next week—and the *haftorah,* the reading from the Prophets, too?"

Kalman unflinchingly turned the pages, found the excerpt from the Prophets, and began reading the Yiddish translation. "And a woman of the disciples of the prophets, the wife of Obadiah, cried out to Elisha . . . "

The teacher stared, openmouthed, and the children gaped. Kalman surveyed the room triumphantly.

It was a great victory, but no good came out of it. The next day the teacher informed Jonah that Kalman had outgrown his *heder.* Jonah then enrolled Kalman in a Talmud class, where all the boys, who were a few years older, considered it an affront to their dignity to have a five-year-old brat in their class.

Kalman kept pace with the other boys on the subjects of the Bible and Rashi commentary, but Mishna was entirely unfamiliar to him. Aware that everyone hoped he would fail, he studied even when the teacher was not watching him, and he wouldn't join in the games the boys played under the table and behind the rebbe's back. When he didn't understand something in the text he asked questions, and then he asked questions about the answers, until even the teacher lost patience. Eventually he learned enough that he no longer had to ask questions to follow the rebbe.

The other boys now realized that this upstart knew as much as they did, and they made his life even more miserable. Before class or during recess, the boys horsed around and wrestled with each other, mostly in fun but sometimes in earnest. There was no way they could fight with Kalman, who could do nothing but sit. It often happened, however, that one of the boys would "accidentally" bump into him and knock him over. He would have endured all this gladly if any one of them had talked with him or had a good word to say about him.

•　•　•　•　•

When the teacher noticed what was going on, he lectured the boys: "You are a gang of heartless scoundrels! How can you not feel sorry for an orphan—and a crippled orphan at that?!" But even before the teacher had finished reproaching them, one boy thumbed his nose at Kalman and another stuck out his tongue. But the teacher's words hurt him even more than their taunting gestures.

Kalman had just about gotten used to the Hebrew Mishna text when they began to study the Aramaic Gemarah. Many of the words were similar to those in the Mishna, but others were as foreign to him as Chinese. He didn't always catch the rebbe's translation or remember it when he did hear it. It was difficult for the other boys too, only they could afford not to care what it meant. But he *had* to know.

He tried asking Jonah, but sometimes the Aramaic words were unfamiliar to his grandfather, too. Once, when the rebbe said the word *kaka,* the boys laughed so loud that Kalman didn't hear the translation. He asked an older student in the synagogue, but he didn't know what it meant either. Kalman screwed up his courage and asked the Rabbi. The *shammes,* standing nearby, also laughed at the word *kaka.* But the Rabbi sat down with Kalman and answered him with great patience:

"It depends on where the word occurs and in what form. K-A-K or K-A-K-I can mean a white goose. K-A-K-A means neck. However, KA-AKA means tattoo—a kind of writing etched into the skin—something Jews are not permitted to do. What is your name, little boy?"

"Kalman."

"Kalman who?"

Didn't the Rabbi have eyes? How many cripples were there in Dombrovka? Or was he pretending that Kalman was just like all the other boys? Finally Kalman answered, "I'm Kalman—old man Jonah's Kalman."

"Oh, Reb Jonah's grandson! If you continue to study this way, you'll be a rabbi yourself some day and help other Jews understand the Torah." The Rabbi rose, and Kalman moved aside to make way for him. But the Rabbi continued: "Come with me, Kalman, I want to show you something."

He led the boy to the bookcase, took out a volume, and showed it to him. "You see this? It is the *Sefer He-Arukh.* It's a kind of dictionary of all the words in the Gemarah, in alphabetical order." He opened the book and helped Kalman find the root K-K. "But if you have a question, don't be shy. And, if you wish, come in sometimes and I'll examine you in your studies."

Not long afterward, Kalman took up the Rabbi's invitation. The Rebbetsin even gave him an apple and a cookie. He was so proud that he boasted about his visit in the *heder* the next day, but the boys only laughed: "And maybe it was *you* who examined the Rabbi, Kalman?"

Later, when the boys were playing soccer, one boy threw the ball at him, possibly intending to hurt him. Kalman reached up and caught it, but couldn't kick it back. The boy came over to get the ball, and Kalman hoped to hear him say it was a good catch. But apparently his classmate could not forgive his boasting. "If you weren't a cripple, Kalman, which would you rather be: a rabbi or a soccer player?"

Kalman realized that it was utter folly for him to show off his cleverness. At that moment he swore to keep his mouth shut and pretend to be a dunce like everyone else, but it was hard to restrain himself.

Then came the incident with the burrs. By now, he was almost a member of the Rabbi's household. The Rabbi was the only person in the world he loved, and he was sure that if the Rabbi had been his grandfather, life wouldn't have been so bitter.

He was now studying with Mendel the Talmud teacher. The boys in the class who harassed him also tormented a boy named Shloimele, calling him "Red Chicken" or "Red Pig" because of his red hair and freckles. Kalman sat beside Shloimele and tried to make friends with him. On the other side of Shloimele sat Beryl Bass. Beryl butted Shloimele and said, "Go wash your shitty face!" Shloimele started to cry, but stopped in surprise when Kalman said, "Beryl Bass, with a head like an ass, has touched your face, you had better go wash it!" The other boys smothered their laughter as the teacher entered the room, but the nickname stuck: "Beryl Bass, with a head like an ass!"

The truth was, Shloimele wasn't very smart. When the other boys teased him, he waited for Kalman to tell him how best to respond. On the day of Tisha b'Av, everyone went to the synagogue, where the men sat on the floor reciting lamentations for the destruction of the Holy Temple. Outside, the boys were fooling around. Kalman, skillfully ducking the seed-burrs the boys were pelting him with, didn't think he had anything to worry about from Shloimele; after all, Shloimele was his friend. But Shloimele, apparently trying to ingratiate himself to the other boys, stuck a handful of burrs under Kalman's shirt. The more Kalman scratched, the more the itching spread around his body. "Scratch, Kalman, scratch!" the boys taunted him. "Your lice will eat you up alive!"

He went home, washed, put on a fresh shirt, and the itching let up a bit. Shloimele's betrayal, however, left an itching in his head that was impervious to scratching. His usual fantasy of an older brother who would avenge him brought him no relief—he would have to fend for himself.

There was an abundance of plum trees in the vicinity of Dombrovka. In the town itself there was a sugar refinery. Since plums and sugar were both plentiful and cheap, every housewife had a supply of plum jam in her pantry. Dvosha, the woman who came in every day to cook and clean for Jonah, had put up plum jam for him and his grandson. Kalman knew that Shloimele had an insatiable sweet tooth; whenever he brought bread and plum jam to class, he shared it with his friend.

After the incident with the burrs, Kalman thought of mixing some poison into the jam before giving it to Shloimele. Let him croak, the redheaded pig! Obtaining the poison would be no problem—Jonah sold rat poison in the store. But Kalman knew that he couldn't carry out that plan, no matter how outraged he was, though it gave him malicious pleasure to think of it.

The next morning, Kalman was watching Jonah mixing up a powder with water—a laxative he took every morning—when the answer popped into his head. A little of that powder in the plum jam and that traitor Shloimele would be shitting in his pants in front of everyone!

As he expected, Shloimele gobbled down the Kaiser roll he offered him so fast that he didn't notice any difference in taste. Soon after, Shloimele stood up to ask the teacher's permission to leave the room, and Kalman knew that the laxative was having its effect. He quickly moved off the bench and, before Shloimele could get the words out of his mouth, Kalman was already out the door with a desperate, "I've got to go right away!" There was only one outhouse in the courtyard, and, on general principle, the teacher never let two boys go out at the same time, because they might use it as an excuse to stay outside and play. Shloimele continued to plead for permission to leave the room, but the Rebbe's rule was ironclad: "As soon as Kalman comes back . . ."

By the time Kalman finally returned, the cramps in Shloimele's stomach had overwhelmed him, and he soiled his pants before he reached the door. "Shitface has a shitty ass!" the boys mocked, as Kalman observed the scene with an innocent look.

He had designed his prank well and had executed it to perfection, but the result was just the opposite of what he had planned. Because he was Shloimele's best friend, the teacher instructed him to take the sick boy home. All the way along Wilki Street, the mess dripped down Shloimele's pants; his face was ash-gray, his red earlocks turned dirty brown with perspiration, and the tears running down his face looked red as drops of blood. Kalman, taking pity on him, went into Jancze's feed store and got a bundle of straw to wipe the excrement from Shloimele's shoes.

Shloimele did not return to the *heder* the next day, or the day after that. Several days later, Ita, Shloimele's redheaded sister, appeared at the *heder* to ask the children to recite psalms and pray for Shloimele, for he was very sick. The following day, all the children went to the synagogue to recite psalms with the congregation in front of burning candles. The boys stood around the prayer leader, and the Rabbi noticed that Kalman was weeping uncontrollably. After the service, the Rabbi tried to console Kalman: "The One above will certainly listen to the prayers of the children, who are pure and without sin. He will undoubtedly send a cure for Shloimele's illness."

But the One above, it seemed, paid no attention to the prayers. A few days later, Kalman, along with the other boys from the *heder,* attended his friend's funeral. After Shloimele's father said the Kaddish, the teacher appealed to his pupils: "Boys, many things can happen among friends. If any of you ever quarreled with Shloimele, if any of you ever said a bad word to him or about him, come closer now and beg forgiveness at his open grave."

None of the children moved. Each clod of earth fell on the coffin like a thunderclap. All the mourners held their breath.

"Go near the grave and beg his forgiveness," Kalman prodded himself. "You didn't say any bad words to him, you just killed him!"

He had edged toward the grave when Ita started wailing: "Look, none of his friends ever quarreled with him. No one ever wanted to harm him. Shloimele was goodness itself, an angel from God, why do we deserve such cruel punishment?" The whole family began to sob: "An angel from God! Never quarreled with anyone!"

"Beg forgiveness before it's too late," Kalman kept telling himself. But everything within him froze. He could neither move a muscle nor utter a sound. And he barely got home on arms that seemed to have lost all their strength.

That night he couldn't fall asleep. When his eyes finally closed, frightful nightmares gripped him: he was on his way to *heder,* he was in Jancze's feed store, he had to go and get some straw. In the store there were great heaps of sacks of oats, bundles of hay, he had to get some straw . . . The big brown seed-oil cakes smelled like—like freshly dug earth. Where was the straw? Suddenly, the shutters of the store slammed shut behind him, the heavy doors banged shut. He went further into the darkness; he had to find the straw. He bumped into a stack of seed-oil cakes and knocked them over; the cakes hit the floor, sounding like clods of earth falling on a coffin. Stacks of seed-oil cakes marched toward him. A freckled hand reached out of the bundles of straw. Kalman retreated, but the hand grew longer and longer, and seized him by the neck. He wanted to scream for help! But the bony fingers tightened around his throat and choked off his voice. From all the bundles of straw, from all the sacks of oats, from all the stacks of seed-oil cakes, long, bony fingers stretched out toward him. The straw and the oats turned as brown as the seed-oil cakes, then they turned into seed-oil cakes and fell upon him with a dull thud, like clods of earth falling onto a coffin. HELP!

He woke up in a cold sweat, afraid to open his eyes, and afraid to keep them shut in case he fall asleep again. For the first time since he had arrived in Dombrovka, he crawled into his grandfather's bed. He was grateful for Jonah's snoring—anything except the sound of seed-oil cakes thudding down onto floorboards . . .

When he finally fell asleep, the dream recurred. And it recurred night after night, in various guises. Every detail of the dream became so familiar to him that he could not longer distinguish between it and reality. Night and day intermingled in a cruel nightmare.

Jonah realized that something was wrong with Kalman. Dvosha noticed that he left the food on his plate. Was he sick? They called Leiybush Feldsher, the town barber-surgeon, who applied his usual remedy, cupping. They summoned the doctor, who prescribed cod-liver oil. When Jonah forced him to swallow it, he vomited it right up. They ordered him to stay in bed, but now he didn't want to miss a single day in *heder,* nor did he skip any opportunities to go to the synagogue for the daily services. He didn't want to be left alone, he was afraid to fall asleep . . . He ate little, and seldom said anything. The dark grief in his eyes reminded Jonah of his wife, Liebele, when she got depressed. Kalman followed his grandfather to the synagogue for the Shabbes services, but hardly moved his lips at the prayers. Jonah asked the Rabbi's advice.

"He's not eating, you say?" the Rabbi responded. "Maybe he doesn't like Dvosha's cooking. Kalman loves to eat with us." He approached the boy. "Kalman, it's true you're a big boy now, but you can still come to see me once in a while so I can examine you in your studies. Or you could just drop in for a visit—we are distantly related, did you know that?"

Kalman nodded his head.

"It so happens that the Rebbetsin has prepared a very delicious tsimmes. Why don't you come and eat with us? Your grandfather won't mind."

Kalman didn't answer.

"And there's a kugel too, a noodle kugel. I remember you used to like that very much."

The Rabbi started to walk away, but Kalman didn't move.

"Well, Kalman?"

"I'm not hungry," Kalman finally replied in a low voice.

"When have you had to be hungry to eat my wife's kugel? Come, Kalman, don't be stubborn." The Rabbi waited, and Kalman had no choice but to follow him, but he barely touched his food. During the *zemirot* he moved his lips, but soundlessly. After the meal, when everyone else had left the table, the Rabbi asked him to come into his study.

"Proverbs advise us that if we are worried about something we should talk about it to someone. Can you tell me what's troubling you, Kalman?"

How could he tell the Rabbi what he had done?

"I know what happened to your friend," the Rabbi began, consolingly. Kalman almost jumped out of his skin. How could the Rabbi know?

"It's a great accomplishment to become attached to a friend and to love him as David and Jonathan loved each other. But the Almighty knows better than we do what is right. Maybe Shloimele was destined to have a life full of troubles, and the Father of Mercy took him up to Himself in order to save him from that—"

"Why didn't he save *me* from that?" Kalman's accusation was almost a scream.

The Rabbi put an arm around him. "I know, Kalman, how bitter it is to lose a loved one." The warm hand on his shoulder released something inside Kalman. His whole body shook. The Rabbi drew him closer. The boy's useless legs dragged behind him, and he hung limply in the old man's arms. His face buried in the Rabbi's silk Sabbath coat, he choked out his story, exactly as it had happened.

"Kalman, Kalman, you're such a clever boy—how did you ever convince yourself of such foolishness? Shloimele died of pneumonia, God protect us. A laxative has nothing to do with the lungs. He must have already been walking around with the disease for several days when he fell ill at the *heder* . . . "

A huge rock rolled away from Kalman's heart, but he could not stop crying.

"Maybe you should have begged his forgiveness," the Rabbi added, "but it's not too late for that. Those who are in the next world can still hear us. Do it now, Kalman. I'll say the words and you repeat them after me, all right?"

Kalman nodded.

"*Mes tohur Shlomo ben Yaakov* . . . "

Kalman broke into sobs again.

"If it's too hard for you to say the words aloud, say them in your heart. In the next world they can hear the voice of the heart too. I'll start again. *Mes tohur habachur Shlomo ben Yaakov*—I, your friend Kalman son of Boruch, beg your forgiveness for all the wrongs I did to you both deliberately and unintentionally. And for all the good things I did for you I beg you to bestow loving kindness upon me and to intercede for me in the next world."

That night Kalman finally slept without dreaming. He slept through the night and the next day. When he opened his eyes, Dvosha was standing at his bedside.

"The Rabbi's son Berish is here. The Rabbi wants to see you."

Although Kalman felt weak, he hurried to the Rabbi's.

"Kalman, I've got to go to the cemetery. I always ask someone to accompany me. Will you come with me?"

"I haven't said my prayers yet. I just woke up."

"Have you said the Shema?"

"I was asleep. When Dvosha woke me I got dressed and came right over."

"Say the Shema. The Rebbetsin will give you a glass of milk. You'll finish your prayers when we get back."

At the cemetery, the Rabbi suggested to Kalman that he stop for a moment at Shloimele's grave. Kalman was able to beg for forgiveness, saying the words out loud without crying.

On the way back, they happened to pass Jancze's feed store. The Rabbi held Kalman's hand as they went inside, and then asked questions about every sack and bundle—what it was and how it was made. He said that he smelled a foul odor in the straw and asked that everything be moved and inspected. Jancze shrugged: "The hay smells of clover, and even the seed-oil cakes are fresh." But the Rabbi insisted, and so Jancze moved everything around.

Kalman's eyes went from the Rabbi to Jancze and back again, trying to fathom what was going on. He thought the Rabbi meant to intone some sort of incantation, some formula to drive away evil spirits, but the Rabbi wasn't moving his lips. Only later did Kalman understand that the Rabbi wanted him to see that Jancze's store contained only ordinary bundles of straw, without any bony fingers. There was nothing there for Kalman to fear.

3

Kalman grew up to be a quick and vigorous person. As his legs and feet didn't move at all, he was forced to slide along the ground, propelling himself with his hands and arms and swinging his legs in a semicircle, but he always arrived at his destination faster than people who walked normally. In the winter, Kalman moved about the streets on a kind of little sled that he had made.

Whenever a new shelf had to be put up in the store, he was the one who did it. He mended his own clothes and even repaired his own watch. There wasn't anything his deft hands couldn't do. And quick as his hands were, his mind was quicker. In the wink of an eye he could calculate the most complicated sums. Any time someone would enter Kalman's store, they would find Kalman with pencil and paper, working with figures. It's true that he had enlarged his grandfather's store, but he spent more time with his calculations than with his customers.

"The squire with all his riches does not do this much calculating," someone told him. "I'll be richer than the squire," was his answer.

One day, Kalman the Cripple went to the mayor of Dombrovka

to complain: "In our days, people in the smallest villages have electricity, but here we are still breathing the soot of our kerosene and carbon lamps."

The mayor explained, "The sugar factory refuses to sell power even to the squire's court."

"Then someone else must," said Kalman.

"And where would we find 'someone else'?"

"Right here in Dombrovka."

"Now you're talking nonsense. Who in Dombrovka—"

"Me."

The Mayor thought this was one of Kalman's jokes, but Kalman continued. "I am ready to build a generating station, but collecting the payments every month from the consumers is a matter for City Hall, not for a Jewish cripple. If Your Honor would agree to—"

"Collect payments for a Jew? How could I do that?"

"That's true," Kalman admitted. "Your Honor cannot be involved in such things. But suppose the generator belongs not to me but to the city, as it really should?" Kalman elaborated, providing the mayor with an estimate of the income the monthly payments for electricity would bring in and what the expenses would be. He also proposed that the city pay him for the generator by monthly installments over a period of twenty years, after which time it would belong to the city.

This plan would have to be approved by the regional and provincial offices, as well as by the Minister of the Interior. Since the city fathers were intimidated by these high officials, Kalman found a distant relative to tend his store while he himself got involved with the negotiations.

The winter was rough, heavy snowfalls made the roads arduous, but Kalman made frequent visits to Warsaw. When the melting snow turned the roads into swamps and made them impassable, he still found ways to get to the capital.

The townspeople who had been excited when they heard about the project had given up hope that it would ever materialize. But when the summer days cut short the hours of darkness, and no one thought about electricity, the news came that Kalman finally got what he wanted, an official agreement with the town, duly approved by higher authorities.

The Vistula Valley was the fruit belt of the area, with orchards on both sides of the roads which Kalman traveled. The trees kept changing colors as if to remind him of the passage of time. Branches were still bare when Kalman began his trips to the higher authorities. Soon the branches were adorned with rich foliage and sprouted with colorful blossoms. The blossoms' petals fluttered down, coloring the grass like a carpet as they gave way to little fruit. The fruit ripened, was picked and was already for sale in baskets alongside the road, but there was still no sign of the generating plant.

Kalman threw himself more energetically into his own business. All the wagon drivers in town worked for him, hauling from the railroad station manufactured goods from Lodz, leather from Strikow, ironware from Grzybow Square in Warsaw. It was said that merchandise came from as far away as Berlin. Where Kalman stored it all no one could figure out; it was as if that crooked little house had a bottomless pit. People thought the shelves in the store would collapse from too much weight, but actually the store was half empty.

The calendar was losing pages as the trees lost their leaves again, and still there was no sign of the generating station. Kalman sat at the counter in his store. His ungainly, towering young relative, "my partner Yosl," as Kalman called him, wandered around the place not knowing what to do with his clumsy, oversized hands. Yosl was not very bright, but he had the useful talent of being able to sense "sticky fingers."

And then the citizens of Dombrovka began to notice that Kalman was receiving a lot of visitors from out of town. It seemed that every day an elegantly clad businessman would appear at Kalman's store carrying a briefcase. Only later did people learn that the briefcases were full of overdue notes. Kalman, it seems, had bought a lot of goods on credit and then had simply not made any payments.

Kalman handled creditors by pointing to his own paralyzed legs. "Why are you picking on a poor cripple like me? Speak to my partner about it . . ." And Yosl would appear in the doorway. "Yosl, this gentleman here has come to collect money from you. Yosl, I think that fellow over there in the corner just slipped something into his pocket." Even if the peasant was the size of an ox, Yosl would grab him by the collar and toss him outside, adding a boot in the rear.

"Yosl," Kalman would continue, "this gentleman has come all the way from Warsaw because we owe him money. Do you have any money, Yosl?"

"Got no money," Yosl would growl threateningly as he advanced on the gentleman with his fists swinging.

The creditors then wanted to seize the generating station, but they discovered that all Kalman had was the contract to build it, and it became obvious that he had used the contract as a bluff to obtain more credit. Eventually, the creditors stopped demanding and started begging: they were ready to settle for fifty percent. Kalman agreed to buy back his unpaid notes for half the amount of the debt, but since he had no cash, he proposed to pay with new promissory notes! Most of the creditors opted instead for twenty-five percent in cash, choosing not to hold notes that might not even be worth the paper they were written on.

And so the fastest growing town in the Duchy of Lowicz had another distinction—the town with the biggest bankruptcy.

If Kalman the Cripple had tried to enter the Dombrovka synagogue, they would have thrown him out in disgrace. When someone does a lot of business with a firm for many years and then goes bankrupt, he might be forgiven. Kalman, however, had gone to people with whom he had never dealt, had bought goods that he didn't need, and had paid with "customer's notes" which had really been signed by Yosl. This was blatant thievery.

4

The town was still grumbling about Kalman's bankruptcy when he surprised them with his benevolence to little Berele, the porter. A stranger might have thought that a sack of grain was passing by itself. Dombrovkites, however, knew that the burden concealed Berele, carrying a load bigger than he himself. The contents of the sack were destined for Kalman's store.

"Berele, if we didn't keep a sharp eye on you," Kalman quipped, "you'd pick up the whole globe and carry it away on your shoulders."

And Berele, who loved a good joke as much as the next man, would reply: "I'm descended from ants, my friend."

"An ant," retorted Kalman, "has three backs, so if one back breaks under the load, it still has two left. And besides, an ant has six legs."

"So I'm only one third of an ant—two legs and one back."

Berele could laugh at himself, but earning a living was no joke. Although Dombrovka was a city now, its inhabitants were still hard-working people with broad shoulders and powerful legs. If he tried to charge more for his services, they would start carrying their own bundles. The joke about ants gave him an idea, though. If he could scrape together enough money to buy a cart . . . Four wheels, added to his two feet, would make six, and he would be able to haul loads many times his own weight, like an ant.

Berele had no money, but he had plenty of patience. He began collecting cast-off parts from broken wagons. In a split hoop from a big wheel there was enough metal for a small wheel. The same with a spring, a bolt, a crossbar, a shaft. As for axles, he wanted new ones, so he saved his pennies. He lent a hand at the cartwrights; he pumped the bellows at the blacksmith's. It took time, but the cart was built. When Berele took up his position between the two shafts and harnessed himself to his wagon for the first time, he pulled it through the streets of Dombrovka as if he were in a parade.

One spring morning, Kalman was taking the sun in front of his store when Berele came up the muddy street dragging a heavy load on his wagon, sweat pouring down the stiff hairs of his beard, and Kalman could not resist the urge to tease him. He called out, "Is your horse sick today, Berele?"

"I'm not too sick to be my own horse," Berele replied.

"Four-footed horses need to make a living too."

"Not at my expense! There isn't always enough to fill the belly of this horse," said Berele, pointing to himself with a laugh.

"With a real horse you'd be able to make ten trips in the time it now takes you to make one." Kalman's tone was mocking, but he was serious. He could not understand why people around here failed to see any further than their noses. They toiled mightily with their hands while their heads stayed fast asleep.

Berele felt no malice in Kalman's teasing and he joined in the game. "Buying a horse is no big deal, but where would I get money for a whip? A driver without a whip is like a roof without a chimney. Anyway, who wants to mess around with horses? When my wife complains that I don't bring home enough I have an answer for her, but how do you argue with a hungry horse?"

This fellow's no fool, Kalman realized. "I'm serious. How much would it cost for an old nag to pull that tiny wagon? You could borrow a little money and pay it back from your increased earnings."

"Who would lend *me* money?" asked Berele, growing serious too.

"You could put up some collateral against the loan."

"My Tsilke was an orphan when I married her, so there was no one to give the bridegroom a gold watch. In return, I didn't buy her a string of pearls, not even one silver candlestick. I could pawn my poverty, but no one has ever loaned a grosz on a pledge like that."

"Have you ever tried? In this world you've got to try."

"Then I'll try now. Panie Kalman, sir, I know that people borrow money from you. Would you lend money to a rich man like me?"

"You see, Berele, it's worth a try. Yes, I will. I'll lend you a hundred. You can pay me back five zloty a week for twenty weeks."

Berele was terrified by this tremendous financial transaction. "And what if I don't earn anything one week? We're in the middle of an economic crisis right now. Or I could get sick, God forbid."

"If you ever need to skip a payment, the sky won't fall down."

"And what about feeding the animal? And the interest on the loan?"

"Don't be a coward, Berele. With a horse you'll be able to earn a lot more than you do now. And did you hear me say I would charge you interest?"

"That goes without saying."

"Consider it a friendly loan—no interest."

"You're not making fun of me? Why do I deserve a loan all of a sudden?"

"Don't be a shlemiel, Berele. You argue with me as if I were trying to rob you of your grandmother's inheritance. Ask around for an inexpensive horse and then come to me for the money . . ."

This conversation took place at the time when Kalman was about to go bankrupt. He was full of scorn for the suckers who had given him so much merchandise on credit. He needed money to finance his generating station and he would take it wherever he could. So why was he suddenly giving away a hundred zloty as a "friendly loan," Kalman asked himself.

The generating-station project was a business gamble, but the loan to Berele was just stupid. The horse might drop dead before Berele had managed to pay back the first five zloty. Why have I suddenly become so philanthropic, Kalman wondered. This started out as a prank on Berele. Oh well, Kalman the Cripple enjoys a prank even at his own expense.

5

For a pittance, Kalman rid himself of all his debts except one, a substantial one. All the other creditors stayed in Dombrovka for days, pleading, threatening him with lawsuits, whining that he was reducing them to penury. But Mr. Feinsilber was a proud and haughty man. He came to Dombrovka dressed immaculately, with a bowler hat and a silver-handled cane. His moustache was waxed, and his neat little beard was brushed stiffly to either side of his chin. Entering the store, he said, in German, *"Sie sind ein Dieb, sie sind ein Schwein!"* You are a thief, you are a pig! And, thumping the floor with his cane as if he were signing a verdict, he pivoted sharply, marched out, and went immediately back to Lodz.

When this happened, Kalman laughed it off. But when he wanted to start up his business again, his hands were tied as long as his unpaid notes remained in Feinsilber's possession. He wrote Feinsilber that he was ready "to do the impossible" and redeem the notes at twenty-five percent of their face value. The stubborn creditor did not deign to reply. Kalman could not bring himself to pay the debt in full, so he decided to travel to Lodz and pay Feinsilber a visit.

He was on the way to the railway station when he turned and went home for more cash. His plan was to lay money down on the table—he knew well he couldn't talk himself out of this situation. As he closed his door for the second time he paused, and then he went back inside once more and looked at a box full of pieces of jewelry that had been given to his grandfather as pledges and never redeemed. He selected a pair of pendant earrings with blue stones and a string of pearls. These items, added to the cash he had, amounted to about forty percent of the debt, which was the most he was ready to pay.

Herr Feinsilber sat behind a massive mahogany desk smoking a fat cigar as Kalman recounted a heart-rending story about his orphan childhood, his struggle to earn a living, and his burning ambition which had driven him too far and caused him to lose everything. He sensed that his near-perfect use of German was making a favorable impression on the resentful merchant, who was probably a Litvak but who sprinkled his speech liberally with German words to display his superiority over the other Jewish manufacturers of Lodz.

Kalman laid his money on the desk and looked at Feinsilber sadly. This was every cent he could scrape together, he said; he might not even have enough cash for the fare home. Then he produced the jewelry with a dramatic flourish. *"Und dieses Schmuck . . ."* And this jewelry. This was all he had left from his sainted mother, but he was ready to add it to his payment if Feinsilber would retract his insults, the words *"Dieb"* and *"Schwein"* that he had shouted in the store.

Feinsilber replied that he was not given to lightly insulting people. But when a customer buys something on credit and never pays him a grosz, then he was indeed a—

"Bitte, Herr Feinsilber, I beg you, do not insult me again. I am a whipped cur as it is."

Feinsilber finally agreed to accept the cash Kalman had offered. He would leave Kalman with his mother's jewels, but he would not retract his insults.

Kalman stuck the jewelry into his pocket and tore the notes into tiny bits. A sardonic grin appeared on his lips as he switched to Yiddish. "I really don't know how to thank you enough for having said *Dieb* and *Schwein* in German. If you had called me a *ganef* and a pig in Yiddish I wouldn't have been able to bear it. Nevertheless, Herr Feinsilber, I still need money for my generating plant. For each thousand that you return to me you can call me *Dieb* and *Schwein* again, and even tack on the word *ganef.*"

Feinsilber's mouth fell open.

"And if you return all the money to me," Kalman went on, "you can spit in my face at the same time."

Feinsilber regained his composure. "Stefan! Stefan!" he called. "Come in here quickly. Throw this miserable wretch out!"

"Herr Feinsilber, permit me to make one other observation," Kalman remarked coolly as he propelled himself out of the office. *"You* are a real *yekke putz*—yokel!"

Having paid off his last debt, Kalman filled up his shelves again. The Jews in Dombrovka felt deeply ashamed, as if they too were somehow guilty. People said it was always the same hulking peasant who tried to pocket something whenever a creditor was in the store, in order to give Yosl a chance to put on a show of strength and scare the creditor away . . .

6

Kalman sat behind his counter and gazed with satisfaction at his restocked shelves. Now he had both the contract for the generating plant and the money to build it. All those high-and-mighty Lodz businessmen were nothing but a bunch of suckers. When he had planned the bankruptcy he had never imagined it would all go so smoothly. He was already the wealthiest Jew in Dombrovka, and once the generating station was finished . . . He thought of how unhappy he'd always been that he could not stand as tall as other people; but once he was rich everyone would look up to him. His legs weren't as important as his head—it was more useful to out-smart the others than to outrun them. He thought of those big-city merchants who were out to dupe him when they stuck him with secondhand merchandise or out-of-fashion goods, and it reminded him of the anti-Semitic joke about the Jew and the Gypsy: A Jew wants to sell a horse to a Gypsy. A Pole standing nearby is curious to see who will get the better of whom. The Jew asks a ridiculously low price for the horse, and the Pole calls him aside and tells him, "That horse is worth a lot more!" The Jew replies, "I'm selling him cheap because he's lame." The Pole runs to the Gypsy: "The horse is lame." The Gypsy confides to the Pole: "The horse is limping because he has a nail in his hoof." The Pole runs back to the Jew: "Your horse is limping because he has a nail in his hoof." The Jew says, "I put the nail there myself, to make it appear that the nail is the cause for the horse's limping." The Gypsy buys the horse anyway. Afterwards, the Gypsy whispers to the Pole, "The money I paid for the horse isn't worth a plugged nickel—it's counterfeit!"

7

One might have thought that there were quite a few Matuses in Dombrovka, but in fact there was just one Matus, with many nicknames. He was called Matus Hopper, because he limped on his right foot; Matus Pulpit, because he liked to lead the services on the cantor's pulpit; Matus Goat, because he kept one; and Matus Glazier, because that was how he earned his living. His birth certificate said he was Matus Lifschitz, but hardly anyone knew him by that name.

Matus lived at the edge of town, where there were broad ditches overgrown with grass on either side of the road. It would have been a sin not to graze a goat in the ditches, especially considering that Matus's income was meager, and without the goat there wouldn't have been enough milk or cheese for the six mouths in his family. All year long they ate dairy meals, but around Passover a baby goat would be born, sometimes two, and the meat of a young kid tasted like the fruit of Paradise.

Replacing broken window panes and grazing a goat might have provided enough to sustain the Matus family if three of his daughters had not had, like their father, one leg shorter than the other. Those poor, limping young women should at least have a decent dress to wear. And his youngest daughter, who wasn't lame, and who was as pretty as a picture, shouldn't walk around in rags either. And on top of that, his wife, Tsippe, was always bungling things. When she milked the goat and carried the pail into the house, her foot would catch in the doorway and the milk would spill. When she finally put some milk to boil, it either ran over or was so badly scorched that it was inedible. When she hung up a bag of cheese to dry, the string would break and the cat would have a feast.

The oldest daughter, Kayleh, had a speech defect and couldn't pronounce the letter "K," so that her own name came out "Tayleh." But she was as agile as her father and had the same golden hands, if only she could find something to do with them. Other poor girls from town went off to Warsaw to serve in the homes of the rich, but Matus didn't want his Kayleh to be a servant-girl. That station in life, along with her limp, would make it impossible for her to find a husband.

If people hadn't had such bad things to say about Kalman the Cripple, Matus might have considered him and Kayleh a match. On the other hand, people talked just to have something to say. Why would Kalman rob the world when he earned a good, honest living anyway? If he had been a drunk or a carouser, one might believe these things. But no one had ever seen Kalman drunk, and the unfortunate man couldn't go out carousing, even if he wanted to. Maybe those stories were plain rumor mongering: Kalman had gotten rich, and people were jealous.

Matus proposed to Kalman that he hire Kayleh to help him in the store. The business was growing; another hand would be a blessing. Kalman said that he didn't need any more help in the store, but he could use someone to run the house.

"What do you mean, run the house? Kayleh is not a servant . . . "

"Run the house means run the house—buy the food, manage the household as if it were her own home."

"And cooking and cleaning and washing clothes?"

"Well, doesn't every woman cook and clean and wash clothes in her own home?"

Matus was pleased that Kalman talked of "a woman in her own home." "But she won't sleep in your kitchen, Kalman. She'll come home to sleep."

"Why should she sleep in the kitchen? It's a big house, she can have her own room."

Matus and his family all lived in one room. For Kayleh, a whole room to herself would be the height of luxury.

When Kayleh moved into Kalman's, the house immediately changed. She repainted the walls and scrubbed the floors and polished them until she could see her face in them. She measured the windows and made curtains out of lace that Kalman gave her from the store. Yosl wanted to help her hang them, but in his clumsiness he ripped one. Kalman laughed, pushed him aside, and helped Kayleh himself. He leaped about the room like a frog, his hands reaching wherever they were needed. Kayleh giggled and a warmth crept into her eyes as she watched him.

Only a week later, someone asked Kayleh whether she was a servant at Kalman the Cripple's.

"No," she replied. "I'm not his servant. I'm Talman the Tripple's fiancée."

•   •   •   •   •

Usually when Matus came home from anywhere, he had to run from neighbor to neighbor looking for his wife. Tsippe couldn't sit still in her own house—she always had something to complain about, and what was the use of complaining if there was no one around to hear you? Now, however, she avoided the neighbors, though her mouth still worked as she muttered complaints to herself and to Him whose Holy Name must not be uttered without first washing one's hands.

On one warm spring morning, doors stood open and the house-wives did much of their work in the courtyard. Tsippe was trying to churn up some butter, but she moved her tub into a corner away from the others. She churned away with the pestle to the rhythm of a prayer-tune and lamented softly, "Woe to my dark, hidden secrets which nobody in the world must know."

Although the day was warm, Tsippe wore her heavy shawl over her head and shoulders as though it would cover her secrets. As she beat the butter, her shawl kept sliding down and she kept pushing it up over her wig. Pieces of butter were forming in the tub. She thought about the borsht she would whip up with the buttermilk— she had already reckoned up how much butter she would sell and how much she would keep—when her shawl began to slide down again. She gave it an upward tug—and it shoved the wig right off her head and into the tub. She didn't know which calamity to be-moan first—the spoiled butter, the soiled wig, or the sin and dis-grace of her naked head, exposed in the middle of the courtyard. As she stood there wringing her hands, the cat ran by.

"She's got my piece of meat! Stop her, that thief!"

A dog started chasing the cat and they both vanished from sight. Tsippe ran into her house to see if there was anything left in the soaking-pail where she koshered her meat. They had planned to keep the baby goat until the holidays, but since they needed a few zloty Matus had the animal slaughtered and they were preparing the meat for the market. Tsippe was soaking only the head and lungs for her-self. Nothing was missing from the soaking-pail, but all the good meat they were preparing for sale was gone. "I accept the losses with humility, dear God," she moaned. "May it serve as a reprieve and absolve us from our sins. But that greater shame and punishment! Woe unto me and my hidden secrets that I dare not reveal to another human soul!"

When Kayleh disappeared from Kalman's house and from Dom-brovka, people caught on to the hidden secrets that Tsippe was mut-tering about.

When Matus went to talk to Kalman about marriage, Kalman was furious. "What do you want of me? Why don't you stop picking on a poor, defenseless cripple?"

"It didn't happen by itself," Matus pleaded.

"Of course it didn't happen by itself. But why pick on me? I have a partner, Yosl."

"If he's not lying," Matus later explained to Tsippe, "if, God forbid, it's the truth, then it's like a sore on top of a blister. If Kalman is making it up, if he had the gall to make up such a terrible lie, then there's nobody even to talk to."

"A terrible trouble, an awful calamity, woe unto us," Tsippe wailed.

"Hush!" Matus pleaded. "Pinch your cheek and give it color."

"When the heart is full the eyes run over, and I'm not even allowed to cry? Oy, with the disasters that have struck me, I'll be spared the tortures of the grave. May that cripple hurt like I'm hurting—may he lose both his arms too . . . "

"Don't, Tsippe. Cursing is a sin. May the One Above help us now. If only we could have a marriage ceremony to wipe out the shame and disgrace . . . "

Again Matus went to talk to Kalman. If only he would marry her . . . he could divorce her the next day. A child would be born, his child, let it not be born a bastard. "Kalman, I know you have a heart. Have pity on God's innocent creature."

A malicious grin twisted Kalman's lips. "God makes innocent human beings into miserable cripples and human beings make God's innocent creatures into bastards. Should a man be more righteous than God Himself?"

"Don't talk like that Kalman, you'll bring down a terrible punishment on yourself, God forbid."

That silly glazier should marvel to see me punished, Kalman reflected. Is he still trying to drag me under the wedding canopy? He grimaced: I'll grow a new pair of legs before they get me there . . .

8

The people of Dombrovka had begun to ridicule Kalman's boast about building a generating station for the town. But one fine morning, workmen began digging a foundation for the building. Kalman fussed around with papers and plans, and when people asked him what was going on he told them this was the building for his power plant. He began to make frequent trips to Warsaw to confer with the lawyers who were drawing up his agreement with the mayor. "The Pan has a good head on his shoulders," one of the lawyers remarked.

"And good-for-nothing legs," Kalman retorted.

"Did the Pan ever study law? The Pan made several interesting points."

"Everything can be found in books, Panie Attorney. I want to put in a clause that the name of the factory be 'Kalman the Cripple's Electric Generating Station.' Maybe the street could be called Kalman the Cripple Street? What is the Pan's opinion?"

•　•　•　•　•

Kalman's crooked house was again on everyone's lips, this time because of his partner, Yosl, or Yosl Golem, as he was now called. Yosl left Dombrovka, and when he had not returned after several days people concluded that Kalman had fired him, no longer needing him, since his business was now honest. But just as Yosl was fading from memory, he returned—and he brought a wife with him.

As Yosl was tall and broad shouldered, so Breindl was short and slender, with a pretty face and a shapely figure. "A big noodle and a tiny *farfl*," people said when they saw the couple, but it was said in envy. They said she had no brains, but anyone who talked to her knew that wasn't true. So why had she hooked up with a *golem*, a brainless hulk like Yosl? Maybe he was just lucky—after all, Kalman had taken him on as a partner; what could be luckier than that? As they said, "If it's meant to be, you don't have to be smart."

•　•　•　•　•

The roof had not yet been built onto the power station when wooden poles were unloaded on Lowicz Street. Within a few days, goats were frolicking on the poles, *heder*-boys were measuring them with their feet and trying to guess whether the poles would reach higher than the acacia and chestnut trees that lined the street. But some people were still skeptical: the poles would lie there forever; the whole story about an electrical generating plant was another of Kalman's tricks to wangle new credit so that he could declare bankruptcy and thumb his nose at the world again.

But one morning, as people were leaving the synagogue after prayers, pungent smoke stung their noses. It was coming from big iron kettles of boiling tar. Workmen dipped their brushes into the hot liquid and smeared it on the thicker ends of the poles, which would be buried in the ground.

9

Hannuka wasn't yet over, but an early cold spell held the land in its grip. During the night raging winds wrestled with the roofs, tore at the window shutters, and threatened the chimneys with an eerie howling. The wind finally died down, leaving huge heaps of snow that blocked entrances. The long night faded away with an almost serene quietness. On the fields the seeds nestled safely under a cover of white down, in the orchards the trees swayed with soft movements, as if careful not to shake off the sparkling white trim acquired during the snowfall.

Somewhere a cock pierced the night with a single crow, a moment of muteness, and soon all of Dombrovka resounded with the answer, as the night turned pale and receded, chased by the cocks' chorus. Light cracks appeared in the window shutters, the chimneys became alive with smoke and warmth, which melted the gray frost that had settled on the rooftops.

It was a market day, and the people were up early: one has to go to the synagogue before putting up the stalls. They were still wrestling with the frost-covered outer shutters when the town was shaken by a thunderous crash. Smoke reached the nostrils with a biting sensation. The alarm bell sounded. A fire? Where? A pillar of dust rose over Lowicz Street, but there was no red glow in the sky.

The house of Kalman the Cripple tumbled and crumbled down into a heap of rubble, smoke, and . . . dust more than smoke; it seemed that the tumbling walls suffocated the fire. What did it do to the three people inside?

Removing some of the debris, they found Yosl crushed under a huge beam. The barber-surgeon found faint signs of life in Kalman and Breindl. The local doctor did what he could, and then had them taken to the hospital in Lowicz.

When Kalman regained consciousness he was in great pain, but he couldn't help noticing the irony of his situation. His wasted legs had remained whole, except for a burn where his trousers had caught fire. But the sound part of his body was seriously damaged. His right arm was broken, his ribs were cracked, his flesh lacerated. Had anything remained intact? Kalman wondered. The doctor listed his injuries and Kalman summed up the answer: yes, his head had remained intact so that he might better understand how crippled he now was. It seemed that he would have to be carried or pushed around in a wheelchair.

For Breindl things hadn't gone well either. Her broken legs were not the worst of it, the doctor said. They still couldn't tell the extent of her injuries. Evidently she could see and hear, because she was able to follow instructions. But not a sound came out of her mouth—had she lost the power of speech? And was the loss physical or as a result of the shock of the accident? Kalman hoped it was permanent, so that no one would ever have to learn what happened during that tragic night.

Kalman left the hospital and returned to Dombrovka, over his doctor's objections—his bones were mending, but they were not healed; the burn on his leg was still festering; his back was still weak. But Kalman insisted that he couldn't leave his business unattended any longer. What business, wondered the doctor. The store lay in ruins, the power plant couldn't be finished while the whole town was under three feet of snow, so what was the rush?

Kalman had had the very same debate with himself, and the answer was his grandfather's gold pieces, which were now lying under the debris of his house. If no one knew about them, no one would go digging in the snow, that was true. Breindl, the only person who did know, lay in the hospital speechless. Nevertheless, he preferred to be back in Dombrovka. Kalman the Cripple and Yosl the giant, he mused, but who had survived? Apparently, at that terrible moment he had had enough sense not to be positioned directly under a beam. If one's head is in the right place one can crawl to safety out of the world's worst troubles.

10

A distant cousin came all the way from Warsaw to visit Kalman. Kalman had never heard of this person and knew that he hadn't come to visit but to see how close he was to the inheritance. The relative had learned about the accident from the newspapers, which had taken the occasion to write about Kalman's accomplishments and the power-station project. When Kalman's mother had been stranded with a sick child, no cousins had shown up. When the sick child had been left an orphan, no relatives had appeared to claim him. A cripple has no relatives. But a power plant does, even if it belongs to the cripple.

Kalman's dreams were beginning to be fulfilled, though. Every one of his get-rich schemes had included the hope that he would be written up in the newspapers, and that one of those papers would eventually reach his father. When his father read about the achievements of his son, he would remember that he had a share in him and would come running from wherever the devil had taken him to. Did he miss his father? Oh, no. If his father had any sense, he wouldn't dare show his face anywhere near his son.

11

Even when he was a *heder*-boy, Kalman realized that life was passing him by. The other boys ran out to play in the meadows, swim in the river, skate on the ice. He, Kalman, had his great moment when he managed to construct a wooden sled which enabled him to get around even when there was snow on the ground. People called him a "cripple with golden hands." That was his first triumph.

As he was growing up, the other boys started talking about girls, and the girls started swaying their hips when they saw the boys watching. But they didn't pay attention to him—no girl ever "showed" him anything, or encouraged him to put his hand on a "soft place." Girls looked at him with revulsion or, at best, pity. He had his tricks, though. He might "accidentally" bump into a girl on the street and his head would end up under her dress. He found a way to climb a tree near the river and hide in the foliage for hours until the girls came down to swim. From another hiding place he managed to peep in a window and watch a girl getting undressed. He sneaked over to the window and tossed a live mouse into her room. The girl ran out of the room squealing and half naked, and he deemed it a great triumph.

But these pranks left Kalman empty. The fantasy that when he got rich his father would appear was the best of his reveries; it warmed and excited him; it had brought him Yosl, it had brought him bankruptcy, it had brought him a generating plant and—it had smashed his bones. And still his father hadn't come.

He still hadn't found a way to scavenge the treasure that was buried beneath the snow-covered ruins of his house. He thought of building a fence around the property or getting a vicious dog, but that would give away his secret. At any rate, he knew that he still had enough money in the bank to complete the generating plant, even if his gold pieces were stolen. However, he soon learned that people were cutting down the posts, and the police were looking the other way. The city had already given up on the power station. But they didn't know Kalman the Cripple!

Kalman was now living in a rented room in Dombrovka, with a nurse to take care of him. Judging from his fervor, it appeared that he would actually be able to claw his way out of the pit he was in. Two weeks after he was released from the hospital, workmen were again stringing wires along the poles on Lowicz Street, in spite of the cold. Kalman had his bed pushed close to the window so he could look out and enjoy this triumph.

Maria, the strict nurse, permitted Kalman no visitors. But once, when Maria was out shopping, Matus the Glazier managed to sneak into his room.

"Reb Matus? Oh, I owe you money for putting in the windows at the plant. You must have thought it was a lost cause, eh? Don't worry—I would have come back from the grave to finish this project."

Matus counted the money, but he remained at Kalman's bedside. Kalman guessed that Matus wanted a few zloty extra because he had waited so long for his money. He felt rather friendly toward the glazier because the matter with Kayleh had been so quickly dropped. Kalman put another ten zloty in Matus's hand. "This is for waiting for so long . . ."

But Matus still stood there. Did he want more?

"Ten zloty is a nice bonus," Kalman said, indicating that he had reached the limit of his generosity.

"Thank you very much, Kalman. Ten zloty is enough. It will come in handy, especially the way things are going these days."

"Is there something else you want?"

"As a matter of fact—"

Kalman gave him a stern look. Matus was not going to start up again with that old story?

"Kalman, you've just been granted a great miracle. You stared death in the face—may God protect you—and yet you escaped. You must have some special favor in the Almighty's eyes. Tell me the truth now. Kayleh swears by her life that Yosl never touched her. I'm not demanding anything from you. I only want to know one thing: did you make up the story about Yosl because you didn't want to marry her? Or were you suspicious for no good reason? By my life— and yours, Kalman—you're going to tell me the truth!"

"What difference does it make now?"

"A big difference. Maybe not for you. But Kayleh swears she thought you were going to marry her."

"I never promised her that."

"She admits that, but she was convinced nevertheless."

"Am I obliged to fulfil her daydreams?"

"No one's asking you to marry her now. But my family is the laughing stock of Dombrovka. Moyshe Longlegs doesn't let me lead the afternoon services any more. He yelled at me, right in the syna- gogue, saying my daughter is a whore."

"Moyshe is still the big shot in your synagogue? He must think the notes he owes me are buried under the ruins of my house. Don't worry. The notes are safe in a bank in Warsaw. Tell Moyshe I can put him out of business any time I please."

"It's not just what other people are saying, Kalman. It's a shame and a disgrace for us. At first I couldn't eat or sleep, but now I believe my daughter."

Maria returned, and Matus rushed on to his main point. "Kal- man, I swear to you, I only want one thing from you—for you to admit that your suspicions of Kayleh were unfounded."

Matus waited. Kalman sat mute. Maria crossed her arms and stared at Matus, waiting for him to leave. "Kayleh has a good job in Warsaw, and Zelikl is a happy, healthy child," Matus managed to add before Maria grabbed his arm and propelled him to the door.

"A happy, healthy child," Kalman chuckled bitterly. "Out of two cripples . . ." He suddenly yelled, "Where is he? Why did the Pani put him out? Why is the Pani standing there like a dummy? Call him back! Run after him and bring him back here!"

A few minutes later Matus stood before him again.

"Please sit down, Reb Matus," Kalman said affably. "A person comes to visit and my nurse chases him out—I'm like a prisoner in her hands . . . "

Matus sat on a chair near the bed and waited for Kalman to tell him why he had called him back. But Kalman said nothing.

"Is there something you wanted to tell me?" Matus finally asked.

"I just wanted to say—your Kayleh—you know her better than I do. If you believe her, I do, too."

Matus leaped from his chair and seized Kalman's hand. "Kalman, you've granted me new life! May God grant you a speedy recovery!"

Kalman had only wanted to weaken Matus's complaints against him, but perhaps he had said more than he had intended. He yanked his hand away impatiently, to Matus's surprise. To restore his goodwill, Kalman smiled. "You said things weren't going so well. Maybe I'll find some work for you."

Matus left, marveling at Kalman's generosity.

What had occurred to Kalman was that there was probably only one man honest enough—or foolish enough—to be entrusted with the job of digging his gold pieces from under his house, and that was Matus. Although . . . anyone could be tempted to steal, and who had a better excuse than Matus? He would convince himself that he was doing it for his grandchild, Kalman's son and heir by the law of God. No, Kalman decided, he wouldn't rush into it.

Matus visited Kalman often. Kalman tried to buy Matus's friendship by paying him to run errands. And Matus, for his part, always found an opportunity to work Kayleh's name into the conversation. Sympathy was cheap, and Kalman provided it in abundance. He was "deeply hurt," he said, that Matus would even entertain the slightest suspicion that he, Kalman, had made up stories about Kayleh and Yosl. He himself had been shamed and persecuted all his life—why would he disgrace someone else for no good reason? And yet . . . a healthy, handsome strong young man hanging around the house all the time, and he, Kalman, nothing but a cripple. "Am I not correct, Reb Matus, that Yosl was a much more attractive man than I?"

"I'm lame myself," said Matus, pointing to his leg, "but you should have seen my Tsippe when she was young. Believe it or not, people used to stop and stare at her in the street, that's how pretty she was. And my Raizele . . . "

"Maybe you're right. I don't know what Kayleh ever saw in me. She has a face like a doll . . . "

Matus was so moved that his eyes grew moist. "Kalman, we can still set things right. I won't deny that Kayleh was furious after you voiced your suspicions about Yosl—we couldn't even mention your name. But she has a pure soul . . . "

Kalman retreated. "You don't have to tell me about Kayleh's virtues, Reb Matus. But Kayleh and I as a match—it doesn't make sense. Two cripples going out dancing? The whole town would laugh. And it would be bad for business, too." Matus's face turned gray, and Kalman tried again to retrieve the situation. "But more important than anything is *menshlichkeit,* decency."

"Kayleh's child is your own flesh and blood."

Kalman knew he shouldn't have let the conversation go this far, but since it had he shouldn't have said that he had no intention of marrying Kayleh—not before the gold pieces had been found. Oh well, let Matus think that Kalman was infatuated with her; later, when it no longer mattered what that silly family thought of him, they could call him a traitor, a crook, a liar, and a thief.

"I beg you, Reb Matus, when you see Kayleh please tell her that I am not so black a devil as she thinks. I too have been nursing a broken heart ever since that time. It's hard for me to talk about it, but if Kayleh could read my thoughts she would certainly not be angry with me, that I can swear to you."

As he said the word "swear," a new idea flashed in his head, but he needed time to think it through. "Please come back first thing tomorrow morning. I've got something very important to tell you."

Matus appeared the following morning immediately after services. Although Kalman was aware that this meant that Matus had not yet had breakfast, he moved directly to the business at hand.

"Reb Matus, I'm a sick man, much sicker than you think. I have no family. To whom shall I turn, all alone and tied to this bed? To whom am I turning now? You're the closest person to me in all Dombrovka. You'll do a great *mitzva* and I'll pay you well for your trouble . . . "

"Helping a sick person is indeed a *mitzva,* Kalman, but you needn't pay me for that. If you have work for me, that is something else."

"You need a livelihood, and I don't expect anyone to work for me for nothing. The store is in ruins, but the Almighty doesn't desert a cripple. He punishes with one hand and rewards with the other."

Again Matus's eyes grew moist. "If there's something I can do for you, just say the word."

"If there's anyone who doesn't believe that the One Above sends the remedy with the sickness, let him talk to me. But what I have to say to you now is a deep secret, and it must remain a secret."

"Don't worry. I know how to keep secrets."

"Sometimes you can't trust even yourself, right? Most of what I learned in *heder* I forgot long ago, but I do remember this much: although everything is contained in the Torah, and Jews must observe it, our sages built a fence around the Law because a human being cannot trust himself completely. But I am keeping you from your breakfast. Why don't you go home and eat, then come back here with a Chumash."

"A Chumash?"

"Yes, you bring a Chumash and have your wife bring along her woman's bible, *Tzena Ur-ena*. She must have one, for how else would Kayleh know all those Bible stories she told me? Yes, bring your children too. I wouldn't ask you to keep secrets from your family."

Matus stood wide-eyed and openmouthed.

"Don't worry, Reb Matus, I haven't taken leave of my senses. I can't say any more now than I've said already. But you'll soon see for yourself. You'll save me and I—well, you'll see . . . "

As soon as Matus got home, he told Tsippe to find the girls. His breathless excitement alarmed her.

"Matus, what's happened?"

"Nothing bad, God forbid. Just the opposite. Go call the children."

"Matus, you're white as chalk. I won't go until you tell me!"

"Of course I'll tell you! Do I ever keep secrets from you? But you're standing there instead of getting the girls, so how can I tell you?"

"Oh my God! It must be something terrible, I feel it in my bones! I'll faint right here. How can I go out there scared to death?"

"Your health should only be as good as the news! You should have heard how he talked about Kayleh!"

"Who? What did he say? Must I drag it out one word at a time?"

"What do you mean, who? I told you where I was going, didn't I? And how can I tell you when I don't even know myself. All I know is it's a big secret. And you should've heard what he said about Kayleh."

"That wicked crook? That treacherous liar? May someone be saying Kaddish for him very soon, please God . . . So what do you need the children for?"

"He wants us all to come and he'll tell us."

"Tell us what?"

"If you keep standing there like a stubborn mule, we'll never know!"

Tsippe ran out to the courtyard, crying, "Freydl, Chaya, Raizel, come quick! Kalman wants to tell us all a secret!"

•   •   •   •   •

Kalman knew that for Matus and Tsippe an oath was a sacred thing. To violate an oath was to sell your soul to Satan. They would have to swear on a holy object—a scroll of the Torah, maybe, but where would he get one? If they swore in the synagogue, the whole community would know something was afoot. He would have Matus swear on a Hebrew Bible and Tsippe on her Yiddish Bible. So, Kalman thought, his head was still working well—he had found the best way—the only way—to gather up his gold pieces without any loss at all.

But when Matus and his family, dressed in their finest clothes, arrived at Kalman's door, they found it locked. They learned from the neighbors that the police had taken Kalman and his nurse away.

12

Two months after the fire, Breindl was still in the hospital, but she felt much better and the doctor believed she was ready to hear the truth about her husband: "Only you and Kalman survived."

"Kalman is alive?"

"She's talking!" The doctor tried to get her to say something else, but her eyes glazed over and her lips were sealed again. Not until later that evening, when a nurse came to see how she was feeling, did Breindl ask:

"Is he here in this hospital?"

"Thank God, he didn't suffer," the nurse said, being sure Breindl was asking about her husband. "A big beam split his head open and that was the end."

"When?"

"There were no signs of life when they found him."

"But the doctor told me—"

"Unfortunately, no signs of life. Only the Pani and the Pan—what is his name?"

"I'm talking about Kalman."

"Oh, him. Yes, he was here. But he's already gone home."

"Home? That scoundrel—he's gone home? Yosl is in his grave and his murderer has gone home?" Breindl began to thrash about so violently that it took a strong sedative to quiet her.

The following morning she began to talk again. She asked to see the police, because the house had not collapsed of its own accord—Kalman had murdered her husband and had almost killed her too.

Kalman was brought in, but he was able to post a modest bail and remain free. As soon as he returned to his bed, he sent Maria to fetch Matus. If Breindl was talking, he must act immediately.

Matus, Tsippe, and their three daughters swore they would say nothing and immediately got to work. They dug in the snow, they moved piles of debris. Since Matus had already visited Kalman and was known to run errands for him, no one wondered why he and his family were now working for him, cleaning up the debris of the collapsed house and preparing the lot for a new building. Matus avoided other people, and he even stopped going to the synagogue. Tsippe didn't dare reply to a simple good morning, because the oaths she had sworn to Kalman dictated that she would burn in hell if she broke her word. Tsippe had expected another kind of secret from Kalman, something to do with Kayleh; but she knew that it would come eventually. After all, he had trusted Matus with this job, a task for only the closest relatives.

Matus and his family worked like mules for three days digging in the rubble, moving planks, chunks of stucco, and heavy beams, but they found nothing. The little crowd of spectators melted away after a while, and Matus began to wonder if this wasn't a useless task which was overtaxing the strength of his wife and daughters. But Kalman wouldn't let him stop; the night of the fire was still vivid in his head—when the old beams had started to shake it had rained gold pieces. Old Jonah had squirreled them away in cracks in the ceiling.

Finally, on the morning of the fourth day of digging, Tsippe cried out, "Matus, I am fainting!" Matus rushed over to where she was digging, hushing her frantically when he saw the glitter at her feet. He filled his pockets with gold pieces and ran to Kalman's house.

By the end of that day, they had found so much gold that Kalman was sure they had gotten it all. But the next morning Matus found more; and that evening he found paper rubles that would have amounted to a small fortune if the paper banknotes hadn't lost their value. Kalman wondered where his grandfather had gotten so much money. He couldn't have earned it in the store—had he had another business? Had he inherited it? Had he robbed a bank? And why did the old miser take the secret with him to the grave? With such a fortune Kalman could have built the power station without his tricky bankruptcy.

Over the next few days the flow of gold from the ruins slowed to a trickle, but Matus started bringing Kalman documents that he found wrapped in rags or folded up and stuffed into tin cigar boxes or empty Wisotsky tea tins. Kalman guessed that many of these were certificates that were now worthless, and wondered how Jonah could have been so crazy as to allow these treasures to rot away in secret. And he wondered where they had been hidden so that he had never found them.

One of the tin cans was packed tight with notes and scraps of paper all bearing the same signature. Kalman spent an entire night trying to decipher the name, and he succeeded as dawn was breaking. Stefan Pakula? That was the squire of the Dombrovka court! When had Jonah had dealings with that Jew-hater? Could it be that Pakula had owed money to Jonah and had stopped paying after Jonah died? Kalman found one paper dated from before the Great War. At that time the old squire, Davidson, had still been alive, and Pakula had been his employee.

If these really were the squire's notes, and if he was under the impression that they had been lost or destroyed, it would be better to keep them hidden until after the trial, when Breindl's charges against Kalman would be dismissed, for the squire and the judge were probably cronies.

Kalman was in no hurry for that trial. Breindl was very sick— maybe she'd croak—may the little bitch be found a *shriven lich* in a desolate ditch! He found it hard to believe that he had been crazy about her. Bringing her to his house was no more than a prank, a practical joke . . . and in no time the sober, cynical Kalman was nuts about her. He could see that she was cute. But he wanted to believe that he was immune to a woman's shtick, and nursed himself with the smart aleck joke, "if I need a glass of milk once in a while, I am not going to buy a cow." It was an excuse for his damn pride and the fear of rejection. The little bitch had taught him a big lesson: no female would ever again weaken him. To hell with his cracked bones and burnt leg, as long as his head stayed intact and free of emotional attachment. He knew how to get what he wanted, and God help anyone who got in his way . . .

13

That evening, Matus hung around longer than usual, shuffling his feet and looking uncomfortable, until he finally blurted out, "If I have no time to work at my trade, I don't have money to feed my family. You've got to give me a few zloty!"

Kalman couldn't believe his ears. This jerk Matus was no smarter than his daughter Kayleh—here he was handling piles of uncounted money and he hadn't skimmed off a grosz for himself! "Do you know how much money you've brought me?" he asked.

"How should I know? I couldn't stand in the street counting it."

"You came right here? You never stopped off at your house, or anywhere else?"

"Why should I?" Matus sounded insulted.

"To get a drink of water. To stop at the synagogue for afternoon services . . ."

"I haven't been inside the synagogue since I started this job for you."

"Why not?"

"People talk, they ask questions. And I swore a sacred oath to keep your secret—I even avoid talking to people in the street."

"How much do you want, then? How much do you make a day as a glazier?"

"I work alone at my trade, and glaziery is different from dragging beams around and pushing wheelbarrows full of rubble . . . "

"How much do you want?" Kalman asked again.

"We all worked, Tsippe, Freydl, Chaya, Raizel. Their hands are all scratched up—"

"So how much do you want?"

"Whatever you give me."

"And if I give you one zloty?"

"I know you won't cheat me."

"How do you know that? You hear what people say about me, don't you?"

"One person says bad things, another good. Like Berele the porter."

"What does Berele say?"

"Berele would tear the eyes out of anyone who says a word against you. 'Kalman made me stop being a horse,' he says."

"What does he mean by that?"

"He still tells the story of how you offered to buy a horse for him so he wouldn't have to pull his wagon himself."

"He paid me back every grosz," Kalman recalled, pulling out his wallet.

Matus stared in disbelief at Kalman's outstretched hand: two crisp hundred-zloty bills!

"Kalman, I'll turn over every stone, I'll sift through every inch of dirt, nothing will be lost."

Kalman, who only a few hours earlier had been so glad that he was not encumbered by emotions, now marveled at the words which came out of his mouth. "This is just a down payment, Reb Matus. Listen to what I am saying to you. Forget about glaziery! Starting today, you have a job with me, and you won't lack for anything. And do they still prevent you from leading the services in that synagogue? Soon they'll be begging you to. Listen—one of these days Moyshe Longlegs will bow down before you and plead, 'Reb Matus, would you please do us the honor of leading the afternoon services?' Remember what I'm saying, Matus . . . "

Tears welled up in Matus's eyes, and Kalman was surprised to find his own eyes grow moist. True, he needed Matus now, but he had spoken only to soften Matus's heart—and his own heart had melted like butter on a hot stove.

But he didn't have to wait long to see his emotions backfire: Matus embraced him and pleaded, "Kalman, my dear Kalman, be a father to your child!"

For a moment, Kalman was speechless. Then he quickly suppressed the harsh words that rose in his throat. He needed this simpleton now as much as he did his own life.

"Listen to me carefully, Reb Matus. I already have one foot in the grave—I might as well think of marriage as of going out dancing. There will be time to think about this when . . . if . . . I regain my health . . ."

14

Among the papers Matus found in the ruins of Kalman's house was the photograph of a baby. Kalman did not recall having seen it before. Had it been among his grandfather's important documents? Was that old misanthrope really sentimental enough to keep a toddler's picture among his treasures? On the back of the photograph was the inscription, "This is my Kalmandl at the age of one," and it was signed, "Boruch."

Kalman was amazed that this happy baby with the plump, healthy legs sticking up in the air was himself. He became completely distracted from his gold and his certificates. "My Kalmandl" —once there had been a little boy whose father had called him by an affectionate name and had his picture taken so he could show him off. This child had a mother too, and even his grandfather, who lived far away, kept the photograph among his precious possessions—no wonder the baby was happy!

Kalman left the picture on the table, where he could see it to admire it, and it was there when Matus came in the next morning. Matus snatched it up and hurried to Kalman's bedside: "Where did you get this?"

"You brought it to me."

"I did? No! Never!"

"It was among the papers you brought yesterday."

"Impossible! What would it be doing among the papers?"

"Do you know who this is?"

"Do you know?"

"Read the other side."

Only now did Matus notice that it was an old photograph. The ink of the inscription had already faded. His hand trembled as he handed the photograph back. Kalman started to ask what was wrong, but Matus suddenly dashed out the door. Just as Kalman was about to send Maria after him, he rushed back in and handed Kalman another photograph.

"How did you come by this?" Kalman demanded.

"It's my grandson, Zelikl, my Kayleh's little boy." Matus's voice choked with emotion.

Kalman stared at the two pictures a long time, comparing the features. It occurred to him that it would have been better if the child had Kayleh's features and his brains, rather than the other way around . . .

Maria came over to see what he was staring at. He pointed to the new photograph: "Not bad for Kalman the Cripple, eh?"

15

The date of the trial was approaching, and every few days a new examiner showed up. Kalman was not the only one they assailed with their questions about everything under the sun; they also questioned people who had nothing to do with him directly. They even went to Matus for Kayleh's address. Kalman wondered who was out to get him: was it the Mayor trying to get rid of him so that he wouldn't have to pay for the power plant? If so, the joke was on them, because Kalman wouldn't lift a finger until the court absolved him of all guilt. But all the same, he would obviously have to hire a good lawyer.

The lawyer asked Kalman whether he had any close friends who could serve as character witnesses. Friends, Kalman replied, no, he didn't even have relatives. He had had a distant cousin, Yosl, whom he had taken into the business, but the poor fellow had died. It was only after the lawyer left that Kalman remembered that there was someone who would vouch for him—Matus. But there was one problem with Matus—he couldn't tell a lie, especially after taking an oath. And in court you are under oath to tell the truth. No doubt they would ask Matus about Kayleh, and he would use the opportunity to deny that there was a "partner" named Yosl. In fact, Matus should be sent out of town. But what about Berele the porter? Berele would only have to repeat what he kept telling everyone about the tremendous favors Kalman had done for him. At the time Kalman had thought it was foolishness, but apparently even his foolishness had paid him off handsomely.

Besides, he now had enough gold to buy as many friends as he wanted. He had neither the time nor the patience to court individuals, but he could do something big for the community and, in one gesture, capture the hearts of all the Jews in Dombrovka.

Matus had gone to Warsaw to put the squire's notes in a safe-deposit box in Shereshevsky's Bank, in Kalman's name. He came back half-frozen after traveling from the train station for almost three hours in an open buggy. As he warmed his hands at the brick oven, Kalman asked him, "Matus, what does the Jewish community of Dombrovka need?"

Matus didn't understand the question. "What do we need? The same thing all Jews need—salvation. Grabski's Hearse is killing our business." Finance Minister Grabski had invented a new way to drive Jews out of business: he levied impossibly heavy taxes on Jewish merchants, and when they couldn't pay the bailiff came with a wagon and expropriated their merchandise. Just as the community burial society's hearse signaled the death of a Jewish soul, "Grabski's Hearse" meant the death of Jewish businesses.

"Even without Grabski's decrees, may there soon be an end to our exile and all our troubles," Kalman sighed sanctimoniously. "I'm talking about something else now. I was in a terrible accident, and with God's help I came out of it alive. But I still need Divine mercy, both for my health and for the slanders that crazy Breindl fabricated about me. A poor man donates one candle to the synagogue. Thank God, I can afford more than that."

"Give them a whole kilo of candles."

"No, Reb Matus. I need a great deal of help and I want to do something really important."

"Well, the community needs a synagogue. And a *mikveh,* a ritual bath. That Jew-hating squire won't stop his dirty tricks until he executes his whole plan to the end."

"Oh, Reb Matus, what a wise man you are!"

Matus didn't see great wisdom in what he had said, but Kalman asked no more questions. He just encouraged Matus to take off his boots, unwind his leggings, and rest his chilled feet against the tiles of the oven. Matus warmed himself thoroughly, and then went home.

As soon as Matus left, Kalman began to scheme. He would kill two birds with one stone. He still had to take care of the details though, and he was in no hurry . . .

•   •   •   •   •

When the Jewish community had wanted to build a synagogue, all of Dombrovka still belonged to the "nobleman's estate," and that estate belonged to Davidson, the Jewish landowner. The truth was, though that he wasn't much of a Jew. No mezuzas hung on the doorposts of his palace; he never set foot inside the Dombrovka synagogue; and, though he spent his winters in Warsaw, he apparently never entered the Warsaw synagogue either.

A committee of respected Jews, headed by Jonah, had gone to see Davidson. It must be said that he never turned away the Jews who came to ask him for something. On this occasion he immediately called in his estate manager and plans to build the synagogue were discussed on the spot.

It never occurred to anyone to ask the squire for an official transfer of the property. For one thing, there was no one to transfer it to—there wasn't another individual in Dombrovka whose name was as good as the squire's. For another, the lumber for the synagogue building was hewn from Davidson's forest, and the bricks were from his brickyard.

The town was further improved when a large square was paved for a marketplace, and Tuesday and Friday were designated as auction days, and every fourth Tuesday became market day. People came from all over to buy and sell—the peasants their crops, the Jews whatever the peasants needed for their homes and farms. The synagogue had been built on a side street, but now the side street had become part of the marketplace, so the synagogue stood on a more prominent site than the church. The Jew-haters in Dombrovka couldn't stand this, and the worst Jew-hater in town was Stefan Pakula, the husband of the old squire's only daughter, Jadzia.

As Jadzia grew up, anyone could see that she hated Jews like poison, but no one stopped to think that the land on which the synagogue, Study House, and *mikveh* sat was still registered in her father's name. The squire died young, and his land and inheritance went to Jadzia. People said that her conversion and her marriage to the anti-Semitic hoodlum Pakula had driven her father to his early grave.

Apparently, Pakula's attorneys advised him not to take the matter to court. Jews who seemed to know said that as long as the synagogue building was standing there was nothing he could do. Only when the structure itself had to be rebuilt could he get his hands on the land. In the meantime, he simply made trouble. His workmen came and dug ditches in front of the synagogue and the bathhouse, making it hard to enter. At the bathhouse, not a week went by that a "careless" pickax didn't puncture a water pipe. It was feared the constant digging would undermine the foundation of the building.

Kalman was preparing himself to battle the squire. It seemed as if he was never happy except when he was plotting to trip one up, trap another, and show a third up for a sucker. And now it was the squire's turn.

Generally, the squire was in Dombrovka only during the summer; he spent his winters in Warsaw or abroad. But this winter, it happened that he had invited a whole party of guests to his estate to join him hunting in his forests. Dozens of elegant sleighs arrived with a great clamor and tinkling of bells. The noise woke Kalman, and he moved into action. Maria delivered a note to the squire's court, advising that Kalman wanted to see him. She returned without a reply.

"What did he tell you?" Kalman asked.

"Nothing."

"The Pani did not wait for an answer? But I told you—"

"I waited and waited and waited. The guests were all over the place, the servants kept running back and forth, but no one paid any attention to me. Finally someone asked me what I wanted. I said I was waiting for a reply from his Most Distinguished Pan Squire."

"And?"

"The person went away, came right back, and led me out to the gate."

"What did he say?"

"Nothing."

"The Pani will have to go back with another letter."

"I'm a nurse, not a messenger."

"This time the Pani will not wait for an answer. Here's five zloty—the Pani should not have to go all the way to the squire's court for nothing."

The new letter read: "To his Excellency, the highborn, noble, and gracious Pan Pakula: I humbly beg the exalted and highborn Pan Squire to kindly do me the honor of permitting me to see him concerning certain notes and documents of the years 1904–1905 which are made out to my grandfather, Jonah Swerdl, and signed by the highborn Pan Squire. Since these documents are in the custody of an attorney and the attorney plans to initiate certain legal actions, it is of utmost importance that his highborn Excellency, in his noble generosity, allow me to see him immediately, without delay.

"I remain the honorable Squire's most humble servant. With sincere respect, Kalman Swerdl, 27 Lowicz Street."

Had his right hand not still been in a cast, Kalman would have rubbed his palms together in glee with this letter: calling the squire "highborn" of course rubbed in the fact that he wasn't highborn at all, that in reality his status and possessions came to him through his Jewish wife.

The next day, a messenger from the squire appeared at Kalman's, announcing that the squire was ready to meet with him. But now Kalman was in no hurry. When he had sent his letter it had been a sunny day; now, with the wind and snow, he could not leave his house—he was a sick man, perhaps the squire would consider coming to see him. When the messenger left, Kalman hurt his bruised ribs laughing as he pictured the fury of the squire—the insolence of that little Jew, suggesting that the squire come to see him!

The weather improved, but Kalman informed the squire that he was still not feeling well enough to venture out. In this way Kalman postponed his visit from day to day for a week. Finally, a messenger came to announce that the squire was about to return to Warsaw. Kalman replied that fortunately his legal matters were being handled by an attorney in Warsaw anyway. The squire must have been dying to find out what documents Kalman had in his possession, because he sent his own coach to fetch Kalman, and Kalman finally let himself be persuaded that the closed coach would transport him comfortably to the squire and take him home again.

The palace was quiet; all the guests had departed. Only the squire and a few servants rattled around in the enormous building. This was the setting for a contest between two master manipulators, each trying to ferret out what the other knew. The squire denied that he had ever borrowed money from Jonah. Yes, they had jointly agreed to provide the Russian army with flour and meat for the

Manchurian war front with Japan. Actually, it was the squire's deal; Jonah was only supposed to help him.

"A thousand pardons, Most Distinguished Pan Squire, but all this happened close to thirty years ago. The Squire looks not a day over thirty himself."

This attempted compliment did not sway the squire. "I was actually in my early twenties, but I already had a reputation and important contacts. The contract was in my name."

"I know, but my attorney says—"

"What does the Pan's attorney say?" the squire almost jumped down Kalman's throat with curiosity.

"These matters are much too complicated for me. If his Excellency wants to know the truth, I must confess I didn't understand what the lawyer said. He used so many legal terms I couldn't make head nor tail of it."

"As I said, it was my contract—a tremendous deal. And, as well, I managed all the affairs of the old squire. I didn't need to borrow money from anyone."

"But the Most Distinguished Pan Squire signed—Oh, I forgot— at that time the Most Distinguished Pan Squire was not yet a Most Distinguished Pan Squire."

The squire's face turned a fiery red, but he only muttered from behind his moustaches, "Didn't borrow, never borrowed. If I signed, maybe as security, as a guarantor for the partnership."

"Then his Excellency must surely have my grandfather's notes and guarantees. My attorney has not yet looked over all the papers." Kalman laughed. "The papers might have grown moldy in the Warsaw Bank and I wouldn't have known anything about them, but when they started that latest business with our synagogue, it occurred to me that maybe there was something in my grandfather's papers about the land for the synagogue. They tell me that Jonah visited the old squire frequently."

"There's nothing in the books about a synagogue."

"My grandfather was a careful, prudent man. He would never have started building if he hadn't had the requisite documents."

"The Pan has found a document?"

"Everything is in the hands of my lawyers. He must have found something. He asked me to write him about every action taken against the synagogue."

"Why do you keep it so dirty that it's a disgrace to the city?"

"That's something I would undertake to correct, for your Excellency's sake. Even if I pay for it out of my own pocket, I will fix everything up and renovate the building so that it will not be a disgrace."

The squire wanted to know who Kalman's lawyer was, but Kalman had a sudden lapse of memory—he slapped his forehead in frustration. All he could remember was that his office was on Leshno Street.

Several days later, a load of lumber was left on the snow outside the synagogue, to be used for a new floor; Kalman sent Matus to tell Moyshe Longlegs that as soon as the weather warmed up he would pay for a new roof to be put on the building.

"That Kalman will ruin us all yet!" protested Moyshe Longlegs. "It's dangerous to call the bear out of the woods!"

"It's all arranged with the squire," Kalman assured everyone, but they would not have been so reassured if they hadn't heard from other sources that Kalman had actually visited the squire, riding in a coach sent by the squire himself.

16

Only a few weeks earlier, if Kalman had invited Reb Aaron to his home, the old Hassid would have declined the invitation; Kalman was well known as a scoffer and a libertine. But now he had dared to talk with the squire about the synagogue and had even donated generously out of his own pocket for its reconstruction. It was possible that all the things said about him were pure libel. Or, on the other hand, perhaps he had become a penitent after the One above had rescued him from death beneath the ruins of his house. And was it not written that a true penitent can sometimes earn a better place in the next world than a man who has been righteous all his life? And so Reb Aaron accepted Kalman's invitation immediately. He was certain that Kalman wanted to speak with him about assuming certain fasts and mortifications of the flesh as penance for his previous sins. What else would a young man like Kalman have to talk about with an old man who for the last twenty years had been sitting in the Study House over the Talmud or reciting psalms from dawn to midnight, fasting every Monday and Thursday and on the eve of every new moon, and eating meat only in honor of the Sabbath?

Kalman did indeed begin the conversation with a ritual question, which he should perhaps have asked the Rabbi instead of Reb Aaron. Kalman's grandfather, may he rest in peace, was a very humble man. When he was still alive, he ordered his gravestone, and even paid the stonecutter in advance to add, on the day of his death, an inscription to go with the letters that mean "here rests." His unpretentious gravestone was made of sandstone, which was so soft that the wind and rain were wearing away the inscription. Kalman wanted to know whether it was permissible to put up a larger, more beautiful gravestone to replace the old one.

To the reply that yes, this was permissible, Kalman asked further whether he should have the words "He dealt with everyone honestly and with integrity" inscribed on the stone. He asked this question, he said, because someone had dropped a hint about his grandfather which disturbed him. This person had said that in a grocery store in a one-horse town, which Dombrovka was at that time, no one could have amassed such a fortune. True, Grandfather had loaned money for interest, but the question remained: where had he gotten the money to lend?

Reb Aaron, who had known Jonah when they were both boys, assured Kalman: "You don't have to worry, my son. Your grandfather never did anything against the law, God forbid. Whenever he loaned money for interest, he first made a contract stipulating that he would be a partner to no more than a certain percentage of the profits made on the borrowed money. Other people permitted themselves to take interest even when there was no profit, but Jonah, may he rest in peace, never did that. He might have given a little more to charity, but that's something you could correct. You could give to charity from your grandfather's inheritance, for the sake of his soul."

"But I still don't understand," Kalman insisted. "Where did he get all that money?"

"It's no mystery. A wartime contract with the army. He would have become another Rothschild if it hadn't been for that nefarious Pakula who robbed him and ran away to Paris!"

•　　•　　•　　•　　•

Reb Aaron kept trying to cut short his story so that he could return to his books at the Study House. Kalman promised to provide coal for the Study House for the whole winter if Reb Aaron would tell him the whole story with all the details.

Reb Aaron was certain that the Swerdl family had some special grace in heaven. Jonah's grandfather had built the first synagogue in Bilgoray; Jonah had helped to build the first synagogue in Dombrovka. And now his grandson had the privilege of saving the synagogue and contributing to its renovation. And thus the merit of his forefathers had stood him in good stead. It was not so much that he had survived the collapse of his house, for of what significance is life on this sinful earth anyway? This is only an anteroom, a passageway to the true world and eternal life. At any moment, he, Aaron, was ready for his soul to return to its source. He would thank and praise the Creator if now, this instant, he could go to his old friend Jonah in the true world and bring him the news that his grandson had returned to the path of his ancestors . . .

Kalman lost the train of Reb Aaron's words. A new image of his grandfather had risen before his eyes: a tall, slender man with shining eyes and a warm heart. It seemed that his troubles had transformed that vibrant young man into the morose grumbler who shoved his gold pieces into the chinks of wooden beams. But at least he had had faith. What would remain of Kalman, his grandson, when bitterness further contorted his body and eroded his mind?

Book Two: The Swerdls

1

Kalman had disliked his family name, Swerdl, ever since he could remember. He detested the boy in *heder* who mockingly rhymed the name with words of derogatory meaning. A silly word like Swerdl, "little sword," simply begs for mocking doggerel. What sort of idiotic ancestors had saddled the family with such a name, and how had the name of a deadly weapon come to represent a clan devoted to serving God and studying the Torah? Perhaps the squire would like to swap names with him—nobility was, after all, granted for exploits of the sword, and these had symbolic importance in the ceremony of the investment of a new noble. For the upstart squire of Dombrovka the name Swerdl should be worth its weight in gold. How, then, had it fallen to Jews, who recognize only nobility of the spirit?

Kalman traced the history of his family up to the first Swerdl, in the city of Bilgoray. His great-great-grandfather, Shmuel Boruch, had been a military supplier, and had begun selling provisions to the Russian army during the Crimean War, in the days of Nicholas I. After the Bulgarian uprising against Turkish rule, when Serbia and Montenegro started a war against Turkey, Shmuel Boruch was awarded larger contracts by the government of Alexander II. Russia did not officially enter the war against Turkey until a year later, but the bread the Serbian soldiers ate, the rare piece of meat for the Russian "volunteers," and many of their weapons reached the front lines through the efforts of Shmuel Boruch from Bilgoray. Reb Boruch would have been just as happy to be released from the contract. In the offices of the Tsar one hand didn't know what the other was doing, but every hand was open for a bribe. Luckily the Turks surpassed the Russians in corruption and disorganization.

In March, 1878—just before Passover, 5538—the "old Jew" (as Bismarck called the Earl of Beaconsfield, then Prime Minister of the British Empire) dispatched the British fleet to rule the waves of the

Black Sea, where the Russians had only a few ships. Without this waterway, the Russian army at the front was cut off from supplies. But, with the help of the Jewish communities in Rumania and Bulgaria, Boruch found partners in those countries and guaranteed the delivery of provisions to the front.

The chief of the Russian Army, Grand Duke Nikolai, the Tsar's brother, summoned Boruch to Petersburg and greeted him with the good news that the Tsar wished to present him with the Golden Cross. Bowing low before the Grand Duke, Boruch said, "Gracious and highborn Prince, the honor you do me is more than I deserve. It is every citizen's duty to serve his Tsar and his fatherland. I was only doing my duty. Giving me the award will bring honor to all my brothers of the Mosaic faith. But I am afraid to accept a cross, which is so sacred to Christians, lest in my ignorance I mishandle it."

So instead of a cross, Alexander II gave Shmuel Boruch a little golden sword. His community was extremely proud of this award and called him "Shmuel Boruch with the *shverdl.*" In time it became Shmuel Boruch Swerdl.

Bilgoray was a thriving Jewish community: it had a rabbi who was a renowned scholar and a member of a distinguished family; but it had no synagogue. No matter how many times the Jews appealed to the Mayor for permission to build a house of worship, they were turned down. Reb Shmuel Boruch traveled to Lublin to speak to the county chief. He did send the required documents to the governor of the province; and the governor did pass them on to the mayor of Bilgoray; but in Bilgoray they got buried in files. As the years went by and the community grew, the Jews continued to knock on the doors of government offices, and even tried bribes, to no avail. It was said that some hard-bitten bishop had made up his mind that only Christian houses of worship should be erected in Bilgoray.

When Reb Shmuel Boruch learned that Grand Duke Nikolai was scheduled to travel through Bilgoray, he suggested to the rabbi that they secretly prepare to lay the cornerstone of a synagogue.

"Without a permit?!" The rabbi was incredulous.

"With God's help we will build without a permit."

A big parade was organized in honor of the illustrious guest. The city fathers welcomed the Grand Duke with music and flags, the priests with icons and crucifixes, and the Jews, represented by their rabbi and leading citizens, with a scroll of the Torah. Among these leaders was Reb Shmuel Boruch, wearing, for the first time in memory, his golden sword. When the Grand Duke beckoned to him, Reb Shmuel Boruch came forward and handed him a golden pail and a golden trowel, on both of which was engraved the Romanov coat of arms, and said, "The Jews of Bilgoray have delayed the construction of their first synagogue until this memorable day of his Excellency's visit to our city. We will start building today to mark the great honor which the highly esteemed Grand Duke has brought to the city of Bilgoray. We humbly request his Excellency the Grand Duke, in his graciousness, to accept this pail and trowel as a memento of this most auspicious day. The parade will be passing by the site of the synagogue, and may we be so bold as to request that the hero of our country's great battles do us the honor of laying the cornerstone? It is a House of God, He who is the hero of every battle."

The city fathers and the ducal retinue heard very little of Reb Shmuel Boruch's speech. They were irritated that this Jew should take up so much of the Grand Duke's time; but there was nothing they could do about it, the Grand Duke having consented to hear Reb Boruch out. And when the Grand Duke did indeed agree to lay the cornerstone of the new synagogue, no further permission was needed from local authorities.

Reb Shmuel Boruch donated a copper roof for the building and arranged a grand housewarming party for the entire community when the synagogue was completed. At the party he danced a great deal—too much for a man of his years—and in the middle of a dance he collapsed and fell unconscious to the floor. The next morning, as he was preparing to leave for Warsaw, his family begged him to postpone his departure until he regained his strength; but he insisted that he had a mission in the city that affected the welfare of an entire Jewish community. In Warsaw he collapsed again, and this time he did not recover.

The biography of Kalman's great-great-grandfather and the origin of his family name closed with the passage: "To enter the eternal world while in the performance of an important *mitzva,* a good deed, is a distinction granted only to a righteous man" like Reb Shmuel Boruch.

2

Reb Shmuel Boruch had been a loner and a man of few words. Kalman Mordecai, his youngest son, had gleaned very little about his father's business. But, having spent the first years of his married life in the home of his wife's father, he had learned something about the lumber business. When the inheritance was distributed among the heirs, Kalman Mordecai took his share in cash and invested it in the purchase of a large forest near Bilgoray. Since the law made it impossible for a Jew to buy land, Kalman Mordecai actually leased it and bought only the trees, with rights to the lumber for fifty years. By the time his family moved into the house in the forest near Bilgoray, a sawmill was in operation, producing building materials for the surrounding region. Not far away, a distillery made whiskey from the grain growing in the nearby fields.

Since Jonah was the only son of Kalman Mordecai, his bar mitzva party was the talk of all Poland. Relatives came from all corners of the land; and even beggars arrived from everywhere, knowing that they could eat their fill at the festive occasion, and receive generous alms as well. Afterward, Reb Kalman Mordecai brought in Reb Shimshon, a scholar from Lublin, to continue Jonah's Jewish education.

Reb Kalman Mordecai, like his father, was a generous man. He was always entertaining visitors—representatives of a community in Eretz Israel, emissaries from a yeshiva (an academy for higher religious studies), messengers from Jewish towns that had been hard hit by fires. Individuals in trouble also found an open heart here and a generous hand. People came to Reb Kalman Mordecai and his wife, Genendel, in all kinds of emergencies, and no one left empty-handed.

As Reb Kalman Mordecai's wealth multiplied, so did the number of buildings in his courtyard. Genendel dressed as befitted the wife of a squire, but she conducted herself as a pious Jewish woman. Because she spoke in a scholarly manner, often quoting the Torah, and because of her charitable deeds, she was called "Reb Genendel," though this scholar's title was usually given to men only. Reb Kalman Mordecai added a new line of merchandise; Reb Genendel arranged the wedding of another poor Jewish bride. Once, when she and her husband were seated inside their carriage, about to drive to the city for a celebration, a Jew from Bilgoray came running up with the sad tale of a sick, lonely widow who needed urgent help. Reb Genendel immediately suggested to her husband that he go ahead without her, because she had a greater *mitzva* to perform. She stepped out of the wagon and sent for the *shochet,* the ritual slaughterer. They slaughtered a young hen, and Genendel tied an apron over her silk dress and helped her servant-girl cook up a fresh chicken soup. Not until she had delivered the soup to the sick woman did she start out for the celebration.

Reb Kalman Mordecai was often away on business trips, and when he was at home he was never idle. He hurried from the distillery to the sawmill, from the sawmill to the forest—he had to decide which trees were to be cut down and which left standing. When he was in his office there was always someone with him: the bookkeeper wanted to show him an account, the steward consulted with him about the new seeding, and there were always decisions to be made about how much credit to extend to a new customer or how hard to press for payment of an old debt.

Reb Genendel, for her part, was busy with the big household and with charitable affairs in nearby Bilgoray, as well as in more distant places. People wrote, sent telegrams, or even special messengers: a Jewish town had burned down and needed help; a Jew imprisoned on a false charge had to be ransomed. Here, a sick and impoverished scholar needed an operation; there, a father blessed with many daughters needed money for dowries. Something had to be done about these situations, and it seemed to Reb Kalman Mordecai that his fortune was a holy trust, and that the One above had chosen him and his wife to distribute His treasures to the needy.

Not having any brothers or sisters, Jonah would have loved to help his parents, but a young man must study all day. They had gone to great lengths to obtain an exceptional teacher for him, but Jonah had never been an eager student, and he was even less so since whiskers had started sprouting on his chin. He had little patience for sitting over a page of the Talmud, but he was always ready to pick up a toolbox in the workshop near the sawmill. He built a special lectern for the prayer-leader in the synagogue prayer house, and he designed and built a table on which to unroll the Torah scrolls. These were all good deeds, and Genendel was proud that Jonah had a talent for everything, but how could you compare building a pulpit to studying Torah? They had been blessed with abundance; let Jonah gather Torah so that he might have both Torah and Gedula, spiritual and material affluence.

3

It was the harvest season, and Jonah disappeared for hours at a time. The High Holy Days were approaching and he had to learn three

tractates of Gemarah and their commentaries. Tractate Rosh Hashonah had to be completed before the New Year, and within a week
after that he must learn Yoma for Yom Kippur; and when would
time be found to learn the Tractate Sukkot in the four days between
Yom Kippur and Sukkot? All three Gemarahs lay on the table, Reb
Shimshon waited, and Genendel dispatched messengers to look for
Jonah, but no one could find him. Who would have thought to seek
him out among the peasants in the field? The peasants told how he
helped to build haystacks, saying he tossed the hay better than the
farmers. And one continued: "And madam, the forest-warden's daughter
had piled up a big bundle of branches, too large for her to lift to her
shoulder. The young boss, who was passing by, helped her tie the
rope around the branches and hoisted the bundle to her shoulder as if
it were a bunch of feathers. The girl was so touched by the young
squire's assistance that, had it not been for the weight on her back,
she would have bent over and kissed his hand!"

Genendel was perplexed. Maybe they should send him to a yeshiva . . . She was alarmed by her own thought, for she would miss
him terribly were he to go away. Reb Shimshon had told her once
that he had a son about Jonah's age, so she asked her husband if he
thought it would be a good idea for the boy to come and stay—
Jonah needed friends his own age.

●　　●　　●　　●　　●

Aaron, the teacher's son, arrived just after the holidays. The two boys
studied together and became good friends. But Genendel and her
husband were not pleased with the strange ways Aaron brought with
him from the court of a Hassidic rebbe. Aaron and Jonah now fasted
every Monday and Thursday, eating only after sunset. On Thursday
evenings they went back to the study-house after breaking their fast
to continue their studies. At midnight they went to the ritual bath
for ablutions. They immersed themselves in the *mikveh* and then
continued to study the mystical teaching of the Kabbalah all night
long.

"It's not right to fill every hour of the day with Torah," Genendel
argued, "the night was given to us for sleep."

But Jonah had a ready answer: Aaron had shown him a passage in
the Zohar praising those who study during the night. The angels in
Heaven ask, "What is that sweet sound we hear?" And the One

Above answers, "It is the voice of my children, who are now studying the Torah . . . "

Discussing the secret teachings of Kabbalah enchanted Jonah. Actually, Aaron did all the talking, and Jonah did all the listening. But that had always been his nature, and he had grown even more taciturn since he had, under Aaron's influence, become an impassioned Hassid. This would not have disturbed Kalman Mordecai, but Reb Shimshon complained that the boys spent too much time talking about ethics and not enough time studying Gemarah. No sooner had they finished grace after a meal than they were off to the study house.

One morning after Aaron had gone Jonah remained to tell Genendel that he wanted to spend a couple of weeks at the court of a Hassidic rebbe. Genendel took this opportunity to have a serious talk with her son.

"God blessed us with prosperity," she said, "but you are our most precious treasure. It is a special gift from the Creator, blessed be His name, that you have entered upon the path of Torah. But to really become a 'man of Torah' one must work hard. They say that when the great rabbi, Akiba Eyger of Posen, was a boy, a friend tried to persuade him to visit a Hassidic rebbe. Akiba Eyger, however, was a diligent scholar and resented having to waste time traveling.

" 'How long does it take to become a Hassid?' the young Akiba asked.

" 'The moment you start to believe in the Rebbe and start to follow his ways, you are a Hassid,' came the quick reply.

" 'But to become a scholar takes years of study,' retorted Akiba Eyger. 'So I will first try to become a scholar, and if I ever decide to embrace Hassidism—in one moment I'll be a Hassid.' "

Genendel concluded, "The greater a scholar you are, the more potential you have to be great in everything."

"Am I going to be a rabbi?" Jonah asked.

"Since when is Torah the exclusive property of the rabbis? Studying Torah sharpens the mind. And it is written, 'Torah leads to good deeds.' "

"It is certainly a blessing from on high that I am privileged to study Torah in great comfort, but money and luxury also bring great temptations. The Talmud says that it was possession of all that gold which led the Jews in the wilderness to build the Golden Calf. Aaron is helping me to forge weapons against the Wicked Temptations."

"Do I have anything new to tell you, Jonaleh? I draw my knowledge from the *Tzena-Ur-ena,* the women's texts, whereas you are learning directly from the source. I once read in a sacred book that it is for the sake of the Torah that the Almighty saved the Jews from their tribulations, and the Wicked Temptations therefore cannot exercise dominion over them. So you see, Torah is the best defense against the Wicked Temptation."

"There you are right, Mameshi," Jonah admitted, and thought to himself that now would be the right moment to convince his mother that it was not necessary to spend so much time at the table during meals. At Genendel's table one did not eat in a hurry. Every day the table was set as if for a festive meal, with a white tablecloth and the best dishes; one might think the housewife here was trying to show off her wealth. Aaron had, in fact, complained: "A Jew must study Torah and not waste his time keeping up appearances." Now Jonah repeated this to his mother.

"You told me once," replied Genendel, "that we dip the first bite of bread in salt because the table is likened to an altar and the meal to a sacrificial offering. And the Torah says, 'You shall prepare all your sacrifices with salt.' How much more so is this true when there are guests at the table? Charity is certainly as important as sacrifices."

"First comes Torah, then marriage, and only then good deeds," Jonah reminded her.

"Who am I, a mere woman, to argue with you about such matters? But the holy books tell us that Torah is only a path to good deeds. As the prophet said, 'And what does your God require of you?' I don't recall the exact words, but all that God requires is that we act justly and perform charitable deeds. Torah is light, charity is life. The holy books say that when we give charity, and thereby enable the poor to live, the Almighty is particularly careful to keep the benefactor alive."

"What does that have to do with spending so much time at the table?" Jonah could not keep the impatience out of his voice. "It is true that we must satisfy our bodily needs, but stuffing one's stomach is the height of gross materialism and sensuousness."

"Studying Torah is not enough, Jonaleh. One must also learn how to put one's learning into practice. The verse says, 'Break your bread with the hungry.' The holy sage, Reb Shimon ben Yochai, learned from that verse that it is not enough merely to hand the poor man a piece of bread. Breaking bread with him means to sit down with him at a nicely prepared table, talk to him, listen to him, and make it an event, as you do for an important guest. And just as at the altar in the Temple the choicest portion was reserved for the Almighty, so at the table-altar one must give the poor the choicest portion."

"And who says you shouldn't?"

"Just imagine, Jonah. You invite an important guest, you serve the best food, but you yourself run away from the table and leave the guest sitting there all alone. If giving to the poor is like giving to God, then both of them are guests at your table—the poor and the One Above. Your Tateshi, bless him, has to travel all the time and is rarely home. And I am a mere woman, who cannot sit at the table with strange men. God Himself sits at our table—would you run away when such an honored guest comes to visit us?"

"But why must the meal go on and on for such a long time?"

"In order that the host may have time to socialize with the guest. You know better than I that giving is not enough; you must also console the unfortunate person who is in the position of receiving. In this week's Torah portion we read, 'Therefore I command you, saying, open wide your hand . . . ' What does that word 'saying' mean? I once read a beautiful explanation of that. You shall say to the poor person: you too will one day open your hand to give charity. Today you receive from others, tomorrow God will help you and you will give to others. The giver has to be careful not to hurt the pride of one needing his help."

"The Talmud says," agreed Jonah, "whoever gives money to the poor is blessed with six blessings; whoever also consoles the poor is blessed with eleven blessings."

"There! You see, my son, you know it yourself. Unfortunately, we were not blessed with many children; they were taken from us as soon as they were born. But our compassionate Father in heaven had mercy upon us, and you remained with us. We still need many blessings and much favor in the eyes of the Lord."

Genendel strove to lead her household in the paths of pious Jewishness. If some people cannot carry out all the lofty principles because of poverty, they at least have some justification. But she, to whom God had given all the means and all the possibilities, what excuse would she have when she was called to account for her conduct on earth? Soon Jonah too, with God's help, would be a householder; he should become accustomed to the ways of charity. Good deeds are no less important than studying Torah.

4

One day, Reb Kalman Mordecai returned from a trip to Warsaw with good tidings. He wished Jonah mazel tov—a betrothal contract had been written, and Jonah was now engaged. Genendel informed her son that his fiancée was a pretty girl from the esteemed Davidson family. True, Reb Hertz, the girl's father, was not as wealthy as the other Davidsons, "but since the One Above has blessed us with wealth and you are our only son, we don't need to look for a bride with a dowry. She has other virtues, praise God. She is refined and well educated. Her father said she plays the piano, too. A young Torah scholar doesn't really need a piano, true, but you know how these rich folks are . . . Many of the Davidsons own large estates."

5

Jonah was sixteen and betrothed. On the occasion of every Jewish holiday he wrote a letter to his future father-in-law and added a greeting to his mother-in-law and bride. Genendel, whenever her husband went to Warsaw on business, sent along something for the bride—a fan, an umbrella—at first, inexpensive things. Liebele thanked her future mother-in-law each time with a note in Polish or Russian. She wrote her greetings to her future father-in-law, as well as to her intended, in Yiddish, but her handwriting was much more graceful in the non-Jewish languages than in Yiddish.

Then came a day when Genendel suggested that it was high time the bride and groom saw each other. Reb Kalman was opposed. "Marriages are made in heaven, and up there they know exactly what the bride and bridegroom look like."

Reb Kalman Mordecai was a learned man, but his wife was better at finding an appropriate verse or passage to buttress her ideas. "It is forbidden for a man to wed a woman until he has seen her," she said, quoting the Talmud.

"Before the wedding day arrives, much water will yet flow under the bridge," countered her husband.

"Jonaleh walks around constantly in a daze. You said yourself that Liebele is a very pretty girl. Let him at least see her, and his heart will be gladdened."

"Next time I'm in Warsaw I'll mention it to the girl's father."

Several weeks later, returning from a trip to Warsaw, Reb Kalman Mordecai brought back a photograph of Jonah's bride.

•　　•　　•　　•　　•

"With the help of G-d. The third day of the week of the Torah portion, 'And Jacob Went Out,' in the year 5656, in the holy congregation of Warsaw.

"To the young bridegroom, the god-fearing and praiseworthy Jonah, son of the well-known philanthropist Reb Kalman Mordecai and his wife, the exemplary benefactress Genendel, long life to them, may your light shine like the midday sun, and may Jerusalem be rebuilt speedily and in our days, amen.

"I would first of all like to inform you that I, my wife, and our Liebele, are all in the best of health, praise G-d, hoping to hear the same from you and your dear parents, amen.

"Secondly, I wish to inform you that we here will all be happy if you would do us the honor of visiting with us at our modest home on the approaching Sabbath Hannuka—may it bring only good fortune with it. Please advise what day and time you will arrive, and with G-d's help, I will be waiting for you at the train.

"We all send our warmest regards to your parents, may they always be well. Signed with affection, your intended father-in-law, Hertz, son of Reb Yakov Halevi Davidson."

Genendel wondered why Reb Hertz had waited so long to invite Jonah to his home. Reb Kalman Mordecai said he knew the reason. Reb Hertz Davidson might not be a man of remarkable wealth, but he was very proud. He would have waited until he had accumulated enough money to buy Jonah a gift befitting such a wealthy bridegroom.

Genendel had prepared a necklace of diamonds for Jonah to bring to his bride, but now she reconsidered: such an expensive gift might compel the bride's father to spend more on wedding gifts than he could afford. So she put the necklace away for later. In the meantime she would send only a golden brooch, with no jewels.

Jonah was therefore embarrassed when, after he gave Liebele the little brooch, her father presented him with an expensive gold watch and chain and a Vilna edition of the Talmud in leather binding with gold embossing.

As for Liebele, she was even prettier in person than in her photograph. But a strange sort of sadness hovered over her. Did Jonah not please her? From the moment he had arrived, her father talked about visiting a relative—one of the wealthy Davidsons—but later it turned out that this relative had to make an emergency trip abroad. First Reb Hertz couldn't stop talking about the wealth of this relative, who owned so many fields and forests, and then he said it was fortunate that they wouldn't have to visit him because everything in his home was so far from being kosher that it may as well not have been a Jewish home at all. A Jew could not eat at his table, and he would certainly have been insulted if his guests had refused to touch their food.

On his way home, Jonah couldn't stop thinking about Liebele's father: everyone around him seemed to be successful, but his piece of bread always fell butter-side-down. So what? Was wealth the most important thing in life? Reb Hertz was a handsome man, his daughter was gentle and beautiful, they were all well educated; was all of this not enough to make him proud? Why did he feel compelled to brag about his wealthy relatives? Although he himself was a mature young man, about to get married, Jonah mused, he still knew very little about life.

• • • • •

Reb Kalman Mordecai and Genendel invited Liebele to visit their home in honor of Shavuos. When she arrived Genendel was alarmed by her pallor. Here in the forest, if a person had a white skin it was touched with pink freshness—"blood and milk," as the expression went. Liebele's whiteness had no blood. She had a neat, slender figure and gentle features, delicate as finely turned porcelain: look but don't touch, it might break apart in your hand.

Lately, Jonah's body had been acquiring the stoop of a typical yeshiva student, just like his friend Aaron: shoulders rounded, eyes cast down, mouth shut tight. But Genendel noted with satisfaction that ever since Liebele's arrival he seemed to have grown a head taller and he broke into the occasional smile. And although he said even less than before, his eyes spoke for him; his love-filled glances at Liebele were not hidden from his mother's eyes.

Liebele soon sensed Genendel's warmth, and she clung to her. After several days in the village, Liebele's skin began to show a little color, and she learned how to smile. It was a tremulous smile, which barely stayed on her lips. In general, she was a tremulous person— her nostrils trembled, a vein in her forehead quivered, even her hands sometimes shook. Despite all this, she was full of charm: the way she walked, talked—everything about her was graceful and delightful. Even Reb Kalman Mordecai, who was too busy to spend much time with her, expressed his admiration for her cultured manner and refinement. "A Davidson is a Davidson," he declared, "rich or poor . . . "

6

No matter how much Jonah immersed himself in the *mikveh,* he could not wash out of his head the thoughts that were assailing him, thoughts which transported him on wings of joy, but which also cast gloom and terror upon him. Even now, with his fiancée a guest in his home, he and Aaron studied Kabbalah every Thursday from midnight to morning prayers. Aaron sang out the lines from the book about the ecstacy of love, the secret of the kiss, and of eventual union. Together with his friend he swayed over the holy Zohar and ecstatically recited the words, "because the joining of breath with breath takes place only through the kiss, and kissing is done with the mouth, which takes in air and breathes it out again . . . the breath of both partners is joined and they become one, and that is love . . . "

When they read further how the four letters of the Ineffable Name arise out of the holy kiss of love, and how the exaltation in the four letters in *Ahava,* the Hebrew word for love, is the foundation of perfection, Aaron practically achieved disembodiment, as if he were leaving the earth behind and soaring to the upper spheres. Jonah could not elevate himself that high. The Zohar speaks of a kiss between two worlds—the heavenly and the earthly—but alas, in his imagination shone only the lips of his bride, as his lips touched hers.

In a sudden rush of fear, Jonah realized that these thoughts were put in his head by Satan, hoping to make him stumble. His father had told him that one should not devote oneself to Kabbalah so young. The Zohar tells of a love that leads to a state wherein one's body is freed from sadness and filled with gladness, but he was now being assailed by intense sadness because he could not raise himself up to the essence and purity of the sacred concepts. He was being assailed, God save his soul, by a feeling of envy. Aaron too was betrothed, yet no earthly thoughts confused his learning.

Jonah unburdened himself to his friend, and Aaron did not deny that evil thoughts come from Satan and his minions, who try to prevent mortal men from raising themselves to celestial heights. However, Aaron did comfort Jonah with this advice: "There is no force in the nether world so strong that you cannot overcome it with holiness. The Zohar says that when a man tries to purify himself, God helps him. A passage in the Talmud tractate Yoma states, 'when a man consecrates himself just a little, the powers on high consecrate him much, much more.'" Aaron also found in an old book a good defense against Satan's stratagems: whenever strong thoughts interrupted Jonah's studies, he was to wipe his forehead three times from temple to temple, each time reciting the verse from Psalms: "A pure heart create for me, O Lord, and a strong spirit renew in me."

"Jonah's moodiness is not serious, God forbid," Genendel assured her husband. "Even a blind man could see that he and Liebele have found favor in each other's eyes. It is not a sadness; it is a yearning. Why wait any longer for the wedding? This house, thank God, is large enough. Let them be part of our household. In these lovely woods, with food straight from the fields and gardens, Liebele will bloom even more beautifully. May I not sin with these words," she concluded, "but a girl is prettier when she puts a little flesh on her bones."

Reb Kalman Mordecai promised to talk to the girl's father. When he went to Warsaw again, Genendel started readying the rooms for the young couple. She could hardly wait to tell her son the good news, but Reb Kalman Mordecai returned from Warsaw with a refusal.

"Apparently he hasn't saved up enough money for the wedding. That haughty man—God forgive me—will neither give his daughter away without a substantial trousseau, nor will he let anyone help him."

7

Another year went by. The parents of Jonah and Liebele met to determine the wedding date. The groom's father wanted it to be the coming Lag B'Omer, but the bride's father was adamant: not earlier than the High Holidays. Genendel wanted Liebele to spend another summer in the woods—with God's help, she would soon need the strength to carry and bear healthy children. But, since her father was so stubborn, they would have to wait.

Immediately after Shavuos, Genendel began making preparations for the wedding of her only child. The house, in the midst of the fields and forests, looked as if it had naturally grown out of the fertile earth. The birds chirped their melodies in the courtyard, and the rooms were full of the songs of the seamstresses who had come from the village to sew the wedding clothes. The golden stalks in the fields fell before the scythes of the reapers. Reb Kalman Mordecai owned many fields which supplied the grain for his distillery, just as the forests supplied lumber for his sawmill.

One day, Genendel had just returned from the city where she was on errands of mercy and her husband was at the distillery. Jonah had received a letter from his intended, and took it with him for a walk in the woods. A subtle breeze ruffled the leafy branches over his head. Suddenly, a terrifying thunder shook the ground under Jonah's feet. He ran toward home.

An explosion lifted the roof off the distillery and a sheet of fire hurtled toward the sky. At once, the entire building was aflame. Several workers were torn apart in the explosion. Reb Kalman Mordecai had managed to get out of the building, but he was enveloped in flames. Blood vessels in his body burst as he fell to the ground. The blood that spurted out also ignited. The clothing on those who ran over to help him caught fire. He was like a wick dipped in alcohol.

Perhaps something could have been saved, had Reb Kalman Mordecai not been among the first victims. The distillery building was surrounded by trees, as was everything here. The flames swept through the trees, destroying them and whatever had been built amidst them. Fire fighters were called from all over the area. The flames outran them. That night, and for many following (for it was many days and nights before the fires were finally extinguished), the sky was lit as if for a wedding celebration.

When Jonah reached his blazing home, he was diverted to a remote shack where his father's charred body was already lying on the ground covered with his tallis. Outside, the flames lunged at the sky, and down below, at the head of the body, a candle flickered quietly. When Genendel heard that Jonah was coming she quickly wiped her eyes and went out to meet him.

"Jonah, the One Above has called Tateshi to His side."

Jonah remained standing at the open door, staring at the tiny flame of the soul-candle that seemed to disappear in a mist. Jonah shuddered, and his knees buckled. Aaron ran to him and helped him to a bench. The little flame at the head of the corpse emerged from the mist and flickered as if it were beckoning to him.

"The One Above has taken away the crown of our family," Genendel began, and a sob cut off her words. She took hold of herself and continued. "The One Above is a true judge. We shall not complain—it can become an obstacle to father's ascending soul, God forbid. Say the words, my child: *boruch dayan emes,* blessed be the true judge . . . "

Jonah looked uncomprehendingly at his mother. She moved closer to him. "Jonaleh, we have just suffered a terrible blow, but now is not the time to think of ourselves. Father is in danger of the tortures of the grave. We must do all we can still do for him. Say the words, Jonaleh, *boruch dayan emes . . .* "

Jonah's lips moved, but no sound came from them. Genendel refused to retreat. "With the fear of heaven that Father implanted in us we will both say together—say it with me—God is just and His judgment is correct, *boruch dayan emes . . .* "

Jonah finally forced the words out of his constricted throat.

Nothing remained of Reb Kalman Mordecai's property. The families observed the mourning period for the victims and, because sacred objects had been destroyed, they fasted. Three scrolls of the Torah had gone up in flames, and each one of them was associated with Jonah. One had been ordered and paid for by Reb Kalman Mordecai in Jonah's name when he was born; one had been an offering of thanks that Genendel, with God's help, had survived her difficult pregnancy; and the third had been for the occasion of Jonah's bar mitzva. In the last scroll, Jonah himself had written the last few letters. It was indeed a drastic indictment from heaven if, along with the man who had donated them, the Torah scrolls too were burned to cinders.

8

There was not a house left standing in the village in which to observe the period of mourning. Having accompanied the coffin to Bilgoray, the family remained there and observed shiva in the home of a relative. Genendel's lips never ceased their murmuring. Jonah did whatever he was told, but his mind seemed to float around his body, outside of it. His body moved, his ears heard, his mouth spoke, but it was as if he were somewhere outside, observing himself. He kept bumping into things. A lump formed on his forehead, a bruise appeared on his leg, but the pain was outside his mind as well.

When they observed the custom of *kriah,* he felt as if it was not the cloth of his coat but the fiber of his heart that was being rent. The rip resounded in his ears like a thunderclap. The torn lapel of his coat hung down like the head of a sacrificial hen after slaughtering. He stared at it without making sense of it; he felt as if a piece of his own body had been torn away and were flopping outside him like a broken limb hanging by a piece of torn skin.

Not until the fourth day of shiva did Jonah's mind begin to clear. A question, a most difficult question, penetrated his head and bored its way into his mind like a persistent worm. His father, God rest his soul, had been a righteous man, a doer of good deeds, a more than generous benefactor. "And Charity will save from death," said Proverbs, yet his father had been punished with the most horrible death—by fire, at an early age. Why? How could it have happened? Jonah knew that a Jew must have faith in divine justice and must accept judgment even in the most severe punishment. But if a man condemned by an earthly court had the right to ask, "On what basis have you condemned me," then one could certainly ask that question of the heavenly court. Did not the sages say that Torah applies also to heaven?

Mameshi was righteousness itself. She had accepted without complaining the torments of twice losing her newborn child. When she had finally given birth to a living son, she then accepted the fate of barrenness. Mameshi did not seek the idle pleasures of this base world. She never rested for a moment. Whenever she was not busy with charity, she dipped into a *Menoras Ha-mor,* a *Rabeynu B'Chayo,* or other holy books. Even when she was occupied with household affairs, she never stopped murmuring psalms and prayers. Why did she deserve such harsh punishment? There are so many injunctions in the Torah against wronging widows and orphans—why had Fate wronged her and made a young widow of her?

God Almighty! Jonah suddenly slapped his forehead. Instead of examining his own behavior, he had been busy lodging complaints against heaven. Aaron had warned him about this!

Until Aaron's arrival in the village, Jonah had been an observant Jew, but an unsophisticated one. Aaron had opened doors to higher spheres for him. It is perhaps enough to do only that which one is commanded to do out of fear of heaven, but, when one loves the Creator with all his heart and soul, he tries to do much more than he is obliged to. With the strength of holy *kavanot* or meditations, ordinary human beings can help to redeem the Divine sparks from exile, even the *Shechina* itself. Jonah wanted very much to ascend with Aaron to these higher spheres, but (God protect him!) his sinful body kept dragging him down. The thoughts, which needed to be pure, clear, and devoid of every trace of corporality, were tangled up, especially since his betrothal, in matters which it was better not even to name.

Yes, Aaron had warned him, and he had tried to do penance, particularly after that unfortunate incident with the nocturnal emission. Spilling one's seed in vain is a terrible sin. From each seed a human being is supposed to be born for whom a soul is already waiting. What happens to that soul when the seed becomes—nothing? Nothing? From that kind of seed spring evil spirits, God save us and protect us!

Again he confessed to his friend, and again Aaron searched diligently in the holy books. In *Avodas HaKodesh,* written by the kabbalist Hayim Joseph David Azulai, Aaron found what he had been looking for: give charity, observe three days of fasting in succession, stay awake one night a week and do nothing but study and say a special prayer. Jonah took this penance upon himself and recited the prayer with a broken heart: "My flesh and sinews and blood are diminished by my fasting; may this be as pleasing to the Creator as if I had placed it upon His altar as a sacrificial offering. Father in heaven, God of forgiveness, accept my offering, have mercy upon me, and in your goodness gather together the holy sparks which, because of my sin, were spread among the demons (may heaven protect us), and let them arise to a place of sanctification. May benevolent intercessors bring my prayer to You. Protect me from evil temptation and from all sorts of sinful imaginings, and purify my heart to serve you. Amen."

Then he concentrated on all the holy names which were prescribed by the *Avodas HaKodesh,* particularly the name Kra Satan ("tear Satan apart"), but Satan was indestructible; he hid in a corner of Jonah's brain and then suddenly leaped out in all his fearsome height. Aaron had warned him that one must not look at a woman, and certainly not think about her appearance, and most certainly not carry within oneself the shimmer of her hair or the sound of her voice. "The sage Rabbi Jonah says," Aaron emphasized, "that anyone who looks at women is, for that one sin, likened to one who abandoned his faith, God forbid!"

Jonah fasted and tormented himself again and again, yet—Liebele's sad eyes, her soft sweet voice, the trembling of her delicate nostrils, the quiver of her lip—he did not know how to drive those from his mind, and perhaps he did not wish to. Aaron searched through the sacred texts to find more and more rigorous laws and prohibitions, but what he found were more indulgences.

Was Aaron right? Who was greater than Maimonides—was it not said of him that since the time of Moses our Teacher there was no greater leader than Moses Ben Maimon? And Maimonides had ruled that a man must not live like an ascetic. And whoever refused to enjoy the pleasures of God's world—even if only a glass of good wine—was a sinner. The Talmud is full of passages about valuing and appreciating a wife; Liebele had been paired with him by heaven and would soon, God willing, be his wife.

Things may have worked out better if he hadn't tried to climb the heights, if he had remained a simple, honest Jew. But he had become obsessed with becoming a kabbalist, and had embraced the Zohar. Words and ideas about the "sacred bride," about the *Shechina,* were the canvas on which he had painted visions of his earthly bride. By doing this he had desecrated God's honor and His holy Name, and for such a sin the punishment is death!

But why had the punishment not fallen on him, the guilty one?

At his circumcision ceremony, his father had declared that if the child was not destined to live a long life (God forbid!), then he gladly offered his own years as a gift to his son. This explained what had happened now! He deserved to die for his sins, but his father had taken upon himself the punishment decreed in heaven for the son. In this way he was responsible for his own father's death!

But why in such a horrible way? Why such a horrible death?!

On the seventh day of mourning they recited the morning prayers as soon as the dawn broke. Immediately after the final prayer, Genendel asked the worshippers to leave the house, because with their departure the shiva period would be officially over, but she begged them to come right back in again, so that Jonah could lead the reading of a chapter of Mishna for the sake of his father's ascending soul.

One of the men, versed in the Law, objected: "During the first thirty days, it is forbidden for a mourner to study Torah; he cannot even be called up to Torah reading. Torah gladdens the heart, and a mourner must grieve."

But Genendel knew better. "I have the abbreviated book of Shelah, where it specifically states that this is a mistaken custom. My Kalman Mordecai, God rest his soul, was descended from the author of the Shelah."

"Mameshi, you want me to lead the reading, when I can barely recite a chapter of Psalms with the proper devotion!"

"Jonaleh, my son, you see what a fearful indictment it is. Your father, rest his soul, has already reckoned up his accounts and can no longer do anything for himself, so we—you, his only son—must do something for the ascent of his soul. Studying Mishna and giving charity in his name—that's all we can do for him now. Do it, Jonah dear. My heart is crying out for your father's soul."

9

As with Job, one affliction followed another.

During the mourning period itself, people came who had invested their savings with Reb Kalman Mordecai. One was saving up money with the rich man for his daughter's wedding; another had deposited a legacy with him until it could be divided among his heirs. They had trusted Reb Kalman Mordecai more than a bank. When they learned that all his property had gone up in smoke, they came running to demand their due. Reb Yankel, the bookkeeper, assured them that there was enough left for everyone.

"It is the way of business," he explained. "First you fill the larger orders. Then you send them a bill which they are supposed to pay in thirty days, but they don't always pay punctually. Even when they do pay, they give you a note postdated several months. Kalman Mordecai's account books were destroyed in the fire, but, thank God, I have all the figures in my head. With God's help, Reb Genendel will pay everyone back what is owed him."

The creditors knew that Genendel would not take a penny of their money, and this was enough to calm their fears. Reb Yankel agreed to prepare a written list of all the credits and notes that were destroyed, but he was still too upset by the tragedy to think clearly. On the day following the mourning period, Reb Yankel sat down with Jonah to draw up the list, and at the same time give the young man some introduction to his father's business. Kalman Mordecai had wanted his son to continue studying the Torah for many more years, so Jonah knew even less about his father's affairs than his mother, who knew nothing. Reb Yankel was talking about debit and credit, about laws governing the leasing of land when suddenly he clutched at his side. The pain became so intense that he had to lie down with a heated stove-cover. The pains moved from his side to his chest, and he had trouble breathing. A medic was called, and he sent for the doctor. By the time the doctor arrived, Reb Yankel could no longer speak. Before the doctor left, it was all over for Reb Yankel.

Genendel was still busy day and night trying to accumulate merits for the soul of her departed husband. Reb Yankel's death shook her out of her trance. The curse which had descended upon her house had still not lifted, the evil decree had not yet been averted. "God in heaven, if it must strike someone else, let it be me—me— but please spare my child." Only now did she notice that Jonah was dragging his feet as if he had no strength to lift them. His eyes were dull, his skin gray, and he hardly touched the food on his plate.

"Reb Kalman Mordecai earned the privilege of meeting his Maker cleansed of all sin, purified by fire," said the Rabbi of Bilgoray in his eulogy, and he explained that one must have great merit indeed to be absolved of every trace of sin at the threshold of the eternal world.

Yes, Reb Kalman Mordecai, God rest his soul, was a righteous man, may his merits be credited to his son and save him from danger, Genendel prayed. She must pay a little more attention to Jonah. One storm after another upon such a young sapling. May the One Above grant him the strength to endure all the misfortunes.

• • • • •

When the clods of earth fell on the planks of Reb Yankel's grave, the sound reverberated inside Jonah as though someone were knocking on his shutters to wake him up. Reb Yankel was also gone! He was all alone, alone with many heavy burdens. No one would pay Tateshi's debts except Jonah, if he could. And what about Mameshi? He must assume responsibility for her too.

Just when Genendel was at the point of trying to persuade Jonah to stop fasting, she noticed that he was now emptying his plate, and that when he got up from the table his back was again straight and his step firm.

Jonah considered his new situation and came to the conclusion that he must go to Warsaw at once to find out from the customers which ones owed him money. During the thirty days following the death of one's father, business trips were forbidden unless other people insisted. When they learned what was involved, there were indeed a number of people who loudly insisted he go. So Jonah started out on the first business trip he had ever made.

On the long journey from Bilgoray to Warsaw, Jonah reached several conclusions: he was no longer the pampered child of wealthy parents; he was no longer the delicate bridegroom who could expect to live for years at his father's or father-in-law's expense. He was now a man with heavy burdens, and he must learn how to bear that yoke, or he would fall under the weight of his load. He was no longer a seeker after new and esoteric ways to serve the Almighty—and maybe he never really had been that seeker. Instead, he was a simple Jew, and he would serve his God as did every other simple Jew: by studying a section of Mishna, by reading the Torah portion for the week, by reciting some of the psalms . . . If he wanted to do more, his parents had shown him the way. He would run his business with honesty toward God and man, he would work hard—he now had to support two families, and Mameshi must continue to distribute charity with the same open hand she had grown accustomed to having. Jonah prayed that God in heaven would bless his efforts and make them successful.

Then and there he made a vow: if and when he became a wealthy man he would keep a modest home, a simple household; let his children not grow so accustomed to luxury that they would feel lost if the wheel of fortune turned the other way . . .

10

When he arrived in Warsaw, Jonah went to an inn. He could not appear at his in-laws' front door without notice, as much as he wanted to see Liebele. He needed time to think. Besides, he was embarrassed to show up there in his country clothes, which were all he had left after the fire; anyway, a mourner was forbidden to wear new clothes.

But he couldn't leave Warsaw without visiting them once. He decided to take care of the business matters first. And so he had to find the addresses for the few names Reb Yankel had mentioned. From these merchants he hoped to learn the names of other customers of his father's. And so, for two days he ran around the city, stopping only occasionally to enter a synagogue to recite the Kaddish or a chapter of Psalms. On the third day, he sent a message to his future father-in-law telling him that he was in town and wished to visit before he started back to Bilgoray. He waited at his inn for a response.

Reb Hertz soon appeared at the inn. "I read all about it," he explained. "It was in all the papers. May you be spared further grief in your life . . . "

Jonah moved a chair over for his visitor. Before he sat down, Reb Hertz wiped the chair with his palm, blew away the dust that remained, and wiped it once more with his handkerchief. "Did you receive my condolence note? No, it couldn't have arrived yet. I know everything from the papers. When did you arrive in Warsaw?"

"The day before yesterday."

Reb Hertz was indignant. "Well, I understand that you couldn't let us know from Bilgoray that you were coming—who knows when the letter would have been delivered. But here in the city, you should have let us know as soon as you arrived."

"Yes, you are right, Reb Hertz. Everything happened so suddenly."

"Why have you come here, what have you been doing for three days in hiding?"

"I haven't been hiding. I came here on business, and I've been running around for the last two days."

"You don't know anything about business—you should have asked me for advice."

"When I'm ready to do business on my own, I will need and appreciate your advice. But now I'm here only to collect some old debts."

"And?"

"It is not as easy as I thought. Three days from morning till evening and I haven't accomplished much. I was simply in no condition to show myself to anyone, especially—Reb Hertz, you can see for yourself how I'm dressed."

"Dressed shmessed! I understand, losing a father is a terrible tragedy! But you shouldn't worry so much about the distillery burning down. Your father, rest his soul, owned so much property that no matter how much of it burned down, there must still be more left over than other people ever dream of owning."

"Everything was burned to the ground, Reb Hertz."

"What do you mean, everything?"

"Everything—the distillery, the mill, the sawmill, the forest. The coat I'm wearing is all I have left. All the houses went up in smoke. Three Torah scrolls, too—for our many sins—were destroyed."

"What do you actually have left?"

"The earth—the scorched earth. But the land is leased, of course—a Jew cannot buy land in our region. Without the factories, we won't be able to pay the squire his rent. Our only hope is that he will agree to cancel the contract."

"Don't exaggerate, Jonah. We mustn't complain against the Almighty. So you won't have such a big house, and you won't squander thousands on charity."

"Reb Hertz, we don't have any thousands left for ourselves."

Reb Hertz paled. Now he saw it, this pipsqueak who looked so innocent wants to cancel the marriage agreement—now he would want a bride with a large dowry. "A moment ago you said you came here to collect debts. And now you say there's nothing left?"

Jonah told him how little he had actually managed to collect. Reb Hertz listened with mounting suspicion; this young man would have to pay a considerable penalty if he wanted to get out of the marriage contract! "Aren't you going to ask about your bride?"

"In the note I sent I said I wanted to see Liebele. Didn't Reb Hertz read it?"

"You can't drop in on people so suddenly," Reb Hertz said testily. "My house is being painted. Usually I have it done for Pesach, but this year I delayed it so they would be freshly painted for the wedding."

"The wedding doesn't have to be held in your home. Maybe—"

"My Liebele, good health to her, is a sensitive child. This is no way to behave—not with in-laws and not with a bride-to-be. Besides, Liebele isn't here now anyway. It's too hot in the city, and my cousin Miecyslav the Squire insisted that she come to his country estate for a vacation . . . "

11

Jonah returned with seven thousand rubles in his pocket, of which two thousand would go to pay off debts. It was possible to make a small business, even with only five thousand rubles. One could rent a place, fix up a store, and make a fair living. There were merchants in Bilgoray who had started with less than that. Jonah hoped to earn enough money to enable Genendel to resume her charitable activities. Such were Jonah's thoughts on the long ride home from Warsaw.

But during the time he had been away, more creditors had showed up with receipts signed by Reb Kalman Mordecai. Jonah paid them all off, and was left with barely a thousand rubles for himself.

It happened that there was a building with eight apartments for sale in the center of the marketplace. The income from such a building would earn a livelihood for Genendel. But where would Jonah find the money to buy it?

Evidently, the One Above sends down a partial remedy with every disease. While everyone else had been running in panic from the burning house, the devoted servant-girl, Shifra, had grabbed a cleaver, run into the master bedroom, and broken into the metal strongbox attached to the clothes closet. Mameshi's jewelry must be worth a small fortune. Reb Yankel had told Jonah that the necklace she had put away for Liebele was worth six or seven hundred rubles. Then there came in the mail, unbidden, a commission of almost two thousand rubles from a Warsaw customer, which arrived just as the broker was coming to tell Jonah that the building was to be sold to another buyer. Jonah saw this as a sign from heaven; he gave the broker everything he had and promised another three thousand rubles in six months. During the intervening half year, they would certainly be able to find a good customer for the jewelry.

The building had been bought in Genendel's name, so before she signed the papers Jonah had to tell her about the three-thousand-ruble debt he had incurred and how he planned to pay it off.

"Sell my jewelry? Where would I get jewelry?"

"Your jewelry, it was in the box, Shifra ran in for it, you remember . . ."

"All I have is what Tateshi, rest his soul, bought for Liebele—the necklace, a string of pearls, and a gold brooch."

"And your necklace, Mameshi, and the cluster of pearls, and the diamond ring, the earrings, and—"

"The explosion took the lives of Shaya and Wacek. Both of them left widows and orphans. Lazar the blacksmith and his two apprentices were crippled in fighting the fire. Whatever I had left I divided up among their families. I don't need jewelry—you, my son, are my only real jewel."

"Mameshi, we have been left with nothing, absolutely nothing!"

"Don't say that, my son. You mustn't talk like that. Praise God, we were left with our lives and our health. Papa, may he intercede for us in heaven, had bought all those things or inherited them from his mother, may she enjoy a bright Paradise. It was his, and I thank the Almighty that something remained with which to pay his debts. If Papa's distillery caused Libeh-Rochel to become a widow, that's Papa's debt. Reb Yankel, the bookkeeper is also a victim of our misfortune, his newlywed son Hirsh was left fatherless, and his wife is in her third month. I gave them a gold chain and a breast-pin. As I told you Jonaleh, we still have years to live, and during those years we can still accumulate *mitzvos*. Tateshi can no longer give charity, nor can he do good deeds, so I had to do it for his sake. I did everything I could for the ascent of his soul, may he find rest in Paradise."

Jonah pawned the few pieces of jewelry that had been put away for Liebele and borrowed some money to reduce the debt on the building. Again he traveled to Warsaw to look for merchants who had owed his father money. This time, he did notify his father-in-law that he was coming. And he put the betrothal contract in his pocket.

12

As soon as Jonah entered Reb Hertz's house, he noticed that the walls had not been recently painted as Reb Hertz had told him during his previous visit to Warsaw. So it was only an excuse to keep him away from the house. And, come to think of it, the story about Liebele's visit to the country was probably another lie; from what Liebele had told him, she would never have wanted to spend any amount of time with her uncle the Squire in the country. Were these lies deliberately transparent?

And where is Liebele now? This time he notified them about his arrival and the time of his visit. Is Liebele in her room, or is it another visit with her uncle the squire?

Evidently her father had sent her away so that he could interrogate his future son-in-law. Jonah concealed none of the bitter truth. Reb Hertz squirmed in his seat, drummed his fingers on the table, and asked the same questions over and over. So far no one explained Liebele's absence or offered their guest so much as a glass of water. Jonah pulled out the chain with his pocket watch, not to check the time but to show his annoyance.

"I see you rescued the watch," Reb Hertz observed, glaring at the time piece, as if he wanted it back immediately. It was the golden watch and chain he had given Jonah as a betrothal present.

Jonah had an urge to unhook the chain and return it, when the doorbell rang. He held his breath.

It was Liebele. She ran straight toward him, but suddenly stopped, embarrassed. She paused for a second, then slowly walked over to the table. Shyly, almost in a whisper, she murmured something that sounded like "good afternoon."

Jonah jumped up, but he was equally at a loss for words. She was wearing a white blouse. How gracefully the fine lace hugged her wrists and framed her delicate neck. He wanted to ask her how she was, but the words stuck in his throat, although her name, Liebele, resounded deep inside him.

Jonah had foreseen Reb Hertz's attitude, and that was why he had brought the marriage contract, but now, after seeing Liebele again . . . Dear Father in heaven, did you bring us together just to torment me? You blessed me with such deep feelings for her, will you now take her away from me? You are trying me with one calamity on top of another, but I am not a *tsaddik* like Job, I am a plain and simple man trying my best to serve you. Please don't take Liebele away from me.

Liebele went to her room to change. Her father followed her and returned in a foul mood. Silence descended in the room. Mrs. Hertz brought a tray with tea and cookies. When Liebele finally came out of her room, her eyes were swollen. She sat down between her father and Jonah and turned to her intended with a sweet, sad smile.

"Don't be angry with me, Jonah, for writing to you in Polish. I didn't have the words in Yiddish to express my feelings. Did you get my letter?"

Before Jonah could reply, Reb Hertz broke in: "It's still a long time to Rosh Hashonah and it's raining so hard that the crops will be ruined." Then he abruptly motioned to his wife to leave the room with him. Jonah sat there dumbfounded. He realized that he owed an answer to Liebele: yes, he had received her letter, and yes, she was perfectly free to write in Polish if she found it easier to do so. But before he could get the words out, Reb Hertz came to the door and called Liebele out. When she returned a few minutes later, her face was even paler than before. No sooner had she sat down than her mother came in to call her out again.

"Later, Mameshi," Liebele said and remained seated. A vein pulsed in her left temple, and her hands trembled. She poured herself some tea and the glass rattled in the saucer. It was obvious that her father would try to dissolve the match. Was that what Liebele wanted too? Evidently not, but she had no choice in the matter— Reb Hertz would have his way. The truth was that he, Jonah, would find it very difficult to provide for her properly. He had no money, he was not a businessman, and he didn't even have anyone to learn from.

Her parents came back into the room. They all sat around the table drinking tea with such concentration that it seemed like the eve of a fast day. No one uttered a word. When Reb Hertz again signaled his wife to leave the room, Jonah took the marriage contract out of his pocket and laid it on the table before Liebele.

"I've been left without a ruble," he declared. "I cannot ask you to live in poverty with me. I now release you from this contract."

Liebele sat there numbly and watched wide-eyed as Jonah unhooked the chain with his gold watch, and laid it on top of the contract. He wanted to say goodbye but he was afraid he would start to cry, so he turned and started toward the door.

"In whose hands are you leaving me, Jonah?!"

Liebele's outcry stopped him, and he turned toward her. She hastily wiped her eyes and said, "I do not release you!"

Reb Hertz reentered the room. His glance went toward the table, fell on the contract and the watch. Liebele jumped from her chair and thrust them closer to Jonah.

"They belong to you! They're yours! Take them!"

13

When a wedding date had first been discussed, Reb Hertz had insisted on a lavish affair with a big orchestra and a famous wedding jester. He had announced that he would have around two hundred guests from his side of the family, and that the groom's side was free to invite the same number. He didn't care how much he had to borrow, just as long as he could show off for Jonah's family. But now he was the one to propose that, with Jonah still saying Kaddish for his father, an ostentatious celebration would be inappropriate. A simple ceremony at a rabbi's house, with whiskey and cake for the guests, would suffice. Jonah learned from Liebele why Reb Hertz had wanted such a big wedding. It was not just a poor man's pride; Reb Hertz knew only too well how small a poor relative could be made to feel, and he did not want his wealthy in-laws looking at his daughter that way. But now the groom was no less a pauper than his father-in-law. Genendel could discuss the Bible very impressively, but about money she knew nothing except how to distribute it to the needy. She didn't even understand that her son, who had provided her with a livelihood, had done so with his last few rubles and had left nothing for himself.

•   •   •   •   •

During the wedding, Reb Hertz kept mentioning his relative, the squire of Dombrovka, who could not attend because he was out of the country on important business. According to Reb Hertz, the squire had said that a Jew could easily make a living hanging around his court in Dombrovka: his court sold grain, the millers bought grain. When one brings together a buyer and a seller he becomes a broker. If one is smart and industrious he can make a nice living in the brokerage business.

After the squire agreed to receive Reb Hertz and his young son-in-law at his home in Warsaw, Jonah grew so optimistic that he persuaded his friend Aaron to settle in Dombrovka too, because it offered such high hopes of earning a good living. Jonah and Aaron rented an old house in Dombrovka for themselves and their families. At that time, there were almost fifty Jewish families in the village, but there was still no synagogue, no *mikveh,* and not even a rabbi. Jews traveled to a neighboring community to use the bathhouse. When there was a ritual question about a fowl or an animal, they simply gave the doubtful article away to a non-Jew. There was a ritual slaughterer who doubled as a prayer leader. Whenever the Kaddish needed to be recited in the presence of a congregation, a quorum of Jews would gather in someone's home for the service, but the Torah portion was read from a printed bible, not a scroll, because the congregation was too poor to have one written.

Jonah quickly picked up the essentials of brokerage and did in fact earn a few rubles around the squire's court. Aaron, who had no head at all for business, managed to earn a living from teaching. The number of Jewish families in the village of Dombrovka continued to grow, especially after the squire opened a large sugar factory. The growth of the general population now opened opportunities for more merchants and crafts.

Liebele was far from robust. In the first two years of marriage, she became pregnant twice, and miscarried both times. Often she took to her bed, and Jonah prepared the meals.

After three years, Liebele gave birth to twin boys. This would truly have been a blessing from heaven, except that Liebele did not properly recover from her confinement.

• • • • •

To the east and the south the land nestled in the curve of the Bzura River; to the north it sloped downward toward the Vistula. The rippling waters caught the rays of the sun and turned them into golden dancing stars. The valley was a kaleidoscope of brilliant colors: the deep green of the rich meadows was speckled with the coy mauve of clover, tiny blue flowers winked from tawny rye fields, and the golden wheat stalks bowed gracefully to the brashly red poppies. The soil here was fertile, the stalks in the fields heavy with grain, the trees in the orchards laden with fruit, and the water was alive with fish.

The orchards in the Vistula valley were a cornucopia of succulent fruit. The sugarplums were really as sweet as sugar, and the winepears were little jugs of juice. And oh, the "grokhot" apples, the "rattlers." The seeds rattled around inside the fruit, boasting of their pedigree. Truly, there were no other apples in the county with such a subtle taste and delicate aroma.

The region was called Ksienstwo Lowickie, the Duchy of Lowicz. The peasants here, who at one time were serfs of the Duke of Lowicz, were still known as Duchyites. In their everyday, homespun clothes, the Duchyites were no different from other peasants. But come Sunday, a holiday, or a church fair, when they dressed up in their finest, they swelled the streets with the vivid colors of the surrounding meadows. The men's trousers and the women's skirts were made from a special, gaily striped cloth. Their linen was handwoven from their crop of flax. The little embroidered aprons of white organdy, the lace for their blouses, the stiff cloth of their ruffled petticoats, and the brightly colored ribbons and beads which decorated every garment were provided by the Jewish dry goods and fancy goods merchant.

Here, in Dombrovka, Jews and gentiles could not survive without each other. The peasants had to till the squires' fields as well as their own little plots of land. The work was terribly hard: with their sweat, man and beast coaxed bread out of the soil. The trades had to be left to others: the tailor, the cobbler, the hatter, and the shopkeeper were all Jews. In Dombrovka, even the squire was a Jew.

Dombrovka is not easy to reach; it is not near a railway line or a main highway. Its obscurity may be the secret of its existence. For how else is one to explain a large estate, with a castle belonging to Davidson, a Jewish squire, in the middle of the Duchy of Lowicz, only twenty miles from the Cathedral where Jews were once sentenced in blood-libel trials?

The first Jewish families settled in Dombrovka when Jews were expelled from Lowicz in the sixteenth century. Jews were permitted to pass through Lowicz only on foot and with their heads bared. This decree was enforced even more strictly after the church charged the Jews with persuading a Christian woman to steal a Host wafer; they were said to have stabbed the wafer with a knife, causing it to bleed, and to have collected the blood into a vessel for their own ritual purposes. King Zygmund Augustus did not believe this accusation, but the sentence was carried out against his wishes, and Jews were not allowed into Lowicz except during the big fairs. The church fairs were a good source of income. So the Jews lived in neighboring villages and traveled to Lowicz for the fairs. From Dombrovka, for instance, it was only a three hour drive by horse and buggy.

Sometimes, at a church festival, the peasants would leave the services with their ears ringing with tales of the iniquitous Jews tormenting God's begotten Son. They did not always resist the urge to avenge their Lord's suffering. But the next day, a peasant would bring a tub of butter and a dozen eggs to a Jewish dry goods merchant to pay for the scythe he had bought on credit. God's business is one thing, man's is quite another.

14

The esteemed Squire Mieczyslaw Davidson still retained a mental image of his early childhood years, when he sat on the knee of his grandpa the Rabbi, who called him Mottelle. People said, then, that he looked just like his grandfather. It may actually have been that his grandfather had as small a face as his, but he was a tall, patriarchal man with a long, thick beard. He himself, however, had remained short and small-boned, with a face not much larger than his own heavy mustache, which was pointed upward in the fashion of the nobility.

When he married Felicia, she had been a slender young woman, but later her figure had broadened considerably, so that he looked like a schoolboy next to her. Her bosom grew so large that a drunken squire had once joked, "Pan Mieczyslaw never gets wet in the rain—he walks under his wife's bosom."

Pan Mieczyslaw was descended from rabbis and landowners. Pani Felicia herself came from a rich family of lumber merchants, simple people with neither learning nor social status. It was Felicia who wanted more than anything to maintain the regal way of life befitting her wealth. She was constantly arranging parties and dances and would regularly invite the neighboring squires to hunt in the Dombrovka forests. But the real nobility, the aristocrats, would never have deigned to visit the *Zhidek,* squire or no squire. It was the *nouveau riche* who came, those with very little pedigree and less education. Having grown up on the fertile plains of the lower Vistula, they were sturdy men with broad, muscular, peasant bodies. Pan Mieczyslaw was no match for them in his riding skill, his sharpshooting prowess, or in the art of guzzling vodka. Had it not been for his thick, twirled mustache, he would have looked more like one of the lads who tagged along to take care of the horses. Pan Mieczyslaw hated the hunting lodge where Felicia had hung the stuffed heads of wild animals, boasting that these were her husband's trophies. No one believed her anyway.

The Pani Felicia desperately wanted to be accepted by the Polish nobility, and the Jewish merchants in her court were like thorns in her flesh. The neighboring landowners also did business with Jewish merchants, but in Dombrovka even the estate steward was a Jew. When he died, the squire could not find a replacement. Furthermore, those who were available weren't worth hiring. They had in fact lost their jobs because they were either drunkards, lazy, or had "sticky fingers."

Thinking about this, the squire had an idea: why not hire a young student and teach him the business? Then he would not put on airs, but would remain loyal to his employer for giving him the chance to hold an important job.

His first thought was to look for a Jewish student, but people told him all the Jewish students were socialists—and maybe there was some truth in it. The Polish students harassed the Jewish students no less than the Tsarist government did. Only the radical students stuck together—Jews and Poles. So it was only natural that the Jewish students were attracted to the socialists. And that was all he needed—for the police to catch a revolutionary in the court of the Dombrovka Jewish squire.

Pan Mieczyslaw searched a long time before he found a young

Pole who seemed to have the required intelligence and the proper recommendations. The young man did display a keen desire for money, but the squire did not consider that a flaw: that kind of ambition would only make him work harder. It was also in his favor that the young man came from a poor family; he would not look down his nose at the master who happened to be a Jew.

15

Just as in the Scriptures, with a new king came trouble. The new estate manager turned out to be quite capable, but Jews had a harder time around the squire's court. People said the mistress ordered him to treat Jews in this way, but perhaps he didn't need orders for this. The squire himself was either away in Warsaw or the manager simply didn't let the Jewish merchants see him.

The manager had a special grudge against Jonah, and Jonah had let slip the comment that he could not be driven out of this court since he was related to the squire. This even reached the ears of Pani Felicia, who, although a Jew herself, was no less a Jew-hater than the manager.

Now that his family was growing, Jonah did not wish to rely any longer on the fickle fortunes of the brokerage business. His friend Aaron rented a flat of his own, and Jonah opened a little grocery store in the front room of his home. The store did not earn much, but there was food on the table, and Jonah managed to find a bit of brokerage work on the side.

There was a deep affection between the stout Jonah and his dainty wife. The number of mouths in his household increased, but his income did not. Fortunately, he was a good handyman. Once, he would never have thought of doing a thing for himself, but now, as a matter of necessity, he did everything, including repairs on the old roof to keep the rain out.

16

"Children all the world over get sick, but when it hits my household . . . " Liebele lamented, wringing her hands. Both of her boys had come down with the measles, but after a week, Shmulik, the first-born of the twins, had developed pneumonia. The barber-surgeon applied leeches and cupping. The doctor prescribed a cabinet-full of remedies. They rubbed Shmulik's back with an extract of boiled cam-omile, violets, and kohlrabi leaves. Then the doctor performed the special cupping procedure for pneumonia, puncturing the skin so that each cup drew blood.

They did not rely on medical remedies alone. The affliction could have come from an evil eye or a malicious spirit. A messenger was sent to fetch an amulet from the Rebbe of Gostinin, and Reb Aaron's wife chanted a special incantation:

> If an evil spell
> On this household fell,
> If it came with the river's flow,
> the cat's meow, or the rooster's crow,
> If brought with a dog's bark,
> Or Lilith dropped it in the dark,
> If it entered through a limb, nail, or hair,
> Whenever our hearts despair
> And we feel forlorn,
> To you, our Creator, we turn
> And beg for your care.

Father in heaven, God of mercy, healer of all flesh, send Raphael, your healing angel with a cure for the child Shmuel, son of Liebe, and thus fulfill the verse "May the Lord sustain me on my sickbed." Amen.

But there was no sign of the healing angel. The child's tempera-ture rose by the hour. "For whose sins is this innocent child being punished?" Liebele cried, as she rocked him in her arms throughout that long night. She knew she was sinful; she had always complained about her father's ways. But she had also always obeyed him, except that one time, when Jonah's parents lost their fortune and her father resolved to break her betrothal to Jonah. What was so shameful about poverty, she had asked. Unlike her father, who had grown up with riches, she had known it all her life. Poverty was inconvenient, to be sure, but at Jonah's side she was willing to bear it. May the

One Above just grant good health for her children and her husband; the love she and Jonah shared was a blessing from God worth more than precious jewels.

Certainly Jonah had done good deeds, even though he worked day and night to scrape together a living. Through his efforts, Dombrovka now had a place of worship and a Torah scroll. Liebele had been so inspired by her husband's efforts that she used a bolt of satin that Jonah had bought her for a dress to make a curtain instead for the Holy Ark and a mantle for the Torah scroll. She had stayed up nights after the housework was done, embroidering the curtain with a crown and Tablets of the Law and all sorts of flowers to adorn the sacred objects. Now she prayed, may the beautiful curtain she had made for the Holy Ark be counted to the merit of her child. She wished for herself only the merit of the Torah mantle, so that she could enter the next world with at least one good deed to her name.

But Shmulik's temperature continued climbing until the moment it plummeted down—all the way down!

Jonah mustered all his strength to face the tragedy. It was a bitter judgment indeed, but the One Above, in His benevolence, had at least cut the decree in half and let his other son, Boruchl, recover. May God grant that he live to see Boruchl grow up strong and healthy, with children and grandchildren of his own.

Liebele could hardly tear herself away from the grave. She felt as though part of her remained in the cemetery, buried with Shmulikl's little body.

Jonah tried to console her: "The One above will compensate us with new children . . . " And, indeed, new children did arrive. But Liebele's pregnancies left her in a weakened condition.

The neighbors' children rolled in the dirt, roamed the streets half naked, played all day long in the gutters, and stayed healthy and strong. But any illness in the air struck down Liebele's boys. With so much money needed for doctors and medicine, very little was left of Jonah's earnings. Liebele wrung her hands and bemoaned her fate. Why hadn't her father prepared her for a life of poverty? Even after he lost his wealth, he still never allowed her to help her mother in the kitchen: "Liebele's hands should be white and smooth," he would say. He brought in tutors to teach her Polish and Russian; she had had piano, and even singing lessons. Liebele and all her friends knew how to knit and embroider, but for Liebele, her father had hired a special teacher to prepare her to become a "lady." He succeeded in finding her a rich suitor. But the One Above had other plans, and before their wedding day the rich suitor had become a pauper.

Still, complaining is a sin. Boruchl was clawing his way past all the childhood diseases, and was growing up to be a fine, healthy boy. He was already studying Talmud with Reb Aaron, the best teacher in Dombrovka.

•   •   •   •   •

Spring had come late the previous year, and now, 1893 brought no spring at all. By Passover it was hot, and the heat persisted. The fields languished without a drop of rain, the rivers shrank, the wells dried up. By the first day of the month of Tammuz the harvest was in, but it was a harvest without blessing. The stalks were emaciated, the kernels—when there were any—tiny. The wind had blown most of them out of the withered stalks. People feared the coming winter, unaware that something worse than hunger awaited them. Another harvest of a different order loomed: entire communities were to fall under the scythe of the Angel of Death.

By the fast of the Ninth of Av, the Jews of Dombrovka had learned what the cholera epidemic had wrought elsewhere. They did not travel to the stricken cities, they avoided eating heavy foods, they fasted half-days every Monday and Thursday, they recited the psalms, and they hoped—they were, after all, living in a remote corner of the land, well away from the main roads.

Even so, the pestilence found its way to Dombrovka. It began in the cottages behind the muddy road. Then it crossed to the homes of the Squire's farm hands and spread like wildfire through the entire town.

Liebele was terrified. If it should strike her household, God forbid . . . Boruchl was still on the frail side . . . the cholera spread from house to house . . . Perhaps the wisest thing would be to leave the house.

Jonah rented a barn from a peasant whose farm was a full mile away from the last house on Wilki Street. The morning after he moved his family there, he noticed that the farmer's wife would run behind the house every few minutes. It was almost like the prophet's curse against Moab: "A horror and a ditch and a trap: he who runs from the horror will fall into the ditch, and he who climbs out of the ditch will fall into the trap."

They had barely returned to the town when they heard that people were fleeing their homes and settling in empty fields. Liebele had no more strength to run. Whatever was destined to happen, it was better to be at home, she decided, where one could eat a hot meal and sleep in a bed, and where a mezuzza with God's name hung on the doorpost.

Reb Leybush, the village barber-surgeon of Dombrovka, was a highly pious man. On Saturday he himself would go to the apothecary and give the prescription orally, so he would not desecrate the Sabbath by writing. No time was given any longer for such considerations. "Save us, Reb Leybush, help us!" Jews and non-Jews gave him no rest.

In truth, Reb Leybush too was at a complete loss. The cure for diarrhea was emulsion of almonds or the water from boiled flaxseed, but no almonds or flaxseed were available, and the only remedy left was rice cooked without salt. But the dry rice stuck in his patients' throats until they got so nauseated that they vomited it out, with green bile. The remedy for vomiting was vinegar, but how could he prescribe vinegar when their entire bodies, from tongue to intestines, were raw and inflamed? Burning with fever, the sick would cry out for a sip of water, but the more they drank, the more they evacuated and vomited. They could not possibly consume as much as they expelled. Their skin grew clammy, their pulses weakened, until their death agonies began.

Just as Reb Leybush was bewildered by so many patients, the Burial Society was paralyzed by so many corpses. At that time Dombrovka had no Jewish cemetery, and the bodies had to be transported eleven kilometers to Gombin, and Gombin surely did not want to receive any victims of the plague. In the crowded Jewish houses the dead lay in their beds alongside those who still breathed faintly, and those who still remained on their feet did what they could for those who had been stricken.

•   •   •   •   •

When Jonah's mother, Genendel, learned that the epidemic had reached Dombrovka, she sent a telegram from Bilgoray: "Boil the water before you drink it." But in Dombrovka the telegrapher lay in bed dying, and there was no one else to receive the message.

In normal times they would have brought in a doctor from Gombin or Lowicz; now, of course, no doctor would come even if they could offer him a mountain of gold. The squire sent a sanitation expert down from Warsaw, but he seemed helpless. The priest called together a few of his congregants and instructed them about helping the sick. Reb Aaron, who was consulted like a rabbi, also met with a few people near the water pump.

"It is a decree from heaven," he said. "Whoever is destined to be stricken will not escape it, even if he runs to the ends of the earth. But the good deed of tending the sick can help to avert the evil from reaching you."

Jonah heeded these words and joined a few others in burying the dead on a plot of ground belonging to the Squire, promising to pay for the land if they survived the plague.

Day after day passed, and Genendel received no reply to her telegram. After a week, she decided on her course of action. She went first to her husband's grave and urged him to keep an eye on their son from on high. Then, returning home, she packed a couple of holy books, and set out for Dombrovka.

On the way, Genendel stopped to see Dr. Percal, who had treated her many years ago when, after her confinement, she had been seriously ill. Hearing of her mission, the doctor tried to persuade her to turn back. She had no proof, he urged, that the sickness had struck her family. Besides, her son was young and healthy; it made no sense for her, a frail and elderly woman, to risk her own health just to see him. The doctor saw, however, that she was not to be dissuaded and gave her the advice she was seeking: the vomiting and high fever of the cholera drew every last drop of moisture from the body; drinking was the only remedy, buckets of water should be placed at the bedside of each patient.

"Boiled water?"

"Boiled water is for those who are still healthy. For the sick, cold water. Apply ice to their heads and give them pieces of ice to suck on."

"Ice for a seriously ill person?" Genendel could not believe she had heard correctly.

"Yes. Let them chew on the ice, and make them drink, drink, drink! And put salt into the water."

"Won't that make them more thirsty?"

"This sickness drives the salt out of the body, and that can also cause death."

• • • • •

When Jonah saw his mother he cried like a baby. "Everyone is running away from the plague, Mameshi, and you pick this time to come here?"

Genendel was not given to tears, but her relief at seeing her family healthy was obvious. She even consented to let Liebele fix her a meal, although she insisted on reciting the afternoon prayers before she would accept any food.

Much as Genendel feared for the health of her only son, she was still pleased that he ran out immediately to spread the news about giving the sick plenty of water to drink. After all, if a person sits with folded hands when he could be helping to save lives, he loses both worlds—this world of sorrow and struggle and the world to come as well. Fear for the health of her children must have been purposely planted in her by the Almighty so that she would come to this unfortunate place with advice from the good Dr. Percal.

One morning, after sitting up with a sick man all night, Jonah was preparing to go out again. His mother stopped him. "You are too tired now, my son. A tired body invites all kinds of ailments. A few hours' sleep will renew your strength."

"It acts so fast, Mameshi. A man can, God forbid, die in just a few hours."

Jonah picked up a pail and was halfway to the pump when he felt a knifelike cramp in his stomach. The pain lasted only a second. He went to the outhouse and came back a moment later, but before he reached the pump he had to run back to the outhouse. He knew that the disease always started out in a mild form.

When Genendel discovered that her son had been stricken, she arranged for Liebele and the children to stay at another house, for they were not to touch Jonah's clothes or use his utensils. "I will take care of him," she assured them. "I've been out among the sick, anyway."

Jonah drank every drop of the blackberry juice his mother had brought from Bilgoray, but for this disease, the traditional remedy for diarrhea proved ineffective. The vomiting erupted with such force that Genendel feared he would bring up his guts. By evening, he no longer had the strength to open his mouth; she had to pry it open and force pieces of ice into it. When the ice revived him a little, she pleaded, "Drink, my son, drink, my only child, drink!"

For a little while Genendel dozed at Jonah's bedside. It was way past midnight when she awoke. She saw at once that her son's face had become drawn and gray, like a—God forbid! The time was past for Dr. Percal's remedies. Now, the Healer of the sick who is in heaven must intervene! She left Jonah's side and ran to waken Reb Aaron. Now, this minute, they must call together a quorum of ten men, a minyan. There was no other way to save Jonah!

When the men began to assemble in Reb Aaron's house, Genendel was already there, her face buried in the curtain of the Holy Ark, her shoulders quivering with muffled sobs. The long shadows cast by the few candles wavered as the flames flickered, filling the air with a mysterious awe.

The men put on their prayer shawls, covering their heads and eyes with them. After a few moments of silence, Reb Aaron began to chant solemnly:

"May the King who sits upon the throne of mercy, He who treats His children with compassion and mercy, be filled with pity for all His children who have been stricken by the dread cholera, and particularly for Jonah, son of Gitl-Genendel. May it please the heavenly court that, by the authority of the earthly court, and by the authority of the holy congregation here assembled, we hereby change the name of Jonah to Chaim-Jonah. And may he live to celebrate his new name, as Scripture says, 'I will make thy name great, and be thou a blessing.'

"May it be Thy will, Master of the Universe, God of our fathers, that any evil decrees against Jonah ben Gitl-Genendel shall have no power over Chaim-Jonah, because he is as a different person and a new being, against whom there are no decrees. As our sages said, changing one's name annuls the evil decree. May he be reborn, like a new child, to a good life, to long, full years, and may the verse be fulfilled for him: 'I shall make the days of your life full.' Amen."

"Amen," the men answered in unison, as they lifted the prayer shawls from over their eyes and looked around with a feeling of relief and hope. The shadows had vanished, and the first light of the new day glowed at the windows.

Reb Aaron proposed to chant a few psalms before starting the morning prayers. A few of the men exchanged news about their families' health; others were preparing to put on their *tefillin* when Genendel gestured that she had something to add. The men turned toward her as she began to speak.

"The good Lord has invested power in His Torah and wisdom in His sages. Tonight we have invoked their remedies. But that alone is not enough."

The room became suddenly quiet. Genendel continued in a firm voice.

"This congregation of Jews, a holy minyan here assembled, is witness that I, Gitl-Genendel, daughter of Beyla, hereby give away all my years as a sacrifice to redeem the life of my son Chaim-Jonah. Whatever *mitzvos,* good deeds I have done, whatever charity I have given, and whatever merits I have accumulated, they are now transferred to my son Chaim-Jonah."

"Leave something for yourself," interjected Reb Aaron.

"No! I came into this world without any *mitzvos* and without *mitzvos* I shall leave it. Everything I have accumulated, from the day of my birth until today, and everything that I may earn until my last hour on earth, all of it, is given over to save my son Chaim-Jonah. This is a pledge never to be revoked, no regrets, or declarations of annulment shall be valid."

Genendel finished her last words in a hurry, her face twisted in sudden agony as she staggered out of the synagogue.

The entire community prayed for Genendel's recovery. Prior to her arrival with Dr. Percal's remedies, whoever took sick had died. But now, with the drinking of large amounts of water, the number of deaths had decreased.

The One Above finally relented and withdrew the terrible sickness that had taken three hundred lives in Dombrovka. Eventually, Genendel also started to feel better; and Jonah too was able to leave his bed. The dark days receded and the Holy Days of Awe approached. Genendel insisted on returning to Bilgoray for Rosh Hashonah, where she had her own seat in the synagogue, and where she could pray at her husband's grave and the graves of her ancestors. When her bundles were loaded onto the wagon that would take her to the train station at Lowicz, she informed Jonah that she had something to discuss with him, and she asked Liebele to listen as well.

"The One Above has saved us from the sickness, my children, but it has been a costly bargain," Genendel began. "Any years that are left to me, as you know, I have ransomed for you, Chaim-Jonah, for a long and happy life. And in addition to donating my years, I renounced all my merits. In your father's house, Chaim-Jonah, I distributed charity with an open hand, thank God, and I accumulated a whole treasure of merits. Your friend Aaron warned me to leave something for myself. But I have no regrets for not listening to him. I gave everything away, everything I had, and everything I will earn until my last hour, and I praise the One Above that my sacrifice was accepted and approved.

"But now I am in your hands, and only you can save me. We come into this world of vanity only to earn merits and do good deeds, so that we may have something with which to appear before the heavenly court. What will I take with me when I leave this world, and what will I bring with me for the eternal life? You must promise me that when my time comes you will not fail to say the Kaddish for me regularly. If you . . . "

Before Genendel could finish, Liebele broke into tears, her body shaking convulsively.

Jonah tried to calm his wife: "Don't worry, Liebele, the good Lord will grant Mameshi many more years, and she will yet dance with us at many a celebration."

To Liebele it was all becoming clear now. She remembered well from her Scriptures that an animal offered as a sacrifice at the Temple must be whole and complete. Had she, like her mother-in-law, offered everything? No, she had not! When she had needed the Lord's intervention to save her Shmulik and she had been ready to sacrifice her merits, she had held back the merit of the Torah mantle. Her sacrifice had been incomplete and therefore unacceptable. She had had it then in her power to save her sweet little boy, but, in her selfishness, she had missed the opportunity and he had slipped away forever.

17

In *Wisdom of the Fathers* it says, "Because you drowned another, you were drowned; and he who drowned you will suffer the same fate." This is the case for nations as it is for individuals; and it is as true for the times of old as of our day. First the Japanese attacked China and took Port Arthur, China's only warm-water port in the Pacific. So Russia joined with other governments and compelled Japan to return the seaport to China. Several years later, Russia herself seized Port Arthur, became the ruler of Manchuria, and began to extend the trans-Siberian railway line to the occupied areas. So now Japan united with England to stop the Russians, who were also casting a covetous eye on Korea.

Meanwhile, the Japanese built up their military forces to the point where the Russian Minister of War, Kropotkin, was ready to return Port Arthur to China for a good price, namely, a piece of land near Vladivostok. It was evident that everyone was willing to take, but no one was in a hurry to give back. This game went on until a winter night in 1904, when Japanese torpedo boats attacked Russian ships in Port Arthur and started a war.

The matter was widely discussed among the worshipers at the Dombrovka synagogue as they waited for the first three stars to appear in the sky, so evening services could start. Jonah Swerdl suddenly remembered that a war needed suppliers, and that his grandfather had been such a supplier during the Russo-Turkish war; why not use his "ancestral merit" to become a contractor in the Russo-Japanese war? True, this would require much capital.

A relative in Bilgoray had his grandfather's documents of his dealings with the government during a previous war. These papers opened doors for Jonah, but the gentlemen whose offices he visited asked whether he had enough capital for the venture. Governments did not pay in advance, and with "Ivan" one would see a cat carrying a camel before seeing the color of the ruble. The profit margin would be great, but where would the money to start come from? It was a vicious circle: he could not land a contract until he had the necessary capital, but he could not get the capital until he had a contract. Unless he were to find a partner . . .

It occurred to Jonah that he ought to turn to Liebele's relative, Squire Davidson. Pan Mieczyslaw was a pleasant man who was willing to do good turns for people. But his wife, Pani Felicia, suffered from the ignominy of her obviously Jewish name; nor did she find it particularly pleasing that bearded Jews in ankle-length caftans were wandering around in her court. But it would please her if only one Jew would buy up the squire's entire grain harvest and all the cattle he could produce. This would be not only very convenient, but very profitable, too.

Seventy years had passed since the serfs had been freed in Russia. When they had only begun to talk about this in Poland, Mieczyslaw's grandfather, Reb Tevil Davidson, had freed all his peasants and given each one a plot of land to cultivate. When a government decree in 1881 made the land which had been distributed in leases to the serfs their own, personal property, this had already long been accomplished in Dombrovka.

The peasants had large families, and, in addition to working their own little parcels of land, they also worked the landowner's fields, in return for which they received part of the crop. Their well-being was therefore still dependent on the landowner. Elections were held for a community administration, and a village Elder was chosen, but the peasants always voted for the candidates chosen by the landowners. It was the landowner who provided the seed for planting, and by the end of winter the peasants were borrowing potatoes from the court's supply. It went without saying that whenever a peasant's horse died or his barn burned down, he had to turn to the landowner for help.

This particular landowner happened to be Jewish, but when his carriage drove by the peasants would stop and doff their hats, even on holidays when they were on their way to church. The women would bow their brightly kerchiefed heads and adjust their Sunday clothes: blouses made of linen from the flax in their fields; little woolen jackets with stripes of dazzling colors, and skirts of the same material over stiffly starched petticoats. It sometimes happened that one of the squire's coach-horses would kick mud on this holiday attire, but the peasants never took offense at this: a landowner is a landowner and must ride in a carriage. A landowner without a carriage is not really a landowner, and if there were no landowner, from whom could they borrow when their own barns were empty?

Mieczyslaw knew that his grandfather and father had been more generous to the peasants than he could afford to be—Felicia squandered too much money on fancy parties. But now that he had a steady buyer for his grain, he would help his peasants plant more seed, pasture more cows. He would buy the yield from them in advance, making a tidy profit in the resale, and keeping both them and himself happy. With socialists throwing bombs and inciting the peasants, it was better for him that his peasants not go hungry.

Jonah went to a Warsaw bank and assigned to the squire everything that the government would owe him for provisions, and the squire agreed to supply him with grain and cattle, and also to co-sign his loans for the purchase of other goods. Just as all the arrangements had been worked out, Jonah was told that there were too many Jewish contractors dealing with the government and that the quartermaster departments were coming under fire. Perhaps Jonah had a non-Jewish friend in whose name the contract could be made out? The whole deal was in danger of collapsing, but the squire had an idea: his new estate manager was a young student from a poor family; for two or three thousand rubles he would gladly lend his name to the transaction.

Jonah did not think highly of the young estate manager, but the squire had invested a lot of money in this enterprise and he would never have agreed to do it with someone he didn't trust. And so the estate manager, Pakula, lent his name for the contract. In turn, he signed various deeds and assurances testifying that the contracts actually belonged to Jonah and that he, Pakula, renounced in advance any claim against the profits of the business.

Everything was approved and signed, but Jonah experienced a growing sense of panic. He was undertaking to conduct a business involving millions of rubles, a contract with the army in time of war. If he failed to produce, he would be in very deep trouble. And why was he doing this in the first place? He wasn't making a fortune with his store, but he was far from being a pauper. God had blessed him with a second set of twins, two delightful little girls, and all Liebele's energy was spent on them. She had a haunted look about her sometimes; she could not forget the terrible times when they were first married and could not get enough to eat.

A contractor could get rich quickly. Jonah dreamed of saving his money in gold pieces and tossing them into Liebele's apron. Maybe the sound of that clinking metal would drive out her bitter memories and bring back the sweet smile that used to play around her lips in the days when she first visited his parents' house. But he would have liked to consult someone. His father-in-law? No, if Reb Hertz had been a good businessman he wouldn't have lost all his money and remained a pauper. The squire? He left such matters to his manager. Liebele? She was intelligent, educated, but how could she advise him when he didn't dare tell her how risky the business was. The contract was in the name of a Pole, but it was no secret that a Jew stood behind him. His goods would pass through the hands of a lot of crooks and bribe takers before they reached their destination—the authorities would as soon scapegoat a Jew as any of their own. But

. . . this might be his last chance to pull himself up out of poverty for once and for all.

Jonah went to see the Rabbi of Gostinin and laid out all his motives and doubts. But the Rabbi sensed that Jonah had not come to be told yes or no; he had come seeking a buttressing of his resolve—confirmation of his decision. So the Rabbi gave his blessing and said that the Guardian of Israel, who had been with Jonah's grandfather and protected him against misfortune, should also be with the grandson and bless the work of his hands.

18

Jonah suffered many anxious moments until the first transport reached its destination. It took some time and much money before he learned how, when, and whom to pay off, to make things run smoothly.

But as time went on, Jonah did start making money, lots of it. Liebele no longer needed to work so hard: a widow came in to do the housework, and a girl helped out with the children. But Jonah was seldom home; when he returned from his business trips he spent most of his time on his accounts. Sometimes he didn't even go to bed, but caught a few winks at the table with his head on his arms.

Liebele's physical burdens were lightened but she had no friends in Dombrovka—few of the women here understood Polish, and even her refined Yiddish was strange to them. They worked hard, and their plumpness and muscles bulged out of their homespun dresses; but Liebele looked like a thin, little doll in a display cabinet. She had come to Dombrovka a stranger, and a stranger she remained.

When Genendel came to visit, she realized that the other women looked upon her daughter-in-law with contempt. Genendel advised Jonah to save a few rubles to buy Liebele a piano.

"I made a vow not to squander money on luxuries, Mameshi."

"Then renounce your vow, Chaim-Jonah. Besides, a piano for Liebele would not be a luxury but a cure for her illness. She'll play for the children and she'll be happy too."

"We don't have room for a piano."

"You've become a good provider, my son, I can see that. Rent a larger house. Or build yourself one."

Genendel also had some words for her daughter-in-law. "My

child, I know exactly what you're going through. I was in a similar situation myself, once. When my Kalman Mordecai, rest his soul, built the sawmill near his forest, I was in my seventh month. Children should be near their father, so I insisted he build a house near the business and we moved into the forest. Kalman was always busy in the sawmill, and I was at home alone, with no one to talk to.

"Whenever I traveled to the city I missed my house in the village, but when I went home my depression returned. I continued to suffer until I began to think: how could I feel sorry for myself when there were people suffering all around me and here I was in a position to help them? And very soon I had no room for self-pity."

Liebele could it hardly imagine that Genendel had also once been miserable. She felt completely incapable of running a large household and distributing charity the way her mother-in-law had done. Did Genendel know how unfortunate her only son had been in his choice of a wife? Still, Liebele felt better when Genendel was around; she told beautiful stories and parables, and knew exactly what to say to cheer Liebele up. It was too bad that Jonah didn't have that gift— not that he wasn't a good husband, it was just that his lips could not speak his heart's feelings.

19

Before the sugar factory was built, Dombrovka had only three streets. The first houses were built on both sides of Lowicz Road. Behind this road and not far from the Nida River, a branch of the Bzura, lay the bogs. Here poor peasants trampled out a path with their feet and built huts facing their little fields. This track was later named Mud Street. Another road crossed Lowicz Street and ran to the village of Wilki, and most of the Jewish homes were on Wilki Road.

Jonah's business ventures flourished, and Dombrovka flourished with them. A whole industry grew around Jonah's enterprise: in the summer livestock was sent to the front; in the winter they shipped meat, because the cold kept it frozen. The cows were slaughtered by a *shochet,* so merchants soon arrived who sold the top—kosher—parts of the animals in Warsaw and sent only the hind cuts to the front lines. There was a small factory that smoked meat. Now the people of Dombrovka sewed uniforms, baked bread, and smoked meat for the

Russian army. More craftsmen arrived, and on Lowicz Street stores appeared where food, clothing, enamel pots, hardware, and dry goods could be purchased. New streets were laid out around the old. The village became a town, the town a city, and the bailiff a mayor.

It turned out that it wasn't easy to get permission from the authorities to build a Jewish house of worship, so they looked to the most influential Jew in Dombrovka, Squire Davidson. Jonah prepared himself for long, tough negotiations and went to see the squire.

•　•　•　•　•

"The best location for a synagogue is on Wilki Street near Lowicz Road. If the squire would give us a small plot of land on the other side of the ditch, the Jewish community would lay a few pipes for the wastewater and cover them with a paved entrance to the synagogue courtyard."

The houses were built on one side of Wilki street; on the other side, along the entire length of the roadway, there was a deep ditch which, in the spring, filled up with water. Beyond the ditch were the squire's fields.

The squire was indignant. "When did your community grow so rich? There are pipes in my courtyard, lumber in my forests, and bricks in my brickyard. Take whatever you need . . . "

Jonah tried to persuade Aaron to become expert in ritual matters so that he could accept the post of Dombrovka's first rabbi. But the idea frightened Aaron. "With most ritual questions it's never a simple matter. One authority says kosher, another says *treyf.* What does the rabbi do in that situation? Interpret the law leniently and rule it kosher? Suppose the more rigorous interpretation is correct? A whole community could be misled into eating non-kosher food; or if he rules it *treyf* a butcher might lose all his resources, which were invested in the slaughtered animal. Besides, the animal might contain the lost soul of a sinful man, waiting for someone to recite a blessing over the meat so that it can be released. A strict ruling might ruin the whole thing."

Instead of spending his few free days with Liebele, Jonah went looking for a rabbi. His mother convinced him to come to Bilgoray, where the local rabbi's son-in-law had shown himself to be not only a scholar but a man who knew the Law and was considerate of the common people at the same time. "In our difficult times, we need a rabbi who does not isolate himself in the Torah but who is both a leader and a friend to his congregants."

Jonah had wanted to go to Bilgoray anyhow to visit the grave of his father. The young rabbi made a good impression on him, and also on the congregation in Dombrovka when he went there to conduct a Sabbath service. Before he left, Reb Aaron wrote in fine calligraphy, in flowery Hebrew, the act of rabbinical nomination, and all the congregants put their signature on it.

Jonah did not believe in celebrations for their own sake, but he remembered vividly the big party his father had arranged in the village whenever there was a new Torah scroll written for the synagogue. Musicians played, horsemen with flaming torches accompanied the congregation which carried the scroll to the Holy Ark, singing psalms and dancing in the streets.

This time there was a triple celebration. Jonah and Aaron traveled to Lowic to await the Rabbi at the railroad station. In Dombrovka the whole community, even the peasants, turned out to greet him. The Rabbi went first to Jonah's house to add the last letter to the Torah scroll which Jonah had ordered written. Outside, the community waited with a canopy, as for a wedding. They escorted the Rabbi, who carried in his arms the scroll, sheltering him under the canopy, to the new synagogue, which he dedicated. There was much singing, dancing, and unbounded joy. Even the infirm were brought to the synagogue for the ceremony. Jonah invited Pan Davidson. True, he was a squire, but he was also a Jew, and he did not appear.

20

Jonah's enterprises were flourishing, growing from a small-town grocery business to handling enormous war contracts. People credited him with the wisdom of a sage, the memory of an elephant, and the ability of a mathematician. He was a highly regarded member of the community, and in the synagogue he was called to the reading of the best Torah portions. He had bought the house he lived in, and the land behind the house, and was making plans to build a new house on the site. But this was not to be.

The squire's young daughter, Jadzia, started out on a trip to Warsaw but never arrived there. Several days later, people realized that the estate manager had not been seen for a long time. The servants reported that he had not slept in his room for over a week. In answer to his questions, the squire learned that as much as a year ago, when he was away, his daughter had often been seen in the company of Pan Pakula. She had even ridden off with him into the forest for days at a time . . .

The squire screamed bloody murder, stamped his feet, quarreled with his wife, and finally, like a real squire, drank himself into a stupor. When he sobered up, he continued to mutter under his breath: that libertine Pakula would squander the few thousand rubles he had gotten from Jonah in no time at all, and then he would be back begging for a kopek. Jadzia was so spoiled that she insisted on only the best and finest of everything. Oh yes, they would crawl back to him on their knees. He would kick Pakula's behind so hard he would land in the next county.

Jonah hurried to the court: "Esteemed Squire, what's to be done about the contract?"

"When that dog spends his last kopek—don't worry, Jonah, he's a scoundrel, but he won't dare start up with the Tsar and the secret police. He's much too smart for that—may he rot in hell!"

"Still, the business is in his name, and that could be trouble."

"He will try to extract from you a big ransom. I forbid you to give him a kopek, you hear?"

"Fortunes are at stake here," Jonah insisted.

"If you give that bastard one grosz, don't ever come around here again!"

Jonah was worried sick, but how could he argue with the squire?

The full extent of the calamity was discovered when Jonah went to the government to ask for payment, and was told that it had already been made. It took much pleading and some greasing of palms before he was finally shown a receipt signed by Jozef Pakula. The authorities knew that Jonah was the real owner, but Pakula had probably paid them plenty to overlook that fact.

Eventually proper measures were taken to ensure that it wouldn't happen again. Meanwhile, Jonah lost not only everything he had earned, but found himself heavily in debt. And he couldn't even complain: the matter had to be kept quiet or the bank would withdraw the substantial credit it had extended to him. The squire did not cancel his guarantee, on condition that Jonah give him notes for everything he owed him.

Jonah refused to give up, and hung on to his faith in the One Above. But when Liebele looked into his eyes he had to tell her the whole truth. All she did was bow her head and moan, "I knew it would end like this."

21

Jonah's business recovered from this setback, and he continued to prosper, but he was out of town more and more often. Once, when he set out to locate a lost shipment, he ended up in Vladivostok. The long journey was worthwhile: not only did he find the missing goods, he also made contacts at all the junction points, even on the trans-Siberian line. He was on the road for months, however, and as he was on his way home, scarlet fever began spreading virulently back in Dombrovka.

Boruchl was among the first struck. Pan Leybush, the medic, recognized the symptoms, cramps in the belly, throat red as fire, and high temperature, and immediately applied leeches around the throat to prevent the infection from spreading to the brain. A doctor came from neighboring Gombin. On the doctor's advice Liebele boiled half an ounce of quinine in half a quart of water until half had evaporated; she put sugar in the essence that was left, but the concoction was still terribly bitter. Jonah would have known how to persuade Boruchl to take a tablespoon of the foul-tasting stuff every two hours, as the doctor had instructed, but Liebele had no such influence with him.

When the red spots erupted all over Boruchl's body, the fever subsided somewhat. A little epsom salt helped ease the constipation that accompanied the disease, and his throat began to feel better. But as his skin began to peel and the recuperation period began, the two younger children, Beyltche and Chayele, were stricken. At her wits' end, Liebele put ice compresses on their foreheads to keep the fever down, but beyond that she didn't know what to do.

As she sat by her children, Liebele bemoaned her situation. In no other house in Dombrovka was there as much sickness as there was in hers. Her children had been stricken with every illness that was borne on the wind. When would this judgment be filled? And she prayed, "May the tears that pour from my eyes extinguish the fire of my sins, Father in heaven, and may my children not be further punished for my transgressions . . . "

While Boruchl improved each day, the girls worsened. Beyltche developed dropsy. Chayele's throat swelled up so badly it touched her ears. The doctor was too busy in his hometown to visit Dombrovka. Chayele's temperature shot up, her breathing grew more labored, and she rarely opened her eyes. When she began to vomit on an empty stomach, they knew it was a brain inflammation and that the convulsions were not far off.

With one child deathly ill and the other already on the ground with her feet toward the door, as the custom calls for with the body of the departed, Liebele sent telegrams and prepared for the funeral. "When will it be enough?" she asked again, and realized that she was being sinful. "I will not cry, not scream, not complain. At least leave me my Beyltche, dear God . . ."

They could not wait more than three days to have the funeral, so Jonah was not present to say the Kaddish at the grave of his daughter.

When Jonah finally did get home, Beyltche had recovered from the dropsy, but she remained very weak.

"Liebele, my life, I'll never go away again, even if it ruins me."

"My life has grown bitter and my spirit dark. Cursed is the womb that brings forth children for the graveyard."

Beyltche slept more and more. Jonah summoned doctors from Lowic, and when Beyltche showed no improvement he sent for a specialist from Warsaw. He had worked so hard to save his family from poverty, he was ready now to spend all the money he made to save them from illness.

Jonah sat vigil by Beyltche's bed night after night, watching and praying. One morning he awoke Liebele and told her the dreaded news. Liebele only bowed her head and whispered, "I knew it would end like this."

22

Just as the tree whose branches spread out like a shelter over the graves of her children, she did not weep. After the Kaddish, when someone took her arm to lead her away, she looked enviously at that tree—no one was dragging it away from them.

Although Jonah had promised not to take any more business trips, a telegram arrived two days after the funeral: "COME TO WARSAW AT ONCE." Because it was a time of war and this was a matter that had to do with military supplies, he had to go or risk being accused of sabotaging orders. He got permission from the rabbi to depart on the fourth day of the mourning period.

Revolutionaries were agitating against the government more and more stridently. In the larger cities there were demonstrations and riots, and the Tsar's Cossacks found the Jews to be an easy target for retribution. Jonah knew he had to watch his step in his dealing with the government: if he were to make a mistake or default on a delivery, it would be disastrous for him.

$$\bullet \quad \bullet \quad \bullet \quad \bullet \quad \bullet$$

Jonah was again prepared to start construction on his new home, and planned to put his family into temporary quarters, but Liebele wasn't feeling well. She complained of constant pain in her back and legs; she could hardly walk. Jonah took her to leading specialists in Warsaw, but they could not find the source of her discomfort. They advised fresh air and the company of other people; above all, she must stop brooding over the tragedies that had afflicted her.

On the trip home from Warsaw, Jonah reflected on Liebele's repeated response whenever trouble struck: "I knew it would end like this." He had often wondered about it, and now he took the opportunity to ask her. Liebele's only reply was a flood of tears, which did not cease during the remainder of the trip. When she got home she fell into bed and cried into her pillow.

Jonah sat beside her, begging her to stop crying, and declaring that he would not leave her side until she explained those cryptic words to him.

Liebele stopped weeping, her face whiter than her pillow. She began to talk in a low, unemotional voice; not a muscle in her face moved, and it was almost as if her voice was disembodied.

"Even my name is a lie. 'Liebele' means lovely, but I have brought nothing but trouble. The day I was born my father went bankrupt. He betrothed me to rich suitor—and that fortune was soon gone up in smoke. But even in poverty I was happy with you. More than anything else I wanted to bear your children. Now you have a children's cemetery all your own. When you became a contractor and started bringing home a lot of money, I was terrified. You know what happened next. When you finally started climbing up out of debt, the children took sick—two more innocent babies in the ground. Now that things are going well for you again, I'm so frightened I don't know what to do. We have only one child left, our Boruchl, and I pray constantly for him. What will happen next, Jonah?"

"We were stricken with the afflictions of Job," Jonah tried to console her, "but as you know, God finally had mercy on Job and granted him new wealth and new children—"

"I bring you nothing but bad luck, Jonah. The Almighty will grant you new wealth and new children, but that will come later, later . . . "

23

Pakula eventually turned up in Paris. At the casinos in the south of France he had already lost everything he had stolen from Jonah. Jadzia was with him, but she went home after the money ran out. There was a wedding ring on her finger, a crucifix around her neck, and she was in the sixth month of her marriage, her conversion, and her pregnancy.

Mieczyslaw Davidson tore his hair, but his wife argued, "It was bound to happen sooner or later. We are no longer Jews and we are not yet Christians. How much longer can we continue this way? Jadzia is better off than we are—at least her decision is behind her now."

"He's only after my money, that thief! And he'll spend it faster than he gets it!"

Jadzia just wept. So far, Dombrovka knew nothing of this affair.

•　•　•　•　•

Messengers came to Jonah with the request that he sign a paper revoking all charges against Pan Pakula, who was prepared to give him notes for all the debts he had incurred. Jonah refused.

One day, as Jonah was leaving the squire's court, the dogs almost tore him to pieces. Who had let the dogs loose just at the moment he was leaving? Several days later, a gang of peasant boys beat Boruch up and threatened that next time he wouldn't get away alive. Jonah went to Warsaw to see the squire, who convinced him to accept Pakula's notes—after all, Jadzia was the squire's only child. "Whether I like it or not, one day Pakula will become the squire of Dombrovka."

Although Jonah took the squire's advice, he left Boruch in Warsaw with his grandparents. Reb Hertz had refused to accept money from his son-in-law, but now he accepted what Jonah sent to support Boruch, although it was always more than was necessary. Warsaw was the right place for Boruch to be: there, he would advance in both his Jewish and his secular studies.

Things were not going well in the squire's court. Pani Felicia stopped coming to Dombrovka altogether. Pani Jadzia referred to her father as "the old Zhid." The squire refused to hand the estate over to Pakula, but insisted that he work for his keep, managing the sugar factory.

The estate was doing well because of Jonah's contracts; production had increased. But the noble Pan Mieczyslaw was not accustomed to working from dawn to dusk dealing with hundreds of peasants, lending them money for seed, and collecting on the loans. It was also necessary to make decisions about what to plant and where, and which forest to clear, and to make sure that the work actually got done. The squire decided to look for a new estate manager, but this time he would look for a Jew. If Felicia and Jadzia have a fit, let them.

24

Genendel departed this world like the proverbial righteous woman. It was a Friday evening. She had taken a sponge cake and a pot of chickpeas to an impoverished new mother, along with the other things necessary for a *sholom zokhor,* a party for a male child. She had ordered a dozen bottles of beer to be delivered. As she realized that darkness was falling, she hurried home. She felt a weakness in her legs as she entered her house, but she lit the Sabbath candles. Then she went out to get a neighbor, after which she had barely enough strength to get into bed.

"Please get me some water to wash my hands," she asked her neighbor.

When she had washed her hands, she began reciting Vidui, the last confession.

"Reb Genendel, it's the Sabbath now," the startled neighbor objected.

"One should really wait until after the Sabbath, if there is time," she agreed, and continued her confession. The neighbor ran out to get help, and more neighbors quickly arrived. As Genendel finished her confession, they saw that she had done so just in time.

•   •   •   •   •

On the fifth day of the mourning period, a squad of armed soldiers arrived and encircled the house. Two of them entered, shackled Jonah in chains, and led him away.

Jonah supplied black bread for the troops and white bread for the officers. In one of the loaves of white bread, a certain general had found a dead mouse. He had demanded who had supplied that particular loaf, and ordered the man to be brought before him in chains. When the squire heard this news he knew immediately who was behind it: he had mentioned to Felicia that Jonah had found him a new estate manager, and news had evidently traveled quickly back to Dombrovka. Of course, it was Pakula who had put the mouse in the dough and arranged for that loaf of bread to be delivered to a certain person at a certain time. Knowing that Jonah was facing a court-martial and a prison term in Siberia, the squire hurried to speak to the authorities.

As the trial was being prepared, the powers in St. Petersburg noticed an interruption in Jonah's shipments. When they learned about the arrest, they ordered the prisoner delivered to them on the next train. There, Jonah told his side of the story, and the authorities decided that the attempt to discredit such an efficient supplier for the Tsar's army could only be the work of saboteurs and revolutionaries, or even enemy spies. Jonah returned to Dombrovka with a letter stating that no one had the right to arrest him without a special order from the Commanding General in charge of provisions.

More bad news awaited Jonah when he went home: the squire had had a stroke and was in hospital. Although he could move most of his limbs, his mouth was distorted and it was doubtful that he would regain the use of his left leg. In his absence, Pani Felicia dismissed the Jewish estate manager and installed her son-in-law in his place.

Liebele was bedridden, but Jonah hoped that she would improve now that he was home. But she showed no signs of recuperation; every day her face grew grayer, her skin more wrinkled, and she was nauseated to the point where she could hardly eat. The doctors still had no explanation for her illness.

"Liebele, I'm home now. I have a letter from General Koropotkin himself. No one can harm me now." He talked and talked. When he asked if she could hear him she nodded, but she refused to eat. He peeled an orange and offered her a slice, but she clenched her teeth. When she felt his tears falling on her face she opened her eyes. He leaned over her and she pleaded in a whisper, "I can't, Jonah, I can't. My insides twist up when I try to eat."

In the end, the doctor had to force her mouth open to slip some juice or medicine down her throat. She could no longer speak, but her eyes begged Jonah: leave me in peace. Her body shrank to a shadow; the flame of her life sank lower and lower and finally flickered out.

• • • • •

The squire gradually recovered, but he was no longer the same man. Pani Felicia had taken over, and Pakula held the reins of the estate tightly in his hands.

• • • • •

Russia was forced to sue for peace with Japan. When the wars ended, the new settlers in Dombrovka stayed on. The sewing machines of the tailor shops turned out clothing for the market in Lodz and for the bazaars in Warsaw. No one got rich, but there was bread on the table, the rent was paid, and there was even a little money left over for the Hebrew-school teacher. Dombrovka had grown considerably, but it remained a small town on a back road. The sugar factory devoured mountains of white sugar beets; long lines of wagons brought them in and carried away the sugar and waste products. The wheels of heavily laden wagons chewed up the roads, making the mud deeper, but it never occurred to anyone to pave them. The only telephones in town were in the apothecary and the post office, and perhaps there was one in the squire's court. The sugar factory had a power generator, but once the landowner sold the factory to strangers, it became a kind of alien growth on native soil. The townspeople had once appealed to the new owners of the factory to produce electricity for Dombrovka too, but the owners replied that they had come to town only to manufacture sugar, and even on that score they now had some regrets.

Jonah was glad his contract was finished and he would no longer have to deal with the squire's court. Matchmakers came to him with proposals from widows, divorced women, even young women, but Jonah too was no longer the same man. He never built the new house. He reopened his little food store and spent his days sitting behind the counter, unceasingly murmuring into his Psalter.

Book Three

1

When Kalman arranged for a solicitor from Warsaw to defend him against Breindl's charges, the lawyer told him, "You have to act with your defense attorney as with your doctor. If a patient hides something, the doctor could prescribe the wrong medicine—it may even make him worse. The same is true if a defendant hides something: the lawyer might adopt an incorrect tactic. For your doctor and for your lawyer," he grinned, "you've got to take all your clothes off."

Kalman laughed to himself. This big-city lawyer thought he was so smart, but Kalman had already decided on his own tactic. There was no fun in telling the truth, even when he could afford to; and if he expected the court to believe his lies, his lawyer must believe them too. And so must he himself—he had to be well rehearsed for his court performance.

Would a broken-down cripple—a man who has looked death in the eye and who was still very sick—would such a man tell lies? "I don't even know yet whether I'll live to rebuild my home, but I want to go to my grave with a clean name," was what Kalman responded upon the lawyer's proposal for postponement until his health improved. And then he grew indignant: "These libels are only making me sicker! Every day of delay is one day too many! I've got to clear my name!"

2

Two wheelchairs were rolled into the county court of Gostinin. In one chair sat the main witness for the prosecution; in the other, the accused, Kalman. He looked straight into Breindl's eyes without blinking. Could that shriveled-up creature in the wheelchair be all that remained of the once-fair Breindl? Not for a pile of gold would he touch her now. Breindl, for her part, did not look his way even once.

According to the statement Breindl had signed for the police, it appeared that Kalman had killed Yosl in a fight. Kalman's lawyer started the questioning:

"Why did the Pan not rise when His Honor entered the court?"

"I am unable to. I'm a cripple," Kalman replied.

"Since the accident in your house?"

"No. Since childhood."

Kalman's lawyer then asked to have Breindl sworn in and he began his interrogation:

"Was the Pani's husband also a cripple?"

"Oh, no! Yosl was big and strong. Yosl was a giant of a man until—"

"According to the testimony you gave the police, it appears that the semiparalyzed Kalman was stronger than the giant, the Pani's husband. Is that true?"

"He threw an ax," Breindl said in a barely audible voice.

"Who threw an ax?"

"He did," she responded, pointing toward Kalman.

"You saw that with your own eyes? You saw Pan Kalman throw the axe at your husband and kill him?" the lawyer persisted, staring hard at her.

"No. The ax hit the china closet. I heard the crash of breaking glass and I ran in."

"Was your husband inside the china closet? Was he made of glass?" the lawyer quipped. There was laughter in the courtroom, and the judge warned the attorney against cracking jokes in such a serious case. The attorney apologized and continued his interrogation.

"Where were you when you heard the sound of breaking glass?"

"In bed."

"Where was your bed located—in the room where the glass was broken?"

"No."

"Where was your bed?"

"In our room."

"What do you mean by 'our' room?"

"Mine and Yosl's."

"In whose house was the room?"

"In our house."

"You and your husband owned the house? In whose name was the house registered?"

"In his name." Again, Breindl pointed at Kalman.

"Why did you say 'our' house? Had you or your husband bought a part of it?"

"Everyone knew that Yosl was a partner."

"How much did he pay for the partnership?"

"Yosl had no money to pay, but Kalman called him his 'partner.'"

"Is it not true that Pan Kalman contributed the money for your wedding, that he gave you and the deceased a room in that house, that it was his money you spent for food and clothing?"

Breindl did not reply. The judge reminded her that she was under oath and must therefore answer all questions.

"I'll repeat the question," the lawyer continued. "Is it not true that Pan Kalman contributed the money—"

Breindl nodded her head.

"I did not hear you. Please speak up clearly, yes or no, so the Court can hear."

"He should live so long if he—"

"Yes or no?"

"Yes, but—"

"Is it true that Pan Kalman also gave your husband money to buy gifts for his wife—for you? Yes or no?"

"He is a hypocrite, he—"

The judge interrupted her: "The witness must answer yes or no."

"Yes," she whispered.

"You say you were in bed when you heard the crash and you came running, is that correct?"

"Yes."

"Where was the china closet? In which room?"

"In the long room."

"Where was the long room? In the front, next to the store? Or in the back?"

"Near the store."

"And where was your room?"

"Near the yard."

"How far is it from one room to the other?"

"Very close."

"When you ran into the room, where was the ax?"

"I don't remember."

"Please try to remember."

"I can't remember!"

"Where was your husband?"

"In the room."

"Where in the room?"

"In the middle of the room."

"Was he standing, sitting, lying down?"

"He was standing in the middle of the room."

"And where was Pan Kalman standing?"

Breindl hesitated for a long moment, as if she knew it was a trap she must sidestep. She pointed to the defendant: "He was not standing, he's a cripple."

"He was lying down?"

"He was hanging."

"He was what? I'm sorry, I didn't hear you."

"He was hanging."

"I don't understand your answer. What do you mean, hanging?"

"By his hands. From a beam."

"From a ceiling beam?"

"Yes."

"At the other end of the room?"

"Yes."

"He was hanging by his hands from a beam. With what was he holding the ax—his paralyzed legs?"

Breindl did not respond.

"Let me try to understand something," the lawyer continued. "When you heard the crash, you ran in. That's what you said, correct?"

"Yes."

"You didn't walk, you ran. From one room to the other. It couldn't have taken more than a second or two. You will admit that it would be physically impossible for Pan Kalman to throw the ax and then, a second later, in his semiparalyzed condition, to climb up to the beam under the ceiling. Did the Pan Yosl pick him up and hang him up there? I know you did not see it—when you ran into the room he was already hanging up there, isn't that so? Think before you answer."

"He can jump like an evil spirit, like a devil—he is a devil!"

"You mean your deceased husband?"

"Not Yosl! I'm talking about him!" And again she stabbed a finger at Kalman.

"There's no need to shout. We can all hear you. Are you saying that he can throw an ax with his paralyzed feet?"

The prosecuting attorney objected that Kalman's lawyer was badgering the witness, and the judge sustained the objection and ordered the last question struck.

"You said that Pan Kalman was hanging under the ceiling from a beam. Did he, like Samson, pull the beam down and that's when the house collapsed?"

Again, the prosecutor objected and the judge sustained the objection, adding that Kalman's lawyer should restrict his interrogation to questions of fact.

"Let me rephrase the question. Pan Kalman was hanging on the beam. Pan Yosl was standing in the middle of the room on his two strong legs. From somewhere an ax fell into the china closet. Who could have thrown it?"

Breindl did not answer.

"Did you yourself throw the ax?"

"No."

"Did your husband throw the ax?"

Again, no response.

"Did your husband throw the ax?" the lawyer repeated.

Still she did not answer.

The judge admonished Breindl: "The witness must reply clearly and plainly to every question."

Breindl's face tightened, her shoulders began to shake, then she broke into spasms. The judge adjourned the proceedings.

3

When Kalman had first heard about Breindl's accusation that he had killed Yosl, he had been outraged. He now realized that her lies were to his advantage. She was undermining her credibility as a witness, and her testimony would now carry little weight even if she told the real story. If you resort to lies, Briendl, he thought, I can outdo you a hundred times, and make my story credible with a careful blend of fact and fantasy.

The next morning when the court reconvened, the defense attorney advised the judge that his client wished to make a statement. After Kalman was sworn in, he declared, "I've been a cripple as far back as I can remember. Soon after I took sick my father disappeared. I can barely remember him. My grandfather brought me up and he is gone now as well. Yosl was a distant cousin, but the only relative I had. When he got married I was happy for him—for his happiness that a cripple like me cannot have. I felt that he loved me no less than I loved him, until that night, that terrible night . . .

"At the time I told the police that the house collapsed of its own weight, because it was a very old house. But in fact Yosl had suddenly gone berserk and had become violent. When they told me he was no longer among the living, I thought to myself, why blacken his name? I did this also for Breindl's sake. If she had made Yosl happy, then she was as dear to me as he had been. I don't know what's come over her."

The prosecutor interrupted Kalman's narrative. "If it please the Court, the witness is making unfounded allegations against another witness. Objection." The court sustained the objection, and Kalman continued with his statement.

"Your Honor, the unfounded accusations against me compel me to reveal the part of the truth I had, till now, wished to conceal. Yosl suddenly went out of his mind. I don't know what happened between him and Breindl in the privacy of their room, but he ran into the room where I was sitting and began hacking away at the posts that support the building. I tried to calm him down. I talked to him as if he were a child. He ordered me to shut up. When I didn't, he threw the axe. I barely managed to jump out of the way. The axe hit the china closet. The rest you know. They found me—and Breindl—half dead under the ruins of the building, and he himself—it's very painful for me to talk about it . . . "

During Kalman's testimony, Breindl's face remained expressionless, with blankly staring eyes, as if she could not hear what he was saying. Only her eyelids fluttered. A deadly silence descended on the courtroom when Kalman finished. Even the judge was so moved that he proposed an adjournment until the next morning. The prosecutor, of course, did not want the proceedings to stop at that point; he was most anxious to hear what his witness would reply to Kalman's testimony.

*   *   *   *   *

Again they rolled up Breindl's wheelchair. The prosecutor reminded her that she was still under oath, and asked:

"Did the Pani hear what the previous witness said?"

"Yes."

"Does the Pani have anything to say in response?"

"Let him say what happened the night before."

"Can the Pani tell us?"

"Let him tell it."

The judge turned to Kalman: "Does the Pan want to testify about that?"

"What would there be to say about the night *before?*" Kalman replied with feigned innocence.

"Does the witness wish to say any more?" the judge asked.

"Let him say what happened the night that Yosl was away in Warsaw," Breindl insisted.

Kalman merely shrugged. His attorney proposed that the proceedings be adjourned.

"If the Pani has nothing further to say, I will adjourn the proceedings to a later date," the judge warned her.

The prosecutor asked for a few minutes to consult with his witness. The defense attorney objected that the prosecution had no right to coach a witness—she had indicated she had nothing further to say. The judge asked Breindl once more if she wished to tell the court what had happened the night her husband was away.

"He—he raped me," she blurted out in a choked voice that sent a chill through everyone's spine.

Kalman requested to be recalled to the stand. The judge reminded him that he was still under oath.

"Poor Yosl," Kalman began. "I thought he had suddenly gone mad. A simple man, but a good soul. How could something like this happen to him? Was it possible that it was not Yosl but Breindl who had gone crazy? Had she invented some story to drive him wild? But where had she gotten such an insane idea? Unless Yosl took sick that night and Breindl—but what do I know? A house fell in on her—maybe a beam struck her on the head—"

"Objection!" boomed the prosecutor. "The witness is making insinuations. Let him stick to the facts and stop speculating on what might have happened to other people!"

Kalman shrugged. The judge sustained the objection.

"Your Honor, the whole city knows I've been paralyzed since childhood. Breindl had two strong arms and two healthy legs. What she is claiming is an obvious physical impossibility—"

"It was not the first time!" Breindl screamed. "He did it to Kayleh too!"

The prosecutor asked for a postponement so that he could arrange for Kayleh to testify. The court granted his request.

4

When Kayleh heard that she would have to testify about what had happened between her and Kalman, she said she would sooner kill herself. It was explained to her that the trial was not taking place in Dombrovka but in the district court at Gostinin. This was small comfort to her, since half of Dombrovka went to Gostinin to watch the trial. She wept day and night and said she couldn't talk about that night in front of the whole town. However, when she was called to the witness stand she threw back her shoulders and held her head high, with her usual coquettish little skip she walked up to the witness stand. No one from Dombrovka, no one even in Gostinin was wearing a more attractive ensemble than she that day. She had on her bonnet with the bright-colored feather (she secretly blessed her mistress in Warsaw for this fine hand-me-down with which she was attempting to mask her embarrassment). Kalman tried to catch her eye to give her a little smile, but she avoided looking in his direction.

After she was sworn in, the prosecutor asked her to describe what the defendant had done to her:

"Tell us what happened, in your own words."

"I have nothing to tell."

"Did the defendant Kalman Swerdl rape you?"

"No."

The murmuring in the courtroom reached such a pitch that the judge banged his gavel for order.

"Does the Pani have a child?" the prosecutor continued.

"Yes, sir."

"Whose child is it?"

"Mine."

"Does the Pani have a husband?"

"No, sir."

"Were you living at Kalman Swerdl's when you became pregnant?"

"Yes, sir."

"Did he attack you?"

"No, sir."

"Did he rape you?"

"No, sir."

"Did he marry you?"

"He was supposed to."

"Oh? Tell us about it."

"There is nothing to tell."

"The Pani said he was supposed to marry you. Did he promise?"

"I don't know."

"Did he promise to marry you or not?" the prosecutor asked.

"Everyone knew I was Talman Talita's girl," Kayleh blurted out, unable to pronounce a "K."

The prosecutor continued his interrogation: "Please try to remember: what did he promise you?"

"Everything."

The titters in the courtroom were silenced by the judge's glare.

"Try to remember what the defendant told you—his exact words," the prosecutor pressed.

"He said I had beautiful eyes."

"What else did he tell you?"

"I tan't say it before so many people."

"The Pani must tell us. This is a courtroom," the prosecutor insisted.

"He taught me how to tiss—"

"The Pani means 'kiss'?"

"He said I was a good student."

"Anything else?"

"Oh, yes!"

"What else?"

"I tan't say it. It's not nice."

Again the judge intervened and warned her that she must tell everything that happened. Kayleh could only point to her breasts.

"Did he ever say, 'I will marry you'?"

"Not in those words, no, sir."

"What words did he use?"

"He tissed me—and all the other things—"

"That night, when he came to the Pani—"

"It was not only that one night."

"When he came to you the first time, did you ask him whether he would marry you?"

"It's not nice to ast a testion like that."

"Did he give you to understand that if you did what he wanted you to do, he would marry you?"

"I understood that myself."

The prosecutor wiped his forehead. "The child—whose is it?"

"Mine."

"Who is the child's father?"

"It has no father."

"What man did the Pani sleep with before she became pregnant?"

"With Talman."

"With who else?"

Kayleh's eyes flashed angrily. She leaped from her seat as if to leave the courtroom, and the court reporter jumped up to stop her.

"I did not tome here to be insulted!" she cried. "So what if I'm a mother? Suppose I was divorced?"

The prosecutor tried again. "Does the defendant pay you any support for the child?"

"No."

"Why not?"

"I don't want his money."

"The Pani does not want Pan Swerdl to support the child?"

"No."

"But he is the child's father, is he not?"

"My Zelitl has no father. Only a mother."

When Kayleh was excused from the stand, Kalman couldn't help but compare her with Breindl. Tense and scared as Kayleh was, her face broke into a smile from time to time. Sitting there before the court in the elevated witness chair, dressed in her secondhand Warsaw finery, she had looked like a real lady . . . until she had opened her mouth. He could have overlooked her short leg, even her speech impediment, if only she weren't such a silly, stupid cow . . .

5

Kalman's lawyer next called a character witness. Little Berele was proud to know that so many fine gentlemen were paying such close attention to him, as if he were a renowned sage.

"Tell the court your name," the attorney instructed his witness.

"Berek Bilcher. Everyone calls me Berele Porter."

"The Pan is a porter?"

"I was. He—Pan Kalman—changed that for me."

"What do you mean?"

"Because of him I'm not a porter any more, I'm not a horse any more."

"Explain what you are saying, please."

"At first I used to carry the loads on my back, then I built myself a little wagon, but I was the horse, I used to harness myself into the wagon and pull it."

"And?"

"I don't know how to say it in Polish. In Yiddish I made up a little rhyme—Kalman Swerdl stopped me from being a *ferdl*—a little horse." The courtroom erupted in laughter.

"How did he stop you from being a horse?"

"He loaned me the money to buy a horse and he didn't charge me any interest and he gave me work so I could pay back the loan."

"What kind of work?"

"Carrying his goods. And he paid me more than anyone else does."

"Are you a relative of Pan Kalman's? A friend?"

"Me?" Berele chuckled. "No. Who am I to be a friend of his? He's an educated man, with newspapers and books and things like that."

"Then what made you think of asking him—a stranger—for a loan?"

"Who says I thought of it? And even if I had, would I have had the nerve to ask him? I didn't even have anything to give him for security. When Pan Swerdl told me he would lend me as much as a hundred, without a pledge and without interest, I thought he was kidding me. But he has a heart of gold."

"Your witness." Kalman's lawyer handed the witness over to the prosecutor, who began the cross-examination:

"This man with the golden heart who you just referred to—did you know that he went bankrupt under very suspicious circumstances and ruined a lot of people who had trusted him?"

Kalman's attorney objected, but the judge overruled the objection and instructed Berele to answer the question.

"I heard something about it, but you know how people talk. If it's true, it couldn't have been Pan Kalman's idea."

"Whose idea was it, then?"

"It's not nice to say bad thing about the dead, but if that Yosl hadn't been so stupid, I'd guess it was his."

"But if it wasn't Yosl's idea and it wasn't Kalman's idea, whose was it?"

"Maybe it was Breindl's. I was always careful not to go into the store to buy anything when she was behind the counter. She always charged more and never gave me as good a measure as Pan Kalman did."

"The bankruptcy took place before Pani Breindl came to Dombrovka."

"Is that so? Well, what do I know? I only know that to me he was like an angel from heaven. May I have as many good years left as there are people in our town whom Pan Kalman has helped."

6

The prosecutor recalled Kalman to the stand.

"Pan Kalman, who did the buying in your business?"

"I did."

"Not the deceased Pan Yosl?"

"No, sir. He was not the smartest merchant, but he was perfect for keeping an eye on the store."

"And for frightening away creditors?"

"I don't have to answer that question, but Yosl didn't have a mean bone in his body."

"Can you tell us what his role was in the bankruptcy?"

"He had nothing to do with it. Every business has its ups and downs. But I soon overcame the difficulties. All the debts have been paid, every single one."

"I'll go back to my original question. So you did the buying in your business?"

"Yes, sir."

"Then why did Yosl go to Warsaw? How did you happen to send him away on that day before the tragedy?"

"We needed certain goods and there had been a heavy snowfall that morning. I could never have made the trip myself. So I made a list of the items we needed, along with their prices, and Yosl went to Warsaw to pick them up."

"Isn't it true that you sent Yosl away that day so you could be alone with his wife?"

Kalman did not need his attorney's objection to realize where the questions were leading. He countered with a question of his own:

"Is it so dangerous for two people to be alone together? Maybe I'm the one who should have been afraid to be left alone with her. At that time she had two strong arms and two good legs. Mine were useless. And she knew that I had money and jewelry in the house."

"Is the Pan telling us that he was afraid of Yosl's wife?"

"If I had known at that time what can happen to a normal person . . . She and I were often alone there. For hours after Yosl went to bed she sat with me, talking about this and that. Sometimes we played cards—she was a better player, she beat me all the time. You can ask her yourself about that. She told me things even her husband didn't know. She told me that before she married him she was a servant-girl. The night of the incident, before she went to bed, she told me that her employer and his son had both tried to—am I allowed to mention names here?—I remember his name and it can be checked. Please check it, sir!" Kalman turned to the judge: "Your Honor, maybe she got things mixed up in her head—I mean, maybe she had a bad dream and imagined that what happened with the other employer was happening with me."

He turned toward Breindl and spoke directly to her: "Breindele, break out of your nightmare! I loved you, yes, but as a father loves his own daughter, or maybe as a brother loves a sister. But all those terrible things you're saying are nothing but a bad dream!"

The spectators in the courtroom were moved to tears. Pressing home his point, Kalman laboriously wheeled himself across the room and stopped before Breindl, herself helpless in her wheelchair.

"Believe me, Breindl, it's only a bad dream! I'm willing to find the best doctors to cure you, even if it costs a fortune. Leave it to Kalman the Cripple . . . "

He laid his hands on hers and such a piercing scream broke out of her mouth that the windows rattled. But he wouldn't let go of her hand. Trying to pull away from him, she tumbled out of her chair and fell to the floor, still screaming. The courtroom attendants ran for a doctor, and the judge adjourned the proceedings.

Matus, Kayleh's father, helped the nurse, Maria, take Kalman from the courthouse. Knowing he had won, Kalman could not keep from smiling. Matus, seeing the expression on Kalman's face, felt his skin crawl—that poor girl was probably out of her mind—had Kalman no compassion?

7

The defense attorney wanted to call Matus to the stand, but Kalman rejected the idea. One could never tell what tricky questions the prosecutor might ask him. But just the fact that Matus was always with him was enough to show that there were no hard feelings between him and Matus's daughter. The prosecutor himself was beginning to have doubts about Breindl's charges and she finally admitted that Kalman didn't actually kill her husband but, by raping her, caused the event that led to his death. Kalman returned from Gostinin like a victorious warrior. The wounds in his leg grew more painful, but his head filled with new plans.

The day was mild and sunny, and in the hired sleigh it was a two-hour trip to Dombrovka. For months Kalman had seen the outdoors only through a window, so gazing at the spacious white world through which the sleigh was sliding was a real joy. After all those days in court, the peaceful quiet was delightful. A fresh snow had fallen during the night; not even the horses' hooves could be heard. The little bells on the harness tinkled softly and melodiously, as if part of a distant dream.

Matus, sitting beside Kalman, dozed off and started to snore. What a stroke of genius it had been to hire Matus, Kalman reflected. Intelligence was dangerous; only he who was not cursed with it could be faithful as a dog and work like a mule. Matus was like an open book; whatever was in his mind was also on his face—no wonder he was a wretched pauper. If he, Kalman, could trust him, anyone could trust him with their life. But what had happened with Kayleh? She had avoided him in Gostinin; she had refused to ride in his sleigh, although she was traveling to Dombrovka before returning to Warsaw, where she apparently had a good job. He offered to pay her traveling expenses, but this too she refused. Matus said she had left the child with her mother. It might be worth the trouble to take a side trip to get a look at the little bastard . . .

Evidently, Kayleh was no longer ashamed to be seen with her child, or why would she have brought it with her to Dombrovka? Moyshe Longlegs still refused to let Matus lead the synagogue services, and he had promised Matus to do something about that, but . . . In excitement over the idea that had just struck him, Kalman almost leaped out of the sleigh. Oh, would that be a coup!

•   •   •   •   •

Inspired to do something, Kalman started to burn with his usual impatience for action. He woke up Matus.

"Reb Matus, Reb Matus! Tell me—does Moyshe Longlegs have a son?"

"Two of them. Leybl and Pinchas. His youngest is a girl."

"It seems to me that Leybl, the older one, is ripe for the marriage canopy . . . "

"Leybl is ripe for the army. Moyshe is looking for a bride whose father will be able to ransom his son from the military . . . "

Kalman, overjoyed with Matus's reply, pressed on with a further, "innocent" question:

"Why should a strong, healthy young man like Leybl not serve in the army?"

"You must be joking, Kalman! First of all, the food is not kosher. And don't you know how miserable they make life for a Jew in the army, especially a religious Jew? Before long he'll wish he were dead."

Kalman seemed so delighted with this news that he started whistling, and Matus had no idea why he was suddenly so cheerful.

"Reb Matus, listen carefully and remember where you heard it. The day will come when Moyshe Longlegs will beg you to lead the services. Remember what I'm saying: he will beg you!"

"Eh, Kalman, I have bigger worries. It's true I earn a living from the work you give me, but a man who has grown daughters and no dowries—"

"That's exactly what I'm talking about, Reb Matus."

Matus still did not understand. What did synagogue services have to do with dowries? But Kalman had again sunk back into his own thoughts and didn't want to talk about it any more.

When they arrived in Dombrovka and the road past Wilki Street, Kalman noticed some peasants with pick-axes digging up chunks of frozen earth around the synagogue.

"How dare they!" Kalman cried out.

Matus could not help but marvel at the intensity of Kalman's Jewish feelings.

8

Kalman had not fully recovered from the trial when he sent for Moyshe Longlegs.

"What's going on there at the synagogue?" he demanded. "Why don't you inform the squire?"

"The squire? Those are his peasants out there! They have already broken up and made off with a lot of the boards for the new floor."

"But why are the boards still outside? Why aren't you laying the floor? I donated the boards, are you waiting for me to give you the money for the labor? There are plenty of Jewish carpenters around here who would do it as a good deed. If each man put in a few hours' work there would soon be a new floor—"

"Paying for the labor is not the problem."

"So what is the problem?"

"It's wintertime. If we tear up the old floor we'll sink into the mud. Until the new one is finished there won't be any place to hold services."

Moyshe's explanation didn't make sense, and he had not spoken with his usual bluster; he was obviously not telling the truth.

"The squire's peasants, eh? He'll pay for this, that—"

An obscenity almost escaped Kalman's lips, but before him stood the *gabbai* of the synagogue and there was another, more pressing matter he wished to discuss with him.

"Reb Moyshe, I've been meaning to talk with you for some time. You owe me some money—money that you borrowed long ago from my grandfather, rest his soul. How much more time do you expect me to give you?"

"Panie Kalman, this has been on my mind too. Don't worry, your money is working for you. I know I owe you sixty-eight zloty interest. I remember it very well. If you'll add that to the debt and lend me another thirty-two zloty, you'll have an even thousand invested with me."

"Reb Moyshe, you should be ashamed to make such a proposition to me! Every time you're supposed to pay me some interest you want to add it to the loan."

"I give you my word, Panie Kalman. I had the money in my pocket yesterday. I'm standing there loading goods onto the wagon to transport it to Lowicz, to the annual fair. The goods are already on the wagon—and who do you think shows up like a devil out of the ground?"

"Who?"

"The Treasury bailiff. All he wanted—just listen to this!—all he wanted was to put tags on everything in the wagon, saying 'Sequestered for Taxes.' You know what that means, Panie Kalman? It means that the goods belong to the government and I'm not allowed to touch them until that gentleman gives me official permission!"

"What does all this have to do with me and my money?"

"How can you ask such a question, Panie Kalman, you of all people? The Lowicz fair is worth more than a whole month's business. How could I go there with an empty wagon?"

"So you gave him my money? You owe me more than you do Grabski."

"Grabski will not be Finance Minister forever, and the Jew-haters will not always have the upper hand."

"I can also put tags on your goods, Reb Moyshe."

"How much harder can I work? Do you know what it means to

travel to the markets two or three times a week? You start loading the goods in the afternoon. All night long you bounce up and down on the wagon. You set up the booth before daybreak, and in the evening you load the unsold goods and the booth back into the wagon. All of us work—me, my wife, our three children. The boys should be studying Torah. But we barely find time to step into a synagogue and race through our prayers . . . "

"If only you'd remember to make a payment once in a while, even a small one—"

"I don't always have ready cash, Panie Kalman."

"If things are so bad for you, then I shouldn't even wait with the original debt—the longer I wait, the worse it gets. And now you're asking me to increase it?"

"What else can I do? Just add the interest on. And I've got another problem. My Leybl is due to be drafted a few days before Pesach. I had hoped that he would find a good match and that the bride's father would pay for the exemption, but everything seems to be going wrong. Leybl is a fine boy, and a good student too—I thought the matchmakers would be standing in line . . . "

"It's almost Pesach now, Reb Moyshe. Do you know how the army treats a Hassidic boy in their midst?"

"May God help him!"

"As we say, God always provides the remedy before he inflicts the ailment. You came to me at just the right time. I have a wonderful match for your Leybl."

"All the Jews are plagued these days by the Grabski decrees. This man, the girl's father, will he have enough money to pay the exemption and still have something left over for a dowry so Leyble should have funds to start a business?"

"I'm surprised at you, Reb Moyshe! I would have expected a man like you, the *gabbai,* the head of our synagogue, to ask first whether the bride can run a kosher home, whether she comes from a good family. Aren't these things important to you?"

"Forgive me, Panie Kalman. Of course they are important. My troubles are speaking, not me."

"Then I have a bride for him with all the virtues you could ask for. Her father is a man of means, and he can read the Scriptures from the scroll, and it's a pleasure to hear him lead the services. The young woman is a God-fearing girl with many virtues. As for the dowry, it is two thousand zloty, plus the cost of the exemption for Leybl."

"Are you serious? Reb Aaron mentioned that you are a penitent. May the Almighty gladden you with good news as much as you have gladdened my heart with your words. God grant that something good come from this . . . "

"The Almighty has His messengers—in this case, me. I can help you, Reb Moyshe."

"That's exactly what the holy books say—the One Above sends his blessings through a good person, which means—"

"I studied the holy books myself, Reb Moyshe. I haven't forgotten everything yet. But don't you want to know who the bride's father is?"

"Someone I know?"

"Certainly. You once disgraced him publicly, but in those days he was penniless. Today Reb Matus can afford a generous dowry, and his daughters are making matches with the best families."

"You mean—the Pan is not referring to Matus the Glazier?"

"Precisely. Do you doubt he has the money? I'll advance the dowry myself—I'll even stand behind all his obligations."

"But his daughters are all crip—I mean, they all limp."

"You are versed in Torah and you talk like that? Shame on you! Who was the sage who did the same thing you just did? Just a minute—his name is on the tip of my tongue—ah yes, Elezar ben Shimon."

"What are you talking about?"

"I may be a simple shopkeeper, Reb Moyshe, but I haven't forgotten what I once learned."

Reb Moyshe nodded, and Kalman continued. "The story is that one day Rabbi Elezar ben Shimon was riding on a donkey and feeling pretty pleased with himself—he was coming from his teacher's house, where he had just completed the study of a long portion of Torah. You'll admit, Reb Moyshe, that studying Torah can make a person feel just as proud as being *gabbai* in the Dombrovka synagogue. Be that as it may, as he rode he met a very ugly man and said something disparaging to him. The man said to Rabbi Elezar, 'If you have any complaints, address them to Him who created me.'

"The Gemarah reports that Elezar ben Shimon realized even before the words were out of his mouth how grievously he had sinned in one thoughtless moment. He got down from his donkey, fell on his knees before the man he had insulted, and begged his forgiveness.

You, Reb Moyshe, are a better student of Torah than me, so you must know that He who grants beauty to people is the same One who creates cripples, and to demean a cripple is a grave sin."

"But it's not just the limping. His oldest daughter—you know who I mean—has a—"

"You mean Reb Matus's oldest daughter? She is a fine Jewish girl. She is my bride."

"Really? Then I wish you mazel tov."

"Thank you very much."

"I see that you really became a God-fearing man. One of Matus's daughters—"

"Reb Matus," Kalman corrected him.

"One of his daughters is a very pretty girl, I hear."

"You mean Raizele? She's spoken for. The boy's father is a rabbi. I'm thinking of his second daughter, Freydele. She's even prettier than Raizele. One leg is a little shorter than the other, but with fresh air and good food it may still grow. And her virtuous character—you know her father . . . "

"My son is a good-looking boy, if I say so myself—"

"Reb Moyshe, do I have to tell you what King Solomon said about that? 'Charm and beauty are falsehood and vanity.' You can depend on me. I look at women more closely than you do. All of Reb Matus's daughters, from Kayleh to Raizele, have pretty faces with dimples. If you weren't a Hassid I could go into more detail . . . "

"I don't know, Kalman . . . Panie Kalman . . . "

"In any case, don't forget what you owe me, Reb Moyshe. A thousand zloty is no small sum. If you are in a desperate situation and need help to wipe out the debt I'll do my share, but others should contribute as well; don't expect the full thousand from me. Unless—who knows? After all, I'm something of a relative. If they like the bridegroom—which I can't guarantee—if he finds favor in their eyes, to use a Biblical expression, I'll take the thousand you owe me and give it to your Leybl as a wedding present. And that will be in addition to the dowry Reb Matus himself will give."

Kalman was still chuckling over his performance when all Dombrovka started buzzing. How had all this happened? When had the penniless Matus suddenly acquired his wealth? A lucky lottery ticket? And Kalman—what a turnaround he had made—with his brains, if he decided to behave honorably Dombrovka might yet be proud of him.

9

When the rumors reached Matus's ears, he rushed over to Kalman's house; pushing past Maria, he barreled into Kalman's room, waking him up.

"Kalman, my friend, what's going on here? People are congratulating me all over the place, they're asking me to lend them money, they're setting up a Free Loan Society and they want me to donate a hundred zloty. I tell them I don't know what they're talking about and they say I don't have anything to hide any more, Kalman has let the cat out of the bag. What cat, Kalman? And when did I arrange a match with a rabbi's son? Is this one of your pranks?"

Kalman rubbed his eyes. "Reb Matus, would I ever do that to you?"

"Well, why are people saying all those things?"

"Maybe it will all come true—a pious Jew like yourself should have faith."

"But people are asking me questions that I don't know how to answer."

"Don't answer them, then. If someone says, 'Good luck,' you say, 'We can all use it.' If they ask you for money, tell them you'll think about it—successful men don't make quick decisions. And you have told me that Rayzele is pretty as a princess. Princes are gentiles, but a rabbi—for your daughter a rabbi's son would be most appropriate . . ."

"From your mouth to God's ear. But people will laugh at me behind my back."

"Be patient, Reb Matus, and leave it to me. People have called me every name in the book, but no one has ever said I don't know what I'm doing."

"But I want to understand what's going on."

"You remember how they laughed at me when I said I was going to build a power plant here? I thought to myself, we'll see who laughs last. Now I tell you the same thing: wait and see who laughs last."

Matus had also heard that Kalman had claimed Kayleh was his bride, but he didn't know how to ask Kalman about this. He repeated the story to Kayleh, hoping she would swoon with happiness, but she cried out: "Never!"

"How dare you talk like that! He's the father of your child."

"My child has no father!" she proclaimed, exactly the way she had done in court.

Matus and Tsippe both had words with her, but Kayleh stuck to her guns: she wanted nothing to do with Kalman. When they wouldn't stop pestering her, she decided to return to Warsaw.

Before she left, Matus secretly took the child to see Kalman. Kalman was nervous with him at first, but soon he was smacking his lips and tickling the baby, who giggled just like his mother.

After Matus and the baby left, Kalman couldn't stop thinking about the little tyke, who smiled and cooed all the time. Kalman wondered if he had ever been so contented, and how he came to grow so bitter. But he steeled himself against his feelings. He had no intention of marrying Kayleh. Sure, he would sleep with her—he had no chance at anything better—but he could never spend day after day with her.

He had told Moyshe Longlegs that Raizele was betrothed to a rabbi—or was it a rabbi's son? He'd better find out what nice young rabbis were available, for he could afford to play out this comedy—when the power station was running he would make more in a month than he could spend in a year. And he might as well use his money for these games—after all, to whom would he leave an inheritance?

10

The beadle summoned Kalman to go to the Rabbi. What did the Rabbi want? Money, probably. They always needed something for a penniless bride, for a widow, or for orphans. Or, maybe he wanted to talk about the Free Loan Society. Kalman would put up a good front, at least until his practical joke became a reality. Moyshe Longlegs had still not given him an answer about the match for his son, but the plan was working, it was working . . . Yesterday, when Matus was visiting him, his face had been glowing. He had led the services—not just weekday afternoon services, but the Sabbath afternoon services, with the special prayers and all the rest. And who had proffered that honor to him? The trustee himself, Moyshe Longlegs. With conscription day approaching his reluctance paled . . .

Kalman readily agreed to go to the Rabbi. Matus came along to push the wheelchair and help the beadle to settle Kalman with the Rabbi. Many books and manuscripts lay on the table, and the Rabbi was in the middle of writing a research paper. He had come to Dombrovka as a young man and through the years had earned a reputation in the world of scholarship. It was rumored that he was finishing a book.

"Thank you very much, Reb Matus," the Rabbi said. We'll send for you when Kalman is ready to go home."

Undersanding that the Rabbi wanted to talk to Kalman alone, the beadle too left the room.

"And thank you, Kalman, for coming. It would have been more fitting for me to come to you, because I want to make peace with you."

"The Rabbi wants to make peace with me?!" Kalman exclaimed in real surprise.

"Yes. You gave us lumber for a new floor in the synagogue and we never used it."

"I know. The trustee told me why."

"He didn't tell you the whole story. It was I who opposed the acceptance of your contribution."

Kalman was shocked. "You were opposed? The first time I make a big contribution and you don't want it?"

"You once studied Torah, so you probably remember: the Holy Book warns us that a 'harlot's hire' is not acceptable as a sacrifice or for the building of the temple, and our sages forbade it also for a house of worship."

Kalman was flabbergasted. "What has that to do with me?"

"According to the Ramban, the reason it is unacceptable is so that sinners should not think they have expiated their transgressions and be free to sin again. You went bankrupt, and then suddenly you wanted to become a respected member of the community by making a contribution to the synagogue."

"Who wants to be a respected member of the community?" For an instant anger blazed in Kalman's eyes, but it quickly changed to a look of irony. He had made the contribution when he had wanted people to speak well of him; now that the court case was won he no longer cared. "If that's the case, why does the Rabbi want to make peace with me?"

"The community also had grave charges against you because of

what happened with Matus's daughter. You—who have been punished with a disability yourself—should have had compassion for a
handicapped girl and not disgraced her, and you dishonored Matus
into the bargain. But now I hear that you are ready to make amends
for that. You know very well that repentance is a commendable step
in the process of atonement. When will the wedding take place?"

Aha! It was considered a fait accompli. "What wedding?" Kalman demanded.

The Rabbi was so taken with the idea of Kalman's reformed ways
that for a moment he did not register Kalman's response, nor did he
notice how his hands tightened on the grips of the wheelchair and
how his eyes glistened with rage.

"Whose wedding are you talking about?" Kalman repeated
insistently.

"What do you mean, 'whose wedding?' Yours, of course, may it
be crowned with good fortune."

"My marriage to whom?"

"To your bride, good health to her."

"I have no bride."

"I'm talking about Reb Matus's daughter."

"I have no bride and I'm not getting married."

"But the town is buzzing with the news."

"A deaf man heard a mute say that a blind man saw a cripple
running. The whole story is a lie."

"But didn't Reb Matus bring you here?"

"Matus works for me and I pay him wages. I do him a favor now
and then, when I feel like it. But no one dictates to me what I can or
cannot do."

The Rabbi regained his composure only after some moments.
"Your marriage to Reb Matus's daughter is not some kind of favor.
You know what the Torah says—it is your obligation to marry her!"

"Rabbi, you have mentioned my failure in business; I signed
commitments to pay and did not honor my obligations. Consider this
another bankruptcy. Is this why you summoned me? And Rabbi—
my personal affairs are my own business."

"Every Jew is my business, including you. Should anyone harm
you, that would also be my business."

"You don't have to worry about me, Rabbi. I know how to take
care of myself."

"I'm talking right now about the girl you ravished," the Rabbi said, his voice hardening.

"Ravished? Who told you that? She testified under oath that I did no such thing."

"Seduction is the same as rape. Maimonides says that even if the victim acquiesces to the act, it is still considered rape."

"How do you rabbis know so much about rape," Kalman sneered. "Only those who have experienced it can know—"

Kalman braced himself for the Rabbi to throw him out of his office, but instead the Rabbi began to explain, patiently: "Our sages understood human beings and their behavior. Maimonides said that man is a weak creature, and it is his weakness that makes him self-indulgent."

"You and your Maimonides are right. But I am neither weak nor self-indulgent."

"What do you mean?"

"You know very well what I mean, Rabbi."

"I also know what the Talmud says: if a man refuses to marry the woman, he is to be forced to do so, even if she is lame, blind, or leprous."

"Who will force me?"

"The community."

"I can't be forced to do anything. If you don't want the lumber, forget it. What more can you do to me? Refuse to call me up to the Torah? Not allow me into the synagogue? You know that doesn't scare me."

"A day comes when the strongest man and the worst sinner fall into the hands of the community."

"You won't bury me in the Jewish cemetery?"

"You know that every Jew must be buried, but when someone commits a great wrong against the community the heirs are affected and he is buried next to the fence."

Kalman guffawed. "For all I care, after I die you can throw me on the trash heap." The Rabbi was speechless, and Kalman continued. "Are you threatening that my heirs will have to pay dearly for my burial? I'll let you in on a secret, Rabbi. Before I croak, I'll arrange matters so that nothing is left to inherit. No one threatens Kalman the Cripple. And you know something else? I've changed my mind— don't throw me on the trash heap, throw me to the dogs—let them enjoy themselves, at least."

Kalman had started this speech at a high pitch, but as he went on his voice weakened, and by the end he could hardly hold his head up. The Rabbi called for the Rebbetsin to bring a glass of water.

A moment later the Rabbi's wife placed a glass of water on the table beside Kalman. "Shall I make some tea?"

"No, thank you," Kalman moaned. "Where is that Matus?" He realized that what he had attempted here had been lost from the start. Not that there was anything he wanted to win—but now he just wanted to leave. He used to love the Rabbi, and he still had a warm spot for him, despite this encounter.

"Why not a glass of tea? We have a primus stove—it will only take a few minutes." The invitation for tea this time came from the Rabbi himself, who was standing over him with a look of concern on his face.

"Rabbi, in your heart you are likely cursing the very bones of this hopeless sinner—and yet your Rebbetsin should serve me tea?"

The Rabbi smiled. "I never said you were a hopeless sinner. On the contrary, you have already taken the first steps on the way back."

"Who, me? When did I do that?" Kalman had again found his sardonic tone.

"At first you wanted to be thrown on the trash heap, with no regard for any living creature—then you wanted the dogs to have a little pleasure. Today your heart is open to dogs, tomorrow it will open to human beings."

Kalman's wrath melted like ice in the warmth of the Rabbi's smile. He felt the profound humor in the Rabbi's words, like a slap and a caress at the same time. He hated the Dombrovka Jewish leaders because they were all fools, but this Rabbi had brains. Kalman drank the water; the Rebbetsin took the glass and left the room. The Rabbi was right about one thing—Kalman could no longer control his anger the way he used to—cover it up with a sly little smile so no one could tell what he was thinking. What had happened here was unforgivable—the whole plot against Moyshe Longlegs was falling apart.

"Rabbi, you have the patience of Hillel."

"Well, Kalman, your origins carry a lot of weight with me. Your grandfather did a lot for this community, and also for me personally. Did you know that he built the synagogue? He ordered the first Torah scroll in Dombrovka, written in memory of his children who had died at an early age, and another scroll in the name of your grandmother, may they all rest in peace."

"I must confess, Rabbi, I never thought of my grandfather as a benefactor. I remember him as a morose and grumbling miser. Even for holy books he refused to give me money."

"When you are feeling stronger, I can tell you many good things about your grandfather. He was wrong not to remarry after your grandmother died. A Jew must acknowledge the justice of adversity. He must accept the Almighty's judgment and never sink into despondency. But let's return to what I was talking about before. Kalman, this is not just a matter of Reb Matus's daughter. You're not a boy anymore. You're the father of a child, and your child must not remain fatherless, God forbid. A father doesn't do that to his own child."

"He doesn't? If that's the case, then I'm a bastard myself," Kalman replied with a snicker.

"What do you mean?"

"If my father did this, it's a sign that he's not really my father, so I too am a child without a father."

"What makes you so sure your father abandoned you? Maybe he fell ill somewhere and passed away from grief that his only son was stricken. You know that something like that had happened to his mother. Your grandmother, may she forgive me, brought the Angel of Death down upon herself. That's precisely what broke your grandfather's spirit. It's very hard to make peace with a tragedy that we have brought upon ourselves."

"If my father died, or lost his mind, his pockets would have been searched and something to identify him would have been found. He ran away from me because he was an aesthete—and I wasn't very nice to look at. Even God dislikes a cripple. A Temple priest with a limp was not permitted to perform the service; even a lamb with a defect could not be offered up to God. Do you know, Rabbi, why I befriended Matus? Because he's a good father. He's ready to give his life for his lame daughters."

"Yes, it's an achievement to be a good father."

The Rebbetsin brought in a glass of tea and a saucer of sugar cubes. This was not the first time Kalman had been served refreshments here. He used to come here as a boy and the Rabbi would examine him in his lessons, and the Rebbetsin would serve him the

Sabbath fruit—at that time he was still just a crippled boy who evoked pity. But now—if the Rebbetsin had heard what he had said to the Rabbi she would have thrown the hot tea in his face.

"By the way, Rabbi, about running electric wires into the synagogue—you don't have to worry. It won't cost the community anything . . ."

"We can pray by oil lamps—or even candles."

Kalman almost spilled his tea. "Are you telling me that you won't accept the electricity either? To do that work later will cost a fortune."

"We've gotten along without electricity for thirty years."

"No is no. Where is that Matus?"

•   •   •   •   •

Matus was not to be found. The beadle went to the synagogue and brought back the Rabbi's son, Berish, to help take Kalman home. Berish looked to be around twenty; soon he would be conscripted into the army. He had already been ordained, but older rabbis than he still had no positions. Who could save Berish from the military, Kalman wondered; when a rabbi died, his congregation could not engage another rabbi as long as it must support the widow and orphans. The unreasonably high taxes on Jewish merchants and the boycotts of Jewish stores were destroying livelihoods. If there the Jews were not able to pay taxes to the community it would be difficult to pay a rabbi's salary. The only way the community could afford to take on a new rabbi would be if it had enough money to give the widow a severance payment and buy from her the right to the pension. The Dombrovka Rabbi barely earned enough for himself, let alone something for his son. But if Berish married a rich girl—

"Kalman, you're a genius!" he exclaimed, slapping his forehead. He'd had no luck with his lies because they turned into the truth too quickly—here was the Rabbi's son for Raizele to marry. This match must be arranged even if he had to pay the dowry in dollars. Will this ever be fun!

When Kalman arrived home, a messenger from City Hall was waiting with a letter for which Kalman had to sign a receipt.

"A cripple—and he has dealings with the government," the beadle said to Berish in admiration.

11

As Kalman scanned the letter he felt faint. The letter informed him that "whereas the generating station had not been completed in the stipulated time," the contract with him was hereby canceled forthwith and was no longer valid.

"Pani Maria, please go find Matus and bring him here right away."

"But the Pan must rest now."

"Please go and find Matus."

"No Matus, no anyone. You've already done too much for one day."

"That is for me to decide. Go find him for me at once! No, wait—there is no time for Matus. Help me back into the chair and take me to the City Council office."

"I have to change the bandage on your leg."

"Later, when we come back."

"It's your life, but don't complain to me later." Maria wheezed and panted as she lifted Kalman from his bed to the wheelchair. But no sooner was he in the chair than he asked her to put him back in bed.

"What's the matter now?" she sighed.

"Didn't the Pani say she wanted to change the bandage?"

"I can do it while the Pan is sitting in his chair."

"I will be more comfortable in bed."

"And the City Council?"

"The Council can wait."

"Did the Pan suddenly feel bad?"

"No, I feel good, very good," he laughed, and the color was actually returning to his cheeks. Obviously, whoever was responsible for the City Council letter wanted to frighten him, so he must therefore act as if he couldn't care less. And really, why should it bother him? If the mayor did not take over the power plant and it remained Kalman's private enterprise, would that be so bad? He could easily find a few people to deliver the bills to the customers and collect the money. If someone didn't pay, it would be simple enough to disconnect the current.

The Rabbi would have said, "Whatever the One Above does is

for the good." Yes, he would reply to the City Council's letter, he would agree to the cancellation of the contract. His share of the profits would be greater and the plant would remain his even after the twenty-year period.

Maria came in with an armful of bottles, medicaments, gauze, and absorbent cotton. "Just a moment while I get the scissors," she said.

"Please bring me my pen and the Electric Company letterhead."

"I've got to change the bandage."

"Later. First I've got to write a letter."

Maria shrugged. She knew Kalman's obstinate tone of voice.

Kalman began his letter: "To the highly esteemed Mayor, Pan Kostek Nowakowski, and to the honorable gentlemen of the City Council of Dombrovka." He put down his pen; whoever had masterminded this stunt must be anxious to know how he would react. Well, he wouldn't tell them a damned thing—let them find out for themselves. Meanwhile, let them think he was scared to death.

Now he had to do something to show them that construction on the power plant would continue. What could he do with a foot of snow on the ground? If he delivered the poles to Wilki Street, where the plan called for a second network of electric wires, they would be stolen before the ground was thawed enough to put them up. Well, what if a few poles disappeared—there would be enough profit to cover that and even bigger losses.

12

A tense week went by. When the first load of poles was delivered to Wilki Street the mayor sent a policeman to remind Kalman that the electricity project was dead. Two days later, when more poles were delivered, the mayor came in person.

"What's going on here, Panie Swerdl? You know very well that the city has withdrawn from the project."

"But I haven't withdrawn, Panie Mayor."

"A city council can't be compelled to do something against its will," the mayor said in a threatening tone.

Kalman smiled and replied calmly, "Through the courts, Panie Nowakowski, even a city council can be held to a signed contract.

Even the national government must obey a court order. But who wants to force you to do anything? The generating plant will be a gold mine. Patriotic feelings and good will led me to build it in the first place and give it to the city, but if the city throws it back at me—you may rest assured, Panie Mayor, there will be a power plant, and it will be my power plant."

The mayor left in a hurry. Kalman sent Matus to see where he was going. Pan Nowakowski had made directly for the post office to use the telephone, and Matus reported that he had yelled into the phone and that every sentence had begun with "Most Highborn" or "Pan Squire." So Kalman knew that the squire had declared war, using Nowakowski and the city as his weapons.

Another letter arrived by messenger from the City Council. "Pan Swerdl is requested to remove his property from Wilki Street. The streets belong to the city. No one has the right to set up poles on ground belonging to the city without special permission from the municipal authorities."

Forty-eight hours later came a warning that if the owner of the poles did not remove his property in the next three days, the police would do so.

Kalman sent Maria to the mayor with a note asking him to come and discuss the matter.

After two more days, when the mayor didn't show up, Kalman sent him a longer note: "My attorney in Warsaw is asking me for information about a certain receipt for one thousand zloty. I must consult immediately with the Pan Mayor so that I may know how to respond. In Warsaw they might read something into this that neither you nor I want them to."

The mayor came at once.

"Panie Mayor, I am a man of good will," Kalman began. "In all good faith I offered to give the city the power plant that I am building according to my plan—and for my money. In all good faith I gave the Mayor a thousand zloty in return for his efforts on behalf of the plant. I don't know why my lawyer is interfering in this. On the receipt which the Pan Mayor signed it states clearly that I am giving the money to him in return for various expenses incurred in connection with his trips to the out-of-town authorities."

"How did it get into the hands of an attorney? It was a private matter."

"How could I know that among the business papers I sent to my lawyer there was also a receipt for a private matter? I'm in litigation with the city, not with the mayor. Personally, you and I are best of friends."

The mayor left Kalman's house with a bowed head. A few hours later he returned, reeking of whiskey.

"You can't threaten me, you Zhid!" he muttered. "Dombrovka is in Poland, not Palestine! I won't let a Jewish cripple lead me around by the nose!"

"Lead you by the nose, Panie Mayor? On the contrary. Dombrovka suffers from the fact that the world doesn't know such a place exists. This Jewish cripple will make Dombrovka famous. They will talk about Dombrovka in the courts, they'll write about it in the papers, there will be an interpellation in the Sejm. The Pan need not worry about the receipt. My lawyer now says that since the Pan traveled to Gostinin twice on business for the power plant—once to Lowicz and once to Warsaw—it was proper for me to refund those expenditures. That is, unless the Pan also submitted the same expense vouchers to the city treasury?"

The mayor turned red and raised his fist, but he checked himself, and restrained himself from striking Kalman.

"Pshakrev!" he spat. "You can never trust a Jew, cripple or not!"

"But a mayor can be trusted," Kalman said coldly, "especially when you have his receipt."

He braced himself for the mayor's fist, but Nowakowski's shoulders slumped and he lowered himself into a chair. "What can I do?" he groaned. "Don't you think I want the power plant too? But I can't defy the squire, you know that. As long as he wants me to be mayor, I'll be mayor. As soon as he doesn't, I'll fly out of there like a wood chip off an ax!"

"Dombrovka is no longer the squire's personal property and we no longer have serfs. Poland is a free country; people can vote for whomever they please."

"The serfs may be free, but even a cow knows where her trough stands. Who are the wealthier peasants in Dombrovka? Those to whom the squire gave another piece of land—to pay out on long term. Who are the ones in this community who can read and write? Those whom the squire let off from work so they could attend classes."

"I didn't know the squire was such a benevolent man."

"Benevolent? It's his own bastards he sends to school, and he always gives the extra land to the young man who marries a big-bellied bride—and everyone knows who gave her the big belly . . . "

"I thought the nobles no longer had the right of the first night—"

"What right! If the highborn squire takes a liking to a girl, her parents, especially if they are poor peasants, are not likely to object. And he takes the most beautiful girls—at least, if he desires one, the peasants think she's beautiful. The girls even brag about it!"

"Not one of them has ever refused? Not one young man ever protested?"

"A peasant's piece of land is his heart. His possessions are his two hands to work it. When a young man marries one of the squire's girls he receives not only the extra piece of land, but also a strong wench to help him—the squire is fond of healthy, sturdy girls. But the Devil can drive a man to madness, as once happened with a certain Maczek Bodula. Strong as an oak, young Maczek was."

"What happened to him?"

"He was an honest fellow, but too crazy about this girl for his own good."

"She didn't want him?"

"She wanted him, all right, but when the squire cast his eye upon her—well, Maczek was a damn fool and complained too much about it, and—" He paused as if searching for the right word.

"And?"

"And a nobleman can do whatever he damn pleases. And a mayor should keep his fool mouth shut. Anyway, who knows whether the gossips tell the truth—no one actually saw Maczek being pushed into the river; maybe he jumped in and drowned himself."

"The squire had a hand in this?"

"I'm only telling you what I know; what I don't know, I don't tell. But I will tell you that it's not smart to talk too much and fight wars against the squire. No one has ever won such a war."

"The Pan Mayor is correct. We don't have to tell all the stories we hear. But we can think about them. What do you think about this Maczek story?"

Kalman asked Maria to bring in the whiskey bottle and then sent her back out of the room. The mayor wiped the whiskey off his moustaches and became even more circumspect.

"I'm not going to repeat everything the peasants babble."

"Absolutely, Panie Mayor, nothing but old wives' tales."

The mayor retreated. "The peasants are not fools, Panie Kalman."

"But I don't believe this story about Maczek."

"Do you know something about it?"

"Peasants come into the store, they talk."

"So you know the whole story?"

"But I don't believe it. A young serf doesn't start a fight with a squire."

"The squire wanted to give him a piece of land, a big farm. A real son of serfs would have grabbed it with both hands, but Maczek had a nobleman's temper."

"That is a dangerous combination."

"If you know the whole story, you certainly know that Maczek was born about four months after his mother's wedding, and that the squire was then only a manager of the old squire's estate."

"And the squire didn't know he was taking his own son's girl to bed?"

"Of course he knew! Who sent Maczek to school? Even Maczek knew it. They say he went to the squire to tell him he wanted to get married, and he asked for a piece of land."

"He went to him as one goes to a father?"

"Exactly. It was a stupid thing to do. The good father wanted to see the girl, and Maczek himself sent her to him. Maczek was crazy about her—and she affected his father the same way. You should see her now—just another fat-assed peasant woman. But then, in all of Dombrovka—and even in Warsaw—no girl could compare with her!"

"And the illustrious squire killed his own bastard?"

"Not all noblemen are like our upstart. He is . . . yes, our squire has so many bastards. And if one of them rebels against him—you especially should remember this well—if anyone rebels . . . "

"And did the girl keep her mouth shut?"

"Hella? Maybe she was afraid, or maybe—who knows? There are still some women around today who wiggle their behinds with pride because twenty years ago the squire took a fancy to them. In any case, she did receive a piece of land, and a husband too, and what's buried in the ground is best left buried."

"What does the squire have against the power plant? His court would benefit from it too."

"You have gotten too involved with that synagogue. You don't go to services anyway; what do you need a synagogue for? And on the squire's land—it must be gone before the president comes."

"The president? Of Poland? He's coming to Dombrovka?"

"It's a big secret. President Moscicki will be coming to hunt in the squire's forests, and he will be staying at the court. The president has a son—and the squire has daughters. But I'm talking too much again—"

"The squire said this?"

"The squire doesn't talk about such things. But I would be a fool if I didn't know . . . "

13

That squire was worse than a gangster! He lured his son's bride into his bed and then got rid of the son; even robbers and cutthroats spared their own kin. The squire was a very dangerous man, and Kalman knew he had better watch his step.

Matus took the gold and the important papers to Warsaw. The squire's unpaid notes were safely tucked into a safe in Shereshevsky's Bank, but what help was that if the squire liquidated Kalman? Kalman's blood froze at the thought, but suddenly he laughed out loud. It was a real joke, a riot. If his grandmother was a Davidson, the squire's wife was a relative of his. Would the squire be among those claiming part of his legacy?

Yet this was far from a laughing matter. The squire would set all Dombrovka afire as long as Kalman too went up in smoke. But if the squire was hoping for a match between his daughter and the president's son, he wasn't so smart after all—the president would never agree to a marriage with the granddaughter of a Jew, even if a mountain of gold came with the match. But the squire would stop at nothing to get what he wanted—Kalman was indeed playing with fire, he who had prided himself on his cautious, calculating mind.

If the squire was starting up with the synagogue business again, and wasn't afraid of what Kalman might do with his unpaid notes, then he must have a plan. Kalman must leave someone behind who could sue for payment. This very minute he must record everything and turn it over to a prominent lawyer for safekeeping—he dared not put it off even to the next morning.

Kalman had had to write with his left hand since a bone in his right arm had been broken in the accident.

It was hard, tiring work, and his hand cramped up often, so that he had to stop and rest. But painstakingly he listed everything the squire owed him and noted where the documents were now stored; should anything happen to him at the squire's hand, let the authorities know who had done it, and why. At the end of his document he added, "Whoever inherits my estate shall not touch a penny of it until Stefan Pakula is brought to trial."

Rereading what he had written, he underlined the final sentences in red ink. He pressed the pen down so hard that it split apart, staining the paper. This gave him an odd feeling of satisfaction, as if the paper were the enemy and the ink were blood. He felt relieved, and was about to call Maria to help him into bed, when a new terror suddenly struck. What if he were too late? Something could happen that very night. The document must be gotten out of the house—who could he give it to? Not Matus; everyone knew that Matus was his employee, and if everyone knew, the squire knew too. Who else could he trust? Not a soul! He had never needed friends and so he had none. *The Wisdom of the Fathers* said, "Buy yourself a friend." Friends didn't just appear when one needed them. "Buy" means give friendship in order to cultivate a friendship towards you; it is give and take. When had he ever done anything for someone just for the joy of doing it, and who had ever done anything for him in that spirit?

Berele the Porter? Too small an individual to keep such a big secret. Matus was the only one left. He wasn't too smart, but he had kept the secret of Kalman's gold pieces. Moyshe Longlegs? He still owed money that he had borrowed from Kalman's grandfather, and Kalman wasn't dunning him for it. Maybe—

But he was forgetting someone. There were two people in Dombrovka who had helped him. The Rabbi and his wife had been so kind to him when he was a helpless, crippled child, that he had often been moved to tears. Many a night he had dreamt about all the nice things he would do for the Rabbi when he grew up to be big and strong. Yes, he could trust the Rabbi, and he would give the document to him. The cunning squire would never think of searching the Rabbi's house. But how would he get it there? Maria? If this house were to go up in smoke, both he and Maria would go up with it, and there would be no one left to reveal his secret. And he could not send it by messenger; he himself must deliver it directly into the Rabbi's hands.

"Maria, Maria!" He called so loudly that she came running in, alarmed. "Maria! Today is the anniversary of my blessed mother's death. I must go to the synagogue and say a prayer."

"The synagogue? A prayer? Just yesterday the Pan sent me to the store for ham."

"Ham is ham, and a mother is a mother. The Pani must take me over to the synagogue. Matus will bring me home."

Maria brought him to the synagogue, and the worshippers helped her wheel him inside. They were in the middle of a service, but Kalman's entrance caused a stir. His defense of the synagogue building was apparently not such a simple matter—now he was actually coming to pray.

● ● ● ● ●

Kalman caught Matus's eye and indicated that he wanted to speak with him.

"Tell the Rabbi I have something urgent to discuss with him, but not until everyone leaves."

Kalman's sudden appearance aroused such curiosity that the congregants did not hurry home, as they usually did after services. When the Rabbi finally approached him, a few people were still left in the synagogue.

"I seem to be completely out of place here,"

Kalman said to the Rabbi.

"Every Jew is a welcome guest in a Jewish house of prayer."

It was more than an hour after evening services, and although there were still a few worshippers in the synagogue, Kalman had managed to tell the Rabbi what the problem was and had even surreptitiously slipped the document to him. But the Rabbi wanted to read it before Kalman left.

"Let Matus take you to my house. It's a dark night, no one will see you. I'll stay here a little longer, so that no one will suspect anything."

"You say, 'Whoever inherits.' Who is this 'whoever?'" the Rabbi asked when he finished reading the document.

"I don't know, Rabbi. I have no close relatives."

"When there are no heirs, the government takes it all. Is that your intent?"

"No, not at all!"

"Then write in a name and a date and I'll sign as a witness. If you want, you can change the name later on. You should have a notary draw up a legal will for you."

Kalman's first impulse was to name the Rabbi as his heir, but then the Rabbi could not sign as a witness. It might be better to name the Rabbi as executor and let him distribute it according to his best judgment. But then, if the Rabbi were the executor, he would give the entire estate to Kayleh and the child. Oh well, he might as well skip the middle step and name her himself. And so he wrote, "It is my wish that after my death all my property shall go to Matus Lifschitz, his daughter Kayleh, and her heirs."

He handed the paper to the Rabbi, happy with what he had written. By naming "Kayleh and her heirs," he had given his estate to the Rabbi's choice, but he had confessed to nothing. And he could always change it if he wanted to.

The Rabbi witnessed the document and promised to send it to Kalman's lawyer in Warsaw. Kalman impressed upon the Rabbi that it was a very important and dangerous errand. "People say the squire hired someone to drown his bastard son. A man who does that to his own kin . . . "

Kalman stopped midsentence. He noticed a grimace on the Rabbi's face. Kalman could hear him soundlessly say, "I know another father who doesn't care a bit about his illegitimate son . . . "

There was a long silence, and then the Rabbi called Matus in to take Kalman home. As Kalman left, he turned and said, "What you had talked with me about that time, Rabbi, I've been thinking about it . . . "

•   •   •   •   •

Was he really considering marrying Kayleh, Kalman wondered? He needed the Rabbi's friendship now at all costs, and he was rewarding that friendship with counterfeit coin—he was as big a con man as the squire. Would he be capable of drowning his own child? God forbid—being indifferent was a far cry from being a murderer. And yet, the story of the squire and Maczek recalled a story in his own life; it had been a distant relative instead of a son, and he didn't kill him, but it ended with death all the same.

Kalman shook his head. He had vowed to purge the nightmare of Yosl and Breindl from his mind. But what of his own son? The squire, when he took a wench to bed, rewarded her afterward with a husband and a piece of land. He even sent his bastards to school. But what was Kalman doing for his bastard? Kalman tossed and turned in bed, unable to sleep. He woke Maria, who fixed him a glass of warm milk laced with whiskey and honey, and he finally felt drowsy.

But then the real nightmares started: he was Kalman the Cripple, but he was also a squire riding a horse. He galloped into his court-yard, over to the cow barn. He inspected cow after cow, felt their udders, hefted them in his palms. Yes, they were heavy with milk. The cows marched past him, then the farm hands, then the wenches—a parade of naked breasts, one after the other. He weighed them in his palms, yes, they were ripe and ready for the plucking, and all eyes were upon him, full of lust, begging, "Take me!" He pointed with one finger and galloped away, riding straight into—what place was this?—his grandfather's house! She was already waiting for him in his bed. He wanted to undress her but she insisted she first had to change the bandage on the Pan's leg and—and her breasts were large, immense, and he said, "Pani Maria, not now," but she pushed a brown nipple into his mouth. He gagged and woke up with a start.

What a ridiculous dream, but so real! Such broad-hipped peasant girls, such full, hot breasts—he could still feel their weight in his hands . . .

He tossed and turned. He could have been a squire. His grand-mother came from a family—no, his grandmother was from the im-pecunious Davidsons, but his father's grandfather had owned forests and other properties. Everything could have been his, he would have been a squire and galloped around on a horse if hadn't been for the fire that consumed everything. Living in the fresh country air, he would not have been affected by that cursed disease that had attacked him in Warsaw. He would have spent his days riding from one end of his estate to the other, and whatever wench he cast eyes on . . .

Was it the whiskey? He tried to retrieve the images of his dream, tossing from side to side.

The creaking of his bed wakened Maria. "Is the Pan not feeling well?" she asked as she stood in his doorway. "I'll turn on the lamp."

"No, the light hurts my eyes."

"Another hot drink?"

"No, thank you. Please sit down beside me." No wonder that in his dream it had been, finally, Maria. "When the Pani has to fasten her blouse in front, can she reach the buttons?"

"What is the Pan talking about?"

"The Pani has such a high bosom—I'm asking if her arms aren't too short to reach the buttons on her blouse."

Taken aback, Maria said nothing.

"Men go wild over women's breasts," Kalman added. "The bigger the better."

"My sainted husband used to say that, too," she said, sitting on the chair next to his bed.

"He was lucky, goddam it. A bed full of wife! Why didn't the Pani ever marry again?"

"One drunk in a lifetime is enough . . . "

"How many years has the Pani been without a husband?"

"More years than the Pan has lived."

"And the Pani never feels the need for—" he stretched out his hand and pinched her arm. "A good-looking woman like the Pani has no admirers? Impossible!"

"What's the use of discussing it? I'm a grandmother now."

"A good-looking grandmother!" He pinched her waist, let his hand slide down to pinch her bottom.

"Panie Kalman! What do you think I am!"

"The Pani is a nurse and I need a cure. Come, Maria, come into bed with me."

"Why should I?"

"I desire you, Maria!"

"But why should I do it?" She jumped up. "I'll get the Pan an aspirin."

She left his room and came back with a lamp. If she had come in with a lamp before, he wouldn't have made such a fool of himself; in her nightshirt she looked even worse than in her clothes. Her "high" bust was not high at all, but hung down to her belly. Her dishevelled hair, her—thank goodness she had rejected his advances.

She handed him a glass of water and some aspirin powder.

"Thank you, Pani Maria. I don't need the aspirin. I told the Pani what I need. It's worse than a sickness. If the Pani could find a pretty girl for me—I'll pay well. I'm ready to spend a hundred, if—"

"A hundred! Why didn't you say so before?"

He thought she had not wanted to go to bed with a cripple, but she had only wanted to know what was in it for her. But whatever he had imagined of her as he was lying in the dark, in the light of the lamp he would give nothing to have her in his bed.

"I'm feeling better now, Pani Maria. Please take the lamp out with you."

She went to the table, picked up the lamp, and left the room. Had he insulted her? He couldn't get along without her help— should he call her back?

The light went out in the next room. He heard the slap of her bare feet on the floor. A moment later she was in his bed, beside him under the covers. She was no longer wearing her nightshirt. Her feet were cold, but her body was hot. Blessed was the darkness, which covered everything Kalman did not wish to see.

Maria snored like a cow. When she awoke, light was coming through the window. She was so ugly, Kalman thought as he watched her leave the room. The fat seemed to be fermenting on her body—what a belly—if only she had put on her nightshirt before she got up. Kayleh—how had he been dissatisfied with Kayleh? She walked with a limp, she couldn't pronounce a "K," but she had a fresh, pretty face, and she had closed her eyes shyly when he had undressed her . . . He had laughed to himself when she had gazed at him with that calf-love. But he was worse than a calf, he was an idiot! Fat old Maria wouldn't sleep with him unless he paid her, but the innocent young Kayleh desired him and trembled at his touch. Yet it was Kayleh whom he had driven from his house . . . If he had knees that could bend, he would run to her and kneel before her, begging her to come back, come back . . .

14

Maria protested: it was too dangerous to travel in this cold weather. If he was so determined to take his own life, she wanted no part in it. Kalman wasn't moved by her threats. He hadn't intended to take her along to Warsaw anyway. Matus would be accompanying him.

After the doctor removed the cast, Kalman felt the strength returning to his right arm. When he was able to use both arms again, he could move around on his butt. The burns on his leg weren't completely healed yet? So he wouldn't move a mile a minute and he'd be careful not to irritate the wound. This was still better than depending on Maria to take him to the bathroom.

To get to the railroad station at Lowicz, Matus rented a carriage with the top up, but Kalman ordered the top put down. It was cold, yes, but the sun was shining brightly. The air pinched his nose and the tips of his ears, but it was good to feel the sunshine on his face again.

Arriving in Lowicz, Kalman went directly to the hospital. There the doctor examined him and assured him he was healing well. The leg was taking a little longer because the blood circulation there was weaker. True, his knees were locked, but he should still try to move the legs as much as possible. Sliding on his behind? Fine! Would Kalman please show how he did that? Good, very good! It was very important to keep pushing his legs forward, even if it hurt a bit. Maria was still with him? Good. A proficient nurse, but he should be careful. She had the reputation of being a bit greedy and a little crafty, too.

•   •   •   •   •

In Warsaw, Kalman drove first to the square at Iron Gate at Number One, to the bank of the Shereshevsky brothers.

The square bubbled with tumult and commotion, a bustling commercial arcade whose roof is the open sky. Shopkeepers grabbed customers by the coattails. Vendors hawked their wares at the top of their lungs. Licensed peddlars stood near their stalls, dancing alternately on one foot, then the other, all the while slapping their arms to keep warm. Those who couldn't afford a license kept their goods on flimsy two-wheeled carts so they could make a quick getaway at the first sign of a policeman. One eye was always on the customer, who might have sticky fingers; the other darted all around, on the lookout for cops. Somebody spotted a blue uniform.

"Six!" came the signal, and the illegals started running in all directions.

"Hot bagels! Fresh bagels," one youngster shouted. He didn't have to flee until the very last moment. He could even lose, himself in the crowd and brazen it out: "My mama sent me to buy bagels!" His pretext might work—his entire stock was in a paper bag.

But evidently it was a false alarm.

Again the portable "shops" were ready for business. A valise opened up and there was an assortment of neckties, bow ties, gloves, pocketknives . . . A man opened his coat and a selection of watches was pinned to the lining. An old woman with a round tin can in one hand and a wooden box under her arm sold regular herring from the can, smoked herring from the box. Her competitor, who had a larger stock, was eager to tell you about it:

"Herring! Herring! Herring! Salty and peppery, smoked and pickled, schmaltz herring, marinated herring! Herring with roe! Herring with milk! All kinds of herring! I've got it!"

"Sour tomatoes! Sauerkraut! Sour, ladies! Cook up some sweetness in your life with a sour *kapushniak!*"

"Beans, ladies! Round ones, long ones, lima beans! Kasha-Manna! Semolina! Millet! Groats for a *krupnik!* Soup barley! Kasha! Kasha! All kinds of kasha!"

"Socks, mister! Stockings! Strong as iron! Your shoes will wear out long before these stockings do!"

After Kalman had run this gauntlet and gotten to the bank on the corner, and the heavy door closed behind him, he felt as if he had entered another world. He slowed down instinctively and straightened out his coat. Some people even removed their hats there, although it was a Jewish bank. Outside, people were screaming themselves hoarse, but inside the same people spoke slowly and softly, as if they were confiding a state secret.

• • • • •

Kalman took the document he had written out for the Rabbi and placed it in his safe-deposit box. He had also prepared a paper authorizing Matus to open the box in the presence of a bank official. He still had to see Pan Rafal or Pan Michal Shereshevsky. Pan Rafal was out of the country. Pan Michal was busy. In their stead, a tall, distinguished looking official met with him and gave him the advice he was seeking. In a matter like this, it was worthwhile getting in touch with Attorney Apollinari Hartglass, who was once a Sejm deputy. Should anyone try any underhand tricks, the Pan Hartglass could have the matter investigated by the Parliament.

15

At home, Maria never let him get out of bed; here in Warsaw he was constantly on the move. Since the doctor had advised him to move around, why should he baby himself? It was the bone in his left arm that was broken, and the pain was acute in both arms, all the way up to his shoulders. But Kalman kept moving. Whenever Matus offered to help him, he waved him away. When his elbows started hurting, he rested a few moments, gave himself a push and was moving again. Kalman the Cripple had a high pain threshold.

Kalman had written to the squire at his Warsaw address asking for the exact date of the president's visit to Dombrovka. He was ready, he said, to exert every effort to have electricity in the squire's palace in time for the president's visit. In the same letter he had also mentioned that he was planning to be in Warsaw and would telephone the squire as soon as he arrived in the city.

The man who answered the phone asked him to wait. When he came back on the line he informed Kalman that the squire was not available at the moment but suggested that Kalman try again in about an hour.

"Try again in an hour" meant that the squire was up to his old tricks. Well, Kalman Kalika would pay him back in the same coin.

"I'm staying at the Hotel Bristol," he replied. "I can wait here only an hour for the Pan Squire to call me back." And he hung up.

The squire did not call back—he came in person.

"How does the Pan know about the president's visit?" he asked even before he was inside Kalman's room.

Kalman was pleased that the squire had addressed him formally, not as if he were talking to one of his "serfs" in Dombrovka. Still, Kalman evaded the question and went straight to the point, even though the squire had taken a seat before being invited.

"I do not underestimate the Pan Squire's position and I would not want the Pan Squire to underestimate mine. The Pan Squire's strength lies in his wealth, status and influence—which extends all the way up to the head of the state. Paradoxically, my strength lies in my weakness. A sick man, a cripple, will win the sympathy of the judge, the journalists, and even the deputies in the Sejm—if it ever comes to a parliamentary interpellation. The fact that I have no position in the community is also a virtue in a sense—I have nothing to lose but my life—and even that is insured for a quarter-million. It's not for the sake of my heirs that I'm paying all that money for insurance, but only because the company that has to pay out such a tremendous sum will want to know exactly what happened—and why."

"I don't recall that the Pan was ever one of my friends," said the squire, "and I see no reason why I should know about the Pan's life or his life insurance."

"And I see no reason why we should be adversaries when it's in everyone's interest to cooperate. I'll speak bluntly; I know the Pan Squire is a hard man to hoodwink. The Pan Squire knows I'm not a man who can be bought and sold for a fiver."

"And I'm not a man who can be threatened with nonexistent notes. I'll be blunt too. I see no sense in continuing this conversation."

"Begging the Pan's pardon, but those notes are hardly nonexistent. They sailed on a ship to England. My grandfather, through his local bank, sent the originals to their main office in London. I've already learned a few things about this from my grandfather's papers. It is now thirty-five years since he sent those documents to London, and the bank wants to know what to do with them. I've asked them to send me copies."

"Copies of false papers!" the squire almost shouted. He jumped up from his chair, his face suffused with a beet-red glow. "Your grandfather—" he reverted to the familiar "you"—"your grandfather was a—" The squire interrupted himself and concluded, "They are false documents, false notes, forgeries!"

The squire had been on the verge of insulting Kalman's grandfather but stopped himself just in time. The mighty Pan Squire was obviously scared; a scandal now might ruin the whole presidential visit. Kalman was strongly tempted to say something else that would further enrage the squire, but the merchant within him won the upper hand:

"The Pan Squire has no reason to be angry. My instructions to London and to my local lawyers are that they are to take no action, none whatsoever. I feel I can profit more by cooperating with the Pan Squire."

Kalman's guest took a deep breath and sat down again. "If the Pan wants to do business with me . . . I deal only with friends. The Pan must first give me the docu—the so-called documents."

"I am my grandfather's heir through my father, and my father disappeared without a trace. I can go through a trial for the sake of my father's estate, but to give it away for nothing would involve a long legal process, or a special law in the Sejm to permit me to do it. It's in nobody's interest to drag these things out into the open. And the Pan Squire is not so naïve as to think that I would do that even if I had the legal right. That's my trump card—and the Squire has a quick temper." The little imp inside Kalman was victorious as he added: "People who holler don't bite. Anyway, I don't believe everything that people are saying about the Pan Squire."

"Saying about me?!" The squire's eyes almost popped out.

"I don't believe any of it."

"What are people saying about me?"

"Something wild—that the Pan Squire—well, it's not even worth repeating—"

"The Pan has already started—he might as well finish it."

"People are saying that his Lordship took his own son's wife to bed and—"

"I don't even have a son, goddamnit!"

"They say this about an illegitimate son. And then—"

"Damn it to hell!" The squire's face again turned brick red. "Who dares to spread such—such—"

"Terrible lies!" Kalman concluded for the squire. "I told my lawyer not to believe a word of it."

"Your lawyer? How did it get to a lawyer?"

"One of our Jewish writers says that the truth walks on foot while the lie gallops on horseback. The Honorable Pan Squire shouldn't take it too seriously. I told the lawyer that things like that might have happened during the days of serfdom, maybe during the rotten Tsarist regime, where anybody and everybody could be bought. But our Poland is a free country with a free press. Any wrong done by a high aristocrat or an important authority can be brought to public attention through an interpellation in the Sejm."

"Are you threatening me, Jew?"

"Who, me? Oh, the Pan Squire thinks I mean—. Would the president of our Republic associate with the Pan Squire if such idiotic rumors had any basis?"

"The Pan must tell me this instant where these lies come from— if he really wants to do business with me. We'll tear out that liar's tongue and roast it!"

"The Illustrious Squire should not excite himself like this," Kalman interrupted. "Now I'm beginning to understand how a lot of those lies get started. When the Pan Squire is angry he lets some harsh words slip out, like 'tear out his tongue'—"

"Don't teach me how to speak, Jew!"

"I'm someone who hopes to do business with the Squire and is interested in his well-being for my own selfish motives."

"The Pan must tell me now where that filth is coming from or I won't stay here another moment!"

"I'll try to find out, even if I have to stay in Warsaw a few more days."

"From whose poisonous lips did the Pan first hear it?"

"It came up during a talk with my lawyer. Exactly who said it I can't remember. I've already told you that as a fellow townsman of the Squire's I warned my attorneys not to pay any attention to it."

"Who are your lawyers?" A flush appeared again on the squire's face. "I'll call my own attorney. Spreading malicious gossip and making libelous accusations is punishable by law."

"That's exactly what I told them. I'm on the Pan Squire's side and I hope it never comes to the point where my lawyers have to tangle with the Pan Squire's lawyers. And about the electricity for the Pan President's visit, the Pan Squire needn't worry. True, I'm not finished yet with the Pan Mayor. I don't know yet whether I'll renew the contract with them—I can find more influential partners. But there will be electricity in Dombrovka. It's been approved in all the offices—from the *starosta* in Gostinin to the Minister of Interior in Warsaw. Noboby can stand in the way of progress forever."

The squire understood very well that Kalman's honeyed words were really hidden threats. Kalman had apparently not been frightened off by the squire's display of righteous indignation. Maybe the friendly approach would be more effective.

"Yes," he said evenly, "but electricity or not, in honor of the president's visit, Lowicz Street will be named Moscicki Street. Other high government officials will also be there, along with princes of the Church. It is intolerable that on the central square of the president's street—on my piece of ground—there should be a Jewish synagogue standing half in ruins!"

"The Pan Squire is certainly correct there," Kalman hastened to concur. "In honor of the president's visit the building must be renovated, a new floor put down, the walls plastered, and—Panie Squire, the synagogue is two to three hundred meters away from Lowicz Street. They could plant trees there, bushes, so that from Lowicz Street all you could see would be a garden; the main entrance to the synagogue is on Wilki."

"You're not a—the Pan has a good idea. My people could plant a little garden there and put a fence around it, so the grass won't be trampled."

"And so there won't be a thoroughfare from Lowicz Street to the synagogue," Kalman seconded, to show that he understood what the squire was driving at. But he was ready for such a compromise. "I'll call the secretary of the Kolo—the Jewish deputies circle—and have them withdraw the interpellation in the Sejm."

"So—it's the Pan who's behind that Jew-agitation?"

"As I said, we live in a free, democratic Republic. I'm sure the Pan Squire takes pride in that . . . "

"I don't know who invented the story that I'm an anti-Semite." The squire's tone became confidential. "The Pan will never guess who I'm inviting to the President's Ball!"

"Who?"

"Solomon Pitel."

"The shoemaker?"

"He's also a musician."

"Oh, yes. He plays at peasant weddings."

"He knows a lot of local folk tunes. We need to show the president some of our local folk art. Pan Pitel has played for me on more than one occasion. And Pani Barecka is coming especially from Warsaw to teach the girls of my court the local dances. She's Jewish too."

Kalman was on the verge of saying, "And the hostess, whose married name is Pakula, is also a Jew," but he thought it best not to try the squire's patience too much. "I'm beginning to believe," he said instead, "I'll be able to do business with the Pan's court, just like my grandfather did in his day. And I'm talking about big transactions—"

The squire grew positively gracious. "Perhaps I'll invite the Pan too. Let the Pan President see how a man, cruelly punished by Fate, has, by dint of hard work, advanced himself in our little Dombrovka, educated himself, developed himself into a successful industrialist and merchant . . . "

The squire was already at the door when again the spiteful little imp inside Kalman took over.

"Would the Pan Squire be so good as to give my cousin my regards?"

The squire wheeled around. "I know the Pan's cousin?"

"My grandmother was a Davidson, of the Warsaw Davidsons.

One of them was a banker, one was a scientist—he settled in Paris, and the third one was—the Squire of Dombrovka."

The squire fled as if someone had scalded him.

16

Kalman was pleased with himself and exhilarated from his little game. The squire would not have come calling on a Jew in hotel room and would certainly not have tolerated all these hints about his adventures if he weren't scared out of his wits. Any hint of scandal now and the president would cancel his visit.

The squire must think that this Kalman the Cripple is a fanatical Jew ready to do battle in defense of Jewish interests. In truth, why had he suddenly become such a fighter for the synagogue, a place in which he hadn't set foot for a long time? If there was ever a parable for the fate of the Jewish people, it was Kalman the Cripple himself. The nations of the world hate the Jew and persecute him—just as the other boys in the *heder* had hated him and made his life miserable. The teacher had pleaded with them to have pity on this weak, helpless child. But people look down on weaklings. The more cowardly the individual, the more he takes out his frustrations on someone who is weaker than he, and blames him for all his troubles. If all the Jews were like Kalman the Cripple, Kalman Kalika, and avenged every wrong done to them, that would be the end of all the anti-Semitic tricks against them.

The God whom all the Jews think of as their father had abandoned His children, leaving them to the mercy of a rotten world, just as his father had done. Every Jew should be a chunk of bitter horseradish, just as he was. Every Jew should execrate God's name and hate Him with the kind of fierce hatred he felt for his father, may his name and his memory be eradicated!

His fists, which clenched convulsively whenever he swore, relaxed, and he began rubbing one palm against the other, pinching and cracking his knuckles. No, no, no! He was not like his father! Hadn't he named Kayleh and her bastard as his heirs? True, the paper he had asked the Rabbi to sign was not yet his last official will and testament, but who else could he make his heirs? His cousin, Jadzia Davidson-Pakula?

Evidently the squire didn't love his wife, the convert, any more than he loved any other Jew. She wasn't so smart if she had allowed her father's vast fortune to fall into the hands of her slick husband.

•   •   •   •   •

Matus returned from his errands carrying a Yiddish newspaper. Kalman had already read the news in a Polish paper, so he only checked the advertisements and found what he was looking for. Careful not to let Matus see what he was doing, he tore out the page with the "Matchmaker's Corner" and put it in his inside pocket.

A bellhop brought the coffee and cake that Kalman had ordered. As he put the cup to his lips he felt a sudden surge of fear. He had threatened the squire too recklessly, had played on his nerves too brazenly. This sudden affability of the squire was a bad sign. The Jew had hinted at a suspicious drowning of one of the squire's illegitimate sons, and yet that autocrat had ended by intimating that Kalman would be invited to court! The squire must already have arranged Kalman's demise; it could even be done right here in this hotel. It would be a simple matter for the squire to bribe a hotel employee to do the dirty work. He must get out of this place at once.

He lifted the receiver to call the Grand Hotel for a room, but decided against it; the operator might be listening in.

"Reb Matus, please go out and get me a carriage, I'm moving out of here."

"There is no train till eight o'clock this evening."

"Go down and find me a carriage."

"Now?"

"Now!"

Matus was accustomed to Kalman's caprices. He went out into the street. When he returned, Kalman's bags were already packed.

At the Grand Hotel, only one small room with a single bed was available. Matus himself solved the problem.

"Kalman, all this time you've been managing without me. Maybe it's better that way. I can stay with a relative—and it will cost you less."

Matus helped Kalman up to his room. It was on an upper floor and the door had a good strong lock. The only window in the room faced Jerusalimska Avenue, a busy, noisy thoroughfare, but this suited Kalman fine.

"Reb Matus, you can go to your relative now, or go see Kayleh. I'll manage here by myself. But don't tell a soul where I am!"

"Kalman, do you want to see the child?"

"What child?—Oh, the child. Will Kayleh be able to get away from her job?"

"Kayleh? No. I'll bring him myself. Kayleh won't come."

"Let her come, too."

"She won't come."

"How do you know?"

"When she gets stubborn—"

"How do you know she'll get stubborn about this? Did you ever ask her?"

"Remember the trip home from Gostinin? She preferred to bounce around in a wagon rather than ride with you in the same carriage. She doesn't even know I brought the child to you that time."

"And if she did know?"

"She wouldn't have let me do it."

"She wouldn't have let you bring the child to his own father?"

"Remember what she said in court—that the child had no father? She still says so."

"It was her idea?"

"She's angry because of what you said about Yosl. She almost went out of her mind, God forbid."

"Tell her I want to apolgize."

"Moyshe Longlegs says you call Kayleh your 'bride.' When I told her that, she swore—'over my dead body.'"

"Kayleh?" exclaimed Kalman incredulously.

"She's so stubborn—it's not proper for a Jewish woman."

"She'll get over it. And the child does have a father, remember? A father who has already willed his child a big part of his estate. Ask the Rabbi—he'll tell you."

"What are you saying, Kalman? May you live to be a healthy father to your son, but dear Kalman, who's chasing after your money? Keep it, but give Zelikl your name. The way it is now, everybody knows there was no wedding canopy."

"You told me yourself she doesn't want one."

"Just say the word to the Rabbi. Our Rabbi—long life to him—

knows how to talk to her. And as I told you once before, Kalman, if you don't want to live with my Kayleh, we can go back the next morning for a divorce."

"I didn't expect this from Kayleh—" Kalman was still shocked by her unrelenting anger.

"May no girl ever be tested with such a disgrace. She loved you very much, Kalman. She was ready to give her life for you, otherwise what happened would never have happened. My Kayleh is not a loose woman, Kalman. That's exactly why she's so angry. Don't think I didn't try to defend you. I told her everything you said to me—that with you a cripple and Yosl a strong, healthy man, you were—how did you say it—you were eaten up with suspicion. She didn't want to hear anything about that. But the child—I can bring him here. I'll tell her I'm taking him to my relatives—"

"No, Reb Matus. She might find out about it—and she has already suffered enough because of me . . . "

17

As soon as Matus left, Kalman was sorry he had sent him away. If the squire was really as vindictive as people said, he might have someone watching the Hotel Bristol, and that person could have seen the squire's enemy moving to the Grand. And now that the squire knew where he was, he would find a way to carry out his plan. Kalman Kalika was now a greater threat to him than that peasant lad whom the squire's flunkeys had drowned.

"No panic, Kalman!" he chastised himself aloud. Kalman Kalika never was—and never would be—a coward! Squire-shmire! And if that scheming nobleman did manage to outwit him, so what? The world would exist with one cripple less.

Meanwhile, even that gimpy Kayleh couldn't stand his mug.

Maybe he ought to leave his estate to that old hag Maria. He poked fun at himself, maybe he even ought to marry her. She charged him a hundred zloty a night. By making her his wife he could save a lot of money . . .

For much less than a hundred he could buy a younger and prettier one than Maria. Come to think of it, why not?

He called a hotel porter, gave him five zloty and asked him to send up a young and pretty girl. She'd be a whore? And what was Maria? She also did it for money.

He had barely managed to take his clothes off when someone knocked at the door. He took out his money to pay for the "service" and looked around for a place to hide his wallet, but the knocking was growing more insistent. How could she have come up here so quickly—did she have a steady job at this hotel? He stuck the wallet under his pillow, called out "Come in" and pulled the blanket up to his waist, to hide his legs.

When she saw that he was already in bed, she grinned. She locked the door from the inside, came closer and held out her hand.

"My name is Kazia. Thirty zloty."

"You'll get forty if I'm satisfied," he said.

She took off her coat and threw it over a chair. Again she held out her hand. "First the money."

Kalman looked her over. Young, perhaps, but already a seasoned veteran. Where had the porter found this bargain?

"Forty zloty," she said, leaning over him. The smell of heavy perfume and cheap whiskey sickened him. Were these the odors of syphillis or gonorrhea? That was all he needed!

He handed her several banknotes. She counted them and began to unfasten her dress.

"Thank you, you may go now," Kalman said.

"You don't like me?"

"It's not that. I'm just not in the mood."

"You don't like me, ha?" she screeched. "You'll croak before you find a younger one than me, you son-of-a-whore! You know how old I am? Not even twenty-three!"

"When did you start your career—while you were still in your mother's belly?"

That was a stupid thing to say. He must have hit a raw nerve. Or was she one of those hysterical types? She began screaming so incessantly that soon she was frothing at the mouth.

"Stop that! I didn't mean to insult you! Of course you're young! Anyone can see that!" He tried to pacify her. He was certain that all the hotel guests were now standing outside his door and any moment the hotel detectives would burst in, while she stood there with her dress unbuttoned.

"Here! Look, you bastard! Your own sister didn't have a body like this! Your mother didn't have white skin like this! And your bride won't have tits like these!"

"Please stop yelling!" he pleaded. "What did I do to you? I'm a sick man. Before I sent for you I felt like it, now I still want to, but I can't. And I paid you your money, didn't I?"

She continued to scream. He uncovered his legs.

"Look I'm a cripple! I want to, but I can't!"

She stopped in the middle of a screech. Finally she believed him. "Give me another ten and I'll show you you can do it."

He gave her the ten zloty and assured her that it wasn't even worth the effort—God Himself couldn't even help him do it now.

She stared at him searchingly.

"Kazia, do you have an address where you can be reached?"

She gave him an address.

"Thank you," he said.

"Write it down," she insisted.

"I'll remember it." Oh, will I remember it, he said to himself when she left the room. Thank goodness she hadn't asked him to repeat the address. It would have started all over again. No sooner had he locked the door behind her than there was another knock at the door.

"Who's there?"

"Do you have a bathtub? I want to get washed."

"There's no bathtub here."

"Then I'll use the basin. Open the door!"

"There's no basin, and the sink is stopped up." He was afraid she would start screaming again, but it grew quiet. Apparently she had decided to leave him alone.

Yosl used to tell him all kinds of success stories about the good-looking streetwalkers in Warsaw. There was only one drunken whore among the lot of them—and Kalman Kalika had found her.

When Matus came back the next morning he found Kalman at the telephone. "You can stay out for another couple of hours," Kalman told him, putting his hand over the mouthpiece.

He had been calling various marriage brokers. Could they find him a young Torah-scholar from a good family? The young woman was attractive, despite a limp. Her father was a well-to-do leader of the community who conducted services in the synagogue occasionally and could even read from the Torah. The girl's father was ready to buy a military exemption for the young man and would give him a dowry of three thousand zloty. If he wished to continue his studies, his father-in-law would gladly support him.

It would be a fitting thing for Kalman Kalika to do—find husbands for Freydl and Chaya. Then Moyshe Longlegs would really be left speechless.

18

When Kalman returned from Warsaw, Maria was genuinely pleased to see him, but she stood as if transfixed when she realized he was moving about without help from anyone. Did this mean the end of a lucrative position for her?

She put up something for lunch. She offered to change the bandage on his leg, but Kalman muttered "later." After he had eaten he again began preparations for taking care of his leg, but this time he dug a piece of paper out of his coat pocket and handed it to her.

"The doctor prescribed a new salve."

"Why didn't the Pan say so before? The apothecary is closed now."

"The old salve was good enough up to now, it'll be good enough until tomorrow."

Matus said good night and left. His exit seemed to serve as a signal for Maria.

"Why did you stay away so long?" she burst out. "You said you would only be away for one day! I was afraid you'd gotten sick there!"

"Make it snappy with the bandage," he replied coldly. "I'm very tired."

He was able to undress himself now, he told her. She refused to leave his side, however, and insisted on helping him. She even tried to flirt with him, which only made her look ridiculous. As he got into bed she tickled him, but he acted as if he were dead.

"If you want me to," she whispered, "I'll come back later."

What a vulgar cow! To get rid of her, he said: "No, thank you, you're too rich for my blood."

"If it's going to be a regular thing, I'll take only seventy-five," she leered.

"When I want you, I'll call you . . . "

The fire in the stove was blazing hot and soon the down quilt became uncomfortable. He awoke and turned over. The bed creaked. In an instant, Maria was at his side.

"Do you want something?"

Even before he could respond, she was in his bed.

"If you're still tired, don't worry. Working in hospitals, one learns a lot of positions."

"And I always thought hospitals were only for sick people," he groaned. But he submitted. Better an old hag than a young syphilitic.

It was close to Purim. The snow had already started to melt, but under the snow the earth was still frozen hard. They could still not put up poles for the electric wires, but Kalman's people were already working in the squire's court, drawing wires into every room of the palace. The snow-covered piles of dug-up earth around the synagogue square suddenly vanished and no one knew who had carted them away, just as no one knew who had put them there in the first place. The Rabbi received an official invitation to be a member of the delegation that was to receive the president on his arrival in Dombrovka. And near the ruin that had once been Kalman's house, they began stacking up red bricks for his new home.

19

Maria was redressing Kalman's leg when Kostek Nowakowski entered. "What an honor—the Pan Mayor himself paying me a sick call," Kalman said, trying to guess whether he had come to renew the contract or whether the squire had started a new campaign of intrigue against the power station.

Maria, a native of Lowicz, was not overly impressed by the small-town mayor and continued fussing with Kalman's leg. Behind her bent back Nowakowski signaled Kalman to send her away.

"Would the Pani please hurry," Kalman obliged. "The Pan Mayor is waiting."

The Pan Mayor practically ushered her out and closed the door.

"State secrets?" Kalman asked with a smile.

Nowakowski went directly to the point. "Panie Swerdl, the last time I was here I was a bit under the influence—"

"A mayor is still a human being—he's allowed to have a drop now and then."

"A mayor, when he takes an extra drink, should stay home with his lady . . ."

"On the contrary, Panie Mayor. People say that after a couple of drinks a man lets all his troubles out on his wife, so it's better not to be with her."

"Malicious tongues! May they all wither and drop off! It's my enemies who invented that story—that I beat my wife when I drink. Jaga is the prettiest woman in Dombrovka."

"What do I know about such things? I don't have a wife. But I hear that every husband does it. What do the peasants say: 'If a husband doesn't beat his wife, she feels ignored.'"

"A man smacks his wife once in a while, she gets over it. But when one says things he shouldn't say—well, Panie Kalman, walls have ears. If I said anything like that, I wish the Pan would forget it. A dog's bark and a drunk's word are of equal value."

"We Jews say just the opposite. What's in a man's heart when he's sober, is on his tongue when he's drunk. From a drunkard you can always learn the truth."

"The honorable Pan Squire has always been good to me. I wouldn't be Mayor of Dombrovka if it weren't for him."

"The Pan Mayor is too modest. The Pan holds the highest office in the city because the citizens elected him. And they chose the Pan, and no one else, because he is recognized as as important person in his own right, because he knows how to preside over the meetings of the city council. Most of the peasants around here can't even sign their own name."

"I thank you for that, Pan Swerdl. Exactly what I tell my old woman. But the Pan Squire is unhappy with my Ksienzacki accent all of a sudden. Peasant Polish, he says. And even if it is, what of it? More than half the people around here are peasants, or their parents were. But the Pan Squire has been picking on me lately. Somebody in the neighborhood has a tongue . . ."

"The Pan has nothing to worry about. The president knows he is coming to the Ksienzacki region and he expects to hear the accent; he probably enjoys listening to it. The Pan Squire has even invited a Jew from around here to the festivities because he can play Ksienzacki tunes. Warsaw Polish? The president can hear that any day of the week from the people around him."

"The squire has invited Solomon Pitel? The one who scrapes his fiddle at peasant weddings?"

"If he hasn't invited him yet, he will soon. When Kalman the Cripple makes a statement, he knows what he's saying."

"And how does the Pan know?"

"The Pan Mayor can depend on me." Kalman tried to steer the conversation toward the crucial point. "I'm sure the Pan remembers our little difference of opinion—the Pan Mayor said there would not be a power station and I said there would. Well, they are now drawing the wires into the squire's palace. Whether I'll really give the station to the city, I don't know yet. My lawyer has the Mayor's letter canceling the old arrangement."

"And what does the illustrious squire have to say to that?"

"The Pan knows that better than I do. Doesn't he take orders from him?"

"He has said nothing to me about the power station. He says nothing about the elections for mayor, either, but he always finds an opportunity to remind me that a mayor should know this and a mayor should know that. I guess he wants to show off for the president—that he educates his farmhands. If only I were one of his bastards—he sends them all to school—"

"Since that letter was sent out he has said nothing at all about the power plant?"

"He says he's making new arrangements with the Pan, but he doesn't even say whether the electric project is on or off."

"There! The Pan can see for himself. Today the squire says one thing, tomorrow he says the opposite. And the Pan is worried about something he mentioned casually and has probably forgotten he ever said it!"

"Next time the Pan speaks with the squire—a good word never hurts—and I won't forget it. I was the bailiff here when Dombrovka was still a village. I've been the mayor ever since it became a city. How can I suddenly go back to being an ordinary farmer again? On second thought, maybe it would be better that the Pan say nothing. Don't even mention my name. With our illustrious squire you can never tell what's good and what's bad. And the elections will take place soon—"

"Everything will be fine, Panie Mayor. There's nothing to be afraid of."

Kalman could not recall having said anything that could hurt the mayor, and he had a good memory. But if that Kostek keeps babbling like a brook . . . if he talks against the squire to one person, he has probably done the same with others. One drink is enough to loosen his tongue—and he drinks too often.

20

Kostek's grandfather, a serf of the old squire's, had been given five acres of land when he was freed. By dint of hard work on both his own farm and the squire's fields, he doubled the acreage of his property so that Kostek's father inherited ten acres of it. Even this was not sufficient to support his two sons and four daughters, and so once again everyone in the family had to become the squire's farmhands. When the daughters got married, they were compensated for their portion of land with money, in order to keep the farm for the sons.

Kostek grew up tall and broad shouldered, but he was not as good a farmer as his short and skinny younger brother, who could toil from sunup to sundown on a long summer day and be none the worse for wear. A typical peasant, he knew how to save his pennies. Kostek on the other hand had a different set of virtues. He could read from the prayerbook, and with his fine voice sang in the church choir. He also had a knack for organizing the young folk of the parish.

Accordingly, the priest recommended Kostek to the manager of the squire's estate, who promoted him from farming to working in the storehouse for tools and equipment. The pay was not great here either, but Kostek quickly learned how to pick up an extra zloty. Most of the peasants, too poor to buy their own farm equipment, borrowed tools from the estate. Just as they received a portion of the crop from the squire's fields where they worked, they also paid out a portion of the crop from their own fields cultivated with the squire's equipment. With a strong horse and a sharp plow the work goes faster and more easily, and Kostek was in a position to do favors for whomever he pleased and whenever he wished. A peasant gives nothing for nothing and doesn't expect to get anything for nothing. In return for his "favors" Kostek received gifts—eggs, a chicken, a sack of groats. Kostek, though still a very young man, wielded power and people began to look up to him.

Of his father's property, Kostek inherited five acres of the land; a peasant, after finishing his own work with the good tools Kostek had chosen for him would take them to Kostek's farm and do the work there before returning them. One hand washes the other. That's how it goes in a village whenever it's time to pluck feathers and remove them from their spines, or put on a new roof, or build a barn. Kostek knew how to manage his affairs.

When Kostek married the prettiest girl in the village, the squire informed him that he was willing to sell him ten acres of land which could be paid for in installments. These extra ten acres gave him real status as a property owner. With fifteen acres of land being culti-vated for him by others, and a position in the squire's court that brought in further income, one could foresee that in time Kostek would become the wealthiest landowner in the village, next to the squire, of course.

Having so many years to pay for the ten acres was very appealing, but Kostek felt uneasy. He was nobody's fool. The squire didn't throw around acres of land for no reason. At first Kostek thought the land he was getting was sandy or swampy, but when the boundary stakes were hammered into the ground and a row of trees was planted to divide the squire's land and Kostek's new acreage, he knew that the squire was not deceiving him as far as the richness of the land was concerned. Where then, was the deception? The estate manager told Kostek that the squire was rewarding him for loyal service, but Kostek knew very well that his loyalty had been to Kostek No-wakowski alone.

Had the squire given him the land, or even mentioned it, before the wedding, Kostek would have been suspicious. There was talk in town about the squire's "generosity." But on his wedding night, his pals had gotten him good and drunk. A clever wench, that Jagosha of his—what one didn't know, wouldn't hurt him. To com-plicate his troubles, Vladek was born seven months after the wed-ding, and, as you would expect, the infant was tiny. Jagosha laughed at his accusations: when you guzzle less vodka, you'll be less suspicious.

•   •   •   •   •

What a nag! The complaints she had against him! Was he a drunkard before he married her? Would the Pan Priest have recommended
him to the squire's manager had he been a drinker? Certainly not,
but now he had good reason for taking to the bottle. Kostek hated to
be fooled.

Dozens of girls walked home from church on Sundays, but everyone had eyes only for his Jaga. She had a graceful walk. When she
wore her Ksienzack outfit over her well-starched petticoats, her
striped, pleated skirt swirled around with waves of bright colors. She
had such a glint in her eyes that it set you ablaze like a spark on a
haystack. True, he thought she was still very attractive, but a woman
is a woman—for the best horse and the prettiest wench you sometimes need your whip.

When a dark suspicion creeps into the brain, it can't be washed
out with soap, nor burnt out with acid, godammit. Jagosha bore
him three more children. Not one of them looked like Vladek, the
one born after only seven months. And none of the others acted like
Vladek, who was lazy, sly, and stubborn. Jaga had the gall to say
that he was exactly like his father—Kostek. Hadn't the squire
given him ten acres of land only for the purpose of keeping him at
court? Would the squire want to keep him at court if he were a lazy
man?

"Jesus! If you know why his Lordship gave you that land, why do
you drink like a fish and pick on me and never have a kind word for
Vladek?"

"He could have kept me in the court just as well with five acres
of land. Five acres he gave me for my virtues; but for whose virtues
did he give me the other five?"

"Boozer! A man's yapper is like a tin rooster up on the roof—it
turns this way and that way and spins in all directions. You're only
looking for excuses for your guzzling. You took your vows not with
me but with the bottle. Ten acres are not enough for you—you'll
drink them all away yet!"

He raised his fist. "My drinking is my business, you slut!"

It always began with a complaint. If she didn't have such an
insolent mouth, it would never have gone beyond talk. But she always said something calculated to infuriate him, as if she were delib-

erately inviting the blow. More than once she had come to church on Sunday morning with a black eye.

"What happened, honored Pani?" people would ask.

"It was so dark I bumped into the sideboard."

The Dombrovka wags said that the mayor must have a house full of sideboards.

21

Jan Czaplik was a quiet lad. The squire had recommended him for a job in the mayor's office, and the mayor was pleased with him. He wrote a fine, elegant script. He had completed two years of high school but never boasted of his achievement. He followed orders and became an expert at covering up his boss's errors.

Then all of a sudden this quiet, loyal boy became a candidate for mayor of Dombrovka. Kostek was angry at first. Then he laughed the whole thing off. Better Janek than someone else. Who'd ever vote for a kid not even dry behind the ears yet? The squire would certainly oppose him. The president was due to come to Dombrovka and the squire would want to present to him a mayor who was a respectable man of property, not a yokel, not a young shnook like this Janek.

All his cronies said the same thing. Kostek had enough experience in elections to know better than to make a big issue of this. But the minute the elections were over he'd throw this Janek out so hard that he'd break his neck. He really ought to start looking for a new secretary at once.

That Jew Kalman, who at first had made light of the whole business, was now trying to get Kostek all upset about it. "If your secretary is one of the squire's people—maybe even one of his bastards—then silence may not be such a good idea." But what did this cripple know about elections?

Kostek Nowakowski dressed up in his Sunday best, with his black capote and its colorfully embroidered belt, even though the weather wasn't really warm enough yet to go out without a topcoat. He set out for the mayor's office—which also served as the polling station—strolling leisurely, like a man of substance coming to claim what is rightfully his.

No election literature was printed in Dombrovka, because most of the voters were illiterate. And because they could not write, either, the voters were handed printed slips with the names of the candidates. Each voter then placed the slip of his choice in the urn. Kostek was astonished to find that all the way from the marketplace to the mayor's office schoolchildren were pressing slips of paper into the hands of the passersby. Whose arrangement was this? Taking one of the slips, he read it, incredulous. The name on the slip, in big black letters, was JAN CZAPLIK. He took another slip and another, and on each one was the name of his opponent. He forgot that he was supposed to be walking in a leisurely gait to his office. He ran from one child to the other, looking for a slip with his name on it. There was not even one.

"Panie Psiodovniku," he asked the policeman at the door of the mayor's office, using his full title, and not the usual Stakh. "Panie Psiodovniku, why aren't there any Kostek Nowakowski slips here?"

"Oh, there are, there are!" the policeman assured him, with no trace of his customary servility. "Inside, there are."

Inside he asked for a Nowakowski slip, was given one, and he cast his vote. Then he summoned Woiczech, the custodian of the building, and asked him to bring a few packs of Nowakowski slips. It took an inordinately long time for Woiczech to find them. Usually Woiczech himself would have offered to bring the package to the Pan Mayor's home. Today he placed it on the table near Kostek and disappeared abruptly without even bowing or saying the farewell, *dowidzenia*.

What had happened here overnight?

When he returned home, Jagosha served him a good lunch, but he couldn't swallow the first bite until he had downed half a glass of vodka. When he drank the other half, the world began to look better. After his lunch he felt so relaxed that he lay down for a little afternoon nap. His dreams must have been sweet; because he slept soundly until evening.

When he awoke, no one was home. Everyone was probably at a neighbor's, celebrating his reelection. He smiled. What was there to celebrate? It wasn't the first time, or the last. Kostek Nowakowski and Dombrovka had grown up together—who could separate them? He stretched contentedly, draped his sheepskin coat over his shoulders, and walked to his office.

Even before opening the door he heard the commotion inside. Hurrah! Cheers! Why hadn't they waited for the honoree? As he pushed the door open, his heart nearly stopped. A sea of hands was lifting Janek high in the air, setting him down, and raising him up again.

"Long live the mayor!"

The mayor? The mayor was still standing at the door.

The mayor, the new mayor . . . There could no longer be any doubt about what had happened. Little Janek is easy to lift up; they had never lifted Kostek in the air like this—Kostek was too solid a person. . . .

Janek caught sight of him and, pulling free of the hands that were holding him, came running up to Kostek and led him to the front of the room. He clapped his little hands and the crowd grew quiet.

"Panie Mayor," he said, calling his former employer by his lost title, "Panie Mayor, whatever I know, I learned from you. I hope I shall continue to enjoy the Pan's friendship and fatherly advice."

The ex-mayor was so bewildered that he nodded assent. The crowd applauded. Someone brought him a tumbler of vodka, but he did not touch it. He could only shake his head from side to side, as if he had suddenly lost the power of speech. Then he turned and went out the same door through which he had just entered.

The cool breeze sent a shiver through his body. He turned up his collar, drew his head in, and buried his mouth in the warmth of the fur. A disaster for Dombrovka. The town had had a real leader, a father who worried about his citizens as if they were his own children; an administrator who had transformed a decrepit village into a thriving town. Now it would be governed by that fourflusher's—by the squire's stupid little messenger boy, and everything would go to rack and ruin.

Actually he shouldn't give a damn. Over the years he had bought additional land, planted more fruit trees. He owned the biggest farm in the neighborhood, second only to the squire's, and the biggest orchard, second only to the priest's. But Dombrovka would never be the same. Maybe he ought to sell everything, move as far away as he could, and let them beat their heads against the wall here. Let Dombrovka go down the drain together with its old squire and its new mayor.

Passing the liquor store, he noticed light coming through the cracks of the closed shutters. The law prohibited the sale of alcoholic beverages on election day, and besides, it was after business hours.

But that Jew Shimek always acted as if the law didn't apply to him. The little Jew used to fawn on him and give him gifts of expensive vodka; now that lousy traitor would probably do the same for the new mayor.

He slipped into Shimek Unger's store through the back door, as he had done so often before. Shimek was taking bottles out of boxes and arranging them on the shelves. Who had emptied these shelves on an election day? Goddamn them all with their drinking and celebrations! They would all live to regret this day, the dirty scum!

He went over to a shelf, took down two liters of Wiborowa Vodka, the best in the house, and stuck a bottle under each arm. Would the Jew ask him for money, or wasn't he aware yet of the election results? It would cost him a lot more than the vodka was worth if he dared to ask Kostek Nowakowski for money. Mayor or not, he could still send a policeman to write up a complaint and make a charge. His police could always find a reason to fine somebody . . .

"Dobranoc!" he said, as he went out, and Shimek returned his "good-night." The Jew did not run out after him to demand payment. For citizens of Dombrovka, Kostek Nowakowski was still head of the town.

22

The lights were on in his house and he heard the sound of people talking. In no mood for socializing, he went into the barn behind the house and stretched out on some hay. He clamped the two bottles of vodka between his legs, so that they wouldn't get lost in the dark.

When he had snatched the bottles off the shelf in the liquor store he was in a hurry, Devil knows why. When you buy real monopoly liquor you should check the seal. He didn't recall seeing the red seals on these bottles. Could these be Wiborowa bottles which the Jew had filled with homebrew? Everybody knows that Jews are swindlers if you give them the opportunity.

He picked up one bottle and smacked its bottom sharply. The cork popped out. The aroma was good, very refreshing. He put the bottle up to his mouth; the taste was bracing. The weariness in his limbs began to recede. No, that Jew wouldn't dare to swindle the mayor himself.

He had intended to take only a sip, but the cork had flown out into the darkness. Could he stand the bottle up on the straw and go look for it? Wiborowa is not a vodka you spill on the ground. Was it really worth more than the plain monopoly vodka? After the first couple of swallows he thought, yes, it was. But after he had downed a little more, he wasn't so sure. Vodka is vodka, Wiborowa or any other kind.

He came to several other conclusions. It is easy to run a large farm when other people do the work, when the squire's court provides the best horses and the most modern equipment. Now that he was no longer their mayor, would these clodhoppers plow his fields? They were doing it as good neighbors, they had always said, good friends, good cronies. Eh, don't be silly! He was still a crony, a friend, and neighbor. The ones who had worked his fields for so long would still continue to do so. The people would not turn their backs on him overnight.

Maybe this stuff wasn't Wiborowa after all. Maybe not even the regular government stock. Otherwise, why would so many dark thoughts creep into his head like venomous worms? How could he possibly pay for all the little things he had taken from the stores, for every hour of work that anybody did for him, for each little item, for everything? Christ Almighty, where would he get so much money?

His belly was warm but his skin was crawling from all these horrible thoughts, and his feet were freezing inside his boots. What was he doing in the barn, anyway? He owned a warm house, had a bed with a down cover and a juicy woman who could warm his bones.

As he stood up, some of the vodka spilled. The aroma teased his nostrils. Leaving the sealed bottle lying in the straw, he took the open one with him. The house was now dark and Jagosha was probably snoring in their bed. Her husband was suffering the tortures of the damned and there she lay, wheezing like a cow. He had married a village girl and made a mayor's lady out of her—what had she given him in return? Nothing but curses. Every good-for-nothing had a wife in his bed. He had a snake. He could swear she too had voted for Janek. Naturally, if the squire wanted it that way . . . For her, god-damn it, the squire was a god.

He held the bottle to his mouth and kept it upside down until it was empty. He pulled off his boots. Son of a bitch, the things that other wives . . .

Other wives what? What had he started to say? He had forgotten. Damn Jew must have put poison in the bottle, because—

Because what?

Son of a bitch!

"Get your cold feet off me!" Jagosha exclaimed, startled out of a sound sleep. "Oh, it's the ex-mayor?"

Again she was starting in with her needling.

"And you're the ex-mayor's-lady! Get out of my bed, you old hag! Go back to work! You're nothing but a peasant again!"

"Hitting the bottle again? Well, you'd better stop right now. No more free vodka for an ex-mayor!"

"My drinking is none of your goddamn business! I can get all I want!" He picked the empty bottle off the floor and stuck it in her face. "Wiborowa, see! It didn't cost me a penny! And I have another one just like it!"

"It's the booze that did you in, you rum-pot! The squire was getting tired of having a drunk for a mayor!"

"How do you know so well what the squire wants or what he doesn't want?"

"If I said it, I must know it."

His voice rose to a shout. "You're still sleeping with him?"

"Don't holler, you old fool, you'll wake up the children!"

"Whose children? Mine? Yours? His?"

"Starting your old tricks again?"

"Out of all the people in Dombrovka he picked Kostek Nowakowski to be his bailiff, and then his mayor. Why me, of all people? Now you'd better tell me the truth!"

"Because he slept with your wife! And now he's made you an ex-mayor because you slept with *his* wife!"

"Who wants to sleep with that old Zhidowa?"

"When you get loaded you can talk yourself into anything."

Half-frozen from his stay in the barn, it was a pleasure to touch her warm body. He moved closer to her, put his hand under her nightshirt and enjoyed the feel of her breast in his hand. Damn her, she already has grown sons and she's still an exciting wench! But the top cream had been skimmed off by the squire, and who knows if he had been the first.

"Were you with him only once, or did he call you to his bed after we were married, too?"

She did not reply.

"Did he seduce you somehow, or did he only have to wink and you went running to him?"

Still no answer.

His fingers pinched her flesh as he pressed on with his interrogation. "Did you wash yourself at home before you went to him, or did you take a bath in the squire's palace with his wife's perfumed soap?"

"I smell clean enough without any perfumed soap!"

"Did he play with you first, or did he just do it and then send you away?"

"Only a pig like you would do it the way you did on our wedding night!"

"So he did play with you, eh?"

"Yes, he played with me!"

"And you enjoyed it, ha?"

She did not reply.

"And with your husband you don't like it, is that it?"

"My husband stinks from vodka and runs off at the mouth!"

He slapped her face. "A husband is a husband, vodka or not!"

She leapt out of bed.

"Where are you running to, you bitch?"

"I hope your hand falls off, you crummy wife beater!"

"When your husband wants you, you obey!"

"To hell with you, you old souse! Take your lousy bottle into bed with you and make love to that!"

"Jaga, come back . . . Jagosha . . . "

She ran out of the bedroom and turned on the lamp in the kitchen.

He stormed after her. "Goddamnit, it's the middle of the night!"

She held a wet towel to her face.

"It's the middle of the night, Jaga, come back to bed!"

"You hurt me—you blackened my eye—"

"Before the squire sends for you again it'll be all healed up. He won't be in Dombrovka until Easter."

"The squire was here for the elections, you lamebrain!"

"How do you know that? You know too much about our squire."

"And you don't know your ass from a hole in the ground!"

In only his undershirt and his drawers he ran out to the barn for the other bottle. When he returned, his wife was back in bed, and the kitchen was dark. He found the matches and relit the lamp. He felt cold, but he had no further desire to get into bed, and he was too lazy to heat up the kitchen. Grabbing his sheepskin jacket, he threw it over his shoulders, wrapped his legs in Jaga's heavy shawl, and sat down for the night in the kitchen, with his bottle. He felt unbearably sad. And the more he drank, the sadder he felt . . .

23

When he returned to the bedroom, Jaga was already fast asleep. He moved closer to the bed, holding the lamp in one hand and shaking her with the other. She awoke, covering her eyes with both hands.

"Are you crazy? Turn it off!"

"I only want to ask you one thing."

"Get that lamp out of here, you damn fool!"

"I only want to ask you one thing."

She raised her head and blew at the lamp. The flame flickered, but immediately righted itself.

"I only want to ask you one thing."

"Get that lamp out of here!"

"Look me straight in the eye and tell me one thing."

"You drunken sot!"

"Only one question: Is Vladek my child?"

"No! And put that damn light out!"

"The squire's?"

"The squire's," she lied spitefully. "Now will you leave me alone?"

"Did you sleep with him after the wedding too?"

She reached toward the lamp, but he pushed her hand away.

"Did you?"

"Leave me alone! You said only one question!"

"Just this: You slept with him after the wedding too? Yes or no?"

"Yes, every night. I've just returned from the palace."

He turned out the lamp, turned on his heel and on shaky legs left the house.

•   •   •   •   •

She could not fall back to sleep. When she turned on her side, she saw, through the window, a light in the barn. That stupid drunk would start a fire yet. She got out of bed, and on the way from the kitchen she threw a shawl around her shoulders and walked barefoot to the barn. The dog stirred in his kennel but went back to sleep.

From a distance she heard the creak of metal. Coming into the barn she found Kostek at the grindstone. One foot was pushing the pedal up and down. The grindstone was spinning rapidly. He was sharpening an ax.

"In the middle of the night, you drunk?"

He went right on sharpening the ax, as if he hadn't even heard her.

Somewhere in a dark corner a mouse was gnawing on a board. At the other end of the barn the hens were asleep on the rungs of a ladder. The lamp, suspended from a nail above the door, threw a streak of red on the grindstone as it drew sparks from the metal and scattered them all around Kostek's towering figure.

"Has the devil gotten into you?" Jaga cried out and crossed herself. "The night is nearly over and you haven't had any sleep."

He paid no attention. She moved closer and tugged at his sleeve. He raised the ax menacingly. For the first time she noticed that he had put on his best linen shirt and a Ksienzacki vest with embroidered flowers.

"Dressed up like an undertaker? What for?! There's no midnight mass in church tonight and you're not going to a ball in the squire's court. Come to bed, Kostek." Her tone had grown softer, almost inviting. "When you sleep it off you'll feel better. Come!"

She threw him a glance full of promise and again moved a little closer. He raised his foot as if to kick her and she noticed he was wearing his new boots, too.

"Crazy bastard! He's out of his mind!" she said under her breath. He put his foot down again on the pedal and the wheel spun faster.

Jesus Maria, what was she to do now? If the straw did not ignite from the sparks, he would set it on fire with the kerosene lamp.

"Kostek, sweetheart, we drink and we sleep it off, we quarrel and we make up, but if you send everything up in smoke—"

He continued his sharpening.

"Sober up, Kostek. Sweet Jesus! You're playing with fire in a barn full of straw! What will we have left to live for? You're not the mayor any more!"

The stone scraped louder on the ax blade. A stream of sparks sprayed in her direction. Alarmed, she screamed. He laughed.

"Get the hell out of here, you whore, or you'll be the first one to burn!"

She moved away from the grindstone.

"Coward! Weasel! Out!"

She did not move.

He put the ax down and reached for the lamp. "I said—out! Move—or I'll break this lamp over your head!"

"Kostek, you don't know what you're saying, you don't know what you're doing! Come to your senses, Kostek!"

"Kostek Nowakowski always knows what he's saying—and he knows damn well what he's doing! Nobody can start up with Kostek Nowakowski, not that sissy Janek and not his boss—that poisonous snake in the court! Ha! Nobody has ever spit in Kostek Now-akowski's face and gotten away with it!"

"God in heaven! What are you saying? You're sharpening the ax for—for—it's the middle of the night, why are you sharpening the ax in the middle of the night?"

"It's none of your goddamn business! Go back to bed and snore—it's the middle of the night!" He returned his attention to the grindstone.

"You'll rot in jail, you lunatic!"

"Rot in jail? I don't care. Just so long as that lousy devil rots in the ground, six feet under! I'm going to split his filthy head in two!" Again he raised the ax and waved it in her direction. She took a few steps back. She was at the doorway when he leaped across and blocked her way.

"Oh, no, you don't! You're not going to warn him! I'll chop your legs off before you take the first step!" He raised the ax.

She was too scared to scream, too petrified to move. He stood across from her with the ax in his upraised hand, relishing her terror.

In one of the darkened windows of the house a light came on. Someone had been awakened by his yelling. Jaga could see a face pressed against the window. A moment later a door creaked. Vladek. Thank God.

"Mama, what's wrong?"

The ax had grown heavier. Kostek's arm had begun to drop. A rooster crowed suddenly and flapped his wings. Kostek turned around and raised the ax higher, as if he felt threatened from behind. Jaga used the moment to escape.

"Run! He's gone crazy!" she warned Vladek, who had come out only in his underwear.

"I'll finish you all off," Kostek ranted, "you and your bastard together!" He lunged at them.

As she ran, her shawl slid to the ground. Kostek tripped over it and fell.

Once inside the house, she locked the door. Vladek wanted to go out again and close the shutters. It was too easy to knock out a window and climb into the house that way.

"Leave him be, Vladek, he'll soon sober up."

"Come, Mama!" he urged, pulling her by the arm. They ran into the front room and locked the door behind them.

"Wait, Vladek. He's so wild now, I don't know what—" She ran into the other rooms to wake up the children. When they were all together in the front room, Vladek slipped out, put up the iron grates on the windows and locked the shutters. When he came back into the house they again locked the door and pushed the sideboard up against it. Jaga gathered all her children around her and tried to calm the youngest, who sat crying on her lap.

•   •   •   •   •

Kostek had slid to the ground feet forward. His head had hit an icy pile of snow hardened by the early spring weather. He saw stars and a pain exploded inside his head. When the ice deadened the pain somewhat, he tried to sit up, but his right leg seemed to have fallen asleep. His hands kept sliding over the mud and snow. He managed to raise himself up a few inches, but fell back again. As he struggled to get up, a searing pain stabbed his right foot. Damn it to hell!

After a while he tried again and this time he got himself to a sitting position. He bent over and touched the sore spot on the foot. The boot was covered with something warm and sticky. That lousy ax must have fallen on his foot. Sonofabitch, his new boots!

When he tried to stand up he fell to the ground again. Dragging himself on his behind he inched his way back to the barn.

His foot must be swollen. If that goddamn boot weren't pressing so hard against the swelling, the pain wouldn't be so bad. As he tried to pull off the boot, the pain was so excruciating that his hands

jumped away reflexively. But he had to find out what was wrong
with his foot, didn't he? He was sitting in something damp—was it
blood?

How could he see, when that lousy lamp was hanging so high up
that no light reached the floor? If only he could stand up for a second
to lower that lamp . . .

"Jaga! Goddamn your hide, Jaga! When I need you, you're never
around!"

He managed to drag himself directly underneath the lamp, but
his own shadow blocked the light. What was that he heard? The
rustling of a dress? His tone grew milder.

He held his breath, strained his ears. A deathly stillness.

The rooster again shattered the silence with a sharp squawk and
his brothers took up the cry. Kostek hunched his shoulders, as
though all the chickens were about to attack him at once.

He had to get that lamp down lower. His eye fell on the pitchfork. If he could get close enough to it to pick it up it would be easy
to stick one of its teeth into the ear of the lamp, take it off the nail
and—yes, he must get that goddamn lamp down—.

•　　•　　•　　•　　•

With their heads nestled in their mother's lap, the children in the
front room fell asleep again. Vladek busied his head by inventing
ways of pilfering a few zloty and running away from home. He
scratched his head, spit, and could not decide whether to tell his
mother or not. The dog was barking incessantly. At whom? His own
master? Had even his dog turned against the mayor? Jaga wondered.
Or had Kostek sobered up and gone away?

"Mama, do you think he went to the squire's court?"

"And what if he did? It's not so easy to get close to the squire."

Vladek again sank back into his own thoughts. Jaga's eyes began
to droop . . .

An uproar, penetrating the closed doors and window, finally
reached them. Fists were hammering at the front door. A multitude
of fists. Vladek put his ear to the door and hurriedly began pulling at
the bolts. The door was flung open.

"Christ Almighty! Everything's burning and they're lying in here
snoring!"

After the elections, having celebrated until a late hour, many of the townspeople had not awakened at their usual time. Before anyone smelled smoke and before they could trace where it was coming from, the barn was already enveloped in flames, the roof was burning, and beginning to sag. The firefighters barely managed to save the cows. Of the barn, only ashes remained, and of Kostek Nowakowski, only a charred skeleton.

All the praises which Kostek had so longed to hear while he was alive now poured down on his coffin. From the church the procession went past the mayor's office. The priest and the new mayor spared no words of praise for the "Father of Dombrovka" and more than one person shed tears.

Kalman too attended the funeral. The squire, who had also come to pay his last respects, gave Kalman a friendly nod—from a distance.

24

Even before they were able to wish Matus mazel tov on the engagement of his daughter Freydl, they heard he was already making arrangements for the wedding. What was the hurry? Did Matus again have some kind of embarrassment that had to be covered over as soon as possible?

Matus did not divulge that it would never have occurred to him to have the engagement and the wedding in the same month, but that Kalman wanted it that way. And how could he not follow Kalman's wishes when Kalman was the one who had arranged the match, given him the money for the dowry, and promised to cover all the expenses of the wedding?

The women attached themselves to his wife Tsippe, hoping that out of that babbling mouth it would be easier to discover the truth. But Tsippe no longer complained about "hidden secrets." She kept on spitting three times against the Evil Eye, blessed everyone she spoke to and piously hoped that "every Jewish daughter should get a husband like my Freydl did, may God grant it should happen to your children too."

The wedding feast was to take place in the Study House, so Kalman hired carpenters to put down a new floor, and it was finished in a few days. All the prominent housewives got busy preparing the meal, as if Freydl, God forbid, were a poor orphan whose wedding was the responsiblity of the entire community. Matus and Tsippe ladled out money as if it was growing on trees. The ordinary housewives plucked the feathers out of slaughtered chickens. The more pious housewives watched over the koshering of the meat. All the women arranged among themselves who would cook what. In Glika the baker's oven they roasted geese and ducks, baked cakes and all kinds of cookies. The women themselves didn't know why they were so excited; only a few noticed that Kalman was directing the entire operation.

"Is the wedding for one of the Rothschild children or for a daughter of Matus with the lame leg?" a skeptic asked. But everybody loves a party. And the Jews, with their precarious livelihoods and all those government decrees desperately need a little celebration once in a while.

Kalman even asked himself why he was being so extravagant. "Pretend it's a stage play," he answered himself and enjoyed it more than one of his successful practical jokes.

The Rabbi came into the study house when Kalman was there with the carpenters, planning the arrangement of the tables for the wedding feast. The Rabbi called him aside.

"Kalman, when I was at the cemetery yesterday, I stopped at your grandfather's grave and brought him the good news that you are walking in the paths of your forefathers, praise God."

The spiteful imp in Kalman almost prodded him to say, "My forefathers can stay where they are—six feet under," but he did not utter the words. He only smiled. He was even pleased that the Rabbi was pleased.

There were moments when the whole affair seemed to Kalman too good to be true. The bridegroom had already been excused from military service, so what was his hurry to catch this gimpy girl? Had they asked for a larger dowry, he would have given it to them without quibbling. Matus, who had been negotiating with the groom's father, had come out to report that he had offered a year's board for the groom, and his father had demanded three. "Agree to it," Kalman had told Matus.

"And they insist on an early wedding date."

"Good, very good." Kalman was pleased; there wouldn't be time for regrets. But why was the groom's father in a hurry? Were they hiding some dark secret that might be uncovered if they delayed the marriage?

And come to think of it, was he himself concerned only about Fredyl? There was another limper—Chaya. After Chaya came Raizel. And with Raizel there wouldn't be any problem at all. When Kalman Kalika gets something into his crazy head . . .

25

When the groom's family rode into town in their carriages, all Dombrovka came out to look. In the second carriage the groom, his parents, his two brothers, and a sister were all dressed to the nines. Kalman's doing? So why hadn't he clothed the people in the first carriage? Distant relatives?

There were disparaging skeptics, but most of the spectators stood there with their mouths open at the sight of the bridegroom. Girls from respectable homes forgot their modesty and stared out their windows. Mothers of marriageable daughters wished: "May my child do no worse!" In his long, black silk coat, the bridegroom looked taller than he actually was. His face was pale and elongated. The bloom on his cheeks was so pink it seemed painted on by an artist. A youthful beard was sprouting on his chin, and his dark brown eyes were glowing intensely beneath his festive fur hat.

At his reception, when the talk turned to Torah, it became evident that his relatives were learned men. One of them was a *dayan,* an assistant rabbi. When the Rabbi referred to something in the weekly Torah portion, the groom added an observation of his own. Even before his wedding speech, he was demonstrating proficiency in talmudic texts. One could see he wanted to say more, but he began to cough, as if he had caught cold on the road.

The Rabbi rubbed his palms together, delighted that such a fine young man was going to be one of his congregants. Aside from the seventy-year-old Aaron, no Torah scholars lived in Dombrovka. Mostly the Jews there were workingmen. The few merchants toiled at transacting day and night in the marketplace, a labor often harder than a craftman's trade. Matus limped from guest to guest, happiest when he could repeat something he had learned during the week. Let his in-laws see that he wasn't a complete illiterate.

The reception took place in the Rabbi's courtroom, and the "seating of the bride" in the women's synagogue. Everyone was positively agog during the ceremony. Shoes that Kalman had ordered for Freydl from a Warsaw specialist almost concealed her lameness. She wore a white bridal gown, a crown, and a veil unlike any ever seen before in Dombrovka. All would have gone smoothly but for the clumsy mother of the bride who stepped on the train of the dress and ripped the lace. Luckily the bridesmaids caught the bride by her arms, preventing her from falling across the threshold of the synagogue. This would surely have been a bad omen.

As was the custom, at the reception the young men sat at the table with the bridegroom, since he was still an unwed male like them. The guests did not enter until the moment when the groom would begin his wedding speech. Matus whispered to the Rabbi that Kalman had not arrived yet, and it was not right for the bridegroom to begin without Kalman present. The Rabbi asked the beadle to go and find Kalman. During the day everyone had seen him. He had been in the synagogue giving orders about placing the plates, the glasses, the knives and forks, the silver candlesticks—everything was his responsibilty. They had seen him at the tables in the women's synagogue before the guests' arrival. They had also seen him near the Rabbi's home. And suddenly—no Kalman!

Matus sent the beadle out again to ask Tsippe. But she knew nothing. Soon, however, Raizel brought news that Kalman was still at home. When she appeared at the door, the lively conversation around the table suddenly ceased. Was this because a girl must not enter a room where men are present? The Torah scholars lowered their eyes toward their beards and tapped the table impatiently. It is doubtful that the young men did the same. Dressed up in her pretty frock, with a garland of flowers in her hair, Raizel looked like a bride herself. The Rebbetsin led her into another room.

The Rabbi's home was a short distance from the synagogue but the melting snow had filled Wilki Street with puddles. Raizel's shiny patent leather shoes got muddy, and her dress splattered. The Rebbetsin helped her clean up her shoes and dress and admired this "beautiful flower" that had suddenly bloomed in the house of a poor man.

Matus wanted to rush over to Kalman's, but the Rabbi told him it wasn't proper for a host to leave his guests.

"Berish," the Rabbi told his son, "would you please go over to Kalman's and tell him we're waiting for him. Tell him I sent you."

Berish went into the other room for his coat as Raizel was leaving. They almost collided.

"Just getting my coat," he apologized, his face turing red. "Mazel tov," he added, when her back was already turned.

Raizel walked slowly toward the women's synagogue, trying toavoid the puddles on the unlit street. Someone stopped her with a question.

"Perhaps the young lady knows which house is Kalman's?"

She recognized the voice.

"I will show the gentleman."

"The lady will soil her shoes again," he said shyly.

"Lowicz Street is paved," she replied and walked further with him, although they had already reached the synagogue courtyard.

Lowicz Street was paved with cobblestones, and there were no mud puddles, but where Wilki Street ended and the paved street began, lay a deep pool of mud. Raizel's foot slipped and she would have fallen had she not instinctively grabbed Berish's arm.

Knowing that a young Hassid is not allowed to touch a woman, she released it at once. But then Berish took her arm and gave her a gentle lift: "The lady can easily jump across the puddle to the pavement . . ."

Kalman could hardly believe his eyes at the sight of Berish and Raizel. He had already gone to bed. He had suddenly felt ill, he explained. Such an illustrious wedding and he couldn't be there. The two messengers were departing when Kalman called Berish back and told him in a whisper: "I thank the Rabbi very much for sending for me. But a cripple cannot enhance a celebration. Please tell the Rabbi I said that."

Again Matus insisted on going to fetch Kalman, and again the Rabbi restrained him. "It is written in *Sefer Hassidim*—*ritsono shel odom zehu k'vodo*—we must respect a person's wishes, especially when we wish to do him honor."

The Rabbi thought he knew why Kalman did not want to attend. Whoever introduced him to the in-laws would have to explain his relationship to Matus. Someone might slip, or maliciously reveal a secret about what had happened between Kalman and Kayleh. I should have insisted that he go through the marriage ceremony with Kayleh before they brought these new relatives into the city, the Rabbi reproached himself.

26

Even before Raizel and Berish had closed the door behind them, Kalman was rubbing his hands together, pleased with himself. "It's working . . . Maria! Where the hell are you, you old hag? Bring me the vodka!"

Maria placed a bottle of Wiborowa next to his bed.

As she started to leave the room, he said:

"A glass for you too, Maria—it'll warm your old bones. Do you want to earn seventy-five zloty?"

"What makes you so cheerful today, cripple? It's not your wedding."

Kalman no longer had her turn out the light when they were in bed together. Insulting each other had become part of their foreplay. He studied her body, found all its faults and called each by the nastiest names he could think of. And she returned the compliments. On this night his words were nastier than ever.

"Fat pig! If I could only cut off a piece and fry it with an onion, maybe it would taste better!"

"I thought only your legs were kaput. If you've lost your sense of taste you're just a lump of lard."

"You won't last long in this business, you old whore! Everything on you is hanging down so low it's scraping the ground. You're falling apart—don't you smell the decay?"

"I sure do—from your rotten legs! What's going on in your head nobody can see, but your brains must be all rotten too!"

"You're right there, you foul-mouthed fishwife! Something must be wrong with my brains if I pay an old bitch like you seventy-five zloty. In the old Tzar's days, I am sure, you sold yourself for a few pennies!"

She punched at him with both fists. He pinched her flesh so hard that she screamed in pain.

"Cripple! Blockhead!" She bit him so savagely she drew blood.

From outdoors came the happy sounds of wedding music. He had brought the bride and groom together, arranged the wedding, paid the musicians, but now the merriment taunted and embittered him beyond endurance.

"Shut up, you piece of shit!" He slapped her hard. "You're not even a good lay!"

"What did you say?"

"I said you're a piece of shit!" His tone grew angrier, more in earnest. "And get the hell out of my bed!"

Still under the impression he was teasing her, she moved closer, her breasts almost suffocating him.

"Get away from me, I said!" He pushed her away so violently that she fell off the bed.

It took her a few moments to catch her breath. She struggled to her feet.

"You stupid bastard, you almost broke my ribs!"

"Don't worry—they're well protected by that tub of fat." He turned his face to the wall.

She hurled herself upon him with such force that the bed groaned.

"Go away!" he pleaded. "I don't want to now."

"But I do! You're the one who started it. You can't stop now!"

"Aha! Now you will have to pay me seventy-five zloty!" Kalman said.

"Thirty-seven-and-a-half! You're only half a man!"

"This half a man doesn't need you at all—not at all! You hear me?"

Only then did she realize he was no longer playing a game.

"Son of a bitch! With these Jews you never know where you stand!" She started walking toward the door, then wheeled around. "But you'll pay me for today—seventy-five zloty and not a grosz less!"

Kalman did not reply. She locked the door behind her.

The wedding ceremony must be over by now. The music reverberated joyously. Kalman burst out crying. Sobs shook him. Tears flowed and he could not stop them . . .

When his weeping finally subsided, he could not understand what had happened. He did not even know if he really felt so bad, or—who knows?

27

A crazy night. Judging by all that went through his head, hundreds of hours should have passed, yet it was still night. Anyone privy to his thoughts would have had him locked up in a madhouse. One minute he was an angel who wanted to nestle the whole world in his arms; the next minute—better not to repeat it. Dr. Jekyll and Mr. Hyde were being played out in him. Or was it maybe a tale from an old morality book—the Evil Impulse and the Good Impulse in mortal combat, and he was the battlefield.

The wedding music had ceased and he was still tossing. But in a bad dream, anything can happen. In the few hours that he lay twisting and turning in his bed he had shot and killed the squire, choked Breindl to death, raped Raizel, built a new synagogue, created a free loan society with his own funds, sent the Rabbi to the spa in Marienbad for a cure, and—given Breindl a large dowry so she could marry a rabbi.

Now that his head had cleared up, he might be able to fall asleep, but that old cow in the next room was snoring so loud she had given him a headache. He must get out of bed and close the door to her room. He went through the doorway and a moment later was in her bed. Even though she was still half-asleep she muttered, "A hundred zloty . . ."

He felt something hard against his ribs. A little sack. He closed his fist around it and slipped quietly out of her bed.

"You'll bust and then you'll be back with the hundred," she scolded.

Inside his room again, he locked the door, opened the sack and looked at it by the light of a match. Gold pieces! Russian gold pieces! Where had she gotten them? Had she too searched under the ruins of his house? Or had she stolen them right here in this house before Matus moved the gold to Warsaw? What else had she stolen?

He was back at the door when he thought better of it. During the day she probably carried this under her big bosom. When she woke up she would look for the sack. Let her look. Let her come to him and ask . . .

He had barely stuffed the coins back in the sack when he heard a commotion in the next room. Quietly he moved to the door and flung it open. With a lit candle in her hand she was searching underneath her bed.

He thought she would be embarrassed but she raised her head, demanding:

"My sack!"

Flabbergasted by her shamelessness, he kept silent.

She sprang up with a shout: "My sack of gold!"

"Gold?" he asked naïvely. "Where did you get gold?"

"You took it! Give me back my gold right now, you thief!"

"Where did you get Russian gold pieces?"

"Give it back to me, Zhid! It's my inheritance from my husband. Don't make me take it from you by force!"

"You said your husband was a drunk and died in the poorhouse."

She ran past him into his room, began searching the bedclothes, throwing every piece to the floor. Feverishly she ripped the coverlet and a flurry of feathers filled the room. She pulled the straw out of the mattress, spread it over the floor, feeling through every inch of it. She picked up the pillows, and tore off their cases, one after the other. Kalman sat by the wall, not opening his mouth. When she had gone through every pillow she turned to him: "Give it back to me or else . . ."

Kalman smiled his little crooked smile but said nothing. She ran out and returned with a cleaver in her hand. Kalman was poised to leap out of the way, but she dashed to the table and tried to push it between the drawer lock and the top of the table.

"I'll put you in jail," he threatened.

"I only want what's mine!"

The lock gave way. She pulled out the drawer. Nothing but documents and paper money. She closed the drawer, opened it again, took out the bills, and began counting it aloud. She counted out a month's wages and added another seventy-five zloty.

"How many times have you done this?"

"I'm only taking what's coming to me." She raised her hand with the money to put it into her bosom, forgetting that she was wearing only a nightshirt. She clasped the money in her hand and moved closer to Kalman.

"Where is my gold? Give me back my gold, you thieving Jew-bastard!"

"If it's yours, you can get it back from the police."

"You have it on you!" she screamed, and lunged at him. He picked up a chair and held it up like a shield.

She ran back to the table, grabbed the cleaver and raised it menacingly.

"Give me back my gold or both of us will die right here in this room!"

"I'll give it to the police. Whoever can prove ownership will get it."

"You'll get your death from me, not gold," she hissed. "I'll—"

Someone knocked at the door.

"It's the police! Open it!" Kalman ordered.

"You can't scare me, Zhid! Nobody called the police." She lowered the cleaver and waited. The knocking grew weaker and finally stopped. They heard footsteps walking away from the door, into the street. Kalman turned, slammed the chair against the window. Matus's face appeared outside the broken windowpane.

"Panie Matus," Kalman said in Polish, "Panie Matus, if she doesn't let you in, go fetch the police."

"I'll let him in," she said, and went to open the door.

"Wait there, Matus! She's waving a cleaver around!"

Maria returned. She had put on a dress.

"What's going on here?" Matus asked, sticking his hand in through the windowpane and unlocking the window.

"He robbed me!" Maria whined. "First he raped me, then he robbed me!"

"And made her pregnant," Kalman added.

"Really?" said Matus, bewildered.

Kalman motioned him to come into the house.

"The Pan must please tell him to give me back my gold," Maria said as soon as he entered.

"Pani Maria," Kalman said, "just as no one will believe that I made the Pani pregnant, so no one will believe that the Pani had saved these 1906 Tsarist gold pieces—exactly the same year that my grandfather hid his away. The Pani knows that there were more gold pieces in the place where she got these, a lot more. If I call the police, the Pani will end up in prison. But I don't want to do that and I won't, if she tells me how they came into her possession."

No reply.

"If Pani tells the truth, she can keep the money she took out of the drawer."

Maria began to sob.

"Where did the Pani get them?"

"The same place I got the money."

"The drawer? You opened it with a cleaver?"

She nodded.

"Pan Matus will help the Pani pack her things."

"I don't need any help."

"But I do. Before the Pani puts anything into her basket, it will go through Pan Matus's hands."

She was already at the door when she put down the basket, walked back to Kalman and said to him softly, so that Matus wouldn't hear:

"I know who's out to get you. If I lend them a hand, you'll be a dead man before you're a month older, you rotten lousy cripple!"

Kalman's flesh crawled. When he had lived in terror of the squire's thugs, he evidently had had good reason. He had been afraid to spend the night at the Hotel Bristol—but the danger was here in his own home.

"You showed up at that window as if God Himself sent you," Kalman said to Matus gratefully.

"I was just walking home from the wedding and I said to myself: Who can understand the ways of the Almighty? Nobody deserved to be at that wedding more than Kalman—and he goes and gets sick. He must be very sick if he decided to stay home. My Kayleh says to me: 'Very sick? Then someone should go and see if he needs help.' So I went, and I knocked at the door and nobody answered. I didn't know what to do. Maybe you were asleep. While I was standing there in the street—bang! a crash of glass, and your windowpane was falling apart."

"And here you thought I was spending too much money on the wedding. Reb Matus, that wedding saved my life!"

"I never could stand that nurse."

"And the gold pieces that I took back from her amount to more than the whole wedding cost!"

"May the One Above repay you for all your good deeds, Kalman. Such a son-in-law, such a wedding, *k'n'hora*—may you be protected from an evil eye. I don't know what to say, Kalman . . . "

"You said that Kayleh sent you to look in on me. She's not angry with me any more?"

"I don't know. She's so closemouthed that I don't know how she feels."

"Kayleh is closemouthed?"

"I know she loves to talk. She still talks a lot, but just let someone mention your name—it would be easier to get a word out of stone."

"Yet she sent you to see how I was?"

"I was so surprised that I ran all the way here. May the Almighty help her, too."

"He will help, He will help. Meanwhile, Reb Matus, I need you to help me. Until we find someone else, you will have to stay with me, day and night. You'll have to sleep here."

"If that's your wish. You're like my own son to me, Kalman."

28

It was the custom to have festive meals during the week of the wedding, at which the *sheva-broches,* the seven blessings are recited. On the third day Matus went to eat with the young couple. Kalman was still upset by what had happened in his home on the night of the wedding. Although he had arranged a kind of "truce" with the squire, he still trembled in fear whenever he heard footsteps near his door.

He rebuked himself. Kalman Kalika, the old Kalman Kalika, had relished dangerous situations. The present one shit himself at the mere sign of a shadow. The other Kalman must have remained underneath the ruins of his house. What they dragged out of there was just another cripple.

Under the ruins? The snow had already melted. He must clean the debris away and start searching before they begin work on the new house. He would have to harness up Matus again, with his whole household. Now that he would be able to supervise the work in person, he could hire a few strangers to help out.

A knock at the door. It was Moyshe Longlegs. Had he come for another loan? He wouldn't give him one damn penny. Kalman slid over to unlock the door.

"Have a seat, Reb Moyshe. You've brought something toward

your loan? I'm badly in need of cash. You can see I have a lot of expenses."

"The One Above will repay you, Panie Kalman. Paying for a bride's wedding is a big *mitzva*. It's a bigger *mitzva* to dress up a bride than to dress up a synagogue, and you've done both. Helping a girl get married is a *mitzva* from which you enjoy the fruits—the reward—in this world and the seed remains for the next world."

"Reb Moyshe, I'm talking about something from which I see neither seed nor fruit. You should pledge yourself to bring me so much every week, so that the debt doesn't keep growing larger and larger."

"I'm in a difficult situation with my Leybl right now. A young man who knows Torah, who would study diligently day and night— must now drag himself to markets and fairs and bargain with peasant women over a pot or a frying pan. May I not be sinning with these words—but it's a hard way to earn a living. And if that's not enough, he'll soon be facing conscription into the army, and I don't even want to think about what can happen, God forbid, if they take him. He won't touch their food, and once they get their hands on an observant Jewish boy they make his life unbearable."

"If you had taken my advice, Reb Moyshe, you wouldn't be in this fix today. I proposed a good match for him, but you looked down your nose on it; the girl's family wasn't good enough for you. Well, now someone else has snapped her up. You couldn't want a better match than Reb Matus made for his Freydl."

"They say the youngest daughter is a real beauty. Ever since the wedding, the women haven't stopped singing her praises. Zalman the Fiddler persuaded her to sing something for the bride and my Sarah-Leah says it was really a pleasure to hear!"

"I've told you before that Raizele is practically engaged. It's true they haven't written the contract yet, but you know by now that Kalman doesn't talk just to hear his own voice. And speaking of voices—all of Matus's children are sweet singers."

"My Sarah-Leah says that the oldest daughter, the one that—the one that's in Warsaw—that she has become a real lady—I mean, she dresses like the Warsaw ladies—"

Moyshe was trying to say something that would please Kalman, but Kalman was more interested in something else.

"No matter how much praise is lavished on the other girls, it still doesn't measure up to Chaya, Matus's third daughter. Whoever gets her for a daughter-in-law will have a world of *naches,* of pride and joy. And as for in-laws, well, you can see for yourself."

"About the youngest I might be ready to talk with my Leybl."

"You amaze me, Reb Moyshe! How can you talk like that when she's already spoken for? That's something I can't do a thing about. But I'll tell you what I can do. Although Chayele is younger and even prettier than Freydl, I'm ready to do everything I once promised you I would: a dowry, a year's board, and exemption from the military."

"You also said that you would give me a wedding present of the thousand zloty that I owe you."

Kalman could barely restrain a smile of pleasure at Moyshe's words. His plan was working! It was moving on course! But he sighed: "Well, what can I do? If I said that, I've got to keep my word."

Moyshe stood up, rocked back and forth on his long legs and stuck the end of his beard in his mouth, as if to suck advice out of it.

"I'll talk it over with my wife," he finally said. "I'm thinking that if you would agree to put out the money for Leybl's exemption, we would agree to wait. And if Raizel's match doesn't turn out—"

Kalman didn't let him finish. "And if it does turn out, you'll have another debt that will never be repaid, is that it?"

Moyshe Longlegs flinched. "I'm ready to pledge—and my Leybl will also sign it—that I will repay you the money, God willing, or else—and you must admit that my Leybl is worth a generous dowry."

"Or else what?"

"Or else, if we don't have the money to repay you, God forbid, well, if the One in Heaven has so ordained—what's her name, the third daughter—Chaya?"

"Reb Moyshe, some people think I'm a scoundrel, but I would never have the gall to suggest anything like that. You're praying that Raizel's marriage should never take place, that a sensitive, intelligent Jewish girl should be disgraced. Feh, Reb Moyshe!"

"I've got to discuss it with my wife."

"Reb Moyshe, you're not making sense. You've clearly already discussed this with your family. You've already admitted that it may have been destined by heaven, so why don't you behave in a Jewish manner? What would you say if I came to you and said, 'Reb Moyshe, I have a match for your Leybl. So far they're not sure they want him, but if nobody else comes along, maybe the girl can be persuaded—"

"I've got to talk with Leybl."

"Reb Moyshe, you're a respected citizen of Dombrovka and I don't want you to have any complaints against me if you're left behind. The Warsaw matchmakers bring so many proposals. Any day now the postman will bring the letter. Any hour a telegram may arrive. I'm not threatening you, God forbid. But you came to me at practically the last minute. A believing Jew like you should see the hand of Providence in all this, a heaven-sent destiny."

On the occasion of the last day of reciting the Seven Blessings for Freydl and her bridegroom the entire town was again invited. It was a double celebration—a *sheva-broches* and an engagement. Matus's Chayele became the bride-to-be of Moyshe Longlegs's Leybl, may good fortune be with them.

29

Matus and his entire household, Chayele's bridegroom included, were again digging among the ruins of Kalman's old house. Kalman was there too, directing the work. Melech, Freydl's husband, also came to help, but as soon as he tried to lift something heavy, the poor fellow broke out in a sweat. He still hadn't recovered from the cold he had picked up on the way to the wedding and was coughing a lot. Kalman wheeled himself over to Freydl.

"Freydl, I don't like the way your husband looks—aren't you feeding him enough?"

"Well, he looks good to me. And to everyone else, *k'n'hora*. All the girls envy me."

"I like him too, but I don't like his cough. Give him lots of milk to drink, cream, butter, eggs—nothing but the best—"

"You think I don't? But these Hassidim! All he does is study, day and night, and when it comes time to eat—a lick and a taste and that's it."

"A cough like that should not be neglected."

"You're telling me? All night long he coughs—"

A devilish flame blazed up in Kalman's eye. "Tell me, Freydl— does he do anything else during the night besides cough?"

Freydl turned red from her throat to the top of the blond wig on her shaven head.

"Please, Kalman, don't say things like that. My Melech may become a rabbi."

"And you'll make a perfect rebbetsin, Freydl, believe me. But even rabbis don't spend all their nights coughing, otherwise where would the sons of rabbis come from?"

"We'll have them, with God's help, we'll have them too." She raised her eyes heavenward, as if she already were a rabbi's wife.

Kalman chuckled inwardly. The One Above may not be ready to help, but I am! Freydl was no smarter than Kayleh, but she was worth a sin . . .

Matus again sifted every bit of mud and every heap of ash through his toughened fingers. They did find a few more coins and a little sack of jewelry. From among the discarded rags, Matus retrieved one which bellied out on a pile of trash. It turned out to be a bag stuffed with damp, decaying documents. Noticing Matus fussing over something, Kalman pushed himself over.

"Papers," said Matus and began pulling something out to show to Kalman.

"Don't pull it, it will crumble!" Kalman merely looked into the bag. The papers seemed to be bonds of some sort. Whether they still had any value remained to be seen. His grandfather had also hidden thousands of Tsarist paper rubles that had become utterly worthless.

When Matus told him that Kayleh had gone back to Warsaw, Kalman was beside himself.

"How many times did I tell you not to let her go back! Here I am going to great lengths to arrange these wonderful matches, and she'll ruin everything! Are you so poor that your daughter has to work as a servant for someone else? It's not nice for the in-laws."

"A housemaid's job is an honest living."

"But not so very respectable."

"The people are good to her. It's not fair to leave them all of a sudden, without notice."

"You're defending her yet?"

"I begged her and begged her not to go back, but when my Kayleh gets stubborn . . . And Kalman, what would you say if I suddenly left you? I know there's no comparison. You raised me up from the dust, and now—. Do I have to tell you what you did for me? So there's really no comparison. But when you do something good for a person, he feels a kind of bond. Just today I learned that even though the Egyptians tortured us, we're not permitted to hate an Egyptian, because they were once good to the Jews, and one shouldn't spit in a well from which he once drew water—that's what the Gemarah says."

Kalman had no patience now for a debate with Matus. What can you expect from these fools? On second thought, what did he really care about Matus and his in-laws? Call it nonsense, call it honesty, but precisely because they are what they are, he trusted Matus and his family implicitly.

And he himself—was he smart only when he arranged malicious pranks and mischief? Was he a fool now, when his schemes were actually making those good-natured, naïve people happy? He had exercised a great deal of cunning, conducted a whole strategic campaign to bring about these two matches. If he succeeded in erecting the whole tower all the way to its apex, it would be a tactical masterpiece. He had conducted the negotiations with the diplomatic shrewdness of a Talleyrand. Is shrewdness wisdom?

Shrewdness can be positive, if the results benefit all sides. Moyshe Longlegs's Leybl had already received his draft number, which was higher than the total number of men who would be called to active duty, so he would stay home. Melech, too, seemed pleased with his wife. And about Matus and his daughters, well, it goes without saying that they were in seventh heaven. Kalman the Cripple wants to arrange a practical joke and it comes out a good deed; he tries to do something malicious, as in the good old days, and it turns out to be noble.

Had the good old days really been so good?

Moyshe Longlegs came to Kalman with a proposition. If Leybl would put his dowry money into his father's business, he would then be a full partner. The sense of it is this: In the crockery business you need a large selection of merchandise. If, in addition, you extend credit to the peasant so he doesn't have to pay until after the harvest, you can triple your sales.

"I thought you wanted him to be taken care of for two years so he could sit and study."

"Exactly. My Leybl is eager to study, and now he has someone to study with. Melech is a real scholar. The two young men have already become good friends."

Kalman himself was suprised that he agreed so quickly to give

Moyshe Longlegs a thousand zloty as an advance on the dowry, although the wedding wouldn't take place until Shavuos. Lately he had been making so much money—what was a mere thousand?

In the bag of damp papers that Matus had found, there were bonds dating the beginning of the century. These were important foreign certificates that were now worth a lot of money. Yes, he was Jonah's grandson, but he would not hide his fortune behind a ceiling beam. When you don't have enough money for what you need, every zloty is a fortune. When you have a lot, the money is valuable only if it can buy pleasure. Why deny it? He got enjoyment out of what he had been doing lately. All these limpers, from Matus and Tsippe all the way down to Raizel, were exhilarated. He got pleasure from watching them babble, laugh, and glow with happiness. He even got pleasure out of Freydl's attempts to mix Hebrew words into her speech as she strove to be a rebbetisin.

Yes, he would carry that out, too. Kalman Kalika was leading a whole townful of Jews by the nose, and not only Jews—the illustrious squire himself would also carry out his role in the play, though he wouldn't know he was doing it . . .

30

Kalman had told the squire that he could not return the promissory notes to him because the real heir was his father. It had only been a pretext, but the squire took it seriously and consulted with his lawyers: what could they do to have Kalman's father declared legally dead? The lawyers told him that such a procedure could take years. It would be worthwhile to investigate the facts. If it was a case of amnesia and the man had been carrying no identification, then it was indeed a complicated process and there would be time then to start the legal wheels turning.

The squire instructed them to get those wheels turning at once and at the same time to get the facts in the case of Boruch Swerdl.

The facts were not so difficult to get after all. Boruch had become deranged. He had wandered around from place to place without being recognized by anyone. Apparently his belongings and his personal papers had been stolen from him. During the War, the Germans had arrested him. They managed to obtain a name and address

from him, or perhaps they found something on him with that information. The address was in Warsaw, but when they brought him
there, they were told that the previous occupant had been dead for
several years. The German authorities then committed him to the
Jewish insane asylum on Bonifraterska Street, where he died a few
years later in a deep depression.

The Rabbi was right. Kalman's father had not run away from
him. He had apparently inherited a tendency to depression from his
mother and, when his child became paralyzed, he had broken down
completely. If Grandfather Jonah had paid as much attention to the
search for his son as he did to his business, there might have been
time to do something. But Grandfather was a morose man himself.

So this was his proud lineage? Maybe he was a little crazy himself? Maybe it would show up in his child? He would surround his
child with the best, he would guard him from trouble and depression. Maybe the boy would inherit the cheerful disposition and the
naïve little laugh of his mother. He hoped so, even if it were accompanied by her sense—or lack of it.

Would he be lame?

So far he was growing normally, both legs the same length. Kalman chuckled as he recalled what the Dombrovka wags said about
Tsippe and her limpers. When she was told that one of her child's
legs was shorter, she rolled her eyes heavenward and said piously,
"Praise God it's only one. The child could have been born with both
legs shorter, God forbid."

When she told Matus that one of the child's legs was shorter, he
asked: "And the other?"

"The other leg is longer." she declared gravely.

"You see," Matus consoled her, "the One Above does no wrong.
Even when he punishes with one hand, he compensates with the
other."

And suppose the boy took after his grandmother Tsippe and her
brains?

Well, rich as he would be, he could afford to be a little foolish.

And it wasn't such a bad way to be. Matus's houseful of dimwits
had a greater capacity for happiness than Kalman with all his brains.
They were all blessed with a talent to enjoy life, and there is no
greater wisdom than that. He had the cleverness and the talent to
trip up his fellows. Was there anything to enjoy in this?

31

Chaya and Leybl's wedding began just as happily as Freydl's, but then something occurred to mar the festivities. During one of his coughing spells, now more frequent, Melech used a white hand-kerchief—and it turned bloodred.

Kalman was the first to notice it and he realized why it had been so easy for him to make such a "lucky match." This time Melech could not stop coughing. Kalman sent for a carriage and instructed Freydl to take her husband home, even though the wedding meal had not yet been served.

The next morning Kalman paid a call on the sick man. He found some excuse to send Freydl away, so that he could remain alone with Melech.

"I can see what's going on here," he said, "but if I'm to do anything to help you, I must know the whole truth."

And Melech told him. His mother, who was present at the wedding, is really his stepmother. The mother who bore him died a long time ago of consumption, when he was still a young child. Kalman could see that Melech too was a victim of the disease. His hope had been, said Melech, that when he left the big city and got plenty of fresh air and good food—but one lung was already infected, God help him.

The doctor advised Melech to go to a tuberculosis sanatorium in Otwock. Freydl wanted to rent a room in Otwock—Melech did not trust the kashrut in the sanatorium and anyway, no one could take care of her Melech as well as she could.

Kalman had a consulatation with the doctor. The doctor's opinion was that Melech must go to Otwock alone. Since the young man always had a temperature, he was evidently more sexually active than was good for his health. And kashrut was not the essential factor in this case. Tuberculosis can be fatal, and good food is a remedy, so Melech was permitted to eat everything. He would have to talk with the young man and warn him against playing with fire.

• • • • •

Kayleh came from Warsaw for Chaya and Leybl's wedding. There was so much to do. Another expensive wedding on Kalman's account.

"Kalman is an angel from heaven," Raizel told her.

"Talman?" Kayleh wondered. "Talman is not such a good person."

"Don't be silly, Kayleh. Whatever he's doing for us, he's not doing for father's sake, or Freydl's or Chayele's."

"No?"

"No!"

"Father does things for Talman, so Talman does things for him."

"Father works for him and is paid well—Father is a glazier. Why a glazier for that kind of job?"

"I don't know. Why?"

"Why? Why? Because you're a dummy! He's not in love with Father!"

"Talman in love? Talman doesn't love anybody!"

"Kaylishe, don't be a little fool. He's spending a fortune on us, did you know that? He's giving a lot of money to charity. You think he's doing it for the sake of his reputation? He gives money to Father, and it looks as though Father is the one who's contributing it. In Dombrovka they think Father is a millionaire."

"It seems Talman loves Father?"

"He's not doing it for Father, that's what I've been trying to tell you! And he's not doing it for Freydl or Chayele!"

"For whom, then?"

"For you! For you! He's good to all of us because he still loves you!"

Kayleh began chewing on the white handkerchief in her hand and did not utter another word. At the wedding itself she sat all alone in a corner, away from everyone. Her mother held out her hand to draw her into a dance; the bride herself came over to invite her; but she shook her head and preferred to remain alone, deep in her thoughts.

32

"Before Kayleh goes back to Warsaw, she'll have to ride over to Gostinin with me," Kalman told Matus and showed him the adoption papers for Kayleh's little boy. He expected Matus to jump for joy, but he merely scratched under his beard and groaned:

"I don't know if she'll want to."

Kalman could not believe his ears.

"I'll be right back," Matus said, and ran out.

Kayleh was not at home. Everybody in the household went out to look for her.

Shortly after Matus left, there was a tap on the door.

"Who's there?" Kalman asked.

A familiar, girlish voice answered "me" so softly that he just about heard it.

"Freydl? Chaya? Raizel? Come in! The door's open."

It was Kayleh. For a long moment she stood near the door. Then she ran over to him.

"Talman, I love you too! I was angry, but I never stopped lovin' you." The words came in a rush and then she burst into tears.

She loved him too? Kalman almost laughed out loud. When had she started believing that he was in love wih her? Almost despite himself, his hand began stroking her hair.

"Sh-sh! Don't cry. What you must have gone through! Don't cry, Kayleh. Everything will be all right."

"Oh, what you must have gone through!" She wiped her eyes. "I was angry with you, but when I heard what happened with the house and everything, I thought I would die."

"But you didn't even want to ride in the same sleigh with me?"

"I don't want to talt about it. Let's never talt about that again!"

"You've gotten prettier in Warsaw, Kayleh."

She tittered. "You should see me in my new outfit."

"I hear you've become a real Warsaw lady."

"My madame is very rich. I've learned a lot."

"She taught you how to wear fine clothes?"

"She gives me her things. And you know I tan sew, I tan fix things over to fit me. Wait till my madame hears—"

"You're going back there? You can't! I've told your father a dozen times that it's embarrassing for the in-laws that you're a servant-girl. We still have to arrange a match for Raizel."

"I'm not a servant in that house, Talman. I'm just lite one of the family."

"I understand you prepared the meal for Chayele's engagement party and that even the squire doesn't serve such unusual delicacies."

"If I had all the things my madame has in her titchen, you'd see—"

"You'll have them, Kayleh, you'll have them."

Her eyes brightened and her color rose. Her face glowed with such a freshness—the extreme opposite of that old pestilence he had kept in his home for so long. Breindl had hairy legs like Maria, but Kayleh's were as silky as the skin on her pretty face. Oh, Kayleh, Kayleh, if you only knew what a cripple Kalman Kalika was inside his head!

Kayleh sensed that he was looking at her in the same way as in the old days, and she lowered her eyes. Kalman's eyes dropped, too, and for a while he was silent, engrossed in his own thoughts. When he looked up again he noticed her gazing at his chest, where the nipples pressed against his shirt. He took hold of her hand and put it inside his shirt. She used to love to comb the hair on his chest with her fingers.

"No, Talman, please—"

"You don't want to?"

"I'm embarrassed."

"We have a child already and you're still embarrassed?"

"We're not married yet. Until I put on a ring—"

"According to Jewish law it doesn't necessarily have to be a ring. You can also be married by coitus—that's what it says is the Gemorrah."

"What does that mean?"

"What we did—"

"It's not right. I want a chupah, a real wedding, like Freidl's and Chaya's."

"Of course a chupah. For the sake of your parents, for the sake of the in-laws. But until the wedding—we don't have to wait, since we already have a child—"

He let go of her hand and put his own under her skirt, caressing her thighs.

"Don't, Talman."

"Your skin is like satin. I'm dying to undress you."

"Father might tome in any minute."

"I'll send your father to Warsaw on an errand. Kayleh dear, don't you remember how good it was?"

His words made her skin tingle. She looked at him with eyes full of love.

It was his body she craved, not his money. She was the only one in the world who desired that body, and his body responded. The sooner her father came back the quicker Kalman could send him away.

33

But even before Matus returned, a messenger-boy from the squire's court appeared at Kalman's door. The squire was in Dombrovka and wished to see Kalman at ten the next morning.

Were those the squire's actual words? If he thought he could summon Kalman like one of his farmhands and decide the time without consulting Kalman, then he still didn't know Kalman Kalika!

The messenger was accustomed to bowing and scraping to the "highborn one," so he probably had put his own awe into the squire's words. The squire was a shrewd man, and now, on the eve of the president's visit to Dombrovka, he would not provoke a new war. Nevertheless, a man should stand on his dignity.

"Tell the squire that ten o'clock is not a convenient time for me. Tell him I will try to be there between eleven and twelve—definitely not later than twelve."

Damn it! Now he really needed Matus's help to take him to the squire's court and bring him home again. Well, Matus would have to make the trip to Warsaw a day later.

Kalman had trouble falling asleep. The nights with Maria came back to haunt him. She was more than twice as old as he. And she was ugly. Had he used her to punish himself? His insults were part of a game, but the names he called her were only slightly exaggerated. All the repulsiveness of her swollen body floated into his memory with a vivid clarity—clearer than when she was present in person. He could almost feel the clamminess of her skin. Kalman Kalika, the wealthy Kalman Kalika, who had a fortune in the bank, who owned heaps of gold pieces and piles of stock certificates, who was erecting a whole electric generating plant that would be a gold mine—the same Kalman Kalika who, with his own money, had bought respectability and honor for the humiliated Matus Glazier and happiness for his handicapped daughters—this same Kalman had bought himself a few hours with a piece of shit, and had paid big money for it.

He tried to drive Maria out of his mind by conjuring up recollections of Breindl. But the Breindl episode, too, had ended in a nightmare.

On that ill-starred night he had enjoyed Breindl's company. It was very pleasant to have such a charming woman in his home; it was very agreeable when she laughed at his jokes, when she admired his wit. When he bought her gifts, it was not a devious means of winning her away from Yosl; he was rewarding her for the youth and joy that she brought into his gloomy and depressing home. All day long he waited impatiently for night to come, so that Yosl would go to sleep and leave Breindl alone with him.

They would sit and chat, play cards, talk some more; but after all the talking, when her eyes started to droop, she would go back to Yosl's bed. Yosl Golem's strong legs were more attractive than Kalman's strong head. Breindl's loyalty to that golem proved anew to him with what disgust she—and everyone else—looked upon him. Is that what had made him so bitter?

Every precious moment with Breindl was eradicated, lost under the ruins of his destroyed house. Not one ounce of her joyousness remained with him, not a trace of anything that could now warm his spirit.

The old Kalman used to brag to himself that he had seduced Kayleh into his bed. He even enjoyed the clever notion about Yosl being his "partner." Crazy! Insane! Kayleh's body was fresh, as if it were all covered with dew, and wafted a tantalizing scent to his nostrils. Perhaps it was the scent of a soap, but to him it seemed the natural odor of youth. It was summertime when she first came to him, but her little breasts were cool, though her belly was a hot flame. Only today he had recalled that her legs were like a child's, without a hair, and it had felt so good this afternoon when he touched them again. Had he enjoyed it as much when she gave herself to him completely, without reservations, and without demanding anything in return? She was overflowing with emotion. No one else could give herself with such fervor as Kayleh. She was so feminine; even her giggling, maybe even her silliness, was full of charm.

But at that time he had been callow and boasting and thought it beneath him to marry a girl with a limp. He was embarrassed that she couldn't pronounce his name properly. But at the same time he had persuaded himself that he didn't give a damn about the world. He was like a young child who smears his face with his own excrement. Everyone laughs, and the child thinks he is doing something funny.

It was good that he could now see everything in a new light. He was a late bloomer, and it was good that he had finally grown up.

Why should he be ashamed of Kayleh? She would be the most elegant of ladies. No, Kayleh, you will no longer have to wear borrowed finery. You will dress yourself in your own imported silks and satins. You will ride in a fancy carriage. You will be such a fine lady that if you say "tarriage" it will become the fashion and everybody else will imitate you. He would no longer call himself Kalika. He would call himself "Talman," and establish the firm of Talman Swerdl and Son. No. Talman Swerdl and Sons. There would be many sons, a whole dynasty. Those who begrudged him his success would not laugh. They would burst with envy.

He felt like saying to Matus: "With me, your Kayleh will be a queen." He was still trying to decide whether to wake up Matus and tell him, when a carriage stopped outside his front door. He did not go out to meet the carriage but hid himself in a corner, so that Kayleh would not see him. He wanted to surprise her. Why was she washing the floor? Kayleh didn't need to wash floors, she was a queen. Yosl came running up with an ax in his hand. Yosl was Kalman's partner, he would chop off half the carriage for himself. He stuck his leg out and Yosl tripped. A crash of glass. Had the ax hit the china closet or had it hit his right leg? Damn! His legs were no good for walking, but they could burn. "It's nothing, Kayleh, the leg will heal. Come on in!" Kayleh slipped into the carriage. A liveried footman closed the door and called out to Matus: "Go!" Matus sat in the coachbox and drove the team of horses. Grandfather Jonah tried to take over the reins but Matus held them tight. Children ran behind the carriage and a rain of gold pieces came down on their heads. He looked more closely. It wasn't Kayleh but his grandfather Herz Davidson sitting next to him in the carriage. "We're going straight to the court," said Grandfather Davidson, the old squire. "We're going to take back the Davidson estate from that scoundrel!"

"Only if Kayleh can be the squire's lady."

"Of course! Who else?"

"She limps and says Talman."

"Talman is the correct way to say it. The squire's lady says it that way, and a squire's lady knows how to speak. Only paupers and common people say it any other way. You hear me, Talman?"

He heard, but Maria was waving a cleaver over his head. And his leg! My God, his leg!

Matus was shaking him awake.

"Was I crying out in my sleep, Reb Matus? It's my leg. It hurts all the way up to my knee."

"Shall I call the doctor?"

"No, it will pass."

Matus went back to bed, and Kalman tried to remember whether he had told him that Kayleh was going to be a queen . . .

34

Handing Kalman an official death certificate for his father, the squire demanded the old notes in exchange.

Although Kalman had slept very little that night, he was feeling well. His nerves were steady and his head clear. He thought for a moment and decided that plain words were in order.

"His Excellency and I both have too much business experience for us to imagine that either of us will get something for nothing."

"The Pan requested it and I planted a garden in front of the synagogue."

"The Pan Squire knows that he cannot remove the synagogue legally and I have my doubts that I will ever be able legally to collect a debt that's so old. But why should I give back those notes for nothing?"

"I won't let you blackmail me!" the squire thundered.

"If we don't have a little patience with each other's disagreements we won't get much done. In the business world there are deals from which both sides can benefit."

"Does the Pan have something specific in mind?"

"I need some time to think about it, but on the way over here I had a couple of ideas. For example, the grain on the Squire's fields. My grandfather once had a contract to buy up all the grain from the Dombrovka court. I'm willing to pay the market price, and I may build a mill in Dombrovka as big as the Milakowski mill in Lowicz."

"The Pan has enough capital for such a large mill?"

"Let's say I can get it. Let's say foreign capital. I said I would build a generating plant—and I kept my word."

"What does all this have to do with the notes?"

"As I said, these are ideas that I still have to work out. Let's say a percentage of each deal would go toward paying off the old debts."

"I don't acknowledge that such debts even exist!"

"I mean that a percentage from my side—let's say a percentage of my profits will go toward these unacknowledged debts. That means I will gradually pay them off myself and return the notes one at a time."

"The Pan said that once before but didn't keep his promise."

"I said only that it was too soon to talk about the notes because the matter was out of my hands. Besides, I don't believe in talk and promises; that's what we have lawyers for. We can work out an agreement where everything will be spelled out in black and white."

"The Pan said before—a couple of ideas. Does that mean the Pan has something else to propose?"

"The sugar factory is on the verge of shutting down. They are laying off people. They are not making necessary repairs to the machines. A third of the arable land in this area is used for growing sugar beets. If these beets have to be transported a long distance to a factory, the cost will eat up most of the earnings."

"And what is the Pan's solution?"

"When the Pan Squire sold the sugar factory some years ago, the buyers paid only a small portion of the purchase price. The rest remained as a mortgage. Things went sour right away. They could barely manage to pay the interest on the mortgage, let alone the principal. The Pan Squire could have foreclosed on the mortgage, but he didn't, so long as they were at least paying the interest. Now there won't even be that."

"What right did the Pan have to look so closely into my affairs? What business is it of his? And how did the Pan learn all this?"

The squire's voice had become shrill and menacing. Kalman decided to drop the hide-and-seek approach.

"The sugar factory is of great interest to me," he conceded. "I know it will be a big gamble and I'm not really ready to pay out all that money. But if the Pan Squire takes over his factory again and sells it to me at a price that would make it worth the risk, I'll pay cash—and as a bonus I'll throw in a few of the old notes."

"If the Pan thinks I'll give away a mortgage of 130,000 zloty for nothing, he's making a big mistake."

"I never give anything away for nothing and I don't expect to get something for nothing. The Pan Squire can hold an auction and sell the factory to the highest bidder."

The squire knew very well that nobody would give a grosz for a bankrupt business. He only wanted to test how much he could get out of this ambitious Jew.

"How much is the Pan ready to pay?"

"I don't know yet, exactly."

"Approximately?"

"I don't want the Pan Squire to hold me to my word, but I think twenty thousand would be the maximum."

The Squire let out a guffaw. "Twenty thousand for 130,000? The Pan does want it for nothing."

Kalman knew that the squire's laugh was forced.

To put up such a factory building would indeed cost more than twenty thousand, but in an out of the way place like Dombrovka, an empty factory building was worth almost nothing.

"If the Pan Squire can get more, I'll be pleased too. My only interest in this is that the factory not shut down. If it does, it will take the economy of Dombrovka down with it. We're in a serious worldwide depression. Even the rich United States of America is in trouble."

"I'm touched by Pan's patriotism," the squire sneered.

"No doubt the Pan Squire can find greater patriots among his friends in the court. I withdraw my offer."

"Was that an official proposal you made?"

"The Pan wants an official proposal?"

"I can always take such a proposition and show it to my financial advisors."

"The proposal will also have a point in it about buying up the Pan Squire's sugar beets and, as I said, returning some of the old notes."

"I'll think about the Pan's proposition."

"I've got to think about it some more myself. What I've said here now represents only my first thoughts on the subject. I have another idea that has nothing to do with money, but I think it will please the Pan Squire and yes, I will be satisfying my own patriotic feelings. But first the mayor has to decide about putting electric lights in the streets, especially Lowicz Street."

"What is your idea?"

"We'll finish all the installations in the homes and in the streets before the president arrives, but we won't supply any current. Even in the Squire's court, on the day of the President's visit, there will be only the kerosene lamps and candles. Just as it turns dark, however, the Pan President will pull a lever and for the first time in history, all of Dombrovka will be lit up at the same time."

"Not bad," said the squire, "not bad."

"If we both think about it in a positive way, the results are bound to be positive too. The fate of Dombrovka is now in the hands of the Pan Squire—and I can help him—."

On the way back from the squire's court the carriage again passed the sugar factory. "They are not earning a grosz," he said to Matus, "and I could buy it for a song. Do you know why they're not making any profit?"

"Why?" Matus wanted to know.

"Because the factory is too far from a railroad line, and with horse-and-wagon—"

"You're going to bring in a railroad line?" In Matus's eyes, Kalman could do anything.

"Not a railroad line, no, but motor trucks, yes, that I can bring in from Italy, from Sweden, and even from America."

"Why can't they do the same?"

"Because they don't have the brains, Matus, they don't have the brains."

"When did you think this all out?" Matus's tone was full of admiration.

"I'm not sure yet that it's such a good idea, but Kalman consults with the sharpest experts."

35

His injured leg was still giving him trouble, so Kalman saw his doctor, who prescribed a new salve and suggested that he go to the hospital in Lowicz and let them look at the leg. But Kalman was too busy now, so instead of sending Matus to Warsaw, he brought a Warsaw lawyer to Dombrovka. The first visit to the squire's court had led to other visits. When people noticed that Kalman was riding into the court every few days, a rumor spread that he was going to buy up all the squire's fields and forests. Nothing was too outlandish to believe about that cripple.

During one of Kalman's visits, the squire reminded him of his promise to put a new coat of plaster on the synagogue walls and fresh paint on the Jewish community buildings, in honor of the president's visit. On the way home, Kalman stopped at the Rabbi's to discuss the matter.

"Kalman, you're doing so much for Reb Matus's family. When will you finally do the right thing by his oldest daughter? Believe me, that will be more appreciated than anything you have done so far."

"Rabbi, I will do the right thing. The Rabbi knows, of course, that she is no longer working in Warsaw?"

"Don't postpone the wedding any longer, Kalman. It's causing the family a lot of heartache."

"I'm building an empire, Rabbi, and Kayleh will be the empress. I'm negotiating to buy the sugar factory. I'm going to build silos for the grain. I'm going to set up a big mill. Soon you will be rabbi of the big city of Dombrovka."

"May the One Above help you."

"I'll need trustworthy, capable people, our own people. Melech and Leybl will also become businessmen.

"Where there's Torah there's wisdom. Some of the biggest merchants in Warsaw are also scholars."

"I still need a good match for my youngest sister-in-law. She's a real beauty."

"So my wife says."

"A sensitive girl with a heart of gold, just like all of Matus's daughters. The man who becomes Raizel's husband—I can also make him into a successful businessman, unless he'd rather be a rabbi."

"That's very kind of you, Kalman. And don't forget what I said about the marriage ceremony."

Kalman couldn't tell whether the Rabbi had taken the hint or not.

Kalman grew impatient. He invited Raizel to come and see him and he didn't mince any words.

"Freydl tells me that when Berish comes to visit Melech, he meets you there and talks with you. What is the situation?"

"What situation?"

"What do you think of him? What do you two talk about?"

"Oh, we talk about everything."

"Everything? You don't talk to Berish about the Bible, do you?"

"That too. When Berish explains things, they're easy to understand. Whatever subject comes up, he can interpret it with a verse from the Torah."

"What subjects come up?"

"Anything and everything. The news in the papers. The latest books—"

"Berish reads books? What kind of books?"

"Whatever he can get his hands on. The books I take out of the library—he reads them too."

"He's no longer a strictly observant Jew?"

"He's observant, but he's intelligent too."

"You like him?"

"Oh, yes! He's religious, but not a fanatic. He loves to sing. He taught me a Hassidic song and I sang him 'Raizele the Shokhet's.'"

"Where have you been meeting since Melech went away?"

"Since then I've only seen him once. He came to ask if we had heard any news from Melech and I happened to be at Freydl's."

"Why don't you go to Freydl's and tell him to meet you there?"

"I'm at Freydl's every day now. She's not feeling very well. If he comes, I won't run away. But to tell him?"

"Freydl is sick too? Tuberculosis is infectious —"

"Every woman feels bad at the beginning—"

"The beginning? Of what?"

"You don't know? Freydl's going to be a mother—"

"Mazel tov! But before she becomes a mother, I want you to become a bride."

"So do I."

"Berish's bride."

"Berish? Why Berish?"

"Why not? You said you like him, didn't you? Isn't his family good enough for you?"

"Why are you angry, Kalman? Berish is a fine young man, but it never occurred to me—no, Kalman, I don't want to be the wife of a rabbi—"

"You just said 'So do I.' Do you have someone else in mind?"

"Kalman, you're questioning me like a detective. As though you were accusing me of some crime. Why are you so angry?"

"I'm not angry. And you know I want only the best for you. Are you going out with someone? My God, a one-horse town like Dombrovka and I don't know what's going on under my nose!"

"I don't have anyone special and I don't know yet."

"Whom would you want for a husband?"

"I don't know yet, Kalman."

"But you're going out with someone?"

"Yes. Zalman. You know him. Zalmat Pitel taught me to read music."

"And?"

"And nothing. He's a good-looking fellow. And he plays the violin well. When he plays a sad tune, your heart melts."

"He kisses you?"

"Kalman!"

"I only want to know how serious it is."

"Only once he kissed me. He's very busy. During the day he works in a shoemaker shop, in the evenings he practices his violin, and on Sundays he runs around the villages learning peasant songs."

"Raizele, take my word for it, Berish's Hassidic songs are a hundred times nicer than the peasant songs, and Berish is a hundred times more handsome than Zalman the shoemaker."

"For me, shoemaking and glaziering are no disgrace. No kind of honest labor is a disgrace. Even to be a servant-girl—"

"For me neither. As you know, for the glazier's daughters I found good matches, and for the youngest daughter I want only the best."

"Has Berish said anything to you, Kalman?"

"To me? Why?"

"You sound as if he asked you to speak with me. We talked once or twice—and that's all there is to it."

"Raizel, he's in love with you!"

"How do you know that?"

"I can tell."

"You're imagining it."

"Raizele, nowadays you can't force anybody to marry against their will. I'm only asking one thing of you—don't drive him away. You know how happy it would make your father if you and Berish—. And me too. I love you like I would my own sister and I only want what's best for you . . . "

36

Matus finally made the trip to Warsaw. Kayleh was supposed to visit Kalman after lunch. He prepared himself like a bridegroom on his wedding night. He put a brand new sheet on his bed and new pillowcases on his pillows. He heated up a lot of water to bathe his whole body and he used a scented soap on his face and hair. When he took off his trousers to change, a disgusting odor almost nauseated him. He leaned over for a closer look at his leg—yes, the smell was coming from his injured leg . . . That damn Maria! She had warned him about this—had she done something to make his leg fester?

All the regularly scheduled carriages to Lowicz had already left. Most travelers used the carriages to get to the railroad station. When there were no trains, there were no carriages. Kalman hired a special coach. In the hospital they would clean up the wound in a few minutes and get rid of the stench. If not, he would have to find an excuse to send Kayleh away. He couldn't let her come near him when he stank!

It was not as easy as he thought. The doctor cut away little pieces of flesh. It left Kalman exhausted. The next day they cut again. The doctor apparently expected it to be a lengthy process—and Kalman had to be in Warsaw the day after to meet with his lawyers and the Squire.

Had he grown accustomed to the odor or was he really so much improved? He was still keeping Kayleh at a distance. "I love you" was the message he sent her through Matus, so she'd know that nothing had changed between them. The infection had weakened him at a time when he had more work than usual. They had completed the power station, they were working overtime to finish installing the lines in the houses and set up lights on Lowicz Street. They had renovated the synagogue. And the walls of Kalman's new house were going up at a rapid rate.

Kalman was everywhere. He already had to attend to the new agreements he had worked out with the squire. The harvest was still a long time off, but he had bought the entire crop, including the fruit in the squire's orchard. Who could he put there to take care of all this? Who? Matus?

Matus. Melech was no longer running a temperature. In Otwock they had patched up his sick lung and sent him home. He could spend the hot summer days in the orchard among the trees. With Melech in the orchard, Berish would come to visit him and Matus who would live there with his whole family, including Raizel. Raizele and Berish in the orchard—something would surely bloom there . . .

Matus was ecstatic. Accustomed to hard work, he had grown tired of doing nothing. He had even had to give his goat away to Berele the Porter, because Kalman asked him to. He couldn't have kept it in the orchard anyway—goats gnaw the bark off trees.

"It won't be for long, not for long," Kalman told him.

"Why not?"

"With a rabbi for your daughter's father-in-law, it will be more appropriate for you to be an official in the community or a *gabbai* in the synagogue, not an orchard keeper."

"You're bringing that up again? Maybe Melech will be a rabbi, God willing."

Shavuos-time the fruit is not yet ripe and there is little to guard in the orchard. But it was a warm spring, Melech needed fresh air, and in the orchard stood a fine house with two rooms and a kitchen. Under Melech's direction, Tsippe koshered the kitchen, including the oven, so she could now cook a meal and a few delicacies for the pregnant Freydl.

The orchard had another advantage. It was close to the sugar factory, where Kalman was now the owner and where he often visited, to see what the new manager was accomplishing. The new man, whom Kalman had brought all the way from Cracow, was a specialist in these things.

Along with the new machines for the factory, a Fiat was supposed to come from abroad, a gift that Kalman had ordered for himself. So far he had not told anyone about this. It would be one of the surprises for Kayleh.

37

Berish was born playful. Even the manner of his birth, at a time when his father the Rabbi already had children old enough to be married, was a bit of playfulness. The Rebbetsin was embarrassed to appear before her grown children with a big belly. But the Rabbi was happy. "If the One Above has seen fit to grant us another child, it is a blessing from His Dear Name."

And Berish's father spoiled him. Whenever he went to a celebration of any kind he brought back a piece of cake for "the child." On Purim every householder sent the Rabbi *shalakhmones,* which is the custom of giving gifts of delicacies to one another on the holiday of Purim. On the plates lay various treats that people rarely savored— imported fruit, preserves, specially baked goods. The Rabbi always put away the very best for his youngest son.

As a child, Berish had an insatiable curiosity. He noticed everything, asked innumerable questions, and learned a great deal quickly.

The Rabbi's oldest son, Shmulik, had already been married a few years when he came to visit for Shavuos. During the night someone knocked at the door. Shmulik awakened. Outside the door stood a peasant in his underwear.

"What does the Pan want?" an alarmed Shmulik asked.

"My cow just calved!"

"Who does the Pan want to speak to?"

"Doesn't the Rabbi live here?"

"What does the Pan want of the Rabbi?"

"The young Rabbi told me that as soon as the brown cow calves, I should come and tell him."

Shmulik thought the peasant was confused. But it turned out that the eight-year-old Berish earned a "brokerage fee" of half a zloty for any calf that he told Sender the Butcher about, if Sender then bought it from the farmer.

At the age of twelve, Berish was already earning money as his father's assistant in writing "documents" for Passover, a kind of sales contract for the leavened products.

The text of the contract is written in a formal Aramaic. Berish soon learned this text and before long the Rabbi couldn't get along without him. It was no small thing, writing contracts for a whole town! Each householder paid the Rabbi and slipped his assistant a few groszy.

Berish had a good head on his shoulders, but he also loved to run around the streets with the other boys. He even played ball with them. The fringes of the little tallis over his shirt, along with his side-curls, would flap in the wind as he ran. He could run faster than any of his playmates. Very rarely did he miss a ball that was thrown in his direction.

His mother was full of reproaches. "You mustn't do it, Berish; it's not nice for a student of Torah, it's not proper for a rabbi's son!" The Rabbi, however, would smile forgivingly and Berishle would go out to play ball again.

He did not attend the government school where boys and girls sat together and where classes were held even on Jewish holidays. A teacher came to his home to teach him Polish and other secular subjects. His quick mind helped him here too. He could write Polish quite well, but speaking the language was another story. He rarely used the language and just as rarely heard it spoken well. But even more than from his teacher, he learned from *Nasz Przeglad,* the Jewish newspaper in Polish, to which the Rabbi subscribed in order to keep his Polish up-to-date. A rabbi has frequent communication with government bodies and has to write the civil documents for the marriages, births, and deaths in his congregation.

The first time Berish had to converse at any length in Polish was when he came to Lowicz with his father on a visit to Moyshe Bilkowski. Reb Moyshe owned one of the largest mills in Poland; it served the entire Lowicz principality. Reb Moyshe was in fact the richest Jew in the area. He was president of the Jewish community in Lowicz and headed most of the Jewish charitable institutions in the city. Berish had never in his life seen the inside of a palace, but he imagined it must look like the Bilkowski home. Through the iron railings of the fence that encircled the place you could see only a thick growth of trees. A gate of symmetrically twisted ironwork opened onto a long lane bordered by tall poplars. And if you went far enough up this lane, you would finally get to the Bilkowski home itself.

High, carved doors. High windows covered with fine chiffon curtains. Spacious rooms, furniture polished until it gleamed, Oriental rugs. Berish walked on tiptoe, afraid to put his whole weight down on such beautiful carpets. Later, when he came to know Reb Moyshe's son-in-law, Yudel Charney, it occurred to him that Yudel was one of those individuals who really were "to the manor born."

Berish was then almost seventeen. Yudel was five years older, but they soon became close friends. Yudel Charney was a voracious reader and wrote poems in Polish and Hebrew. Berish found it remarkable that in the home of the Hassid Bilkowski they spoke Polish more readily than Yiddish.

There were other young Hassidim in Lowicz who were Torah

scholars, but they never read "secular" books, and certainly not po-
etry. University students were usually freethinkers who had no time
for Hassidim or Hassidism. But with Berish, Yudel could talk, study,
discuss Polish literature and even read him some of his own verse.
Yudel spoke Polish correctly and Berish was quick to learn from him.

Yudel's wife had a younger sister who was only a year older than
Berish. When Berish started visiting Lowicz more often, his mother
found herself hoping—who knows? Maybe it was divine coincidence.
Itka Bilkowski was a graduate of the high school. She often flitted by
Berish and Yudel as they walked in the garden, but so far they had
not become friends.

Was it the magic of the Bilkowski home that was drawing him
there? Were his mother's suggestions working on him? Whenever he
thought about Itka his nostrils were filled with the aroma of the lilac
bushes in their garden, and his spirit was filled with the softness of
his own footsteps in their carpeted rooms. Itka was slender and sup-
ple and seemed to float along a few inches above the ground. But
Itka remained the dream of a magical night, a white cloud in the
heavens, floating unattainable and untouchable.

Berish loved music. Yudel had his own gramophone, and it was
here that Berish, for the first time, listened to opera on records.

One day Yudel invited Berish to come with him and spend the
Sabbath with the Rebbe of Ger. It happened quite by accident, or
perhaps Yudel had arranged it, but in any case, on the way to Ger
they heard Cantor Sirota sing in the Tlomacki Street synagogue in
Warsaw, and in the evening they went to see the opera *Carmen.* It
was Berish's first time inside a theater. Merely entering the elegant
opera house opened up a new world for him.

When the curtain started going up, he felt as if he were being
elevated along with the tassles of the satin cloth, as he were hanging
in midair, unconscious of his own body. He was hardly aware of the
music, as though next to Yudel sat the empty shell of his body,
hearing Yudel's voice whispering in his ear, but not understanding a
word of what he said. He sat in his seat and floated through the
theater along with the sounds of the orchestra and the rising and
falling tones of the singers. The stormy applause finally woke him
out of his trance. He leaped to his feet and applauded so wildly and
with such loud bravos that Yudel tugged at his arm to calm him
down.

Both of them very much wanted to go see *Tosca,* which was playing later in the week, but that day happened to be Yudel's fifth wedding anniversary and the family in Lowicz was preparing a little celebration in their home. Berish stayed in Lowicz for the party. When the elder Bilkowskis went to bed, the young people had a little party of their own. Berish sang and Itka tried to accompany him on the piano. He was in a jovial mood and acted out his experiences in Warsaw. He mimicked the exaggerated gestures of the opera singers, quavered like the cantor, and parodied the Polish sermon of the Rabbi-Doctor he heard in the big Warsaw synagogue.

After going to their home for more than two years, Berish felt, for the first time, that Itka thought of him as a friend. The next day, when he was getting ready to leave, she came into the room to say good-bye to him.

From home Berish sent a postcard to thank Yudel and everyone in the family for their hospitality. Yudel's reply was an open invitation: "Please come whenever you can. Itka sends regards and promises to teach you to read music."

38

In the orchard, the cherries, grapes, and gooseberries were beginning to ripen. Bushes laden with strawberries grew inside the fence that surrounded the orchard. The crop was so good that year and the work so demanding that Matus could not handle it all by himself. The entire family helped out. Even Berish, who had come to visit Melech, lent a hand.

Cherries are a delicate fruit. If you pick them too soon, they will stay sour; if you leave them on the tree too long, they will get over-ripe or the birds peck away at them. For Matus a bird had always been a welcome guest. Birds fly like the angels, they fly and sing praises to their Creator. But in an orchard, birds are thieves who devour the best fruits or mangle them with their sharp beaks.

Dombrovka was a small Jewish community, but it had many political groupings, including a branch of Hashomer Hatzair, whose members were eager to learn agricultural skills so as to be ready for Palestine. Raizel got the idea of having a talk with them. They were more than willing to work in the orchard.

These Zionist youngsters loved to sing. So did Matus's household. The two Hassidic sons-in-law looked askance at the practice of boys and girls spending so much time together and putting their arms on each other's shoulders when they danced the hora. But Berish, their guest, kept looking longingly toward the place where the joyous singing was coming from. Raizel's voice could be heard above all the rest.

•　　•　　•　　•　　•

Kalman was furious with himself. What sort of new madness was this? Why had he gotten himself so involved with that houseful of nincompoops? Offer an honor to the unworthy, and he'll feel it's beneath him. Here he was, tormented by an infected leg, and still he was moving heaven and earth to bring about a marriage between Raizel and the Rabbi's son! And she—as if to spite him—preferred that folksinging, fiddle-playing shoemaker!

Why was he so upset that he was almost frothing at the mouth? He was finished with being their guardian angel! He would throw them all to the wolves! And if he stopped killing himself for her sisters, would silly little "Tayleh" refuse to marry him?

He was acting like a child who throws himself to the floor and kicks his feet when his mother takes his toys away. When he first got the idea for that match with Moyshe Longlegs's Leybl, it was no more than a joke. But what hadn't he accomplished since then? How far would his crazy ideas take him? Thank goodness he had never gotten the notion of matching Raizel with the son of Poland's president! In Dombrovka they were saying that the squire was counting a lot on the president's visit. The president has a son of marriageable age, and the squire had a daughter, the mayor said. The truth was that even the squire was building castles in the air. The squire's daughter had a Jewish grandfather and was far from being a spring chicken. It could more easily happen that the young Moszchicki would see Raizel and fall for her like a ton of bricks. Raizel is a—yes, it was not at all difficult to fall in love with Raizel.

Would Raizel agree to exchange her shoemaker for the president's son? He has to talk to her about it. "Once Kalman Kalika gets an idea into his head—", he mocked his own slogan. After he had arranged such prestigious matches for the two gimpies, no one could say that Kalman Kalika deluded himself with idle fantasies.

Aha, now he knew what the real problem was! He himself was in love with Raizel, but his sense of reality told him that that dream must be fulfilled through a third person. Why Berish? Because once upon a time, when Kalman Kalika was still a child, he had had dreams of being the Rabbi's son. Now, the Rabbi's son represented him in his dreams of Raizel.

Yes, he often had delighted in Kayleh's resemblance to her youngest sister, especially when Kayleh was seated and you couldn't see that her right leg was shorter. Kayleh's skin was certainly as satiny as her sister's, her legs were just as shapely and smooth as silk. How often he had boasted to himself that he could see Raizel's nude body in his mind's eye: a narrow waist above round hips, with a beauty mark above the right hip—just like Kayleh's.

Would there be a repetition here of what had happened when he made Yosl his surrogate with Breindl?

And maybe—?

He laughed out loud and all his tensions suddenly relaxed. It was the Rabbi he really loved! He wanted to buy his way into the Rabbi's family! Kalman Kalika never could behave like any normal person. There was a time when it had been sufficient for him to have someone he could hate. His greatest triumph was to make someone so furious they could burst. But lately he was looking for ways to please people—Matus, the Rabbi, Kayleh. The Rabbi even more than Matus and his family. As soon as any new thought struck him, he tried to guess what the Rabbi would say about it. Almost twenty years had passed since the Rabbi had tested him in his Bible lesson and given him a fatherly pinch on the cheek. It must be eighteen or nineteen years since the Rabbi himself had taken him along to the cemetery to beg forgiveness from his departed friend, and by doing so, had released him from those terrible nightmares. How could a feeling of gratitude surface after so many years? Why had he forgotten it, and why had it now come back to him? What was going on in his head? Would it again revert from crazy benevolence to crazy malice?

39

The squire did not forget the "regards" that Kalman has sent to his cousin, the squire's lady; he instructed his employees to keep Kalman away if he attempted to approach the squire's party during the parade in honor of the president. But Kalman did not even go to the parade; his leg was bothering him again. At the festivities for the opening of the generating station, he was represented by his bride, Kayleh.

The pains in his leg bothered him, but he enjoyed the thought of the squire presenting Kayleh to the president. The president would shake her hand and maybe even kiss it, in accordance with the custom among aristocrats. Let the mean-spirited squire look on and burst with envy!

The parade did go past the station, but it did not even slow down there. Kalman resented this, but he had bigger worries. The sugar factory was still losing money, the mechanized mill was already under construction but he still had not found an administrator sufficiently qualified to manage such a large business, whom he could trust. Would he bankrupt himself in those two factories? It would be easier to get the right people for his businesses if he could go out and find them himself, but the ailing leg kept him confined to his bed. He ought to chop the damn leg off and throw it to the dogs! With his knees locked so tight that he couldn't bend them, what the hell did he need his lousy legs for?

He knew he wouldn't do it. He was crippled enough as it was. His legs were nothing but bloodless sticks, but when he lay stretched out in bed he was a whole man, with all his limbs. God forbid that he ever become a cripple with one leg missing!

It was laughable—or maybe it was really something to cry about. On the one hand, he must love Kayleh very much if he could remember every detail of her body so clearly and licked his lips over every charming little thing he found in her personality. He wanted her to have the best of the bargain. He could not bear to have her see him with one of his legs missing, just as now he could not let her come near him lest she smell the putrefaction in his injury.

Kalman sent for Berish. Maybe he would have more luck with him than with Raizel. Matus came back to report that Berish was in Lowicz visiting the Bilkowskis.

"The Bilkowskis?" Kalman exclaimed in alarm. "The old man has a daughter Berish's age?"

"I don't know how old she is, but she's still not spoken for. Maybe they will make a good match."

"What are you talking about!" This Matus didn't have any more brains than his Tsippe!

• • • • •

When Berish returned from Lowicz and came to see him, Kalman plunged right in without any preliminaries.

"The Panna Bilkowski is a nice girl?"

"Itka? The Pan knows her?"

"Itka? I see you're already on a first-name basis."

"When one comes into a house so often—"

"How did you come into that house, anyway?"

"Yudel Charney, the son-in-law, is a good friend of mine."

"What did you say the young Panna's name is again?"

"Itka. I said—when one comes into a house so often, eats at the same table—and she's teaching me to play the piano."

"Oh."

"I'll never be a pianist, but I did learn to read music."

"Raizel can read music too."

"I know. Zalman Pitel taught her."

"How do you know that?"

"What do you mean, how do I know? She told me."

That Raizel doesn't seem to be much smarter than her oldest sister. Why did she have to go around blabbing about it?

"Why does a rabbi need to read music?"

"Father can't read music."

"I'm not talking about him. Aren't you going to a be a rabbi some day?"

"Me? Certainly not!"

"But you have ordination."

"Not everyone who is ordained becomes a rabbi."

"I know. It's difficult to find a post. But when you know how— you'll be a rabbi yet, wait and see."

"Who told the Pan that I want to be a rabbi?"

"You really don't?"

"I don't."

"And what will your father say?"

"*The Wisdom of the Fathers* says: 'Love your trade but hate the rabbinate.'"

"When your father finds out—"

"He already knows."

"And he says nothing?"

"He has made peace with the idea."

Kalman felt as though someone had slapped him. Here he was, building castles in the air so he could have a rabbi for a brother-in-law, and—"What do you want to do, then?"

"I'm leaning toward business. In fact, I've already spoken with Reb Moyshe about a position in his mill."

Kalman's head worked feverishly. Berish would learn the miller's trade, that's good. It was not good, however, that he would be living in Lowicz at the Bilkowskis. The young Panna would teach him piano and teach him until he fell into her hands. My God, something had to be done at once! Rabbi or no rabbi, something had to be done to prevent Berish from moving to Lowicz!

"I believe the Pan sent for me?" said Berish, curious to know what Kalman wanted of him.

"It's tactless of me to question you like this, but I had reason. I never stick my nose into other people's business and I never give people my unsolicited advice. But Reb Matus's children are as close to me as to their own father, and I'm sure they speak as openly to me as they do to him."

"The Pan is doing a lot for them—everyone knows that," said Berish, just for the sake of saying something. He still wondered why Kalman had sent for him.

"Maybe I'm guilty of an indiscretion. It's wrong to repeat something that's been said to you in confidence, but when it's for a person's own good—. Raizele talks a lot about you—"

"About me?"

"Nobody can keep a secret forever. When she saw that I understood what is in her heart, she opened it for me."

"It's about Zalman Pitel!" Berish exclaimed.

"What's about Zalman Pitel?"

"Whenever she talks with me, she mentions his name often."

"You say that Zalman taught her to read music. What does that mean? It means nothing. Panna Bilkowski has taught you to play the piano—does that mean anything?"

Kalman waited for a reply, but Berish said not a word. He tried again.

"And if Itka taught you to pick out a tune on the piano, does it mean anything?"

"It means I can pick out a tune on the piano." Berish was losing patience with Kalman's incessant questions.

But Kalman feigned naïveté. "That's just what I've been saying.

She learned from Zalman, but where her heart is—that I'm sure of . . . "

Berish was still silent. He was dying to know what Raizel told Kalman, but that was her secret, and Kalman had no right to say even what he had said thus far. But still—why had Kalman asked him to come here?

"Do you know" asked Kalman, "why Zalman goes to Warsaw to study music?"

"Yes. He was given a stipend. They say that it was a direct result of his playing for the president."

"With or without the stipend, he wouldn't have gone if Raizel had let him talk to her."

"They talk to each other quite frequently."

"I mean talk about—marriage."

"Marriage? How does the Pan know all this?"

"You don't have to draw a picture for Kalman Kalika."

"Raizel is already thinking about marriage?"

"She's afraid to think about it. She comes from a poor family—and besides, I'm a stain on the family honor."

"You? Lately they've been saying the nicest things about you."

"She's also afraid that she's not well enough educated. And really, what can she have in common with a rabbi's son?"

Berish almost jumped out of his chair.

"What are you saying, Panie Kalman?"

"Just what you heard."

"Raizel said that?"

"Not in so many words, but you don't have to draw pictures for Kalman."

"But—"

"But what?"

"Nothing. It's simply not possible."

"Did she tell you otherwise?" Kalman insisted.

"One senses such things. One recognizes it in a look, one hears it in the quiver of a voice—"

"Raizel must be a good actress."

"Is that so? And I thought it was just the opposite—especially when she talks about Zalman Pitel."

This business with the young shoemaker was apparently much more serious than he thought. He should have given that girl such a good whack on her behind that she wouldn't have been able to sit down for a week. So gimpy Matus's daughter didn't fancy the Rabbi's son? She told Berish her secret about the shoemaker, but to Kalman she didn't breathe a word. Here he was, turning the world upside down for her sake, and she didn't even think it necessary to tell him what everybody else already knew. And now, what a mess! He had gone and told Berish that the girl was in love with him! Well, if Kalman had cooked up a mess, Raizel would have to eat it!

"Listen, Berish, Raizel doesn't have to know that I told you all this. Maybe I told you too much. But leave it to Kalman. I never talk just for the sake of talking."

"I'm afraid, Panie Kalman, that you didn't understand Raizel correctly. I'm almost certain—in any event, I thank you for telling me."

"Matus's children are dear to me. And the Rabbi's children are not strangers to me either. I owe the Rabbi more than anyone knows. If—I mean—if I can ever do anything for you, Berish, you only have to say the word."

"Thank you very much."

"And it's a good thing that you'll be working in a mill. Keep your eyes open, Berish. Dombrovka will soon have a big mill, too, and it would be an advantage to have kinfolk there who know the business. The Rabbi's son is like one of the family to me, even if he does think my Raizel is beneath him."

Berish did not even bother to respond to this dig. As if he hadn't even heard it, he said:

"I won't be able to do that."

"Do what?"

"Eat at Moyshe Bilkowski's table, learn the business in his mill, and then go work for his competitor. It would not be proper."

"His competitor? There are mechanized mills in Sochachow, in Gombin, in Zichlin. Not all the peasants bring their grain to Lowicz."

"Almost twenty-five percent of the Dombrovka grain goes to Lowicz—and that segment you will take away."

"You're already talking like an expert. Exactly twenty-five percent? How did you figure that out?"

"Yudel told me. He also said that if you would build the mill in partnership with his father-in-law, it would be advantageous to both of you. The old man's experience in milling would be useful to you."

"I don't need any partners, thank you. Certainly not a partner who'll want to be the boss. On the other hand—I'll think about it."

The commentator, Rashi, explains how Aaron the High Priest brought about a reconciliation between two men who had quarreled. He went to the first and said that the other begged for his forgiveness; then he went to the second one and told him that the first one begged for his forgiveness. When they learned the truth, it was too late for them to become enemies again.

Kalman had used this method with Berish and now he must use it on the other side. When he'd finish with Raizel, Berish would already be under control. He could have the prettier girl and a mill too . . .

40

"Raizele? I was just thinking about you and here you are. Guess who was here today?"

"Who?"

"Berish, the Rabbi's son."

"Berish? How is he?"

"The Bilkowskis of Lowicz would love to get him for their daughter—Itka—she's just crazy about Berish."

"Who says so? Berish wouldn't brag about such things."

"No, Berish is not a braggart, but with Kalman you don't have to draw any pictures. She's giving Berish piano lessons—he stayed at their house for a whole week. And they're giving him a job in their mill."

"Mazel tov, good luck to both of them."

"And it doesn't disturb you?"

"Why should it?"

"Don't play innocent with me, Raizel. You know he's not exactly indifferent to you."

"I don't know it and you do?"

"A person gets a feeling about such things. One can recognize it in a look, one can hear it in the quiver of a voice." It tickled Kalman to be repeating Berish's own words.

"So, now he is indifferent to the Panna Bilkowski."

"I said she was in love with him. I didn't say the feeling was mutual. Berish is in love, all right, but not with the Bilkowski girl."

"Berish loves noodles—and the Bilkowskis have plenty of flour . . ."

"You're not fooling me one bit, Raizel. Come here, closer. You look like you've been crying—"

She turned her back to him.

"What happened between you and Zalman?"

"All my suitors are going away. Zalman to Warsaw. Berish to Lowicz. So I'm sitting on a stone and weeping all alone, as the song says."

"You're a little too glib today, Raizel. Come here. Turn around. A face like yours shouldn't be kept hidden."

She turned around. He could see the tears brimming in her eyes.

"I'm your older brother, Raizel. So let's speak plainly. You're crying? Tell me now, this minute. How far have things gone between you and Zalman? Has he gotten you into trouble? I'll break his goddamn neck!"

"You mean the kind of trouble that you got Kayleh into? No. Kayleh was sure you would marry her. I'm not sure of anything."

"He doesn't like you? You're not good enough for him?"

"Zalman's real love is his fiddle."

"Then let him marry the fiddle and may they have a lot of children together. You can get a bargain like him any time you please."

"Bargain or not, I still love him." Her tone was so plaintive that Kalman's heart softened.

"You want me to talk with him? I can give him a dozen stipends."

She skipped over to Kalman and kissed him.

"You're such a fine, generous person, Kalman! I can't live without him."

Raizel was already out the door when Kalman slapped his forehead sharply. "Idiot! You worked so hard to make the match with the Rabbi's son, and now you've gone and upset the applecart!" He called after her several times, but she was already out of earshot. What a mess he had made of things! He had convinced himself that he could lead everyone by the nose and then shit on their heads. This Raizele is ready to smile sweetly at him, but on one condition: that he buy her that musician-fellow. The innocent, sanctimonious faces they put on! Clever Kalman believed that all the gimpies had collected the gold pieces for him with clean hands and pure hearts, and that not even one coin had stuck to their fingers. But if he had searched under their pillows he might have found more there than Maria had hidden under hers. Dammit to hell! How could such a shrewd operator as he be so blind? People say: "Too much is not good." These gimpies are too honest, too good, too loyal. No! In this sinful world there are no more saints. Too much of anything is a lie and a pretense. Too good to be true.

Since when can that silly Matus's family twist Kalman around their little finger? Fools and paupers! At least, if they had the sense to take the advice of a man who knows better. Here he was, building an empire for them, and she goes and falls in love with a good-for-nothing who collects ditties from peasants—probably while he's laying the farmers' daughters in the haystacks.

Raizel doesn't want Berish? To hell with it! He had already repaid Matus for everything the old fool had done for him. Given him a job, married off two of his cripples, given them generous dowries—enough! Let him keep his Raizel, his dumb Kayleh, and her little bastard. When they all came to him on their knees to beg his forgiveness, he'd inform them that things could never be the same again. They could all come and work for him—all except Kayleh. Maybe he'd buy her a husband of some sort, like the squire does whenever he makes another bastard. But Kalman was building an empire and must have a wife who's a queen. Unless—if they beg him hard enough—he might agree to marry Raizel.

Anger always filled his head with crazy thoughts, but he was dead serious about getting rid of Matus. If it weren't for his leg he'd get rid of him today. It might even be worth it to bring back Maria, if he could dump that whole household. How much could Maria steal, anyway? After all, he'd been ready to give them everything he owned! Yosl, rise up from your grave and get your revenge! Kalman the bigshot is afraid to touch that dumb gimpie Kayleh because he might not smell so good to her.

No, he wouldn't send Kayleh away until he'd put another little bastard in her belly. Whoever tries to make a fool of Kalman Kalika soon discovers that Kalman has made a fool out of them.

He wanted to build an empire, but the emperor turns out to be imprisoned by idiots. Kayleh, "Talman the Tripple" will show you yet what he's capable of! Drive them out? For the time being, he still needs them. First he'll suck the marrow out of their bones, then he'll give them the boot.

Every surge of anger lifted him out of his seat. He clenched his fists, banged on the table, and finally exhausted himself. When the door opened and Kayleh came in to cook his meal, his whole body was slumping downward. He filled his lungs with air and threw back his shoulders.

"Come over here, Kayleh. I'm hungry for something else now."

Submissively, Kayleh moved closer to him. "Why do you teep postponing the wedding, Talman? I tan't wait any longer either . . ." She lowered her eyes shyly.

Wedding shmedding, he thought. He still felt perverse. Because I need a glass of milk sometimes, does that mean I have to breed a cow?

"If neither one of us can wait," he leered, "what are we waiting for?"

"Oh, Talman, Talman," she groaned. Her breath grew hot. He took her hand, felt her pulse racing.

"Kiss me, Kayleh!"

She leaned over to kiss him. From the neck of her blouse, two spheres danced before his eyes. Even before her lips touched his, he said: "Come!" and moved off his chair. He pushed himself to the next room, where his bed stood.

"In the middle of the day?" she protested, but followed him. He hoisted himself onto the bed and remained sitting. He reached out to Kayleh to pull her closer, but merely held her hand. He looked down at the ground, caressed her hand and entreated her: "Don't trust me, Kayleh! I'm a complicated man with complicated moods and wild ideas."

"You're a tlever and learned man and I don't understand everything you say, but you are my Talman and I'm your Tayleh. No matter what you do, I'm still yours."

Kalman pushed himself off the bed and propelled himself into the front room. Kayleh followed him. "Now where are you running to?"

"The door isn't locked. Your father could walk in on us. Trust me, Kayleh. Yes, you can trust me . . . "

41

Whenever Kayleh suggested bringing the child to him he tried to talk her out of it. And he was right. The sweet little baby turned into a squealing little pig the moment Kayleh placed it in his arms.

"You hold him, you hold him!" he pleaded with her.

Kayleh took a lollipop out of her sack and handed it to Kalman. "Here, you give it to him!"

Even before Kalman finished removing the wrapper from the lollipop, the child's hand reached out for it. Kalman wanted to tease him a little bit, but the baby snatched the candy from his hand and let out another loud squeal.

"Like father like son!" Kayleh laughed. "He'll be just as big a grabber as you are!"

Kalman was pleased. "You take him now, Kayleh. I don't know how to handle a baby."

"Better get used to it, Talman. I'm going to have a lot of them!"

He was afraid the child would slip out of his arms, but he burst out laughing when the warm, chubby little fingers brushed across his face. "Take him," he begged. "I don't have any talent for this."

"You, Talman, have a talent for everything. And so does little Zelitl. He tan already tate the paper off a lollipop by himself. He'll be just lite you!"

The baby started grimacing and squeezing.

"Take him, Kayleh! He's big enough now to ask for the potty!"

Kalman admired the way Kayleh cleaned up the mess. She didn't mind getting her hands dirty. Would he ever be able to do that? Could he ever become attached to a little creature like this and laugh when it peed on him?

Hair will grow on my palm first, he thought to himself.

•　•　•　•　•

No sooner had Kalman fallen asleep that night than he found himself in a tangle of orgies. First it was Kayleh, then it turned out to be Raizel. He swore at the woman with the foulest words, but it only intensified her passion. Can't he feel it, can't he see it in her eyes, can't he hear it in the tremor of her voice—she's simply crazy about him. When he reached out to caress her, she moved away and snarled, "Seventy-five zloty." He threw the money into her face—it was Raizel's face but Maria's body. "I love you," he muttered despairingly, "you're the only one I ever loved," but she brandished a cleaver at him as Breindl stood by and laughed.

It was a repetition of what had happened in his childhood—every night another nightmare. For hours after he woke he couldn't fall asleep again. It drained the life out of him. And he had to keep a clear head on him or else everything would go down the drain. Who could he depend on? Melech could only study Talmud. Leybl could sell a pot to a farmwife. Berish might work out, but Raizel would chase him to Lowicz. Kalman Kalika would be left behind here with nothing but beggars and fools.

Perhaps all his troubles stemmed from the fact that he hadn't had a woman in a long time. He was much too tense. He needed to relax. He was afraid he would repel Kayleh with the smell of his putrid wound? Then why not send for a prostitute? He would pay in advance for her services and she wouldn't have to come back again if he didn't smell good enough for her. The trouble with him was he always had to prove himself. He wouldn't be able to stand it if Kayleh ever looked at him pityingly; if that happened, he would start hating her. But who would care if a prostitute didn't think so highly of him?

When Maria came in, Kalman happened to be alone. She had lost a chain with a medallion of the Virgin Mary. It was no ordinary medallion—someone had brought it back from Rome, blessed by the Pope himself. She simply had to find it.

Kalman suspected immediately that this was only a pretext. She certainly knew that he hadn't engaged another nurse yet. She was probably hoping he would make up with her.

Maria pulled the bedclothes off the bed she used to sleep in, moved it away from the wall and began searching underneath it. She found nothing there.

"The Pani wants to earn seventy-five zloty?" he asked her abruptly.

"You son of a bitch!"

"I'm not your son, I'm your client."

"What does the Pan think I am?"

"I'm not an expert on people; only on money. Seventy-five zloty is a damn good price. Younger ones than you take only ten."

"Not one zloty less than a hundred!"

"You're raising your price? Good. A hundred."

"When?"

"Go lock the door and pull the curtains."

Kalman was already on his bed. Maria started taking off her clothes. How quickly he had forgotten what she looked like! None of the bitter words he used to hurl at her were exaggerations. If he had any strength in his legs he'd kick her so hard she'd fly out the window.

"Please go now," he said as he tossed the banknotes at her. This time she didn't hear even one insult from his lips.

42

He was pushing the workmen to have his house finished for Rosh Hashonah, the Jewish New Year. Why the rush? Damn if he knew what he needed such a big house for. When he first started making plans for the house he still had this fantasy about moving that whole tribe into his home. Now he was bored with them, just as he was bored with the sugar factory he had bought at such a big bargain, and his mounting losses now made it no bargain at all. The mill he was building would run on electricity, but it was really a windmill— it was born of a wind in his hot head.

They were already plastering the walls in his new house. And since he had to be in Warsaw anyway, he might as well take a look at some furniture.

When Kayleh heard this she asked him to take her along. "My madam will help me pick out the furniture—her home is like a palace."

"It's high time you stopped calling her 'madam' You're already no less a 'madam' than she is."

"The Pani will help me, she is a kind woman."

Kalman couldn't help smiling. He recalled how tastefully Kayleh had decorated the dingy rooms in his old house.

"Tayleh has good taste—didn't she fall in love with Talman Talita?"

He agreed to take her along to Warsaw.

•   •   •   •   •

This was going to be his compensation, or a revenge on Fate. On the same spot that the gloomy old ruin of Jonah's once stood, Kalman Kalika would now have a big house with high windows to let the light into rooms full of expensive furniture. How had it happened, really, that his grandmother, a Davidson, and his grandfather, of the well-to-do Swerdls, had stayed in that weather-beaten shack with ground-level windows, even after they became rich again? Were they so deathly afraid of the Evil Eye?

If old Jonah could only rise from his grave now and see it! With the gold pieces he had stuck away in the cracks of the beams they were now buying expensive mahogany furniture, upholstered chairs covered with damask, and embroidered chiffon curtains. Yes, just to spite that old skinflint, he would buy the most expensive things and furnish the house like a palace . . .

Kalman had reserved two separate rooms in the hotel in Warsaw. They gave him adjoining rooms connected by a door. No doubt she wouldn't rape him. Kayleh was very shy, and if he didn't take the initiative . . .

The times he went to Warsaw by himself he had always eaten his meals in the hotel restaurant. Kayleh, however, who refused to eat *treyf,* stopped into a Jewish delicatessen and bought cold cuts and a few rolls. They ate their supper in her room and then went down to the restaurant for tea. When they came back Kalman said good night and they went to their separate rooms.

Kalman, who had been reading for quite a while, had already turned out the light when he heard the scraping of a door and the soft patter of bare feet. He reached out to turn the light on again, but his fingers couldn't find the switch. Someone came into his bed and crept under the sheet that covered him. Finally he found the switch of the bed-lamp and turned it on.

"Do you know what you're doing, Kayleh?"

She nodded.

"I'm trying to spare you. I'm willing to wait, but you—"

"You're mating yourself sit, Talman. I tan't stand the way you loot—"

"I can handle my problems myself. I don't want your pity!" he snapped.

Her big blue eyes pleaded with him, but she said nothing.

I must be firm, he decided, as his mind searched for a way to change the subject.

"You're wearing a silk nightgown? You spend too much on foolish things."

"The madam—the Pani—gave it to me."

"Again with your madam? I told you I don't want to hear that word any more."

"The Pani gave it to me when I told her I was going to get married."

"So why don't you wait till you're married?"

She nestled her head on his arm. "You are my husband."

"Without a wedding I'm not your husband."

"You said yourself that it's also valid with—I don't even know how to say it—"

It was a hot night in Warsaw. He had gone to bed stark naked. Her soft hair tickled his arm. He was dying to move closer to her. Instead, he sat bolt upright, shouting:

"You're a fool, Kayleh! I've told you before and I'm warning you again! You burned yourself once and now you're crawling back into the fire. And what will you do if your belly starts swelling?"

"That's exatly what I want."

"You do? That's exactly why I'm calling you a fool! Kalman Kalika sent you away once before with a belly and laughed at you."

No longer angry, he pleaded with her: "Run away, Kayleh, before it's too late."

She bit her lips and lay there with her eyes shut tight.

"In Gostinin, you didn't even want to hear my name."

From beneath her closed eyelids, the tears began to roll down her cheeks.

"I'm only thinking of your own good, Kayleh."

"I know you are," she whispered. "I love you, too."

When she had first said those words to him he had almost laughed out loud. Now he was so deeply moved that his skin tingled. Maybe it wasn't so much what she said as how she said it. He had never heard a voice filled with so much love. She opened her eyes and gazed at him through her tears. He had never known eyes that looked at him with such devotion, as though she were about to dissolve into a warm cloud and envelop him. Maybe his mother had once looked at him this way. He didn't remember his mother. Maybe that's why he didn't know how to be kind.

"Kayleh, Kayleh dear, I have my good moments, but I can also be bitter as gall and cruel as a cutthroat." Exhausted, he sank back on the pillow. "I don't trust myself, Kayleh."

"I trust you." She turned and held out her hand to him.

Had her arm always been so shapely, so womanly? As she turned, her breasts moved under the nightgown as if they were calling to him. A pleasant fragrance touched his nostrils. Kayleh didn't use cosmetics. With a skin so fresh, they are superfluous. Had she learned in Warsaw to use perfume, or had the scent of her "madam's" perfume lingered in the nightgown?

"I'm not scaring you away?" he asked, his tone now soft and warm.

She shook her head.

"You're not afraid of me?"

"Without you, life means nothing to me anyway."

Why does the world assume that innocence is foolish? There is so much charm and freshness in her innocence, and in meekness there can be more nobility than in arrogance. He had caused her such shame, yet her troubles had not even left a wrinkle in her pretty face. That face beside him, with its shy smile that trembled between laughter and weeping, made him feel noble and kind, made him feel whole and sure of himself. It reminded him of something that had happened a long, long time ago.

Was he trying to convince himself that Kayleh reminded him of his mother, so he would love her more? He already did love her more, because she made it possible for him to persuade himself this way.

He hated his Grandfather Jonah probably because he hadn't wanted to accept the old man as compensation for his mother. First his father had disappeared, then his mother had gone away and left him alone, all alone. Now he was no longer alone.

"Don't be angry with me," he said suddenly, beseechingly.

"Angry with you?"

"For that time, for all the other times."

He puckered up his lips and she understood the signal. Her lips were moist and warm and full. He pulled her closer so he could kiss away her tears. He felt the contours of her body through the flimsy nightgown and was suddenly filled with longing to look at her, to enjoy her body without any obstructions. He raised his hand to slip off the shoulder strap of her nightgown but was suddenly assailed by her shyness, as if he were still a child, or as if she were his mother. He pulled his hand back, reached over to the other side of the bed and turned out the lamp. In the dark, they both grew bolder. Kayleh's tears flowed copiously that night, and so did his, as if an iceberg around his heart were melting away.

From the hubbub outdoors he judged that it must be quite late. Kayleh was still sleeping the sleep of the righteous. From now on he too would be able to sleep peacefully. A certainty had arisen within him that Kayleh had released him from the nightmares that had tormented him night after night, just as the Rabbi had released him—back then in his *heder*-years—from the nightmares that had regularly assaulted him then. The Rabbi was his father and Kayleh is both his wife and his mother. What charm rested on that innocent little face on the pillow beside him!

Had she felt his gaze upon her even in her sleep? She opened her eyes and greeted him with a smile.

"My husband," she murmured, and began to giggle.

No, it was not a silly schoolgirl giggle. Good people usually laugh a lot.

"My little wife," he responded, and he, too, laughed.

Playfully he threw off the sheet that had covered them both. She pulled it back over herself.

"I'm embarrassed," she said.

"With your own husband?"

Laughing, she shook her head.

"Just one little look," he begged.

"I told you—I'm shy."

"Close your eyes, and you won't see me looking!"

She did close her eyes, but immediately opened them again, no longer embarrassed. They stayed in bed, even though he was supposed to have a meeting that day with his lawyer. Dusk was falling when they finally went to get something to eat.

"Kayleh dear, don't worry, you'll be happy with me."

"I'm happy already."

He had forgotten all about the trouble with his leg. Had it healed overnight?

43

The house was finished, the furniture was already on the way, but Kalman began running a fever again. The doctor ordered him back to the hospital.

"Won't this ever end?" Kalman complained.

"I'm afraid the leg will have to come off . . . "

"Is it a serious operation? The truth, doctor, the truth."

"The truth? Operations are always serious. When an incision is made in the body it's a shock to the entire system. But you're a healthy man."

"How risky is it? At least tell me that."

"Your heart is strong. Barring any unexpected complications, you'll make a quick recovery. But put your home in order. A merchant should always leave precise instructions, so that his people will act in accordance with his wishes."

"That will take me a few days."

"We can't postpone the operation much longer. The gangrene won't wait."

• • • • •

When Kalman went to Lowicz, Matus ran to the synagogue to gather together a minyan. Praying for a cure and reciting psalms was all that was left to do.

"Man proposes and God disposes," one of the worshippers sighed. "Builds Pithom and Raamses and yet his life hangs by a hair."

They were already up to the psalms when Tsippe ran into the synagogue, threw herself upon the Holy Ark and buried her face in its velvet curtain.

"Holy Torahs," she sobbed, "save him! He is my child and my salvation. Sacred scrolls, pray for him!"

Like wildfire the news spread through Dombrovka: Kalman was on his deathbed. People shook their heads sorrowfully. Some even shed a tear.

Kayleh accompanied Kalman to the hospital, but he sent her out of the room when the doctor came to unwrap the bandages.

"Looks bad, but it's still a distance from the knee. We can wait until tomorrow," the surgeon decided.

"Go stay with your relatives," Kalman told Kayleh. "A few hours sleep will do us both good." Neither of them had slept a wink the previous night.

As soon as she left, a small-time broker from Dombrovka came into the room. His name was Fishel, but people called him "little Fishele." His small head was always buzzing with big plans. A glib talker, he was expert at wheedling an advance on the broker's fee out of his clients before it became obvious that his "big deal" would soon burst like a soap bubble.

"I came to Lowicz on account of a terrific business opportunity, but when I heard that Pan Swerdl wasn't well and was also here in Lowicz, I said to myself: After all, we're both from the same town, take an hour off and go see how he's doing. Decency before business . . . "

"Thanks very much," said Kalman. "Nice of you to come. And now you'd better hurry back to your business. I wish you luck."

"Speaking of business, I have an interesting proposition for you too—"

"I'm a sick man. My head is not on business now."

"What I'm about to offer you is good for your health and will even hasten your recovery."

"I accept remedies only from doctors, never from brokers."

"Panie Swerdl, there are remedies that—"

"Panie Fishel, I'm being operated on tomorrow—"

"If you'll just listen to me for a minute, you'll feel better."

"Make it short and snappy. No prologues!"

"Prologues are like appetizers—"

"Get to the point!"

"The lesser leads to the greater—"

"Nurse!" Kalman shouted.

"To the point? Good. The point is that a sick man like you needs someone to take care of him."

"I have, I have—"

"I happen to know that you can't stand them."

"How do you know that?"

"Everybody knows that a wise man can't stand a fool. You're a very wise man, and they are a bunch of simpletons."

"You said you had a proposition."

"I've got a wife for you—she has no equal. Pretty and smart and with all the virtues."

"Thank you very much. I'm not in the market for a wife."

"Nobody is ever in the market for a bargain—it just falls into your lap."

"Come see me when I'm all better."

"My enemies accuse me of exaggerating, so you must be thinking that if Fishel says she's pretty—wait a minute and you can see for yourself."

"Good night! And don't come back!"

Kalman thought he'd gotten rid of his visitor, but the door opened again immediately and Fishel brought in a young woman, not bad looking, but small as a peanut.

"This is my daughter Feyge. Well, what did I tell you?"

"So this is Feyge? She looks more like a *feygele*—no bigger than a bird."

"The Pan wants a tall one, so that he'd have to put on his eyeglasses to see her face?"

"Fishel, even without eyeglasses I can see that you're touched in the head. I'm lying here in such a state and you come bothering me with marriage proposals."

The girl pulled her hand from Fishel's and ran to the door; Fishel remained.

"A clever person like you says that? A sick man needs someone to take care of him even more than a healthy one does. The marriage canopy erases all sins. In a few minutes you can be as free of sin as the most pious *tsaddik.* Now is the time when you can use the mercy of heaven. I've already made inquiries—they can perform the ceremony right here in the hospital."

Only now did it become clear to Kalman what Fishel was trying to accomplish—he wanted a quick inheritance. Was Kalman Kalika's condition really that serious?

"Nurse!" he shouted again. "Nurse! Where are you?"

"So what do you say, Panie Kalman?"

"Nurse! Nurse!"

"I sent her away. I told her I was your Rabbi. You know how they are—the priest is more important to them than the doctor."

"You spoke of sin and holiness, and you yourself are a hypocrite. You want to know what I say? I say you should get out of here. Good night, Fishel!"

"A good night and a good morning," Fishel quipped, disregarding the insult. "I know you wouldn't say no. You're a wise man, Kalman. I'll come back in the morning with Feygele."

"What else, without her?" Kalman retorted with sarcasm.

But next morning, Fishel was back and so was his daughter.

"Kalman my friend, the *dayan* and ten Jews are already waiting. They've brought a canopy, a ring, and all the other things. But the guard won't let them in. Tell the hospital people to let them in."

"I suppose she's been to the *mikveh* too?" Kalman asked derisively.

"Fishel thinks of everything. Would I let my own daughter stand under the canopy when she's not kosher?"

"For God's sake, Fishel! Why have you attached yourself to me like a leech?"

"Is that a nice thing to say to your father-in-law? Didn't I ask you yesterday—yes or no—and didn't you tell me to come back in the morning with Feygele? 'What else, without her?' Those were your very words. You can't say one thing and mean another and disgrace a Jewish daughter. For an insult like that you'd pay a heavy fine. Kalman, a *dayan* and ten Jews are waiting outside."

Kalman suddenly changed his tone. "How do I know she can bear children?"

"Her mother, praise God, had seven—"

"But she's so tiny—"

"Good things come in small packages." Fishel was sure he was about to clinch the deal.

"All right," agreed Kalman. "But first we have to put her to the test. You stay here, Feygele, and send your father away."

Fishel's mouth dropped open.

"And if she actually becomes pregnant, then we'll talk about a wedding."

"Kalman—"

"And to make sure you don't accuse me of cheating you on the price, I'm telling you in advance—your grandson will not only be an orphan, he'll be a penniless orphan, because I've already made my will and given it to a notary public for safekeeping. You came a little bit too late, Fishel."

"You shall have no rest in your grave! How dare you disgrace a Jewish daughter like this? The Angel of Death is right outside your door and here you—"

"The Angel of Death is a cat—he might start with the fish and the little bird—"

Fishel was still in the doorway when they came to prepare Kalman for the operation.

"Not today," said Kalman to the nurse.

"But the doctor said—"

"It's my life and I'm telling you—not today."

As soon as Kayleh walked into his room he told her to take a carriage to Bilkowski's mill, find Berish the Rabbi's son and ask him to come to the hospital at once.

The doctor appealed to Kalman not to postpone the operation. "The condition has worsened. It won't do it any good to wait."

"I've got to make certain arrangements first. If it goes quickly enough you can still operate today. I hope the Pan Doctor can help me find a notary."

"The Pan is taking a big risk."

"A notary public will reduce the risk," Kalman insisted.

The doctor shrugged and went to the door.

"A notary, Panie Doctor, please?"

"I'll see what I can do."

The notary was all set to draw up a lengthy document, but Kalman asked him to make it as brief and uncomplicated as possible. The matter was simple. He was leaving all his possessions to only two individuals. Everything he owned—real estate, merchandise, money, valuables, negotiable paper—was to be divided into two equal shares—one share to his bride Kayleh, who would, God willing, soon be his wife, and the other to her son Zelikl, who was also his son. Until the child came of age, his legal guardians were to be Kayleh, her father, Matus, and Rabbi Yitzhak Landau. Berish Landau, the Rabbi's son, would be the alternate, if any of the three guardians were, for any reason, unable to act in that capacity. An amount for charity should be determined by the executors, in addition to sums to certain individuals whose names he would probably discuss with them. The exact amounts would be left to the discretion of the executors and their decision would be final.

When Kalman finished with the notary, Berish had already brought back the *dayan* and the canopy. Between one sob and another, Kayleh begged them to postpone the ceremony until after the operation; she wanted her parents to be at the wedding. But Kalman refused to postpone it any longer.

"It's important because of the inheritance law," he explained, trying to calm her.

"I need you, not the inheritance."

"It's important for the child," Berish interjected.

"For *our* child," Kalman added.

A wheelchair under a wedding canopy.

They led Kayleh three times around the wheelchair in which Kalman was sitting. His body slumping, he summoned up all his strength and held his head high, resisting the force that was pulling it down toward his chest. Was he so desperately ill, or only exhausted? The thread of his thoughts kept snapping and he could barely catch the torn end and hold on to it. If only he didn't faint before the ceremony was over . . .

The reading of the *ketuba* went on and on. In order to keep his head up Kalman concentrated his gaze on the big round clock that hung on the wall at the other end of the hospital corridor. If only he could turn back the hands of the clock of his life! Would it soon stop altogether? On the other side of time, the laughter of a small boy was waiting for him; was it his child's laughter or was it his own childhood innocence that he left somewhere and that was waiting for him out there, out there . . .

The sound of breaking glass roused him out of his reverie. No, it was not the sound of an ax or a cleaver. Someone, in his stead, had stomped on the glass and now people were showering him with words—mazel-tov, mazel-tov! On all sides they surrounded him with good wishes and blocked out his view of Kayleh. A hospital attendant stood behind his wheelchair.

"Kayleh! Kayleh!" he called. Berish took Kayleh by the hand and opened a path for her to the chair.

"Mazel-tov, my wife, mazel-tov, Pani Swerdlowa," Kalman smiled, hoping to bring an answering smile to her face. "Don't be scared, Kayleh, your husband has been in worse straits than this and come out alive . . . "

He seized Berish's hand. "I don't know what I'd have done without you. You've been like a brother to me—the only one here from the groom's side. And please tell the Rabbi—I don't know how to say it—tell him I owe him a lot—"

Doors opened like a massive gate and closed behind the wheelchair, leaving Berish and Kayleh standing on the other side.

"Shall I ever see him again?" Kayleh sobbed.

"With God's help," Berish murmured, "with God's help."

44

Had God listened to Little Fishel when he said a wedding canopy be the best remedy and erase all of Kalman's sins? His leg, after festering for so many months, was healing very nicely. The doctor said that if it continued like this he could go home in a few days. He was still weak, but every day he felt a bit better and a little stronger and his head was again full of plans.

Berish visited him almost every day. In the bustle and commotion before the operation, he had thought only about himself, but now he began to notice that it wasn't the same Berish. His face was drawn, his clothes looked too big for him, and he rarely smiled.

"Don't the Bilkowskis give you enough to eat? You've gotten skinny in this Lowicz."

"They eat very well at the Bilkowskis and the cook at the inn where I'm staying doesn't skimp on the food either."

"You're not living with the Bilkowskis?"

"When I was a visitor here it was different. Now I live here. Only yeshiva boys eat in people's homes. I have a job and I'm earning money."

"And how are things at the mill?"

"It wouldn't be right for me to reveal my employer's secrets to his competitor."

"I couldn't care less about your employer as a competition. I only wanted to know how you yourself are doing. May I speak to you as a friend?"

"Certainly. How I'm doing? I myself don't even know that answer."

"Not easy to become a merchant overnight, eh?"

"Reb Moyshe is satisfied with my work."

"So who's not satisfied?"

"Did I say somebody wasn't satisfied?"

"I want us to be close and trusting friends. You know that I feel like a brother to you, Berish. Do you visit the Bilkowskis often?"

"No, not often."

"You don't? Aren't his daughter and son-in-law your friends?"

"A dark shadow has come between me and Yudel, and I don't know what it is."

"In the mill—are things going well?"

"Yes."

"The old man likes you?"

"He likes my work."

"If you do better work in the mill than his son-in-law, that could be the dark shadow. How's Yudel's work?"

"He's a capable man. If he ever puts his mind to it, I'm sure he'll be successful. But for the time being, he'd rather write poems. He's a talented writer."

"I'm afraid your friend begrudges you your success in the mill."

"But we were such close friends."

"As long as you were admiring his poems."

"I still do."

"Maybe the old man said something about your being better suited to the mill than his son-in-law. Yudel is accustomed to people saying nice things about him, making a fuss about him. Now all of a sudden you're his dangerous competition. And how are you doing with the other daughter?—if you feel you can speak openly to me about it."

"Itka? I don't go there often, so I don't often see her."

"You could arrange to meet outside somewhere, if you wanted to."

"If I wanted to . . . "

"I thought you were serious about her—"

"It's a long way from being serious. She already told me to get rid of my Jewish hat and shorten my jacket. We once met her girl-friends from the *gymnazie* on the street—I could sense that she was embarrassed to be seen with me in my Hassidic garb."

"I had the impression that wearing Hassidic clothing wasn't that important to you."

"It's too complicated to go into now. In general, I guess the father likes me better than the daughter does."

"And that bothers you? You can tell me."

"I think Yudel's coolness bothers me more. He was my first and only friend . . . Or maybe I'm just homesick."

"Then go home."

"I will, for the holidays, but I'm not about to run away from something I undertook to do."

"Don't forget, Berish—you have a friend in Dombrovka named Kalman. I hope I can be as good a friend to you as Yudel was before this thing came between you."

45

It turned out that Kalman had been right about the sugar factory. Located far from a rail-line, the houses were cheap; and surrounded by many farmers' villages, food was cheap, too, and so was labor, so much so that it compensated for the extra expense of transporting the finished sugar to the railroad station. There was now a constant flurry of activity on the roads around Dombrovka. Draft horses with heavy legs pulled wagons overloaded with white sugar beets to and from the factory—grated beets dripping juice. Before the sweet effluence could congeal on the highway it was wiped up by the wide rubber tires of the trucks transporting the sacks of sugar to the railroad platforms in Lowicz and Sochachow. The townspeople said that Dombrovka sugar was already sailing across the oceans to far-off lands. Pan Swerdl had been sick, his soul had fluttered between life and death; when had he negotiated all these contracts with the foreign companies?

At first many people didn't know who this "Pan Swerdl" was. Kalman had grown up in Dombrovka, but no one knew his surname. They had called his grandfather "Old Jonah" and the grandson "Old Jonah's Kalman," or "Kalman Kalika." But who could be on a first name basis with a man who builds factories, does business abroad, and rides around in his own automobile? Yes, Kalman, that is, Pan Swerdl, already had his own automobile, equipped so he could drive it himself, even though he couldn't bend his knees and a piece of his right leg was missing. Nothing, at least, was missing from his head, thank God. So he was a frequent visitor at the plant, and the villagers were already beginning to call him "Panie Dziedzicu" —Pan Squire.

In the Dombrovka synagogue they were predicting that Pan Swerdl, who was a Davidson, would yet bring that name back to the court. They also began calling Matus "Reb Matus." They couldn't stop marveling at his good luck with his sons-in-law and with his business affairs. For the last several years the man who had rented the squire's orchard had been losing money in the business. The first year there was no rain, the second year there was not enough sun, the third year a storm tore all the blossoms off the trees. But with Reb Matus, as the saying goes, "When your luck is running, your ox can calve." How long ago was it that Tsippe used to run around bemoaning her "hidden secret?" Who would ever have believed that such salvation would come out of it? When the One Above wants to send you a blessing, it enters through the door and the chimney.

The whole world was in a deep economic crisis, but in Dombrovka, things couldn't be better. New settlers had come, with new occupations. Pan Swerdl was earning so much money that people uttered his name with reverence, with Reb Matus also sharing the honor.

There weren't enough wagon drivers to cart away all the produce from the orchard, so Kalman sent a truck from the factory. Matus ordered big copper kettles from Moyshe Longlegs, his in-law, and from Lazer the Blacksmith, iron tripods. There was plenty of overripe fruit, there was plenty of sugar, so day and night they cooked preserves. In Warsaw Kayleh had learned to make preserves that tasted like nectar and ambrosia. Tsippe kept cautioning her not to bend over too much; she looked as if she were already in her third month.

Kayleh worried a lot about this; she couldn't forget what had happened in Warsaw. She even whined about it to Kalman. "If the child is born in the eighth month, what will we tell Melech and Leybl?"

"You're big because you're carrying twins. My Grandmother Libe had three sets of twins," he consoled her.

"And if they're not twins?" She was certain that Kalman could do everything, even extend her pregnancy.

"I'm building an empire and I've got to establish a dynasty. It must be twins! Every year a set of twins, yes, Kayleh?"

An entire kibbutz of young Zionists from Lowicz was now working in the orchard. What a bunch! Did they never sleep? By day they worked, by night they danced around a campfire in the middle of the field. Saturday they held special meetings where they discussed, argued, sometimes quarreled heatedly—and danced again. A peculiar lot . . .

Lately Raizel hadn't been dancing with them very often. Her face was tanned by the sun, but it had a greenish hue and she loooked haggard.

"Are you angry with me?" Kalman asked her one day when he came to take Kayleh home.

"Angry? Why should I be angry with you?"

"You never come to visit us any more."

"There's so much to do in the orchard."

"What does Zalman write you?"

"He doesn't write."

"What's wrong? You've quarreled?"

"No, we haven't."

"Then why doesn't he write?"

"Ask him."

"If you wish, I'll write to him."

"He doesn't answer my letters—why should he answer yours?"

"You still love him? You don't have to be ashamed to tell me."

"Ever since he played for the president, he's not the same Zalman."

"Raizele, I don't want to hurt you, but you've got to look the truth in the face. Are you certain he doesn't have someone else?"

"I told you he's in love—with his violin."

"It's a match made in heaven."

"Who? Zalman and his fiddle?"

"You and Berish, the Rabbi's son. He looks the same as you now—pale and haggard. He's homesick, he says. You and I know who he's really homesick for. He's coming home for the holidays."

"And the Panna Bilkowski?"

"By this time she must have realized that his heart is in Dombrovka."

46

When Kalman appeared in the synagogue, a buzz went through the congregation. This was the first time he had attended services on Rosh Hashonah since Old Jonah died. Moyshe Longlegs wanted to show him to a seat of honor at the eastern wall, but Kalman kept insisting that he would be more comfortable close to the door, where he could sit in his wheelchair. Moyshe finally gave in.

For Kayleh, however, Kalman had bought a seat in the Women's Section, close to the wives of the Rabbi and the *gabbai*—the trustee. Even for Tsippe he bought a seat among the notables; after all, she was related to the *gabbai* by marriage.

It happened that the *baal-tokea* was having trouble sounding the shofar, the ram's horn, as if Satan himself had crawled into the instrument and wouldn't let a sound come out of it. Another man tried; perhaps it was clogged up, but he had no more success than the first one.

The shofar is sounded in the synagogue all through the month of Elul. On weekdays sometimes Matus was called on to fulfill that obligation. In this emergency they called on him again. He stepped up on the *bima*, wiped the shofar with his tallis, blew into the opposite end to clear it out, and then wiped it again. When he finally put the mouthpiece to his lips and the Rabbi uttered the instruction *"T'keyah!"* —a clear, perfect note came forth, and then he blew the entire series of notes without faltering. Kalman was delighted with his father-in-law's performance.

At the end of the service, Berish came up to wish Kalman a good year.

"Where are you going tomorrow for the *Tashlikh* prayers?" Kalman asked him.

"Where everybody else goes—to the river."

"There's a stream that runs through the squire's orchard, it's a branch of the Nida. Matus and his family will be there for *Tashlikh*.

"I always go with my father."

"The orchard would be too far for the Rabbi to walk. You could come over after *Tashlikh*."

Together with all of Matus's family, Kalman went to Freydl's for the holiday meal. Before they sat down at the table, Kalman whispered to Raizele:

"Berish will be coming to the orchard after *Tashlikh*."

"How do you know?"

"He asked me if you'd be there, so I know he'll come."

On the first day of Rosh Hashonah it rained. On the second day the Rabbi didn't feel well and Berish couldn't leave him. The day after Rosh Hashonah being the fast of Gedaliah, he stayed on in Dombrovka and went over to Kalman's to explain why he hadn't come to the orchard. Kalman took him for a ride in his new automobile to see the mill he was building and the sugar factory that was working at full steam. On the way back, he stopped at the orchard.

"You'll have to walk home, though," he told Berish. "I've got some business to attend to in the village."

Berish apparently had no objections to that.

When Berish came by, Raizel was stirring a kettle of prune jam with a stick.

"Goodness! What a state you've found me in!" she exclaimed, pulling at her dress from all sides.

"I shouldn't have dropped in on you like this without any notice, but it's not entirely my fault. Kalman let me off here."

"If it's against your will, you don't have to stay."

"If I'm an unwelcome guest," Berish said, his face darkening.

"What are you talking about? I heard you were here in town, but I didn't know whether you'd take the time to visit an old friend."

"A young old friend."

"Why are we standing here over this pot? I'll bring out a chair. The grass is still wet from the rain."

Why sit when we can take a walk, he wanted to say, but she had already run into the house. Of course they couldn't take a walk now—that stuff in the pot might burn.

When Raizel came out with the chair, she was wearing a different dress. The one she'd had on before was made of some coarse, stiff material. She had changed to a frock that clung lovingly to her graceful lines. The short sleeves revealed a pair of shapely, suntanned arms.

"Why don't we go for a little walk," she said. "It's a big orchard."

"I haven't even been away three months but it seems like three years." Berish's voice was suffused with nostalgia as he walked beside her.

"In the meantime," she grinned, "I've become an old maid."

"And an ugly one at that," he grinned back.

"Really?" There was apprehension in her tone.

"And a foolish one, too—if you're taking me seriously."

She grew pensive and put a serious look on her face.

"I'm confused," she said. "If it's foolish to think I'm ugly, it must be because I'm pretty. Shall I be pleased that I am pretty, or sorry that I am foolish?"

"Raizel, this kind of quibbling is more appropriate for a yeshiva student than a—a—." He suddenly grew tired of making these disguised compliments, but didn't know how to steer the conversation onto another track. "Raizel, you left the jam unattended. It won't burn?"

"No, the *powidla* is finished and the fire is out by now. You'll have to taste it when it cools."

"Today is Tzom Gedaliah, you know—"

"You're fasting?"

"No. But just to nosh? Today is a fast, and it is supposed to be a sad day."

"A sad day in the middle of the holidays. Are you staying here for the entire ten days?"

"I'm going back tomorrow. But I'll be here again for Yom Kippur."

"I see you can't wait to go back."

"What makes you think that?"

"The big city and its temptations—"

"Some big city! Lowicz is not Warsaw, though compared to Dombrovka it's a metropolis."

"Yes. I don't know why I stay in this godforsaken place. Do you think I could find a job in Lowicz?"

"If you're looking for a big city, why don't you go to Warsaw itself?"

"You went to Lowicz—"

"I went to Lowicz because I had a friend and a job waiting there for me. In Warsaw I have no one."

"I don't have anyone in Warsaw either. In Lowicz I at least have an aquaintance."

"Yes, you have me in Lowicz . . . " He smiled. How ironic!

The look on Raizel's face changed completely. The current expression, "I have you in Lowicz," meant: I couldn't care less what happens to you. A sort of euphemism for "I don't give a damn about you." Berish tried to explain. "I didn't mean it the way it sounds."

"If that was your idea of a joke—"

Was there a complaint against him festering deep inside her that leaped out in those words? When he had first become aware of his feelings toward her, all she ever talked about was Zalman Pitel. As for Berish, "she had him in Lowicz."

She walked along beside him without saying a word. Unlike Panna Bilkowska, she had never been a student in the Gymnasium. Nor did she have a rich father. Still, Matus's daughters had their pride.

"Don't be angry with me, Raizel. Part of me is still a yeshiva student, it's easier for me to talk about a passage of Talmud than to carry on a conversation with a girl. You're the first girl I've ever tried to get close to—and here I've insulted you twice already—"

And what about Panna Bilkowska, she wanted to ask him. But how could she ask him directly?

"In Lowicz you must meet lots of girls, educated girls that you can even discuss Talmud with—sorry Berish, I don't mean—I say silly things."

"So do I." Berish was still unhappy with himself. Their conversation had gotten stuck in a blind alley. He didn't know what else to say. For a while they were both silent. They had walked down to the river, where there was a bench. Raizel wiped it with her palm, sat down and looked up at him expectantly. Berish remained silent.

"If you've still got the patience, please tell me more about this fast day. In the Polish school they don't teach any Jewish history, and in the Jewish library they have only novels and poems. Or maybe I was looking only for novels and poems. In any case, about Jewish history I don't know much more than a Gentile."

The cloud lifted from Berish's face. He sat down beside her on the bench. He didn't know how to make small talk with a girl, but with Jewish history he was on familiar ground.

"That's really the purpose of the Jewish holidays and fast days," he began. "So children will ask questions and the father will answer."

"You're too young to be a father. In the meantime, maybe you can be a teacher—my teacher?" A smile lit up her face like sun after rain. "I don't know much more than a child," she added, "but I do have a desire to learn."

"It's easier to teach a child." He hesitated. "With a pupil like you, it'll be harder for me to concentrate . . . "

He hoped she wouldn't take offense at that. Had he again put his foot in his mouth? He looked up at her—she was smiling at him. As though they could read each other's minds, they both stood up at the same instant and continued their walk. Suddenly she burst out laughing, just for the fun of it, like a bird who bursts into song. It didn't even occur to him to ask her why she was laughing. Her smiling face was answer enough and they both enjoyed the moment, as if they had been telling each other something and only understood it that instant. He helped her jump over a ditch and his face turned crimson when he took her hand.

"What were we talking about?"

"About the fast day," she said.

"About a pupil like you," he smiled.

"With an empty head."

"With a head of golden hair . . . "

"Did you say you don't know how to talk to a girl? You're a regular flirt."

Berish felt a little peeved that she had interrupted him, that she took him for a common flirt. "Do I know what I'm saying? I hear everybody else say 'golden hair,' so I said it too."

"Berish, that was my unfunny joke. Now we're even."

She still wanted to know about the fast day, however, so he began by telling her the story of the King of Judeah who had not taken the advice of the Prophet Jeremiah and how this had led to a war with the King of Babylonia, a war that Judeah lost. King Jehoiachin and many Jews were taken captive to Babylonia. The conquerors appointed Gedaliah ben Ahikam to govern Judeah, but a band of rebels joined forces with the King of Ammon and killed Gedaliah, and this led Babylonia to drive the last Jews out of the country.

He talked and talked and hoped that she would again break into laughter, which would enable him to loosen up and speak to her more freely. But he had gotten all tangled up in a skein of historical details and she was listening quietly and attentively. In the middle of a sentence he interrupted himself:

"The rest of the story will have to wait until Tsom Gedaliah next year."

"You said before that we have the fast days so that people will ask questions and learn about their meaning. Well, we've already done that, so maybe we can stop now and eat some of the jam? We've walked and talked and here we are back at the pot of *powidla!*"

Her smile made his spirits soar.

"A fast day should be a painful one; on that score I've already transgressed." He wanted to add that just being with her was a pleasure for him, but couldn't get the words out.

"I thank you very much," she smiled. "For me too it was *przyjemnie*—how do you say that in Yiddish?"

"Pleasant, pleasurable, delightful—and as soon as you say it, it will be *przyjemnie* for me too."

As he said it, he worried that she would think he was mocking her use of Polish words, but her lovely face lit up in a smile.

"Are you really going back tomorrow?" she asked.

"I've got to get an early start, but I'll be home for Yom Kippur."

"Yom Kippur I won't offer you any preserves!"

"Yom Kippur, before you finish one prayer you start another one. I'll be in the synagogue all day long."

"A pity. When will you teach me something about Yom Kippur? *Przepraszam*—forgive me, I know Yom Kippur is a very holy day and you won't talk to girls. But you did say that feast and fast days were made so people would ask questions . . . "

"In the days of our Holy Temple, the young fellows and girls danced in the gardens of Jerusalem on Yom Kippur—the maidens in their white dresses—and they made new friendships—"

"The orchard belongs to the squire, but ever since Tateshi took it over it has become a second Jerusalem. I'll borrow a white dress . . . "

She flushed a bright red and stopped talking. What was happening to her? She was being too forward. Was it only a flirtation?

"That's interesting!" Berish exclaimed. "The maidens in Jerusalem wore borrowed dresses too. It was the custom. So that girls who were too poor and had to wear borrowed things should not be humiliated . . ."

She barely heard what he was saying, so intent was she on her own thoughts. It couldn't be only revenge on Zalman, she was too happy, and she wanted to see Berish again. She had been so cool to him; now she wanted him to know her feelings were different.

"Does it have to be only new friendships? I mean in Jerusalem. No, I mean here. From a distance I've known you all my life, but our real friendship is not an old one yet, so it's kosher for Yom Kippur."

"I'll be here again for Succos and stay the whole week of the holiday. Maybe after services on Yom Kippur I'll manage to drop in on Pan Kalman."

"Oh, yes. Kalman thinks very highly of you. When I didn't agree immediately with all the nice things he said about you, he was angry with me."

"I don't know that I deserve all of Kalman's praises, but I won't mind at all if he convinces you—"

"Believe me, Panie Berish. I'm not used to flirting with young men either, but you see, both of us are making progress."

Berish looked at his watch. It was almost time for *minchah*. On a fast day they read the Torah at the *minchah* service. Raizel knew it wasn't proper for the Rabbi's son to be seen with a girl, especially on a fast day. She accompanied him only as far as the gate of the orchard and held out her hand.

"It was *przyjemnie*—I mean, I enjoyed our conversation very much. After services on Yom Kippur I'll be at Kalman's."

47

Kalman left the house and was about to slide into his automobile when he noticed a young woman walking in his direction. Small, but cute, he said to himself; tiny, but every inch a woman . . . If only she were wearing a more becoming dress . . . Dombrovka was a small place and he didn't recognize her, but her face was somehow familiar. Wait a minute, wait a minute.

"Feygele?" he called out as she passed by him. She turned. Yes, it was Feygele, little Fishel's daughter. "Feygele, come over here, please. I want to ask you something."

She approached him and waited. But he didn't know what to ask her. Her father was an observant Jew but she was wearing neither a wig nor a bonnet; that could only mean she was still unmarried.

"Feygele, that time in Lowicz," he said finally, "a miracle happened to both of us. I was cured of my illness and you, Miss, you know that your father was trying to use you to get a quick inheritance and you could have wound up the wife of a cripple for the rest of your life."

"You wanted to ask me something?"

"I only wanted to tell you that your father is capable of ruining your life. You're a very pretty girl—how come you're not married yet?"

"Beautiful mazel, luck, is worth more than a beautiful face."

"Mazel, shlemazel! A person's luck rests in his own hands, you hear? Not in your father's, but in your own! If you let him—"

"My father has a sick wife, and nine mouths to feed, rent to pay, tuition for the children—"

"Feygele, you don't have to pretend to me. My own father is no one to brag about."

"My Tateshi is a good man. If he could do it, he'd fetch the moon in the sky for me."

"Tell your father, Miss, when he stops chasing after the moon in the sky he'll be better able to put bread on the table in the kitchen. A zloty here, a zloty there, is better than a cow who jumps over the moon, and even better than a thousand zloty in imaginary broker's fees."

"Panie Swerdl, you don't know my father. Without luck you have no bread and no honor, either."

"You're already a grown-up, Feygele, a small grown-up," he smiled. "Why don't you go to work?"

"I want to."

"But?"

"Because of my sick mother I can't leave the house. And here in Dombrovka, what kind of work could I find, anyway? At first, Tateshi refused to let me become a housemaid. Finally, he agreed. But big strong girls come here from all over the country. People think that small hands do less work than big ones."

"Why wouldn't your Tateshi want you to be a housemaid? Was he afraid it would spoil your chances for a rich husband?"

Feygele blanched.

"There's no work that is as menial as an empty plate, or as sad as a stove without fire or as unpleasant as the grumbling of a hollow belly . . ."

"It's easy for you to talk, Pan Swerdl. You have cars to ride around in."

Kalman's tone softened. "Pani Swerdlowa was a housemaid too. Now she rides around in her own automobile. If you're ready to work as a housemaid, come tomorrow and talk with my wife. Tell her I sent you. I do know you a little bit, Miss," he added with a smile, "I'll give you a good recommendation."

Feygele turned to walk away. He called after her: "I mean it seriously. You could show your father how to earn an honest zloty."

The young woman left without a thank-you. Kalman suspected that she didn't believe his promise. As he got into his auto, he laughed to himself. Listen to this saint who tells people how to earn an honest zloty! You, Kalman, were a crook in your mother's belly. How old were you altogether when you started "borrowing" your grandfather's cash? And the generating station—was that built with your hard-earned money or was it the "profit" from a crafty little barkruptcy?

Actually, it didn't bother him very much that Fishel was a cheat. But why did he have to be such a stupid and foolish one? How had that famous pickpocket put it? Stealing is an art and you can be proud of it; the trouble is that every bungler who's caught with his hand in somebody's pocket calls himself "*ganef*" and ruins the reputation of the whole craft.

•　　•　　•　　•　　•

Kalman was at home reading a newspaper when Keyla ran in to ask him:

"Talman, you hired a new housemaid?"

"Me? Where did you get—oh! it must be little Fishel's daughter. She's in urgent need of a job."

"How many servants do I need? I lite to do something in the titchen myself."

"Let her help you with Chaya and little Zelikl. All the fancy madames have someone for the children nowadays."

"I'm not a fancy madame and Zelitl is *t'n'hora* big enough to tate tare of himself. And Chaya is too young yet."

"Kayleh dear, her mother is a very sick woman. They have nothing to eat in that house."

Kayleh's heart softened. She went back to the kitchen.

Kalman *Mamzer,* he said to himself. Isn't this the same kind of "generosity" you once showed to Breindl? You're a father now, you want to build a dynasty—and you're going to kick up your heels again and upset the whole pail of milk?

Kayleh came back into the sitting room. "Her father is a broter, she says. Tan't you find something for him too?"

"Kayleh, you have more sense than I do! Give her something to eat and then send her in here." Kayleh was almost at the door when he called her back. "Did you notice what she's wearing? Find something for her that she can make over. She's old enough to be a bride and she's wearing rags."

When Feygele came in Kalman had a plan all ready.

"Do you know little Berele?"

"The coachman?"

"Yes. He was once a porter and dragged big heavy bundles on his little back from one place to another. First he bought a little horse and built himself a little wagon. Now he has four wagons and three horses."

"Why is Pan telling me this?"

"I think your father is right. Being a housemaid will hurt your chances of making a good marriage."

Feygele's head dropped.

"I'm prepared to help your father, Miss. I'm ready to help him get on his feet, the way I helped Berele. Tell him to come and see me."

•　　•　　•　　•　　•

When Kalman made his proposal to Fishel, the little broker shrugged and waved his little hand in the air.

"Berele is a porter, a simple creature."

He could not understand how Kalman could compare him to Berele. Fishel assumed the stance of a philosopher giving a lecture.

"You see, Panie Swerdl, there are various kinds of people in the world, just as there are various kinds of animals. The horse, the donkey, and the camel earn their feed with only one part of the body—the back. So does Berele. He was born, like a donkey, to carry a load. As the saying goes, 'k'chamor l'maseh,' like a donkey to its burden. Of a higher order is the species that earns its bread with a greater number of bodily parts—the ten fingers. But there is an even higher order than that. Again, it earns its bread with only one part of the body—the highest and most estimable—the head. You understand my meaning, Panie Swerdl?"

"I understand you perfectly, but there's one thing you didn't tell me: to which order do you belong?"

Fishele merely pointed to his head.

"And here I thought your Feygele was asking me to help you. If you've got such a brain, and with the brain one can earn a good living, what more do you need?"

"I need a little mazel, and in Dombrovka you've cornered the market on that commodity."

"Why don't you demand your share of it? Summon me to the Rabbi! Take me to court. A man with brains shouldn't let himself be cheated."

"To court? Me? I'm not looking for a fight. Through peaceful means you can get anything you want from me. You know, of course, that I have a claim against you for that breach of promise—and it's not a trivial matter. But did I go to the Rabbi with it? Did I drag you into court? I knew your conscience wouldn't let you ignore such a thing."

"Fishel, from now on I shall talk to you only in the presence of the Rabbi or in court."

"What are you saying? What's going on here?"

"You're the one that's going—now!"

"And what am I taking with me?"

"The same thing you came in with."

"Gevalt! A thing like this hasn't happened since the world was created! You know that I earn my living by brokering and any minute some deal can come up, and yet you bring me here for nothing and waste my time while the other brokers are working on my customers. Do you at least know how much I could have earned in that hour?"

"Certainly I know. Exactly the same as you earned in the previous hour. Bring reliable witnesses to testify how much you earned in the hour before you came here and I'll pay you the exact sum—in cash. Take this into your ministerial head, Fishel: if you don't stop being a nuisance, a leech, an affliction, a real pain in the neck, then don't ever dare cross my doorstep again!"

"Panie Kalman—"

Kalman's voice rose as he jabbed his finger at his guest: "Once before I had you thrown out!"

"But you told Feygele you would help me," he pleaded.

"So long as the little fish with the small head rides on a big horse and brandishes his sword, I don't even want to know him."

"Panie Kalman, I won't say another word. You tell me what you had in mind when you asked me to come here."

"What I had in mind? A little while ago you told me the pretty parable of the horse and the donkey. Now I'll remind you of the one about the camel. You, who consider yourself such a big scholar, must remember the quip in the Gemarah: 'The camel went looking for horns, so he lost his ears too.' If you finally understand that you won't get any horns from me, you can come to my office tomorrow. And bring your daughter along. I don't mind telling you, Fishel— she has more sense than you do."

Feygele arrived at Kalman's factory with her father. Kalman had a whole plan worked out for her. They must buy themselves a small horse and cart. Berele could help them do that. Kalman would pay for it—up to one hundred and fifty zloty. In addition, he would give them credit in the factory for another hundred. The factory would sell them merchandise wholesale. Fishel could sell it in the nearby villages to stores and to wealthy farmers.

"I won't even earn enough for the water in my soup," Fishel grumbled.

"Nobody's forcing you, Reb Fishel. Go in good health."

"I need a few zloty to pay an advance—"

"For what?"

"For the horse and cart."

"Not a grosh. The seller will have to come and show me the merchandise."

A couple of days later Fishel came for the hundred and fifty zloty—he had found a horse and cart.

"I will give the money only to the man who's selling you the goods. Let him bring the horse and cart here."

"Panie Kalman, you're doing a good deed—why do you have to tack a sin onto it? You are humiliating me. I'm the father of the household. You know how terrible a sin it is to embarrass a person. It's like drawing his blood."

"Fishel, start in again with your slippery tricks, and the deal is off! If I have to throw you out just once more, you'll never get inside my house again, I'm giving you fair warning."

"Panie Swerdl—"

"Exactly as I've laid it out. That's my proposition. If you feel this humiliates you, let's forget the whole thing."

Fishel scratched his beard. Afraid to say anything more, he left without a word. But a few minutes later he was back.

"If the Pan will look out the window he'll see my new horse and wagon. I only have to pay the one hundred and fifty zloty."

The horse and cart looked familiar. Berele himself was sitting on the coachbox holding the reins. Beside him sat Feygele.

"Berele's?" Kalman asked.

"As soon as I pay him the money, it's mine."

"When did you buy it from him?"

"This morning. Berele has trips to make. I can't keep him waiting."

"Send him in to me for the money."

"He has to watch the horse."

"You can do that."

"Me? The horse doesn't even know me."

"So go out and tell Berele to introduce you formally."

"You may laugh at me now, but I am scared, horses have such big teeth."

"The horse won't eat you."

"You don't trust me? Send the money out with one of your people to put it right in Berele's hand."

"Fishele, by this time you ought to know that I can be just as stubborn as you. Send Berele in here or the deal is off."

Again Fishel scratched his beard. "As you wish," he said resignedly and went out. After an inordinately long time he came back in with Berele.

"What took you so long?" Kalman wanted to know. "You haven't agreed on a price yet? What's going on here, Berele?"

"The thing is this, Panie Swerdl. Fishel comes and says you sent him to me about getting a horse. So—"

"I told him to ask you for advice about a horse and wagon."

"He did. But one word leads to another. He wants a small horse like mine. He's scared of a big one, he says. He wants to know whether horses bite. I can see he's really scared to go near the animal, so I thought—for me a big horse would be better."

"So you sold him your horse and cart?"

"Not him. His daughter."

"Fishel, you're not going to saddle Feygele with that horse and cart?"

"Panie Swerdl, my daughter and I will work that out between us."

"Berele, are you getting a good price for it, at least? Don't depend on his fairness."

"He bargained with me, but we came to an agreement."

"If I remember correctly, you paid a hundred for that horse."

"You loaned me a hundred. I paid eighty-five."

"Today it must be worth more."

"The horse isn't any younger."

"So how much did you ask him for? For the horse and the wagon."

"The thing is this—er, um—Fishel said you would give me one hundred and fifty zloty—"

Kalman caught Fishel's wink to Berele, saw him tug at Berele's elbow. Why was Berele hemming and hawing?

"Berele, tell me straight! How much are you getting for the horse and cart?"

"Also a whip and a sack of oats and—"

"I'm not asking you, Fishel! Berele, I want you to tell me: how much are you getting for everything—including the whip and the feed?"

"Panie Kalman, you know me—I wouldn't skin anybody. But Fishel—Fishel is paying a hundred and fifty—"

"Is it worth a hundred and fifty? You I trust, Berele."

"Fishel is not buying it from me."

"Didn't you tell me it was your horse and cart?"

"Of course it's mine. Well, it is and it isn't. I mean, it is mine, but I'm selling it to his daughter and he's buying it from her for a hundred and fifty."

"Ah! Now I see. He can swear that he agreed to pay one hundred fifty zloty. And how much did the daughter and you settle for?"

Berele didn't know what to say. Kalman saw Fishel step on Berele's foot.

"Berele," he insisted, "how much will be left for you out of the whole transaction?"

"Eighty-five zloty."

Kalman turned angrily toward Fishel. "And I wanted to teach you how to earn your living honestly!"

"In what book of learning is it written that what you earn from your own daughter is not honest? And since when is an outsider permitted to interfere in a business deal between a father and his daughter?"

"Get the hell out of here!" Kalman shouted.

"You promised me one hundred fifty zloty. Your word should be your bond. A real merchant doesn't act this way—"

"Get out! This minute!"

Fishel turned on his heel and left.

An hour later, Feygele came back alone.

"Panie Swerdl, tell the Pani to hire me. I'll scrub floors. I'll do the heaviest work. I can't stand it any longer!" Her voice shook, her eyes were red and swollen.

Kalman felt sorry for her. "You want that horse, Feygele? Buy it. But you buy it. I'll give you the money. But you can't go out peddling in the villages all by yourself. You're young and pretty. There's no use asking for trouble. You'll have to take your father along. Unless it happens that you get married. If you do, I'll help you find a place to live. And furniture for your home."

He unlocked his drawer and counted out eighty-five zloty, then continued counting to one hundred fifty. As he handed her the money, Feygele grabbed his hand and kissed it. Her eyes overflowed. Embarrassed, she ran out of the room.

Why have I suddenly grown so magnanimous, Kalman wondered. Is it because she's small and pretty—like Breindl? Breindl was smart and vivacious and had a good sense of humor. He didn't know whether Feygele was smart, but she always seemed so sad. Breindl had brought the sound of laughter into that gloomy house of Old Jonah. She had come into the house with laughter and left in tears; she had entered full of life and left as a broken cripple.

Could he be helping Feygele because she reminded him of Breindl? Was he trying to compensate for that other sin? He ought to look Breindl up and do something for her.

48

In Lowicz, the day before Yom Kippur, one of the mill workers caught his arm in a transmission belt. They were able to shut off the power in time to save the man's life, but his arm was almost completely severed.

With the emergency of getting the man to the hospital, Berish lost track of the time. When he caught the coach to Dombrovka, it was already late afternoon. He had not washed or changed his clothes and came home covered in dust; even his eyebrows were white with the powder from the mill.

"Well, did you need this?" his mother chided him. "You could be sitting and studying and preparing to walk in your father's footsteps. A rabbi is king in his own country."

"Mameshi, the age of monarchy is over. The few kings still left are sitting on shaky thrones."

"Don't be so clever with me. You know very well what I mean. Look at the respect everyone has for your father."

"Tateshi is one of the lucky ones. Most rabbis have to put up with one kind of feud or another."

"People love your father and they'd love you too. You're just like him."

"People love Tateshi, yes, but not enough to provide him with a decent livelihood. You think I don't know how hard it is for you to buy yourself a new dress once in a while?"

"Dombrovka is a small town. Tateshi could have gotten a better post, but he's a stubborn man, may God not punish me for saying so."

"Mameshi, it's the eve of Yom Kippur, the Day of Atonement, and I don't want to cause you any aggravation, but you must know that I'm just as stubborn as Tateshi. I don't want to be a rabbi. Tateshi knows how I feel and he doesn't insist upon it—do you know why?"

"Don't think it doesn't hurt him."

"Tateshi knows that although I'm an observant Jew, that's not sufficient for a rabbi. They say that in other countries rabbis go to the university, they study secular subjects. They even allow themselves to speak with women. Here they would drive a rabbi out for doing such things."

"Oh? Speaking with women? Is it that? You must be talking about Moyshe Bilkowski's daughter. If you're thinking of getting married, that's another story altogether. But for a young man who's preparing to become a rabbi—"

"To be a miller—"

"Are you serious about her?"

"About who?"

"Reb Moyshe's daughter."

"You think I went to Lowicz because of Reb Moyshe's daughter?"

"It's not such a bad idea. You could come into an estate."

"Who told you I want to come into that estate?"

"Berish, I'm your mother—you don't have to be ashamed to tell me."

"Mameshi, where did you get the idea that I was looking for an estate? Wealth is not my idea of high society. The home of the Dombrovka Rabbi, even with its leaking roof, means more to me than Pan Bilkowski's palace, and the Dombrovka Rabbi certainly has more nobility."

"Her family isn't good enough for you?"

"And you, Mameshi, you would approve of such a match for me? Itka Bilkowski will never put on a wig, and I'm not even sure of some of the other, stricter things."

"Then why are you staying in that Lowicz place? Oh! It's time to set the table. You still have time to run over to the bathhouse. At least wash up, Tateshi will be here any minute."

·　·　·　·　·

Before going to services on the eve of the Great Day of Judgment, it was the Rabbi's custom to bless his children. Placing his hands on Berish's head, he prayed:

"May you find favor in the eyes of the One Above and of people here on earth; may you succeed in everything you do, but may you always remain a God-fearing man and never abandon our Torah . . ."

In the synagogue the electric lights were on, but it is customary to bring candles in memory of deceased parents. Special tables had been set up, with boxes of sand into which the congregants placed large wax candles that burned for twenty-four hours. The synagogue was packed. The candles began to bend from the heat, melted into each other and sputtered black smoke.

Finished with the *minchah* service, the men wrapped themselves in their white robes and large prayer shawls. A mass of white robed figures rocked in reverential fear, murmuring the *Tefilah-zakeh:* "And thou shalt remove evil from the earth and rule the world with honor . . . " They had completed the service with the "Amen, may it be Thy will" and the Rabbi had slowly ascended the *bima,* the platform in front of the Ark of the Torah to deliver his sermon before the solemn Kol Nidre prayer. A special white curtain covered the Holy Ark. Warm brown eyes shone out of the white figure on the *bima* and looked out upon the congregation with love.

The Rabbi's sermon was brief. It seemed to Berish that his father had not said everything he had intended to say. His entire appearance seemed to have changed in the middle of his sermon. Berish had never seen his father perspire like this.

The elders of the congregation stepped up on the *bima,* opened the Ark and lifted out all the Torah scrolls. Couldn't Reb Moyshe see that the largest of the scrolls would be too heavy for Tateshi? The Rabbi would need every last ounce of his strength to hold it . . .

On the way home, his father complained that he had eaten too much at the meal before the fast, although he hadn't really eaten more than usual.

It was a hot Yom Kippur day and the fasting was very difficult. Even the weeping during the prayers was not as loud as usual.

Yom Kippur is a day when the worshipper must concentrate all his attention on repentance, but Berish could think only of the gardens in ancient Jerusalem and the shade trees in the orchard— Matus's Jerusalem. How had the young men and women actually conducted themselves in the holy city? Did they fast—and dance too? Could they have "turned their thoughts to penitence" while the white dresses of Jerusalem's daughters fluttered before their eyes— those daughters so famous for their comeliness?

In his sermon for the *Ne'ilah* service the Rabbi was even briefer than before. And when he left the platform he stumbled over a step and almost fell. Berish ran over to him, tried to take his arm, but he said, "It's nothing, just the heat," and Berish returned to his seat.

It is customary to open the Holy Ark and keep it open during the entire *Ne'ilah* service. Whenever the Ark is open the congregation must stand, out of respect for the Torah scrolls inside the Ark. But the Rabbi suddenly sat down and remained seated. Well, if one is weakened by fasting, one is permitted to sit. Berish noticed that when the Avenu Malkeynu prayer was recited, his father tried to stand up again, but immediately sat down once more.

The congregation finished the *Ne'ilah* service, called out *Shema Yisroel* once, *Boruch shem* three times, *Ha-shem hu Elohim* seven times—and the Rabbi remained seated throughout. Matus put the shofar to his lips and waited for the Rabbi's instruction *"Tekiah,"* but he sat there silently, with his eyes closed. Berish had started pushing his way through the crowd to his father when the Rabbi slid from his seat and fell to the floor unconscious.

Everyone, assuming that the Rabbi was weak from fasting, called for the shammes to bring over the kiddush wine to pour a little into the Rabbi's mouth. But one of the congregants, a doctor, was already at the Rabbi's side:

"No! Don't give him anything! It's his heart."

Berish decided not to go back to Lowicz until his father had recovered from his heart attack. And he did begin to feel better. On the first day of Succos, five days after the attack the Rabbi sat up in bed and said the kiddush. He recovered so rapidly that six days later, on the morning of Hoshana Raba he insisted on getting dressed and going into the *succah*—it would be his last opportunity to fulfill the commandment of "dwelling in the tabernacle."

It was only a few steps to the *succah* in the backyard. Even that was too much for him. He felt as if his legs had been cut below the knee. His breathing was short. He felt better as soon as he sat down in the *succah,* but after only a few minutes, he went back to bed.

The Rabbi asked that the *Shemini Atzeret* service the next day be conducted at his bedside. "You must rest," his wife pleaded, but he wouldn't budge. He explained to Berish:

"The Talmud says: whoever responds *amen* and *yehey-shmey-rabo* with all his vigor—even if he is a bit of a skeptic—his sins will be forgotten."

"You have no need of that, Tateshi."

"A Jew in exile endures so many dire afflictions that no one can avoid a moment of doubt, a tinge of heresy. Remember that, Berish."

A chill went through Berish's spine; his father was preparing himself for his final journey.

A week later, on the Sabbath, the Rabbi could get out of bed, sit in an easy chair and hold a book. He ate his afternoon meal at the table, his evening meal in bed. Berish sang a *zmiros* and his father hummed the melody. Following the grace after meals, he fell into a deep sleep and did not awaken until midnight.

"Sleep will do you good, Tateshi."

"Bring me some water for my hands. I haven't said the evening prayers yet."

After his father said the prayers, Berish led the *Havdala,* the ritual to conclude the Sabbath, with blessings over wine, candles, and spices. The Rabbi also wanted a *melaveh-malkeh,* the post-Sabbath meal. He ate hardly anything, but insisted that Berish sing all the appropriate songs. "It's too much for you, Tateshi," Berish objected.

"Rabbi Isaiah Horwitz said that the observance of the *melaveh-malkeh* saves one from the torments of the grave. The *sabbat*—'additional soul' does not leave the body until after the meal is finished."

Berish again felt his skin crawl; Tateshi was getting ready . . . Please God, let it be an unwarranted fear.

Tateshi fell asleep in his bed and Berish napped on a chair at the bedside. In his sleep he seemed to hear his father groan. He sprang from his chair and whispered "Tateshi." No response. As he was about to sit down again, he was gripped by a growing fear. He picked up a lamp from a corner of the room and brought it closer to the bed. The Rabbi lay still, his eyes shut. Berish couldn't shake his fear. He leaned over, heard his father's breathing. He relaxed. The doctor had said the Rabbi was improving every day. Tateshi's strange talk must have unnerved him. He recited the Shema and went to bed.

He had just about fallen asleep when he was jolted out of the chair by his mother's cry: "Tateshi is unconscious!"

People came running. The doctor appeared almost immediately. The Rabbi was not unconscious. It was all over. The second attack had been fatal . . .

• • • • •

They put off the funeral for a day, to give the older children time to get there. But not only the children came. Present were rabbis from all the neighboring towns; the deceased had been known as a great scholar, he had exchanged letters on ritual questions with many of the leading sages of the day. Dombrovka had never seen so many rabbis in one place, even at the weddings of the Rabbi's older children.

Monday was Rosh Hodesh, the New Moon day, when eulogies are forbidden. They carried the coffin into the synagogue and recited a few psalms. The children from the Hebrew schools were brought to the synagogue and even the government school excused its Jewish pupils so they could attend the funeral. Every Jew in Dombrovka was at the cemetery. When Shmulik and Berish chanted the Kaddish there wasn't a dry eye among the people at the graveside. Nearby, on his old board with wheels, sat Kalman, close to the ground. His eyes were dry, but he trembled all over. With the Rabbi's death, he was orphaned again.

Kalman wheeled himself all the way back from the graveside to the cemetery gate, where he found a driver from the factory who had been waiting for him in a car. When the driver came over to him, Kalman instructed him to pick up the Rabbi's wife and children. He wheeled himself back home, locked himself in his room, and refused to see anyone—even Kayleh.

Why hadn't he ever told the Rabbi how he felt about him? He had dreamed that with his many generous deeds he would repay the Rabbi for his patience, for his kindness. Why had he waited too long? Whenever some crazy scheme popped into his head he rushed to put it into action, but everything he thought and felt about the Rabbi he hadn't even allowed to pass his lips. He had not even apologized to the Rabbi for his arrogant words when he had said they should throw him, Kalman, to the dogs. How could he have said such a thing to the kind, gentle, and noble Rabbi? That's exactly what they should do with him—throw him to the dogs in the street. He didn't deserve better . . .

49

Shmulik, the Rabbi's oldest son, did not have a rabbinical diploma. The son-in-law, who had been ordained, was the son of the wealthy Borensteins and a successful merchant in his own right. He was unwilling to leave his business and become rabbi in Dombrovka.

It was well known in the town that the Rabbi, of blessed memory, had placed his hopes on Berish; from childhood he had prepared him for the rabbinate. It was also known that Berish was not as pious now as his father had been, but people thought that when he took upon himself the yoke of guiding a whole town's Judaism he would forget about the bit of modern worldliness he had picked up. A rabbi would never look straight into a woman's eyes or hand something to her directly, although people said Berish had been seen doing things like that. But for the old Rabbi's sake, they wanted Berish. And more to the point, how could they afford to support the Rabbi's widow and a new rabbi too? With Berish as rabbi, his mother could live with him and one salary would be sufficient.

There was an obstacle, however: it was not usual for an unmarried man to become the religious leader over a whole congregation of Jews. They would first have to find him a wife. In the meantime he could still rule on questions of kosher and *treyf,* even before he officially became the rabbi of Dombrovka. And for questions that a bachelor wouldn't be asked to rule on, there was Reb Matus's son-in-law, whom the Rabbi himself had held to be a remarkable Torah scholar. They even gave Melech a seat by the eastern wall in the synagogue and began calling him Reb Melech.

The Rabbi of Lowicz had come to the funeral, which meant they knew about it there. Moyshe Bilkowski, however, had not come, even though he considered himself a close friend of the Rabbi. Yudel Charney didn't come either, even though he had received ordination from the Rabbi and often corresponded with him about Talmudic questions. The shiva period had already passed when two letters arrived on the same day—one from Moyshe and the other from Yudel. Reb Moyshe had already heard that Berish would inherit the Rabbi's post, so he added to his words of condolence his hope that the time Berish had spent in the mill would stand him in good stead whenever a business problem was brought to his rabbinical court.

Yudel, in his letter, already addressed Berish as "my good friend the Rabbi," and after he signed it, added a line based on a verse from the psalms—"You are my friend who is as close as a brother." Apparently Kalman had sized up the situation correctly when he said that Yudel resented Berish's success in the mill. But now that Berish was no longer a competitor, it wasn't beneath his dignity to have a friend who had become a rabbi at such a young age.

Berish did not react to all these rumors, nor did he answer the two letters. Everything had happened so fast. He knew what had happened, of course, but he hadn't grasped it yet. His thoughts kept running around in his head and colliding with each other; he could follow none of them through to a logical conclusion.

No one knew how the news had reached even to remote places that Dombrovka was looking for a wife for the Rabbi's successor. Matchmakers from all corners of the country descended on him. Some of them represented families who were offering large dowries; others, daughters with impeccable pedigree lines. Berish couldn't find a place to hide from them as they tried to obtain the first "appointment."

"No appointments during the thirty days of mourning," he insisted.

"Tateshi, may he be a good interceder for us, would certainly have no objection," his mother suggested.

Berish was adamant. "No appointments during the *shloshim*." His mother knew it was useless to try to persuade him otherwise.

One matchmaker tried another tack. "Can we at least make an appointment for after *shloshim?*"

"After the thirty days we'll talk," Berish repeated. And that was the end of it.

Kalman found himself thinking about Berish quite often. If he could have asked the Rabbi what his last wish was, he would undoubtedly have said: "My wish is for Berish to become rabbi of Dombrovka." This was perhaps the only thing he could still do for the Rabbi. He would be active in the young rabbi's congregation and see to it that he lacked for nothing.

Raizel? If she really wanted Zalman, let her have him. Kalman Kalika's backstage maneuvers to bring Berish and Raizel together were over and done with. What the Rabbi had hoped would happen—let it happen. Meanwhile, Kalman would keep his distance.

•   •   •   •   •

In Dombrovka, people locked their doors only at night, but Kalman's new house was so large, and in every room there were so many valuable things, that they kept the door locked at all times and visitors had to ring a doorbell. People said that Kalman had installed the bell just to show off or maybe it was Kayleh's idea. She wanted things to be exactly as they were at her madame's house in Warsaw.

That morning they expected Matus to come from the synagogue

right after services. The bell rang and Raizel, who happened to be there, ran to the door. But it was not her father; it was Berish, and all she could do was stare.

"How are you?" Berish managed to say, and blushed to the roots of the scraggly beard that he had grown since his father's passing.

Raizel was at a loss: how does one talk to someone who is almost a rabbi? When Kayleh saw him, the glass she was holding fell out of her hand and she ran to Kalman's room.

"The Rabbi is here!"

Berish went to speak with Kalman and the women retreated to another part of the house. Even Matus, who had meantime come from the synagogue, would not dare enter.

By calling Berish "Rabbi" Kayleh had raised doubts in Kalman's mind as to the proper way to address him.

"I should really stand up when you come into the room, but you know I can't do that." As usual, he tried to cover up his plight with a wisecrack.

"Why should you stand up, all of a sudden?"

"Because I know you're going to be our rabbi."

"Then you know something I don't."

"The whole community is in favor of it—unanimously."

"Even if only one person is opposed, it's not unanimous."

"And who is it that's opposed?" Kalman was so indignant at the thought that he almost rose from his chair to do battle.

"Me," said Berish.

Kalman slumped back and said nothing for a little while. "But the Rabbi wanted that so much . . . " he finally murmured.

"That's why it's so difficult for me. But Tateshi of blessed memory knew that I had no intention of becoming rabbi. And he didn't oppose my going to Lowicz to work."

"And your mother?"

"I can't pose as something that I'm not, and what I am is not sufficient for the Hassidim, most certainly not for Reb Aaron. Even though he was my father's good friend, he would oppose me."

"With me on your side, you wouldn't have to be afraid of anyone," Kalman declared, throwing his chest out.

"I don't want to make the community over in my image. And I won't allow the community to make me over in their image. I haven't come to this decision lightly. Where Tateshi is now he's not looking for any additional honors, even through his son. Poor Mameshi is so broken up, however . . . But what can I do? I cannot follow any other course."

Kalman was pleased with what he was hearing, but angry with himself for feeling this way.

"And how are things with you?" Berish asked.

"Good. Very good. The sugar factory has become a profitable business. The mill is almost finished—they're already putting the machines in."

"I didn't know things were that far advanced."

"The first shipment of flour sacks has come in. They are already laying up the grain. I'm still looking for someone to work there for me."

"That's exactly why I came here today, Kalman. I'll talk with Reb Moyshe—I can't go back to Lowicz and leave Mameshi here all alone."

"You're certain about it—I mean about not becoming rabbi?"

"Melech is more pious than I am. He's a greater scholar, too. You know he's already ruling on ritual questions. Mameshi won't be a burden to anyone—I'll find a way to earn a living and Mameshi will live with me."

"Berish, Berish! If you want to become a businessman you've got to show a little business sense! Your mother deserves a pension, by right and by law. Unless Melech actually becomes rabbi, of course. Melech was given a generous dowry, and he has a rich father-in-law. He'll buy out your mother's claim and pay her in cash."

"A rich father-in-law?" Berish did not understand what Kalman meant.

"Don't worry—your mother won't be victimized—or my name isn't Kalman Kalika!" He had not called himself "Kalika" for a long time, but what he had just learned from Berish put him in such a good mood that he wasn't picking and choosing his words.

"I will not live on community funds—or on my mother's either."

"You've got a job in my mill, if you want it. Didn't I tell you?"

"You're serious? Many thanks, Panie Kalman!"

"Stop with the 'Panie Kalman.' I thought we were friends—brothers?"

"You're my employer now. I work for you."

"Friends are friends. Listen to me, Berish. You'll have a better position with me than with that high-toned Bilkowski. I'll even send you to a business school, if necessary. I'm building an empire, Berish, and I need my own people, people I can trust behind my back."

Kayleh stuck her head in. "May I bring the Rabbi a dlass of tea?"

Seeing an open door, Matus also poked his head in to ask when Kalman wanted to leave for the factory.

"Come in, Reb Matus, I have some news for you. Berish is going to be managing our mill."

"It's not fitting for a rabbi," Matus ruled.

"Berish doesn't want to be a rabbi, he'd rather be a miller. Where is Melech? I must speak with him right away."

When Berish left, Raizel was waiting for him.

"You disappeared before I could even wish you good morning," she complained.

"Well, I'm here now." He smiled.

50

Whenever anyone talked to him about filling the Rabbi's post, Melech shrugged.

"People will take sides, there will be a controversy, and I don't have the strength for that."

But Melech didn't know Dombrovka. Everyone there was related. How would anyone have found his way to this place in the sticks unless a relative brought him here? The influential people were still the old-timers—they and Dombrovka had grown up together.

The Dombrovkites read in the newspapers about conflicts between Hassidim and its opponents, between the ultraorthodox of the Aguda and Zionists. In Dombrovka there were also conflicts, but they never reached the stage of open warfare. In the voting for the Sejm, everyone voted according to his own inclinations, but for the Jewish community leadership they chose individuals according to their status in the town. From time to time "delegates" came from outside, sent by political parties that believed in militancy. But when the emissaries left, things remained the way they were. There were some who traveled to the Rebbe in Ger and who dreamed of establishing a *shtiebl,* a Hassidic prayer house. There were others who collected money for the Zionist *Keren Kayemet* and supported the young fellows and girls who were training as farmers, and dreamt of re-claiming the holy land from the swamps and deserts. There were even those who were suspected of casting an eye towards the communist system of their neighbor to the east.

Among the recent settlers there may even have been some who had taken part in such clashes where they formerly lived. In Dombrovka, however, practically everyone earned his living from Kalman Swerdl's factories, directly or indirectly. Pan Kalman was now an openhanded benefactor, but the talk was that he could also bear a grudge. No one wanted to risk the modest but secure income they had found here, especially at a time when the whole world was buried in a deep economic crisis and anti-Semites, with the help of the government, were taking the bread out of Jewish mouths.

The tax the Jewish community levied was sanctioned by the government. The mathematicians had already figured out that if the community had to pay both a rabbi and the old Rabbi's widow, they would have to increase the tax by seventy-five percent. And when the government taxing authority found out that the Jewish community was raising its taxes, and the cow let itself be milked, they would not sit by with their hands folded. So Rabbi Melech was virtually a heaven-sent messenger to lighten the load on the community's back.

It happened that at that particular time the movement for a co-operative bank was revived. If one can sell only when the buyer is permitted to pay in installments, how can one survive without cheap credit? A representative of the cooperative's main office in Warsaw came to look into the matter on the spot. Just when everyone thought they had worked out an acceptable plan with him, the honorable gentleman from Warsaw informed them that his organization helped only those who help themselves. If the town could raise a fund of twenty thousand zloty, the central office would match that sum and set up a bank.

Where were the Jews of Dombrovka to get such a fortune? They were on the verge of giving up the whole idea when they heard an automobile pull up outside the meeting room. There was only one auto in Dombrovka. Did Kalman need a loan too?

Kalman had come with a complaint: Was he a citizen of this community or not? What did they mean—giving up the idea of a bank? The Jews of Dombrovka couldn't raise twenty thousand zloty? Well, how much could they raise?

"If we raise ten thousand, it'll be a lot."

"My brother-in-law is going to be a rabbi of this town," said Kalman. "Should I act like a stranger, God forbid? If my brother-in-law's community gives ten thousand, I'll give the other ten, and we'll have a bank."

If Kalman took the community for granted, he did it in a nice way. He hadn't set any conditions. He didn't say "if" my brother-in-law becomes rabbi; he spoke of it as though it were already a fact. In a nice way you could get the Dombrovka Jews to do a lot of things.

According to the law, a rabbi must be chosen in a general election, unless there is only one candidate. From somewhere there appeared a rabbi who wanted to put himself forward as a candidate, against the wishes of the synagogue custodians, but he needed the signatures of twenty-five taxpayers of the community—and he could not get them.

Berish's penmanship came in handy as he wrote in fine Hebrew calligraphy the appointment proclamation for the new rabbi, and Kalman helped him translate it into Polish. Various people came to witness it—everyone wanted his signature on an important document like this—especially since Pan Swerdl would see the signatures.

When the Polish text of Melech's appointment came back confirmed by the proper officials, Kalman insisted that they hold a special celebration, as is done in the big cities. The new rabbi asked the two sons of his predecessor—the heirs to the post according to Jewish law—to come to the celebration and sign a codicil declaring that they willingly renounced their right to the post.

The celebration took place on the first night of Hanuka. The entire community was gathered in the synagogue when a delegation of prominent citizens, together with the deceased rabbi's sons, went to the new rabbi's home to escort him to his investiture. At the door of the synagogue a canopy had been erected. Reb Aaron, the senior of the Elders, carrying a scroll of the Torah, said the blessing and handed the scroll to the new rabbi, who kissed it and started walking toward the platform, accompanied by the canopy and by the singing of the congregants.

After returning the Torah to the Ark the Elders of the congregation led Rabbi Melech to the old rabbi's seat at the eastern wall. The new rabbi's father-in-law, Reb Matus, conducted the *mincha* service. Before the *maariv* service the Rabbi haltingly delivered his first sermon. He kept pulling at the hairs of his short beard as if he wanted to make it longer. Well, no matter. It could hardly be compared to a sermon by the old Rabbi, but everyone was confident that his sermons would improve with practice.

In the Women's Section the new rebbetsin sat in her new wig, which was larger than the one worn by the old rebbetsin, who sat beside her. Her sister Kayleh wore a wide-brimmed hat covering all her hair. Next to Kayleh sat Tsippe, the rabbi's mother-in-law, weeping copious tears; her lips moved continuously, whispered incantations against the Evil Eye.

"Mazel tov, good luck, Rebbetsin," the old rebbetsin wished Freydl when the Rabbi ended his sermon. Freydl burst into tears, grasped the older woman's hand and kissed it.

"Nu, nu, you don't have to do that! You are already a rebbetsin yourself."

After the evening service, the women went home. The men moved into the Study House where a lavish table had been set, courtesy of the Rabbi's brother-in-law.

Both her sons accompanied the old rebbetsin home. At the synagogue she had restrained her weeping, not wishing to mar the celebration, but back in her home, her tears flowed endlessly.

"Take hold of yourself, Mameshi," Berish pleaded, trying to calm her.

"We mortals must accept the Almighty's decrees," Shmulik added.

"It's so gloomy in this house now. I still wake up in the morning expecting to hear his voice chanting the holy books."

"Tateshi lived like a *tsaddik* and gave up his soul like a *tsaddik*. Let us accept the decree of heaven, for his sake." Shmulik wiped away a tear himself.

"Go on, both of you," the Rebbetsin urged, "go back to the synagogue. They'll wait for you." She had suddenly realized that their absence would be noted.

"I don't want to leave you alone now, Mameshi," Berish said. "Shmulik will go back."

"No. Both of you go. In Tateshi's house, with Tateshi's books, I am not alone. And Berish, if you don't mind my saying so, you looked much handsomer during the mourning period when you weren't cutting your beard."

After the meal, Shmulik and Berish walked the Rabbi home.

Inside the house there was a young woman and it seemed to Shmulik that she smiled at Berish.

"Who is that?" he asked Berish as they left.

"The new Rabbi's sister-in-law. Her name is Raizel."

"Matus's daughter?"

"Yes. Reb Matus's daughter."

"I thought all his daughters were lame?"

Berish didn't respond. When they reached Wilki Street he said: "I'm glad you came, Shmulik, I need to talk with Mameshi about something and with you there it will be easier."

"You want to go back to Lowicz?"

"To Lowicz? No. But what you said about my getting married—"

"Yes. Mameshi told me."

"Mameshi knows?"

"She told me during shiva that Lowicz is more than a job."

"Lowicz? What does—oh, Mameshi is still thinking of Itka Bilkowski?"

"That's over?"

"Over? There never was anything to it."

"So what's this about getting married?"

"It's Raizel."

They had already reached home, but Shmulik did an about-face and they walked back a few yards.

"Listen to me, Berish. Don't take offense. I'm going to speak my mind. Tateshi isn't here any longer, so it's up to me. When you were working for Bilkowski, it was the boss's daughter. Now that you're going to be working for Kalman, it's the boss's sister-in-law. I hope that's not the only reason."

Berish burst out laughing. How little his brother knew him if he could suspect him of chasing after money.

"What's so funny?" Shmulik protested.

"You saw her yourself. Didn't you see the reason?"

"I'm not that innocent, Berish. But beauty isn't everything."

"You're so right! She has a lot of other virtues besides beauty!"

"But her family?"

"Shmulik, I'm going to speak my mind too. Your own father-in-law—he's no great scholar of Torah either. But? But he's a rich man, a philanthropist, a leader in the community—I know all that. Raizel's father can interpret a chapter of the Bible, he can read the

Torah, this year he was the *baal-tokeah*—and the sound of the shofar was loud and firm. True, up until recently he was an impoverished workingman, but now he has become a philanthropist himself. It's not his money, of course; he has a lot of influence with Kalman, but his home has become a center of good deeds, Shmulik."

His brother chuckled. "I see it's all settled!"

"Yes. I feel very close to her, almost as if our souls are bound together. That's why I want you to be present when I tell Mameshi."

"Mameshi will be all alone, unless she comes to live with me."

"Mameshi will live here with me, God willing. Kalman loved Tateshi very much and he has a lot of respect for Mameshi. She'll be happy with us."

• • • • •

When Berish and Raizel came to see Kalman they were holding hands. It aroused the wag in him.

"It's not fitting for a rabbi's son and a rebbetsin's sister to be holding hands! What will people say?"

"We'll worry about that later," Berish replied. "Right now we're interested only in what one person has to say."

"Thank you, but why? Will it make any difference if I say no?"

Berish laughed. "No, it won't. But it was a big help when you said yes."

"Kalman," Raizel interjected. "We have uncovered your whole conspiracy! You made sure to tell me what Berish said and Berish what I said!"

"And not always did we say what you said we said,"
Berish quipped.

"Are you both trying to make me out a liar?"

"On the contrary," said Berish, "we're making all the lies told about us come true!"

"Kalman, I love you almost as much as Berish does," Raizel said as she kissed him.

Berish grinned at her. "When I told you I loved you, you didn't tell me I had a rival." He didn't notice how sad Kalman had suddenly become and how slow to respond.

"Does your father know?" Kalman finally asked Raizel.

"We haven't told anyone yet."

"Well, that's not quite true—I told my brother and my mother," Berish added.

"What did they say?"

"Mameshi said it must have happened the first time I saw Raizel in our house, at Melech's—at the Rabbi's—wedding."

"So it's not too soon to wish you mazel tov," Kalman smiled. "Wait a little while, Raizel. Let me prepare the way for you with your father. He's a prayer-leader and a shofar-blower—and his daughter is running around with a fellow and carrying on a love affair . . . "

Since Berish was in mourning, he wasn't permitted any celebrations, but Shmulik stayed in Dombrovka over the Sabbath and on Saturday night they wrote the "interim engagement contract." The wedding ceremony too was performed without pomp.

"For the circumcision I'll make a big party," Kalman promised. "And Raizel, you must provide a son as soon as possible to name after the Rabbi, you hear?"

51

Kalman felt uneasy when City Hall was taken over by the man who was sponsored by the squire. But the new mayor did not accept bribes and supported enthusiastically every initiative that would bring a benefit to the city's economy. The young man was capable, and Kalman could count on his endorsement and even support when he needed the approval of regional authorities. If the squire put in an honest and capable man then perhaps he was not just exploiting the city but was interested in its growth and welfare. It was quite possible that the squire was not as black a character as the tales of the peasants made him out to be.

City Hall was making regular payments for electricity, both the sugar factory and the mill were showing a nice profit, and Kalman was already planning new ventures.

Berish tried to talk him out of it. "What do you need new headaches for?"

"How can a person sit and do nothing? I'd go crazy."

"Nothing? How long is it altogether since you took over the sugar factory? The business was on its last legs when you got hold of it. And now . . . With the mill you worked miracles. Even people who saw it with their own eyes can't believe that a building of that size could be put up so fast. I must confess, Kalman, I myself was afraid that in your great impatience you were wasting a lot of money—sending in so many workers. I was afraid that they would only get in each other's way."

"Maybe I've got more luck than brains."

"You've got both—and that's the secret of your success. But why not take a little rest now and enjoy your success?"

"Even in business, if you don't make full use of your potential—how shall I put it?—it's a sin to let an opportunity slip by. Take the sugar factory, for instance. The Vistula Valley grows the best fruit in the country. When you have fruit and you have sugar, it's a waste not to manufacture confections and candy. The Vedel Company doesn't want to deal with Jews? So along will come a Jew and make better candy than they do. Understand?"

"You're going to build a factory to make sweetmeats and confections?"

"I didn't need to spell anything out for you, Berish—that's what I like about you. But it was really Kayleh who gave me the idea."

"Oh? I didn't know she had a head for business."

"She doesn't. But she had enough sense to make use of the surplus fruit from the orchard and the sugar from the factory. At first she did it only for herself and her family, but it ended up with the preserves and the sweetmeats bringing in a big part of the earnings from the orchard."

"So maybe it's really a good idea."

"And that's not all. The dregs of the sugar factory are grated beets. We sell it for fertilizer. How much do we get for it? Chicken feed. But suppose the grated beets end up as meat. Poland exports canned meat to England and even America."

"How can you make canned meat out of grated beets?"

"Very simply. You put it in the trough, the cow eats it and grows fat. You know how much grass you need to raise one cow? You understand what I'm saying? I'll give the farmers grated beets—free—on account of the cows that they supply me. Any farmer can squeeze another cow or two into his barn. If a farmer gets ambitious and wants to enlarge his barn, I'll even give him the lumber. A peasant doesn't need more than the building materials. He does the work himself—and all his neighbors help him . . . "

"It sounds good, Kalman, it makes sense. But how can you carry all that around in your head?"

"Berish, when I don't have enough to think about, I get sick. And another thing, Berish. I'm waiting for good news from Raizel. I'm building an empire and I must have a dynasty to inherit it all."

"We've been married only three months!"

"Three months after the wedding, Raizel should already be in her fourth month. I thought you'd have a boy to name after your father."

"Raizel wants a girl."

"A girl? Is that so? I need men, businessmen. You can see your-self what's happening. Melech will probably turn out to be a good rabbi, but in business matters he's no great prize. Leybl is a petty tradesman with no vision. Your father was a great scholar, but he also knew people, and he knew the ways of the world. He must have been the wisest and most patient man in the world to make a mensch out of Kalman Kalika."

"You didn't need anybody to make a mensch out of you."

"Kalman Swerdl is a successful merchant, a philanthropist, but Kalman Kalika is a rotten person. Berish, I can reveal this only to your father's son: Kalman Kalika is still deeply imbedded inside me and is only waiting for the right moment to spring out at his vic-tims. For that reason alone it's better that I keep my mind busy with commercial adventures."

"Kalman, I can't stand the way you disparage yourself. It is for-bidden to do that. I don't want to listen to it any longer. And about your businesses: they are all well planned and well managed. And most certainly, they are not adventures."

"Berish, you have too much faith in me and my plans. Remember this. The most skilled mountain climber sometimes takes a false step and slips. And the higher you climb, the more dangerous it is. With business it's the same thing. Something unforeseen can happen at any time and upset the whole damned applecart."

"So why do you need more enterprises—you don't have enough?"

"If three or four are successful and one fails, I'll still make a profit. The reason I can afford to take risks is that I can afford to lose. I'm telling you all this because I'm counting on you—you and your children, who will take after you."

"And what about your own children? The second one is already on the way, *k'n'hora*."

"A dynasty needs more than one prince. And anyway, until my children grow up, I'm counting on you. You're still green in business but you have a good head."

"Your head is even better—"

"When I'm gone—"

"Kalman, you're only eight years older than I am!"

"Don't interrupt. Listen to me. I've written a new will. Each one of my brothers-in-law will get a share, but you will have to be the guardian and top man."

"You'll outlive me, anyway."

"Maybe. But I have a feeling . . ."

"Kalman, I'm not even certain you believe in God, so how can you believe in a silly premonition?"

"I'm speaking theoretically, only theoretically. Well, enough. Let's talk about something more cheerful."

"Agreed! I have some good news for you. Raizel made me promise not to say anything until she's absolutely certain, but from you I don't keep any secrets. It's quite possible that a baby is on the way—"

"Wonderful! And it must be a boy, otherwise I'll be displeased, and next year you'll have to provide twin boys, you hear me, Berish?"

52

How many transformations he had endured in his young life! From a shy youngster to a mean, bitter weed. He who grew up as a thief and a lecher was now an upstanding citizen and a philanthropist. Was he now going through a new transformation? Night after night he was twisting and turning in his bed and getting up in the morning cross as a bear. He would lose his temper too often and make Kayleh cry. True, he couldn't abide fools, but he'd better learn to conceal his dislike of Tsippe. The old cow had grown even more pious than her daughter, the Rebbetsin. In his own house she had become the chief authority over what was kosher and what was not and was driving everybody crazy. What rank stupidity that was—letting his mother-and father-in-law move in with him. He'd have to find a nice way to get rid of them.

He had built a house large enough for everyone to live with him. But Freydl's husband had become a rabbi and must have an "open house" for the entire community. He had settled Leybl and Chaya in another house, so that Moyshe Longlegs should not become too much of a boss here. Berish and Raizel—he would enjoy having them in his house, but some healthy instinct cautioned him to build a separate house for them near the mill. One "Breindl story" was enough!

He must really be in love with Kayleh to be doing so much for her and her family. In her late months she didn't want to wear the special shoes he had ordered for her in Warsaw, so she was hopping around, and her big belly bounced right along with her. Raizel wouldn't hop, but she too would soon have a swollen face and a big belly. He thought about her too much. It wasn't a healthy situation. It was shameful to admit, but lately he couldn't make love to his wife unless he closed his eyes and imagined he was with Raizel . . .

How would this all end? Would he end up in a madhouse, like his father, or fall into a state of melancholia like his grandmother? Maybe this new business would keep him so involved that he'd forget about these unhealthy fantasies. If that Kalman Kalika within him was about to be resurrected, better he should croak . . .

53

A whole series of celebrations came and went. First, an "heir to the throne" was born to the Rabbi. By the time they finished all the celebrations, they were already looking forward to good news from Chaya.

Chaya gave birth to a baby girl and so did Kayleh, to Kalman's great disappointment. Kayleh had been so big that he expected twins. But he soon consoled himself. A boy, if he turned out to have Grandmother Tsippe's sense, well, that would be a disaster. For a daughter, however, he would find a young man with a good head on his shoulders who could run a big business. Let's just hope that the baby girl would grow up to be a pretty young woman. Meanwhile her head was too large and too bald and her nose too thick. Who did she take after, anyway? As far as he knew, both his mother and his grandmother were handsome women. He named the baby Libe-Rochel, after his mother and his father's mother.

They held their family seder around the big table in the Rabbi's court room. In another room, on soft pillows, wrapped in long blankets, slept the three infants. The Four Questions were asked by Raizel, the youngest person present. During the Four Questions, the baby in her belly jumped, as if it couldn't wait its turn. Berish was a bit of a singer, and Matus and his daughters had sweet voices, so the seder lasted until way past midnight. Neighbors who had already finished their own seders stood outside the windows of the Rabbi's house and listened to the singing.

Kalman's Liebele grew up to be a pretty child. Her head had probably been swollen from the delivery. Now she had a pretty head of golden curls and her dark eyes had turned blue. "A picture of Raizel! She looks just like her Aunt Raizel!"

This observation made Kalman very happy.

On one side of the sugar factory the mill was already in operation; on the other side, they started building a factory to make candies. Kalman had already made connections with people who would sell him the cocoa beans. To compete with Vedel he would have to use only the best. They had long had a reputation for making only the finest chocolates.

Plans were also materializing for the canned meat factory. Kalman had begun negotiations for a chemical plant in Lowicz. He worked compulsively, in great haste, as if afraid of being too late . . .

54

"Your head works day and night," Berish warned him. "A normal person has to rest sometimes."

"That's why people say Kalman is not normal."

"Seriously, Kalman, you're an emperor of a financial kingdom. If you wear yourself out, who will manage your empire?"

"You think only a cripple can be an emperor? Why not you? Pretend you became a rabbi and had to run a whole community. Believe me, Berish, running a factory is no more difficult than leading a town full of Jews, every one of whom thinks he's smarter than King Solomon."

"Kalman, I always enjoy your jokes, but when I talk to you in earnest I wish you would take me seriously. You haven't been looking too well lately . . . "

"And here I'm getting ready to compete in a beauty contest."

"More jokes? Your face is haggard. You look like you've lost weight. You have two children and three factories. Enough!"

"Enough what? Children or factories?"

"The children need a father and the factories need a boss."

"There will be more children, God willing, and more factories too. I've told you before—I'm building a dynasty and an empire. Don't worry about me. I only need half the rest and half the sleep of a normal person. Half of my body rests twenty-four hours a day. Don't look so glum, Berish. All kidding aside, I really don't need much sleep. And I know how to stop the windmill in my head and relax . . . "

Berish left dissatisfied. Kalman could see that his friend didn't believe him, but it was true—he did know how to drive irksome or debilitating thoughts out of his head. He had always been a master at daydreaming. In his childhood he had dreamed up schemes to get even with his tormentors. When he grew up a little he daydreamed about girls, mostly sweet dreams about passionate love affairs. But whenever he was disappointed in something he became embittered and full of hurt, even in his dreams.

All that had been in the dim distant past, almost in another life. Nowadays the key to his dreams lay in the leather wallet in his breast pocket. Here at home, or in his factory office, it was enough for him to take two photographs out of his wallet—his Zelikl, one year old, and himself at the same age. One glance at the photographs was enough to free him of all worries. In both of them, the children were naked, lying on their stomachs, their faces beaming, their legs kicking playfully. The little rascal in the new photograph had come to remedy what had gone awry with the child in the old photograph . . .

In his own case, fate had made a mistake, but that was only the rehearsal. Zelikl had come to play the role over again, this time with no mistakes. Kayleh didn't like it when he called the child "Kalmandl." "Don't," she would say, "it's bad luck. Jews don't name a child after a father who's still living."

Foolishness! Superstition! Zelikl was a healthy child and his father was building an empire for him. Zelikl was really another Kalman, but with sound legs and a sound head. The little bastard was really showing signs of brains and character. Let someone try to take a toy away from him! He'd let out a scream that would split the ceiling.

Had he really said once that he had no patience with children until they began to talk sensibly? Even a blind man could see that this little pipsqueak already had more brains than his mother. Would he have the same feelings for his daughter Liebele? Kayleh complained that he never showed the little girl any affection. "A person tan't have only boys all the time," she tried to make him understand.

"God forbid!" he smiled. "If you hadn't been born a girl, there would be no Zelikl."

Kayleh didn't understand the joke. "Now you want only girls? Is Zelitl so bad?"

"Zelikl is good as gold and Liebele is sweet as sugar. You know something, Kayleh? This time you're going to have twins—a boy and a girl."

"With God's help," she murmured.

"I don't need any help. Just you and me."

"Don't, Talman!" His blasphemies always frightened her. She pledged herself to donate another pound of candles to the synagogue.

55

Kayleh had a cold and a sore throat. She gargled with salt water and swallowed aspirin, as the doctor had prescribed, and she also began reciting the Shema prayer every night before going to bed.

"Kayleh dear, it's your sister who's the rebbitsin, not you," Kalman laughed. Kayleh continued to mumble her prayer. Was she doing it as a cure for her cold or was it—? She had become more observant when she was pregnant with Liebele too.

"What are you praying for—a boy or a girl?"

"Twins," she replied, when she came to a place in the prayer where speaking is permitted.

"Why twins, all of a sudden?"

"Betause that's what you want."

"Is there something on the way?"

She nodded her head.

In the middle of the night Zelikl woke up screaming and didn't stop until morning.

"Kalman's pride and joy—what in the world do you have to complain about?" he scolded the child in mock anger.

Kayleh tried to sit the baby up in her lap. "Oh my God!" she cried out, "the child is burning like a hot toal!"

"I told you not to touch him when you have a cold," Kalman rebuked her. "Make sure you don't give it to Liebele."

Zelikl began vomiting. Kalman's heart dropped with each new attack. He could not bear to see the child suffer. He threw a coat over his shoulders and drove to fetch the doctor.

"Nothing to worry about," the doctor reassured them. "Children get over this kind of thing one-two-three."

After three days the medicine worked. The temperature went down—but then suddenly shot up again.

Every morning the temperature was down, but every night the little body was again on fire. The doctor kept reassuring them, but an insane idea took possession of Kalman. "He must get better, completely better! No paralysis! Rather than remain a cripple, it's better that—"

He shuddered. You're a fool, Kalman, a real idiot, if you think that everything will always go the way you want it, that your slice of bread will always fall butter-side up. Somewhere fate has already set up a stumbling block for you. If there is a director in heaven, he's playing cat and mouse with Kalman Kalika.

Was there really a disaster in store for him? If something bad had to happen to his factories, to his wealth, he could live without the empire, but his dynasty mustn't be touched. He wanted more than merely Zelikl's life, though. Anything but a cripple. A sound, healthy, sturdy body—or nothing!

He had convinced himself that he was not a believer, yet here he was bargaining as if someone were reading his mind and listening to his arguments. Soon he would ask Tsippe to recite incantations against the Evil Eye. Better to bring a specialist from Lowicz.

He wanted to send his car to Lowicz for Dr. Jagelski, but the car wasn't even available—Kayleh had sent her father to Zichlin to speak to the Rebbe.

Kalman was furious. "A fool is a calamity! Is it my car or not? Why didn't you ask me first?"

Kayleh burst out crying.

"Why didn't you say something to me?" he repeated, more calmly.

"The poor child is so sit and you—I'm afraid you'll say something that will—in heaven they hear everything and Zelitl needs mercy now . . ." She wept louder than ever.

Kalman wheeled himself over to her and patted her on the hand. "Did I say you shouldn't send a message to the Rebbe? But your father could have—I would have sent him in a truck from the factory. But for Dr. Jagelski I must have a car."

"Talman, I don't know what I'm doing. Save our child."

"Don't be silly. The child is in no danger. I want a professor because of you, to reassure you. I'll telephone the doctor to take a taxi, or maybe he has his own car, anyway."

Tsippe was the first to notice that Zelikl's body had broken out in red spots. She ran to Kayleh with the good news. "It's nothing! Only measles! Nothing but measles!"

Kalman was in the mill at the time, so Matus rushed there to tell Kalman the good news: "It's only measles."

"Is that what the doctor said?"

"Red spots—any woman knows what that is."

Kalman brought the doctor, who diagnosed it immediately. "Scarlet fever."

"Not measles?"

"No doubt about it. Scarlet fever."

"I was wondering if we should call Dr. Jagelski in Lowicz."

"The Pan can bring doctors from Lowicz and from Warsaw, but it still won't be the measles. It's scarlet fever."

The child's throat was so raw that he couldn't drink anything. The doctor's orders were that they must get a lot of liquid into him. Kalman did not even go to business. He sat at the child's side day and night. He refused to rely on anyone else.

Zelikl improved. His temperature went down. His skin began peeling. But his throat was still sore. Whenever anyone touched him the child trembled. His tongue was no longer as swollen or as yellow, but it was raw and red as an overripe strawberry.

Although the local doctor could not hide his chagrin at the idea of bringing in another physician, Kalman sent for Dr. Jagelski. If he could at least ease the child's suffering, it would be worth it.

Dr. Jagelski came. He confirmed everything his colleague had said. He assured them that the worst was over. The Dombrovka doctor looked at Kalman with an I-told-you-so expression in his eyes.

The child's temperature was back to normal, but it was not the same Zelikl. His skin was gray, his eyes lusterless. Kalman brought home boxes of toys, but Zelikl showed no interest. Kalman did all sorts of clownish tricks, but the child did not respond. "God Almighty, what more do you want of me! A long time ago you took my legs. You want more? I'll give you one of these arms for a little smile from Zelikl . . . "

•   •   •   •   •

In the middle of the night the child awoke suddenly. Having no more strength to scream, he whimpered, his little body shaking and quivering with every sob. His temperature had gone up again. The doctor, apparently still smarting from the affront, refused to come out in the middle of the night. "The child is better—must be having a bad dream . . . "

Kalman went to his house himself.

"I can't submit to the whims of every patient," the doctor complained. "There are other sick people out there. If I don't get some sleep now, I won't be able to work tomorrow."

"Panie Doctor, tell me what you want and it's yours. The child is suffering horribly."

Unable to get out of it, the doctor came, intending to take a quick look at the child and go back to bed. But one look was enough to make him take off his coat. "Complications," he sighed after a long examination. He had found a swelling in the left ear. He turned angrily toward Kalman. "When you didn't need them, you brought specialists from Lowicz. Now that there is really an inflammation, you wait till it reaches the brain!"

The doctor left. Kalman sat in his chair, all tied up in knots. An emperor? He could shake the pillars of the world? What good now were all his gold and all his power when he couldn't ease his own child's suffering, even for a moment? He had convinced himself that Zelikl would have things twice as good, to compensate for his father's pains. An inferno was burning in that precious little head. Let a fire destroy all his factories, his whole empire, but let Zelikl's head stop burning. God Almighty, help! Enough suffering, enough!

Automobiles raced to bring doctors, medicines. Messengers traveled to holy rabbis. In the synagogue they chanted psalms. They even sent a messenger to Bilgoray to pray at the grave of Kalman's great-grandmother, the righteous Genendel. A bottomless despair settled in Kalman's bones, but he refused to surrender. He sent telegrams to famous physicians: "Come at once. Will pay whatever you ask." He even sent a dispatch to a business associate in England, knowing full well that there wasn't enough time left for a doctor to come from England. His grandfather, Jonah, had also lost many children—had Kalman Kalika inherited the diseased blood or the bitter luck? No! No! No! If Zelikl should, God forbid—no! He would not be able to stay here alone . . .

56

Zelikl succumbed like a little bird, freed of all pain. Kalman let Berish lead him away from the child's bed. The doctor gave him something to make him sleep—and he took it. He woke up a different Kalman—submissive, quiet. Berish and Matus told him what to do and he did it. At the graveside, Melech said the words of the Kaddish slowly and Kalman repeated it word for word. Kayleh wailed, Tsippe screamed hysterically, and Kalman repeated the words of the Kaddish, but his eyes were dry. Kayleh was grateful that he obeyed the Law and didn't trim his beard during the shiva period, but he threw a great fear into her, and even greater was the fear that his silence threw into everyone else . . .

After the morning prayers on the the seventh day from the funeral, the mourners arose. Everyone expected Kalman to rush to the factory. Instead, he went to bed. Kayleh carried Liebele away from the bedroom, lest she awaken her father with her crying. But when Kayleh looked into the bedroom through a crack in the door, she saw that he was lying there with his eyes open. Whenever she came closer she heard him tossing on the bed; whenever she looked in, she met his gaze.

That night she went to bed early. She was glad he hadn't come into her bed; it was prohibited during shiva, the weeklong mourning period. She got into her bed and left the light on. Today it was permitted. But Kalman stayed in his own bed. The light stabbed at her eyes. She switched it off and turned her face toward the wall. When she awoke, dawn had already arrived. Kalman was still lying there with his eyes open. She climbed into his bed. He moved over to make room for her.

"Talman, the baby just moved, right here!" she said, pointing to her abdomen.

"The baby is dead," he said, his voice empty.

"No, no! You shouldn't say such things! I mean the new baby."

Kalman was silent.

"You want to feel it?" Without waiting for him to respond she took his hand and placed it on her belly. "Wait a moment and you'll feel it too. Now! Did you feel it?"

Kayleh was almost shouting for joy. He could not understand how she could be happy at a time when—he clenched his teeth to keep the thought out of his head. No! Zelikl was not rotting in the ground! Zelikl had become an angel. Zelikl was a soul, a new and fresh soul, and would not suffer any more, would never know pain again . . .

57

Kayleh recalled vividly the miserable months when she was pregnant with her first child. She had twisted and turned on a narrow iron bed in the home of a stranger, in a distant city, without even one person there to comfort her. The child had come as a punishment from God. Now a child was coming to correct an injustice. She must have her Kalman by her side—let him feel it too. She had called him and he had come to her bedside, but he was no longer the same Kalman. He always used to come to her with a joke, a quip, anything to make her happy, to make her feel she was the prettiest woman in the world. Now he said hardly anything. He lay at her side with his eyes deep in his head, looking beyond her, beyond the wall. Twice she had found him at Zelikl's empty little bed. It seemed to her that no matter who or what he was looking at, all he could see was Zelikl's empty bed. Her heart contracted whenever she thought about her firstborn, but something else that belonged to them—to her and to

Kalman—was already growing inside her. She ought to make Kalman feel the same way, but she didn't know how to do it. Kalman was such an educated person—she didn't know how to speak to his heart.

Kalman returned to his business affairs, but the old fire was gone. More and more often he went to see Berish at the mill. Berish sensed that Kalman felt a great need to talk. He wanted to help him begin, but didn't know how.

"Berish, you know, of course, that Zelikl was born before we were married," Kalman said to him once when they were alone.

"I know."

"Born a bastard."

"Not so! The law of *mamzerut* applies only to a child of a married woman, a woman who has a husband and commits adultery."

"I'm not referring to the law. A child without a father is a *mamzer*."

"Stop talking nonsense! Zelikl had a father." Berish spoke with an air of finality, as if he were pronouncing sentence, once and for all. He didn't want to talk about it any more and was glad when someone called him away.

Kalman remained alone in the office, deep in thought. He himself had uttered the wish—"better that Zelikl die than live as a cripple." Children can be cruel. The shame and grief that the *heder* boys had caused him was still deep in his bones. Zelikl had a good head on his shoulders, he would have been a better pupil than the others and for that, the blockheads would have persecuted him. Somewhere, somehow, one of the boys would have discovered that Zelikl was born before his parents were married and would have spread the news in the *heder,* in the synagogue, on the street, and one fine day all Zelikl's friends would have turned away from him and called him bastard. No, he would not have wanted his Zelikl to suffer the same kind of hellish childhood as his father.

The chestnut trees on both sides of the road were rocking their blossoming branches when Kalman and Berish rode home. The wind chased the flowers off the trees, spreading them across the highway, and the car rode as if in a snow flurry, on a white carpet. Berish was enjoying the beauty of the landscape and hoped Kalman was too—he seemed to be climbing out of his despondency. Suddenly, in a voice that sounded as if it came from the grave, Kalman said:

"Kalman Kalika was once able to deceive the world, but he could never deceive himself. Here the victim is no more foolish than the deceiver."

"In what connection are you bringing that up?"

"In connection with what I said at the mill. I was trying to console myself with smelling salts."

Berish knew better than to reply to that. The Talmud says that one should not attempt to comfort a mourner when the deceased is still lying before him, because words of consolation uttered before the mourner is able to accept them only make him feel worse, not better. Both of them were silent, but when Berish got out of the car he squeezed his friend's arm:

"Be strong, Kalman . . . "

58

Kalman did not come to services to recite the Kaddish for his son's soul. Matus wanted to say something to Kalman about this, but Berish cautioned him against it.

"When he's ready, he'll come himself."

So Matus remained the only one to say Kaddish for Zelikl. It was after the thirty-day mourning period when Kalman finally appeared in the synagogue one day at afternoon services and recited the Kaddish in unison with his father-in-law. The next morning he came to synagogue again, and thereafter, every day. Matus was glad to see that Kalman was not skipping a word of the prayers. Kayleh began to realize that Kalman was being careful not to take even a swallow of milk sooner than six hours after he had eaten meat; she used to try to stop him from smearing butter on bread with a meat knife.

In the family they whispered this news to each other, afraid to talk openly about it because it had happened so suddenly. The Rebbetsin, however, did say to him once at the table:

"Kalman dear, since you've become observant, why don't you also stop shaving?"

Berish motioned to her to drop the subject, but she continued: "A beard looks good on a Jewish face—it's appropriate for the Rabbi's brother-in-law and it's appropriate for a father of children."

Kalman raised his sad eyes and immediately lowered them again to his plate, but he didn't touch the food.

• • • • •

Everyone was happy that Kalman had become pious, but Berish was uneasy about it, perhaps because it had happened while he was so despondent. Kalman had loved to spice his language with a witticism; now he "counted his words" and answered only when spoken to. Berish tried to cheer him up with jokes, but he was hardly expert at such things. While in Warsaw on business he bought himself a whole pack of Jewish joke books and he assiduously read the humor page of the Friday Yiddish newspaper, but he was seldom able to weave these things naturally into his conversation. In any case, Kalman never laughed at them.

The business was going well. Long before Zelikl had fallen ill, the squire had promised Kalman that he would use his influence to obtain army contracts for him. During the shiva week Berish had gone out to meet with him—Kalman had left it entirely up to Berish. The squire had managed to get them a contract from the War Ministry to supply the army with flour. A confirmation letter had arrived.

"I think you should write to the squire about this," Berish said as he handed him the letter.

Kalman ran his eye over it and handed it to Berish.

"You answer it . . . "

"If this keeps up," Berish said excitedly, "we'll have to expand the mill."

Kalman did not respond.

"You acted very wisely in buying such a big lot—there's plenty of room to grow. You forgot about that, eh? When you first started planning the mill you told me we would outstrip the Bilkowskis."

"You're the miller, Berish. As soon as you say we need to expand, we'll do it."

Berish tried to use the opportunity to joke about it. "You've made me into a miller and I'm getting gray before my time from the dust. For yourself you took the tasty things—a sugar factory, a chocolate factory, a sausage factory—"

"I made you into a miller? I'm the one who tried to convince you to be a rabbi."

"I had to leave the rabbinate to Melech. He's not suited for anything else. Melech is a born rabbi the same way our father-in-law is a born glazier."

Matus was no longer doing any glazing and Berish hoped that Kalman would come to his father-in-law's defense and point out that he was a born *gabbai*—trustee. But Kalman said nothing. Berish tried again.

"There was this glazier who complained to the town madman: 'In other places the town madman breaks windows and the glazier earns a living, but you hang around idle and I don't have any work to do.' The madman disappeared. Some time later the glazier's wife came running to her husband crying that the madman had broken all their windows. The glazier ran home and on the way met the culprit. 'I told you I had to make a living, so why did you go and pick my house?' 'I did it on purpose,' answered the madman: 'I wanted to make sure they would call you to fix the windows, not your competitor.'"

Berish laughed at his own joke but Kalman was still silent.

"There are some businessmen who actually follow the same policy," added Berish, merely for the sake of saying something.

"I know people who follow the same policy in their personal lives," Kalman finally responded.

Berish took the bull by the horns. "Kalman, for a long time now I've wanted to have a serious talk with you. I'm sure you know the verse, 'Silence is a fence to wisdom.' I always took that to mean that silence is the border where wisdom ends. We're as close to each other as brothers. I used to unburden my heart to you—and you did the same with me. People say the way to a man's heart is through his stomach, but I'm sure that the way to reach a friend's heart is through the lips."

"What do you expect me to say?"

"Don't be so naïve, Kalman, you know what it means to be candid with a friend. If something is bothering you, you've got to get it off your chest. That's what friends are for."

"You want me to be completely candid with you? I'm not sure you'd still be my friend."

"A true friend is like a parent—a father still loves his son even if he becomes a thief—or even a murderer—"

"I'm both."

"A real revolution is going on inside you. There was a time you believed in nothing; now you've become a penitent. How can you be silent about that?"

"Me a penitent? No. You remember what God said to Rebecca?

'There are two nations inside your womb.' Well, I'm carrying a Jacob and an Esau inside me and they are constantly fighting. I never know when Esau will get the upper hand."

"Kalman, that's true in every human being. The Evil Inclination is strong, but it's not always negative. You remember from the Bible, when God saw what He had created, 'He saw that it was good.' Our sages said that this refers to the Evil Inclination too. Without an Evil Inclination we wouldn't work hard and plant fields; without an Evil Inclination no children would be born and there would be no continuity in the world. It was your ambition that drove you to amass wealth—you call it building an empire—but you're using your money to do a lot of good things."

"Not always, Berish. You think I've become a penitent? I want to believe in a 'next world,' in a soul that lives on after death, because without that belief I feel miserable. I say the Kaddish because I want to hold on to the illusion that I'm doing something for Zelikl. This morning, when I put on my *tefillin,* I recited the verse 'And I have bound myself to you forever, I have bound myself to you with righteousness and mercy.' Righteousness? There is no such thing. Mercy? Not to me and not to my child! I was almost overwhelmed by the urge to throw the *tefillin* to the ground and scream, 'No! Not mercy but cruelty! There's no law in the world and no judge!' Berish, I'm vindictive and spiteful. If I were really a believer, I'd have done it."

"Your rebelliousness is a sign that you are a believer. Everyone has moments of skepticism and rebellion. The fact that you think about it is a sign that it matters to you—which is a higher stage than obeying blindly. A Hassid once complained to the Rebbe of Kotzk that he often had sinful thoughts. Like what, the Rebbe wanted to know. I'm afraid to say it, replied the Hassid, even Hell won't wipe out that sin. Tell me what it is, the Rebbe insisted. I keep having these doubts, the Hassid admitted. About what? asked the Rebbe. That there is no law and no judge. Why should that concern you, asked the Rebbe. If it's true, said the Hassid, what's the purpose of the whole world? What does it matter to you? said the Rebbe. If it's really so, argued the Hassid, what's the sense of the whole Torah? Is that your responsibilty? the Rebbe demanded. Woe is me, cried the Hassid, without the Torah, what's the use of living? At that point, the Rebbe assured him: 'If all this concerns you, you're a good Jew. A good Jew may think about the world, must think about the world.'"

Kalman listened to all this patiently, thought about it a few minutes, and then said sorrowfully: "You're talking about philosophical skepticism, Berish. I'm not a philosopher. Let the good Jews worry about the Torah, about the world, about the meaning of life. I want to know only one thing: the meaning of death, of Zelikl's death. I'm a wounded man, Berish, my life is nothing but bitterness."

"And how do you think I felt when my father, of blessed memory, suddenly died? But that's life. Those who remain—"

"Berish, my friend, you grew up in a home filled with love. From my earliest years I have been wronged and embittered. The Talmud says we are punished for sins only after we have reached the age of twenty. I was punished by God when I was still an innocent child, and ever since then I've been systematically and unceasingly punished by human beings. The injustice kept accumulating like pus in my body. You know what happens when you touch a raw wound. I struck back and took revenge. If you knew even half of my rotten tricks you wouldn't want to have anything to do with me."

"I can't stand it when you malign yourself this way. If you once did something bad, you've made up for it a long time ago by your good deeds."

"My few good years began when you came along. A tender new skin had begun to cover my open wounds and I stopped being afraid that the Esau in me would again bob up to the surface. Zelikl's death reopened all my old wounds. I'm burning up inside with rage. The serpent inside me is hissing. I take him with me to the synagogue, I tie him up with the thongs of my *tefillin.* How long will that help? I don't enjoy my wealth any longer. I don't give a damn about all my businesses. I'd put a torch to all my factories if I knew the world would burn down with them. So far the pain is still burning here inside me. I built it all for my Zelikl. Now all my successes are only salt in my wounds."

"Kalman, why are you doing this to yourself? Are you the only one in the world who ever lost a child?"

Kalman did not answer immediately. He lowered his head and closed his eyes. After a moment, his eyes still shut, he murmured:

"I may be the only one who deserved the punishment . . . "

"Kalman, this habit you have of torturing yourself is a sickness. I'm telling you this frankly because I know you have the strength to knock it out of your head. One minute you act as though a terrible wrong has been done to you, and in the next breath you say you deserved the punishment. If you really did commit a sin, you've already paid for it a thousand times over."

"You don't know the half of it, Berish, and I'm not talking about something that happened just once. Your father said one day: 'A Jew would never do such a thing.' But a Jew did do that thing, a Jew who is now the brother-in-law of the Rabbi's son. You remember Tsirel's wedding?"

"You mean Tsirel Rothblatt? Are you the one who did that? What a devil!" Berish exclaimed with a little laugh.

"It doesn't bother you?"

"I was barely thirteen at the time, but I wanted to see Tsirel standing under the wedding canopy. Who knows? Maybe I was beginning to be interested in girls. It's not fitting for a bar-mitzva boy, so I snuck into the women's section of the synagogue in order to see the canopy in the yard. I never really got to see it, but I did see you dragging a sack and when it all happened I suspected you were behind it."

"And you told no one?"

"My father."

"What did he say?"

"That I shouldn't tell anybody."

"The Rabbi knew? Your father was a saint! Believe me, if there ever was a *tsaddik* in this world, it was your father."

"Why did you do it, Kalman?"

"It's a long story . . . "

59

People were chasing him. He wanted to cry out but the scream stuck in his throat and—and he awoke. It took a moment before he realized that he was in his own bed, in his own house, and that the noise was not the growling of a wild beast but the snoring of his wife, Kayleh, who was sunk in the deep sleep of the innocent.

Kalman glanced at his wrist. The phosphorescent hands of his watch pointed to three o'clock. He closed his eyes and tried to go back to sleep, but couldn't stop thinking about the dream. He was now completely awake but the nightmare still hovered over him. He slid out of bed and pushed himself quietly out of the bedroom.

In the dark he found his favorite chair and slowly lifted himself into it. Maybe he should go into the kitchen? He had eaten hardly anything for supper. No, no, he wasn't hungry. If he turned on a light, Kayleh would wake up and start asking questions, make a fuss over him. But she needed her rest now more than ever.

What strange dreams! So many dreams! But one dream had turned into a nightmare. Had he really been dreaming of Tsirel? Why after so many years? Of course! He had been talking about her with Berish. It must be true what people say—think about something by day and you'll dream about it at night. Tsirel was his first love. His first? Was there ever a second? Breindl was only a temporary madness. He loved Kayleh, yes, but that was another sort of love. Naïvely, perhaps, but truly in love, he had been only with Tsirel.

He couldn't have been more than twelve when Tsirel had bumped into him on the street. Was it really an accident—or one of his cunning tricks? No, with Tsirel it had not been a trick. She always walked around with her head in the clouds and never noticed what was going on around her, so one day she bumped into him, lost her balance, and sprawled all over him.

"Oh, what a klutz I am!" she had upbraided herself. She was worried that she had hurt him. She helped him sit up again and walked home with him.

From then on he had nodded his head to her whenever he met her on the street, and she always returned his greeting.

He recalled the color of every dress or blouse she wore until she left Dombrovka. In those days he was still devout and prayed every morning that she would appear in the street in the dress he liked most. Every time he looked at his grandfather's prominent ears he couldn't help but compare them with Tsirel's tiny, delicately shaped ears that seemed to wink at him from beneath her silken brown hair. If he ever got rich—and some day he would surely be rich—he would hang jeweled earrings on those lovely ears, and around that slender, elegant throat he would, with his own hands, hang a chain with a medallion. No, not a chain; a string of pearls. You could hang a medallion on a string of pearls too. The translucent gems would be more suitable for her pearly skin.

It was then that he had begun to have his picture taken several times a week. He had it taken from the chest up, and the result was a handsome youth who would have caught the eye of girls anywhere. Broad shoulders, high forehead, dark knowing eyes. He had the photographs made only for himself—he enjoyed looking at them.

Tsirel wore a blue blouse. The collar that rested gracefully around her throat made her eyes even bluer and added to the charm of her smile. He loved that blouse on her, he dreamed of meeting her on the street dressed in that blouse, he even prayed that she wouldn't grow up too fast and outgrow the blouse.

When that skinny Tsirel started maturing, then she was really something to behold. She didn't grow stout; her body filled out gracefully. How often, from behind a curtain, he had watched her walking down the street, her hips rocking rhythmically. And her legs . . . Legs—especially girls' legs—when they are not the accursed limbs of a cripple, can be so shapely that it takes your breath away just to look at them. The Almighty had taken away the strength of his legs, so He owes him another pair of healthy, beautiful—exceptionally beautiful—legs. He had been an innocent child when he took sick. If there is any justice in the world, he would get a bride whose legs would be so beautiful, so marvelous, that—that—just like Tsirel's!

Was Tsirel smart? At that time he couldn't know the answer to that question; he had never exchanged more than a few words with her. But a girl doesn't have to be smart, especially his girl—he had enough brains for both of them. He would greet Tsirel on the street, they would smile at each other, but he could never get up enough nerve to speak with her. He was afraid to take the risk. Suppose she didn't want to speak with him? His dream would collapse like a soap-bubble . . .

•　•　•　•　•

The time his grandfather had found a copy of the Talmudic dictionary *Aruch* that Kalman had bought with stolen money, the old man hadn't even asked where he got the book. But when the postman started delivering one package after another . . . His grandfather could see that he was burying himself night after night in books— Polish books, German books, and another language that he could not even identify. So one day he did ask him: "Where are you getting the money for all these books?"

"They give them to cripples free of charge," he had explained, deliberately inventing an excuse that the old man wouldn't believe. At that point his grandfather started keeping his money under lock and key.

He bought mainly educational books on mechanics, electricity, and similar subjects. To help pass the time he also read cheap novels about torrid love affairs. Their heroes were knights on swift steeds who fought duels over fair ladies. If he had been such a knight he would always have been victorious. His hands were quick and facile. The truth was, however, that he was too smart to fight with his hands. In a duel of heads he would be victorious even now.

One day he noticed that Tsirel was carrying a book by Stefan Zeromski. He immediately went and bought the latest edition of Zeromski's works, among which was his most recent novel, *On the Eve of Spring.* He read it with enjoyment and realized that a good novel could be as entertaining as a tale of knights in armor. The next time he met Tsirel he would initiate a conversation about Zeromski.

60

His grandfather was never sick. And he didn't look his age. Yet one evening he went to bed early, as was his habit, and never woke up again.

All the "old-timers" in Dombrovka came to the funeral. The newer settlers, however, hardly knew him. Tsirel came to the funeral too. Although she didn't walk all the way to the cemetery, she did stay with the procession for quite a long way. He still believed she did it for him. It would have been a good opportunity to speak with her about Zeromski, but how could he do such a thing while his grandfather was being buried? His grandfather's sudden death had frightened him a little, but Tsirel's presence at the funeral made up for everything.

Since his ambition was to get rich quick, he started enlarging the store. Or was he doing it because he wanted Tsirel to come in and buy things from him? She had come in one day to buy buttons, but instead of talking with her about Zeromski he began leaping around like a monkey from shelf to shelf and showing her every button in the store. There were so many that Tsirel had trouble choosing.

Meanwhile, other customers came in. If he'd only had the sense to leave the latest Zeromski book on the counter—he knew they didn't have a copy in the city library yet. Tsirel had left without the conversation, without the book, and even without the buttons.

Should he send her the book with a note? That was the easiest way. Too easy! He'd have to find the courage to speak to her. But suppose he couldn't? Then he wouldn't be worth talking to. Damn his soul if he wouldn't summon up enough gumption to do it!

The next day—it was bright and sunny—he went out into the street with the book on his lap. Maybe he would meet her. All of a sudden, from nowhere, there was a cloudburst. The rain soaked his clothes—and Zeromski's book. It didn't bother him that he might catch cold—better if he ran a fever and croaked! But he couldn't send Tsirel a water-stained book as a gift.

He ordered a new copy of *On the Eve of Spring* from Warsaw. It took forever to arrive. When it did, Tsirel's mother happened to be in the store. Why not send it through her?

"You are buying enough today for a wedding," he said, smiling broadly.

"For an engagement party," she said. "My Tsirel's getting engaged."

"Tsirel? Impossible! She's still a child." Despite his smile, his tone revealed the insistence of a person who refuses to believe what he doesn't want to.

"She'll soon be eighteen, thank God. The second day of Rosh Hashonah. Not so young anymore."

Later he heard that the groom was a cousin of Tsirel's, that their families had been calling them bride-and-groom ever since they had been young children. Why had she encouraged him, then? That false smile, sweet as saccharine, the coquette with the book by Zeromski—Tsirele, Mirele, Shmirele—I love you like a *geshverele*—an abscess—on the rear end!

The wedding took place a year later. Lively music poured out of the open windows of the synagogue into the streets. Suddenly, through one of the windows, a pillow came hurtling and fell to the ground. For a moment it lay there quietly, then it started thrashing around as if it were alive. "A hobgoblin!" one woman screamed—and fainted. A fearful commotion. The pillow jumped up and ran around wildly. The beadle grabbed the groom's new tallis and threw it over the pillow, but the hobgoblin squirted out and escaped, ripping the pillowcase from the inside. Out leaped an unearthly creature the likes of which had never been seen before. It ran back into the hall, howling like a wildcat. Finally, one brave young man captured it.

The hobgoblin turned out to be an ordinary cat covered with tar. The feathers in the pillow had stuck to the tar, giving it the look of something from the netherworld.

The Rabbi wondered who could have perpetrated such a malicious deed. Then he answered his own question. "No Jew would have the shamelessness to do such an odious thing." But on the pillowcase, written in Hebrew letters, were two words: *droshe-geshank*—wedding present.

61

Kayleh went to bed early. She called him but he remained in his chair. His life passed before him like the pages of a book. He wanted to block his memory when Breindl's face appeared to him; he could neither stop it nor escape it, and everything appeared with such clarity that it seemed to have happened only yesterday. It unfurled before him like a densely written scroll, detail after detail.

When Breindl had come to Dombrovka she could not find enough praise for Kalman. She and Yosl occupied the room that had formerly been Kayleh's, but she felt that the entire house was hers. Whenever she needed to buy something for herself or for the household, Yosl always turned to Kalman, but he never had to wait long for an answer. Whatever she wanted, Kalman paid for; her happiness was his greatest concern. She loved to chat, but Yosl never had much to say, so Kalman was the one who kept the conversation going at meal times. He even lingered at the table with her when there were customers in the store. He taught her to play cards and sometimes the game lasted until late in the evening. Yosl couldn't keep his eyes open. He went to bed with the hens and was up with the first crow of the rooster. Breindl would send him to bed and not go in herself until the card game was finished.

The game was slow, with more chatting than playing. Kalman admitted he was the one who had written the letters supposedly from Yosl before the two had married. Breindl, too, confessed she had paid someone to help her with the letters she had written to Yosl. Kalman claimed he had learned to read cards from a gypsy woman and tried a reading for Breindl. Not sure he was really getting it from the cards, she could not deny that he knew more about her than she had told him. No, she had not worked for Pan Blumenkrantz in his dry goods store but in his home, as a servant-girl. With poverty suffocating her, what else could she have done? A new dress was out of the question. The economic crisis was so bad that even if you offered to work for nothing there were no jobs. In good times she had worked in the same weaving mill as her father—he on a loom and she on a spooler. But now with the machines standing idle, the workers had nothing to eat. Not able to bear the misery at home any longer, she fled to the big city and took the first job she could find.

Kalman consoled her. "There's no disgrace working at a job—any kind of job—"

"The Blumenkrantzes ate very well, and I had a couple of extra zloty to send home. In addition to all the other troubles, Mama grew sickly, otherwise I'd have run back home."

"Why? When you had enough to eat and even saved some money?"

"I was—unhappy . . . "

"Which one bothered you—the boss himself or his sonny boy?"

"Both. Then I read the notice in the paper. Young man seeks young woman up to age twenty-five, must be pretty. Dowry unnecessary. If interested, write to—"

"You remember it all by heart?"

"When I sent off my letter I thought I was wasting my postage, but—look what happened. Tell me, Kalman, were you the one who put that notice in the papers?"

"Yes."

"There aren't many people who would do all that for a friend."

"You think I did it only for Yosl? I like having you here too."

"You're sweet, Kalman, if only—"

Breindl didn't finish the sentence, so Kalman helped her: "If only I weren't a cripple?"

"That's not what I was going to say."

"Breindl, you can be honest with me. Anyway, I know what you're going to say even before you say it."

"You're so clever, Kalman. You know so much. You've got a good head on your—"

"I'm beginning to believe that legs are more important than heads. Every moron looks at me with pity. Have you ever looked at a squirrel, Breindele? A squirrel's head is like a mouse's, and so is its body, but a squirrel can fluff up its tail and a mouse can't. The same person who laughs when a cat catches a mouse, will cry when it catches that little animal with the beautiful tail. The head doesn't matter—the important thing is a fluffy tail . . . "

"You can't really mean that, Kalman. All of Dombrovka admires you, you know . . . "

"You too?"

"Me especially."

"Good . . . "

· · · · ·

A chilly dawn brought an early snowfall mixed with rain. Both men were up, Kalman making a list of the merchandise to be bought and Yosl preparing for his first buying trip in Warsaw. Originally Kalman was supposed to go, but he woke Yosl in the middle of the night to pass on the assignment to him. Breindl was grateful for Kalman's confidence in her husband.

The house was cold. Breindl jumped out of bed to fix a hot breakfast and some food for Yosl to take along. Kalman gave Yosl final instructions, then added: "And buy something nice for our Breindl."

Breindl blushed. "It's really unnecessary. I have everything I need here."

It was a busy day at the store and Breindl had to help Kalman. With the early onset of cold weather everyone was rushing to stock up for the winter.

Up and working since five that morning, Breindl was too tired even to wash the supper dishes, and she went to bed early. She turned down the flame of the kerosene lamp, blew it out, slid under her down blanket and closed her eyes. Suddenly a pinkish glare pierced through her eyelids.

"Is that you, Kalman?" she asked.

"Yes, Breindl." He set the lamp down on the table and pushed himself closer to her bed.

"What's wrong, Kalman?" she cried out in alarm. "Has something happened?"

He pointed to his forehead. "Something is wrong here! This morning I asked Yosl to buy a nice gift for you—I completely forgot that I have a beautiful thing for you right here." And, holding up a string of pearls and a pair of gold earrings set with diamonds, he told Breindl, "They were my mother's . . . "

"Why don't you wait till Yosl gets back?"

"Why? I'll only forget again. You like them, don't you?"

"They were your mother's—you should keep them for your wife."

"My wife, Yosl's wife—what's the difference? You are ours, don't you see?"

"You've been good to us, Kalman. We're both very grateful."

"Do you have pierced ears, Breindl? No? Then you'll have it done—it doesn't hurt at all." He slid back to the table. "The earrings I'm putting over here, see? The pearls I must put around your lovely neck myself."

Before she could answer, Kalman was at her side again. One leap and he was on her bed. He undid the catch on the necklace; she raised her chin, and he fastened it around her neck. His hot breath made her feel suddenly very cold.

"Thank you very very much, Kalman. Good night. I'm so sleepy, I've been up for sixteen hours. Kalman, what are you doing?!" It was an anguished, desperate cry. His arms were locked around her waist.

"I'm mad about you, Breindl!"

"Don't, Kalman! I'm Yosl's wife!"

"Be my wife, Breindl!"

"I stood under the chupah, the wedding canopy with Yosl."

"If Yosl hadn't been there, would you have married me? It was I who put the matchmaker's notice in the paper. I sent you Yosl's picture because I'm a mouse, not a squirrel, because I can't stand under a chupah, my useless legs wouldn't hold me up. But I'm human—I'm a man, Breindl, I'm a man!"

"Tomorrow! We'll talk about it tomorrow—"

"Don't try to sweet-talk me!" He tore open his shirt. "Look, Breindl—above my legs I'm just like everyone else. Feel my muscles!" He grabbed her hand and held it to his hairy chest. "My flesh yearns for your touch—"

Breindl pulled her hand away. "I'm sleepy, Kalman, I can't keep my eyes open. Let me get some sleep. Please. Tomorrow we'll talk."

Kalman threw his legs under the covers. "You see? Now I'm just as handsome as Yosl."

"Let me be, Kalman, I beg you!"

"Yosl has strong legs, but up here," he said, pointing to his head, "he's very weak. His body and my brain make a perfect pair. You'll have the best of both worlds."

"Leave me alone, Kalman, or—"

"Don't scream. Yosl and I—we both love our pretty little Breindl—"

"Please, Kalman, I'm begging you—"

He tugged frantically at her nightshirt, trying to pull it off her shoulders. The fabric tore, exposing her ripe little breasts. His eyes grew wild, frenzied.

"Yosl will kill you—"

"We're partners, the two of us. I'm a good partner and Yosl too—"

"What are you babbling about?"

"Fifty-fifty—the store and everything—"

"Yosl knows?" she cried out in bewilderment. "Yosl knew what you were going to do?"

"A person doesn't give away half his fortune just like that."

"I'll spit in his face, I'll scratch his eyes out, I'll throw acid over both of you!" she howled.

Kalman grimaced. "You'll throw acid? No, I will! Those sweet words of yours while we were playing cards—that was just to tease me? Or to get more out of the sucker? Well, Kalman is not an easy mark! You see that lamp? I'll smash it over your head! One lick of the flame and your pretty face will look like roast beef!" Spittle began to froth around his lips. "People are always ready to take, never to give! But Kalman also can take back what's due him! A partner is a partner!"

The pressure of his arms relaxed somewhat. His tone again grew soft, pleading. "You're a newcomer around here, Breindele. Kalman Kalika is not an insult, it's a business establishment. I'm richer than you can imagine. You'll be swimming in gold. In twenty years the electric station will be earning a fortune. You're wondering how so much has flowed into this lopsided little house? It all came from here, everything was born here, in this head." He raised his hand to point to his head and held her down with one arm. She was frightened by his feverish breath and his cold hands. She watched for an opportune moment to break loose.

"It's my own fault, I know," Kalman was saying. "It was I, I myself who brought you two together. How was I to know that you were so—Breindele, you're not a fool. You and I will put our beds and our heads together and the whole world will be ours."

"I already have a husband, Kalman."

"Just say the word and I'll get rid of that imbecile, that *goylem.*"

Her little fist struck him in the nose; blood spurted and ran into his mouth.

She had hit him in order to confuse him, so she could tear herself away, but the sight of blood frightened her and she bent to help him. The opportunity slipped by. Again the crooked smile returned to his bloodstained face. He slid down, using both hands to force her tightly locked legs apart. She clenched her teeth, pressed her legs together with all her might and flailed away at his head with both fists.

Damn these useless legs of mine, he cursed. How could he overpower her when he had only hands and she had hands and feet? Again he began to plead with her. "Breindele, it was I who found you, who saved you from Blumenkrantz's paws, who gave you everything you have. Why does Yosl deserve your caresses and for me you have only fists? It's bad enough that idiot towers so high above me that I reach only to his backside and he farts right in my face. You know me better than anyone else. I'm crazy about you, Breindl, is that why you're hitting me?"

"I'm a married woman, I'm Yosl's wife—"

"Just this one time and it will be enough for me for the rest of my life. I've never even touched a woman like you. Why am I so accursed?"

"A demon's gotten into you today, Kalman." She tried again to reason with him. "Yosl is your best friend and I know you are his best friend."

"That's exactly what I've been telling you! So why should Yosl mind?"

"If I were your wife, and Yosl—wouldn't you mind?"

"Be my wife, Breindl. With me, you'll live like a queen—"

She tore away from him and tumbled over the side of the bed to the floor. Like a cat he was on her before she could move an inch. She dug her fingernails into his face, she scratched at his flesh, she bit him and beat on him with her fists, but she could not free herself from his grip.

"Kalman the Cripple can take a beating," he said with a bitter smile. "Kalman the Cripple is used to that."

She kept pounding him with her fists until her arms grew so weary she could barely lift them. A deep loathing filled her as her resistance grew weaker. Every fiber of her body writhed in desperation, and with each twitch she felt her strength ebb. Only her eyes stayed wide open and staring. She observed herself as if her eyes were outside her body, passively watching the scene on the floor near her bed . . .

Had her passivity frightened him? Had her helplessness awakened his pity? He raised his hand and stroked her hair. A spark of life and hope began to glow within her again, and she raised her head.

Like a ravenous beast he pounced. Her head fell back to the floor and he howled over her like a stallion in heat . . .

She must have fainted, or gone out of her mind. He raped her again and again. The oil in the lamp burned out and still he did not desist. Daylight was dawning when he sat up and took a last look at her.

"You're a pretty girl, Breindele. You be good to me and I'll be good to you, and we'll all live here together in Paradise. And your Yosl doesn't need to know a thing," he added as he left the room and closed the door behind him.

•   •   •   •   •

Too late to go to bed, too early to open the store. Kalman sat down at the table, rested his heavy head on his arms and tried to catch a few winks. His whole body felt weary, but thoughts ran wild in his head. Plans, plans, plans . . . Like him, the plans had no legs to stand on. Nor did they have a head, which was *not* like him. He'd better get hold of himself. His head was all he had, if he lost that—. The whole town would look on in envy whenever he and Breindl appeared on the street. How had such foolishness crept into his head? Look on and laugh is more like it! If he appeared in the street sliding on his ass, with Breindl walking beside him, and if she really did become his Breindl, they would look at them with derision. Some wise guy was bound to see her as a fortress, easy to storm.

She is honest, she is loyal . . .

Loyal to Yosele *goylem!* If that clever Breindl could tie herself so tightly to Yosl, it only showed that those long-haired creatures, even the ones with some brains, are attracted to males who are strong as oxen and have brawny muscles to flex. If one of those creatures ever got involved with him, it would only be to deceive him. No, Kalman Kalika didn't need people watching him with envy over such things. For him it was enough to achieve his ends quietly, in secret. She'd get used to it and he wouldn't have to use force any more—he would be the silent partner.

He couldn't fall asleep anyway, so he might as well go down to the store and unpack the new shipment that had arrived yesterday. He unpacked the goods, arranged them on the shelves, and by then it was opening time. As he was taking the grate off the door from the inside, a customer was already waiting to come in. All day was like that. Customers came and went and Kalman served them, but quietly, not with his usual banter and loquaciousness. He couldn't get his mind off Breindl. Was he in love with her? Ridiculous! Kalman Kalika was too intelligent to fall in love. How had he ever gotten embroiled in this whole business?

It had all begun with a joke, one of his usual tricks. If he took a picture down to the waist only, being very photogenic, he came out looking like a strapping, handsome young man-about-town. So he had got this crazy notion of playing with the matrimonial ads in the newspaper. This developed into a correspondence with marriage brokers and prospective brides. He mailed out his photograph and in return got back photographs of young women. Inane letters and homely pictures he burned right away. Interesting letters and pretty girls' pictures he saved, and continued the correspondence.

Then, the day a marriage broker walked into the store, what excitement! He had made a special trip from Warsaw just to see Pan Kalman.

"Oh, you want Pan Kalman? I'm very sorry, but he was conscripted into the army."

"He never mentioned anything in his letters about enlisting in the army," the matchmaker had complained, showing him a whole pack of letters tied with pink ribbon.

To console the man, he had said: "When Pan Kalman received the conscription notice he did mention something about getting married. I'm sure he'll get in touch with you when he completes his military service."

Military service?

Why not? Every young man with sound limbs serves in the army. He must ask the photographer if he couldn't borrow a uniform somewhere. In a military uniform he would really look terrific.

Maybe there'd be a war. Then he could claim he was a war invalid. Not just an ordinary cripple, but an invalid, a hero who had sacrificed his legs for the fatherland.

No, he wasn't building castles in the air. When Breindl answered one of his notices in the paper and enclosed her photograph, he immediately wanted to bring her here, but he had the sense to sign Yosl's name to his letter and enclose Yosl's photograph.

Was he really doing it for Yosl's sake?

Only after he had been carrying Breindl's picture in his pocket for a week did he actually speak to Yosl. She looked skinny, but had a charming face and a knowing smile, with two dimples and roguish eyes. He must bring her to Dombrovka at any price, but it was a very high price to pay. He would have to bring her here for Yosl. The first time Breindl slept in his house he . . .

He gave them a room of their own. He lay in his cold bed wretched and miserable, while in that other room . . . Yes, he had to be content with fantasies. If he hadn't learned to live with fantasies he'd have been six feet under long ago. It wasn't difficult for him to immerse himself in daydreams in the dark of night, but during the day, whenever he saw this clever little woman smiling so sweetly to her doltish husband, he almost burst with envy. By God, couldn't she see what an oaf that Yosl was! It must be that only Yosl's big hands and long legs were clumsy, but everything in between functioned quite satisfactorily . . .

That whole game with the photographs had soon begun to bore him. It was he who had first started calling his partner "Yosele Goylem," but Yosele Goylem now had a real, live Breindl, and apparently she loved him. He—the clever Kalman—had only paper brides and paper love affairs. Kalmam Kalika, it's you who are the fool, the *goylem*—the biggest *goylem* in the world!

Breindl was not blind to Kalman's virtues. She laughed at his wisecracks, enjoyed his practical jokes, and admired his deep fund of knowledge—"Kalman knows everything," she said, not without pride. After all, he was her Kalman too.

But last night she had fought him like a tigress. Was it aversion to a cripple? It couldn't be only that. She couldn't stand a word of criticism against Yosl. "He's my husband, he's my husband," she kept screaming. A few months ago she hadn't even known that Yosl existed. Now he was "my husband, my husband." Such loyalty. You aren't worth a hill of beans, Kalman Kalika, if you and all your cleverness are as nothing against a blockhead like Yosl.

Ai, Kalman, Kalman, you're a cripple in your head too. You slither around on your battered backside and sigh like a real lover. What would you do if Breindl came out of her room now and said, "Kalman, I've thought it over and come to a decision. Give Yosl whatever he wants, so long as he gives me a divorce. I want to become your wife—yours alone." What would he do if Breindl said that? Hadn't he decided if he couldn't stand on his own feet he'd stand on someone else's? He would steal, rob, swindle, and grab with both hands in order to live and laugh at other people's expense. Was he ready now to marry Breindl, to sign over his property to her, and then?

Funny! It would have been something to laugh about, if it hadn't been something to cry about. He had promised himself he would never marry, but in truth he had wanted to get married when he was still little. It had happened when his father disappeared. His mother couldn't stop crying and he tried to comfort her: "Don't cry, Mama, I'll be the Papa." She had probably said something about Papa not being her father but her husband, that she was married to him. He had said: "I'll be your husband, I'll marry you too."

Did he really remember that? All his life he had been trying to recall how his mother looked, and now—did he really remember this incident, or was he losing his mind?

He recalled very clearly biting his grandfather's hand when he was dragging him out of the house to go to Dombrovka. Or maybe he only dreamed it. Maybe it was only one of his wild fantasies. In his childish imaginings he was often his own brother. A brother yes, and a father no?

A boy in *heder* had punched him and run away, leaving him helpless. "You won't get away with this!" he had screamed at the fleeing culprit.

"Catch me and punch me back!" the tormenter had challenged.

"You won't get away with it! My brother will catch you in a dark alley and pay you back!"

"You don't even have a brother, you cripple!"

"When my brother comes back from Warsaw he'll show you!"

Later that day he fantasized that he was his own brother, a giant of a brother. He comes back from Warsaw, stands in the middle of the street, thrusts out his massive chest and calls out:

"Whoever hurt my kid brother Kalman, let him come out here now and take his punishment, otherwise he'll get it double!"

*　*　*　*　*

Kalman had something to eat and thought about Breindl, who hadn't had a morsel of food yet today. He felt like going out to the confectioner's to buy her a nosh, but he hesitated to appear in the street with a black eye and a scratched up face. He boiled an egg, smeared some butter on a slice of bread, poured a cup of milk, and put it all on a tray. He ought to carry the tray on his head, as the Oriental women do, so that both his hands would be free to push himself around. It would also bring a smile to her eyes. No, this was a time for solemnity. He balanced the tray in one hand, and with the other began wheeling himself to her room. He even got the door open without spilling a drop of the milk. "Not bad for Kalman Kalika," he felt like boasting, but Breindl didn't even glance in his direction. He put the tray down beside her bed and left the room.

Breindl was angry. Would she keep quiet or would she make a fuss? He had always known how to get around Yosl, but what would happen if this Breindle got him all worked up like a mad dog? Eh, Kalman Kalika had been in tighter spots before and gotten out of them . . .

*　*　*　*　*

A representative of the mayor's office came to see him about the power station and brought with him the magistrate of the village of Wilki, only two kilometers from Dombrovka. The magistrate wanted to know if eletricity could also be linked to his village. The farmers there were willing to pay the monthly bill as well as the installation costs.

Kalman answered on the spot. He'd agree to run the lines to Wilki, but he would not go out to collect the monthly payments. The mayor's office would have to do that and pay him twenty percent more than the rate for Dombrovka, to cover the cost of two kilometers of power lines and the loss of power transferred on such a stretch.

His visitors were hardly out the door when he was again thinking about what had happened during the night. Wishing to drive those thoughts out of his head, he picked up a sheet of paper, sharpened a pencil, and started calculating the cost of running power lines to

Wilki; he had to figure out whether the dynamo he had ordered would be large enough to provide electricity for Wilki too. But he couldn't keep his mind on calculations. The only reckoning that kept creeping back into his head was a spiritual one. No, he had no premonitions and he was not afraid of what might happen when Yosl returned from Warsaw. But he felt as though he were sitting in a movie theater with scenes of his life flashing before his eyes.

The store filled up with customers just at a time when he preferred to be alone and think. He weighed and he measured, he took money and he gave change, but with no enjoyment. He was glad when the time came to close the store. He was dead tired. Breindl had stayed all day in her room. Maybe he should bring her something to eat again. But he was sleepy. If she got hungry, she knew where to find everything. He went to his rooms, and with his clothes still on, he threw himself on his bed and fell asleep.

•　•　•　•　•

Kalman woke up late in the evening. He put coal on the fire in the stove and returned to his calculations on the cost of electricity for the village. Yosl arrived home to find Kalman at the table in the big room over a pile of papers.

"Not asleep yet?" he asked, surprised. "It's almost light outside."

"Everybody in the world can sleep—Kalman Kalika has to keep working."

"You don't have to. You've got plenty already. Who scratched you up like that?"

"It's nothing. A cat. Go to bed."

•　•　•　•　•

Kalman's ears picked up every sound at the other end of the house. The door of Yosl's room was flung open and Yosl ran out. To the yard? The outhouse? Yosl is a dunce, but Breindl had more sense and would keep quiet. Or maybe it would be better if she told him. If she told him, it would resolve itself into an equal partnership . . .

Would he really give Yosl half of his property? True, he had promised the *goylem* he would make him a partner. So what? Kalman has his bagful of tricks, like that bamboozling merchant who claims that his word carried more weight than a promissory note. He signs a note to pay and later says he won't pay. He honors his word, not his note . . .

He had already done more than enough for that idiot. What had the klutz ever done for him? Promises cost nothing. On the other hand, what if . . .

The back door groaned. Yosl was coming back in from the yard. Kalman pricked up his ears. Yosl had not stopped at his own room; his lumbering footsteps were coming straight this way! Yosl paused in the doorway, his hulking body almost pushing out the door frame. The sight of the ax in Yosl's right hand sharpened Kalman's senses to an acute awareness.

"Where are you going with an ax?" he asked, keeping his voice calm, but his body ready to jump.

Yosl said nothing. Kalman examined his position. It was too far to go through all the rooms to the back door, too many thresholds to trip him up in the dark. The nearest way out was through the store, but the front door was securely locked and bolted. Until he'd managed to unlock it . . . He had to play a crafty game here. His tongue was sharper than Yosl's ax.

"How did things go in Warsaw?" he asked. "Sit down here at the table—I've been wanting to talk with you about—"

Yosl took a big step into the room and raised the ax. Kalman leaped up on the table, reached high and grabbed one of the beams that held up the ceiling. Yosl rushed toward him, tripped over a chair and dropped the ax on his own shoe.

"Take off your shoe, now! Put cold compresses on your foot!" Kalman's tone dripped concern.

But Yosl apparently was not badly cut. Picking up the ax again, Yosl lunged at Kalman. Quick as a monkey, Kalman swung from beam to beam, Yosl brandishing the ax a step behind him. Kalman swung to the next beam and the ax blade sank into a support post with such force that the whole house shook. Again Kalman measured the distance to the door. Too far. Too risky. He must win over this *goylem* with kind words. He would wear him down, the same way he did with Breindl, and then . . . Kalman Kalika had overcome greater odds than this . . .

Yosl pulled out the ax with such force that he toppled over backward with a thud. Kalman stifled a laugh and again put a look of concern on his face. But before he could even say a word, Yosl was on his feet again, swinging his weapon. Neither of them uttered another sound. Only the groaning of the beams could be heard, and the heavy breathing of the pursuer and the pursued.

Yosl managed to back Kalman into a corner. Slowly and deliberately he raised the ax. Kalman swung his dangling feet across Yosl's face and even before Yosl turned around, Kalman had got to the other end of the room, hanging onto a beam. Yosl lowered the ax and stood as if rooted to the ground. Their eyes met, the bigger man looking up at the smaller.

"Yosl," Kalman tried once more, sympathetically, but his attacker raised the ax high. Now he's going to throw it at me, Kalman thought, bracing himself. But Yosl was no longer looking at him. He had turned and begun chopping away at one of the posts. The house shuddered each time the metal met wood.

Breindl, in her nightshirt, came running and stopped in the doorway. "Yosl," she called softly. "Yosl, come, let's get away from this place . . . "

The ax whistled louder and faster. "Come, Yosl!" She was afraid to move closer, lest she step into the path of the ax. She was not even certain that he saw her or heard her. The ax did not stop its rising and falling. She wanted to scream, but her throat had dried up, her tongue had grown stiff, she could not utter a sound. She turned and moved away.

"Breindle—" Kalman called. The ax fell with heavier and heavier blows. Breindl ran back to her room.

When the post finally split and crumbled, the whole house groaned loudly. A gap appeared between the beam structure and the ceiling. Objects began dropping to the ground.

"Look, Yosl—money!" A package of Tsarist Russian rubles fell to the floor. Let the *goylem* take the worthless paper. "It's a lot of money, Yosl! Take it! It belongs to you!"

Yosl turned his attention to another post.

Again the entire structure of beams and posts trembled. The kerosene lamp flew off its hooks in the middle of the ceiling, hit the table, fell to the floor, and broke into a thousand pieces. For a moment the room was pitch black, but then light appeared from another source—a patch of floor and a leg of the table had caught fire. Yosl stood and stared at the flames, the ax hanging limply in his hand. In Kalman's corner it was dark. The little flames illuminated Yosl from head to toe and gave him the look of an apparition. Had Breindl threatened Kalman yesterday with the fires of hell, or had the thought occurred to him just now? This massive Yosl with his ax, the spreading fire—he broke into a spasm of coughing—this smoke was choking him. The sound seemed to rouse Yosl from his trance. Again he raised the ax and chopped away at the post.

The old miser Jonah had really hidden away treasures here that Kalman knew nothing about. Packets began dropping from the ceiling. One of them broke open. Coins rolled all over the floor.

"Yosl! Look! It's gold!" Let him take the precious gold rubles. But Yosl continued to swing his ax relentlessly.

The smoke rose slowly but steadily. Kalman could not stop his coughing. "Take whatever you want," he spluttered, "it's a big fortune, Yosl, take it all, and take your Breindl, get away from here before—"

Yosl only swung his ax with renewed impetus.

The fire itself—that would be his salvation, Kalman suddenly realized. It was almost daylight, people would soon be going to the synagogue, somebody would see the fire. The flames were creeping closer to Yosl's feet, his pants would catch fire—

Kalman again started swinging from beam to beam, moving closer to the door. Another post crumbled beneath Yosl's ax and he turned to a third one. The ceiling would soon have no supports at all.

The smoke had reached Yosl's bedroom. Breindl came running out again and stopped short as the fire separated her from her husband.

"Yosl! The house is on fire!" she screamed, as if he couldn't see the flames himself. But he only kept hacking away at the wood.

"Run, Breindl!" Kalman cried. "Run for help! He's gone mad!"

Breindl jumped across the burning floor and grabbed Yosl's arm. The ax flew out of his hand into a china closet, shattering it into bits. "Yosl, Yosl!" she screamed, tugging at his arm. He freed himself, put both arms around the post and pulled with all his strength. Debris fell from the ceiling, thick as rain. Kalman swung to another beam. The wood split and his hands slid downward. He managed to hold on to the edge of the log and could feel the heat on his soles. He hung suspended over the flames, as if he were being roasted alive. Which would finish him first—the fire or the ax? A thousand curses on his miserable life! His feet were no good for walking, but they could burn, just like anyone else's. The flames were licking at his feet, and that virtuous Breindl was standing here, doing nothing. Only a miracle could save him now.

And the miracle happened. So much debris fell from the ceiling that it smothered the flames. But the chunks of plaster were bruising his head, and his hands were growing as useless as his feet . . .

The dust and smoke were so thick that Kalman's eyes closed against his will. Breindl screamed. The walls shuddered convulsively. Kalman tore open his eyelids, but no longer saw anything. A loud crash, another . . . Of the whole house, only a pile of debris remained, and a cloud of dust . . .

62

The rain fell all night, but in the morning the freshly washed sun mirrored itself in the puddles on the rutted highway and dried the mud splattered on Kalman's automobile. He drove into the yard of the sugar factory. The yard was paved, but the cement was already crumbling. Rotten workmen! Cripples! I warned them, Kalman grumbled. I warned them about the heavy trucks . . .

Normally Kalman would put his little platform outside the car, lower himself onto it and make his way into the factory without any help. "What am I, an invalid?" he would laugh. But now, with the big pools of water on the ground, he wanted the janitor to come out and help him. He blew his horn a few times, but they were loading a shipment of sugar and there was so much noise in the yard that he could barely hear the sound of his horn himself.

When he finally entered the factory the sight of Berish turned his annoyance into a smile. Berish had plenty of work to do in the mill, but he kept an eye on the sugar factory. True, Kalman had a sharp head for planning, for building, but for running big businesses good administration is needed, and for that he had little patience. Berish was a gift from heaven. He was loyal and didn't have a lazy bone in his body. He managed the mill, but did no less for the sugar factory than the German, Hoenicke, the renowned "professional" that Kalman had brought from the other end of the country.

Berish showed Kalman a letter that had come from London. Neither he nor Herr Hoenicke knew English, but Kalman was fluent. "I'll just have to learn the language," Berish declared.

"Berish, what would I do without you?

• • • • •

When Kalman went out into the yard again, so many motors were roaring at once that the noise was deafening. As he wheeled himself around on his board he saw a large truck moving in his direction. The driver, from his high perch, could not see Kalman so close to the ground. Trucks on all sides, like great devils of *gehennum*. He shouted, but couldn't even hear his own screams. The massive truck kept coming straight at him. He threw himself to his left, and at that instant the driver heard his cries. He jammed on his brakes and the truck skidded—to the left.

"In this absurd way?"

That was the very last thought to cross Kalman's brain.

• • • • •

All of Dombrovka, even non-Jews, walked in the funeral procession for Kalman. Merchants came from far away to pay their last respects, even a banker from Warsaw. Tsippe kept screaming that it was her fault, it was her fault, she hadn't done enough to guard her family against the Evil Eye. She tore out clumps of her hair, even when her son-in-law the Rabbi emphasized that this was forbidden to Jews. Everyone had tears in their eyes—except Kayleh. She had not yet registered what had happened.

The Rabbi tried to say a few words at the open grave but his tears choked him. Matus summoned all his strength and intoned: *Hashem nosan, ha'shem lokakh.* The Lord giveth and the Lord taketh away, and who are we to understand His ways? Then he picked up the spade and tossed the first handful of earth into the grave.

Following religious law, they also put Berish's gaberdine into the grave, because it had been stained with Kalman's blood as he lay dying.

63

Matus went first to Lenchitz; from there he was directed to Lodz. He rang the bell at the address he had been given and announced who he wanted. He was told to "go around to the back." Matus entered the courtyard, found another staircase and climbed up two flights. There Breindl herself opened the door.

"Praise God that you are standing on your own two feet," he said, happy to see that she was well enough to do so. "Does the Miss know who I am?"

"What do you want?"

"Do you recognize me?"

"What do you want? I'm busy," she said irately, blocking the door.

"I'm from Dombrovka. I have a message for the Miss."

"What do you want of me?"

"I have a message from Kalman."

"What does he want from me now? May he drop dead wherever he is."

"Unfortunately, he is no longer among the living."

"May the earth spit him out!"

"Don't. It's not permitted. I have money for you."

"From him? Tfui! His money disgusts me. I don't want it. And I never want to hear his accursed name again."

"Sinful words, Miss. Kalman died a righteous man and—"

"Righteous!?" Breindl mocked, bursting into hysterical laughter. Matus pulled a package out of his pocket and held it out to her.

"He left this for you."

She stepped back into her kitchen and let him in.

"It's been nearly two years. He had a bad case of blood poisoning—gangrene. They amputated part of his leg. Before they took him in for the operation he called me over and told me that if he didn't survive the operation, to give you five thousand zloty."

"Five thousand!"

"Now this all happened suddenly and he didn't have a chance to speak before he died. I told the Rabbi about it, and Berish, my son-in-law, and they sent me with the money. It's yours."

Breindl stood there with her mouth open. Matus again held the package out to her. "Here, please count it."

She had still not taken the money. The door opened and a short, rotund woman marched in.

"*Kto to,* Bronka, who is this?"

"He's here for me, madam."

"Tell him to come back in the evening, when you have time."

"I never have any time here—"

"If you don't like it here you can take your things and go!"

"That's exactly what I'm going to do!"

"You want to run away, ha? Give me back the twenty zloty that I advanced you. You wanted to run away with my twenty zloty!"

"Panie Matus, give her twenty zloty of my money."

"Does the Pani have change of a hundred?" Matus asked.

When she saw the pack of hundred zloty bills in Matus's hand, the Pani lost her tongue. Matus searched in all his pockets for smaller bills, but couldn't find enough.

"While Breindl is packing up her things, I'll run down and change one of these hundreds." Taking out one bill, he handed the rest to Breindl.

"Here—it belongs to you."

One of those real "madams," he said to himself as he hobbled down and up the steps. A poor child with no luck, that Breindl. Barely recovered enough to stand on her feet and go to work and she falls into the clutches of a witch.

When Matus returned, the madam had noticeably softened.

"You don't have to run away so fast, Bronka," she said. "You can finish out the week."

Breindl said nothing and continued her packing.

As Matus stood and waited, his thoughts turned to Kalman. Even without his many good deeds, with this one alone Kalman was now earning a share in the world-to-come.

"At least stay another week until I can find someone else."

"I gave the Pani back her twenty zloty, so she already has half-a-week for nothing." A mischievous little flame blazed up in her eyes. "The Pani wants me to stay? I can stay for good. Young Mietek is looking for a bride with a dowry. I have a dowry—"

"Listen to what a dirty mouth it has! Came here quiet as a pigeon and now—"

"I really ought to do it, just to annoy the madam, but if I have such a grand dowry, why should I marry a no-good, lazy loafer like Mietek?"

"She doesn't want me here while she's packing, so she can help herself to my things, just like she used to from the pots." The madam's tone grew bitter. "But I won't move from this spot!"

"If I had waited only for what she gave me, I'd already have one foot in the grave. Kalman was nasty, but at least he gave me enough to eat."

Matus could not endure her harsh words about Kalman, so he quickly said goodbye and left.

Epilogue

Kalman's last will and testament was written only a month before the accident. It contained the clause, "If something should happen to me . . ." Was this a premonition or only a shrewdly calculated preparation for any eventuality? In the months preceding his death he had consulted Berish on all his business decisions, shared every new idea with him. He had given Berish a list of all his deposits in various banks, in cash and in notes. He showed him where he kept the keys to his safe deposit boxes. When Kalman decided that Berish should go with him to Warsaw to make all these arrangements, Berish pleaded with him: "Think it over, Kalman, speak with your other relatives first," but Kalman had insisted: "I don't want to repeat the mistakes that my Grandfather Jonah made."

When Berish ran out to the scene of the accident, Kalman was still breathing, but blood streamed from his wounds, and before the doctor arrived he was dead. He died in Berish's arms. Afterward, Berish kept washing his hands and they still felt sticky. The image of Kalman in his pool of blood kept surging up in his mind and his insides heaved. He couldn't touch food for days.

Through his mind he sifted every word that Kalman had spoken in his last weeks, trying to discover what was behind them. Kalman—may he forgive me—was a bit of a braggart. Why, then, had he lately been repeating that he was a reprobate? Kalman had once told him that his Grandmother Liebele had become convinced that it was her unlucky star that brought misfortune upon all those around her. Had Kalman been doing this to himself after Zelikl's death?

No, Kalman's head was clear and sane and consistent. True, after Zelikl's death he had become despondent, but that could happen to anyone. He was the only person Kalman trusted, the only person he listened to; why hadn't he seriously tried to drive the dark thoughts out of Kalman's head? If this tragedy had happened because Kalman had grown careless, then Berish, too, was at fault.

He went to the factories even during the shiva period but he didn't really know what was going on there. The sugar factory at least had a manager. The mill and the other businesses were left rudderless. Hour after hour, day after day, he sat over Kalman's papers. His eyes focused on the lines but his head was elsewhere; he forgot what he was reading even as he read. He tried to involve the brothers-in-law, he asked Raizel to help him, but they couldn't understand these complicated businesses, they hadn't the foggiest notion of what went on there. It would all go to rack and ruin. The thought frightened him. He became so desperate that he telephoned his friend Yudel Charney in Lowicz. Yudel promised to come down for a day or two to see what he could do to help Berish out of this predicament.

Then, when Berish sat down again with the papers to prepare himself for Yudel's visit, he couldn't understand why it had seemed so difficult the day before. Overnight it had all somehow become very simple, and when Yudel arrived, he no longer needed his help. He asked him only about the chemical plant in Lowicz that Kalman had been negotiating to buy, but Yudel knew very little about it. The problem was that Kalman had paid 25,000 zloty for an option to buy the plant, with another 25,000 due at a later date to make the contract binding on both parties.

"You need another burden like a hole in the head," Yudel had cautioned him.

"The option runs out in six weeks. If we don't pay the second 25,000 zloty we'll lose the first 25,000."

"I don't know what to tell you."

"You live in Lowicz. It's easier to take care of on the spot. If you or your father-in-law would agree to become partners, we may be prepared to lend you the money for your share too."

Yudel loved to read and write and study philosophy. When it came to amassing wealth he relied on his rich father-in-law. No, he was definitely not interested in getting involved with a chemical factory.

Berish went to Warsaw to consult with Kalman's attorney. He also asked the advice of Michal Shereshevsky, of the Shereshevsky Bank. They all talked out of both sides of their mouths; they found good reasons for going through with the deal and good reasons for not going through with it. He came back home and called together all the executors and all the heirs. They were afraid even to think about such large sums of money.

As they all left, Berish knew for a certainty that he was the only one who could make the decisions. What would Kalman have done? Kalman would have consummated the purchase—about that he hadn't the slightest doubt.

The chemical plant must be a good business, but . . . but he was afraid he wouldn't know how to run it. Maybe he could find someone who did have experience and sell him the option. He suddenly remembered something. Kalman had once boasted that he could sell the option at a profit. Whom did Kalman have in mind?

What would Kalman do? If there was no buyer, he would pretend he had one! And if he had a rich friend who could create the impression that he was a buyer, he would ask him to go over and take a look and then send in an expert who could ask the kinds of questions that would convince the sellers he was serious . . .

That mission Yudel carried out successfully. They worked out a compromise: Kalman's heirs returned their option before the deadline and received half the money Kalman had paid in.

The successful strategy in getting rid of the chemical plant raised Berish's self-confidence and he began to tackle the work with real enthusiasm.

Everything was ready for the candy factory, even the "specialists," who had already resigned from their previous positions. How could he leave them high and dry? The building grew. The machines had been ordered. With God's help there would be a factory and it would compete with the Vedel Company, as Kalman had dreamed.

With the canned meat factory there were still many problems, but Kalman, rest his soul, had been right—the by-product of the sugar factory could be turned into a valuable commodity. It would be a shame not to do so.

Before the accident, Kalman had already arranged for the squire to breed more cows on his farms. The contract had three provisions: they would buy up all his sugar beets, they would return the grated beets to him for fodder, and they would buy the cows from him for meat. The squire had had good results from his previous business with Kalman. He had good contacts. Maybe he could help get a contract from the army to supply them with canned meat as well.

Berish met with the squire, who, hemming and hawing, finally promised to think about it. Berish inferred from this that they would have to pay him something for his help in getting the contract, even though the squire knew he wouldn't lose any money in this deal. Berish returned from the squire's court feeling satisfied. Kalman had wanted an empire. With God's help, there would be one.

Kalman had also wanted a "dynasty." Berish had reason to believe that the dynasty too would grow. As Kalman had hoped, his baby girl would soon have a brother or sister. Raizel gave birth to a boy, and since there was already a child named after his father, Berish named his first-born "Kalman." At the circumcision party, Freydl announced that she was pregnant, thank God, with her second child. The party took place on a Tuesday, which is a lucky day. An empire and a dynasty, for many, many generations. That's what Berish hoped. But . . .

That was Tuesday, January 31, 1933. As the last guests were leaving, it was growing dark. The new mother fell asleep and Berish picked up the newspaper that he hadn't had time to read that day. A screaming headline across the top of the front page announced that President Hindenberg of Germany had summoned Adolf Hitler and asked him to form a new government.

Reichs-Chancellor Hitler became the new leader of Germany.